Annoure and the Dragon Ships

HEIDI SKARIE

Annoure and the Dragon Ships

Cover design by Deranged Doctor Design
Cover Art by Heidi Skarie
Editor Coleen Rhem

Published by

For information
http://Bluestarvisions.com
Info@bluestarvisions

Publisher's Cataloging-in-Publication Data

Skarie, Heidi
Annoure and the Dragon Ships
ISBN: 978-0-9893365-5-0

Reference
1. Skarie, Heidi 2. Vikings 3. Norsemen religion and culture

To my husband, Jim, who was Thorstein in a past life.
He stole me from England then stole my heart.

Cast of Characters

Annoure - fifteen-year old noble woman from Northumbria
Asa - wife of Walfgar, cousin of Thorstein
Astrid - baby daughter of Asa and Walfgar
Ban - a baby born to Annoure
Bergthora - thrall owned by Ingeld
Brandi - Thyri and Njal's son
Cearl - boy kidnapped from Jarrow
Dahlia - Thorstein's childhood sweetheart and neighbor
Danr - Asa's brother
Dylan - Konungar (ruler) of the tribal community where Thorstein lives
Edgtho - Norseman, Ketil's cousin
Eian - Father Eian, Frankish priest at the monastery in Jarrow
Erik - a Norseman skald (wandering minstrel)
Fitela - thrall owned by Ingeld
Freydis - Thorstein's mother
Garth - Thorstein's father
Gerd - thrall owned by Ingeld
Ginna - thrall on Garth's farmstead
Grandmother - Annoure's Grandmother
Gylfi - a Norseman skald (wandering minstrel)
Herjulf - Thorstein's cousin
Hilda - thrall on Garth's farmstead

Ingeld - Norseman trader of thralls
Iona - thrall owned by Ingeld
Jamsgar - Norseman Priest
Kalsetini - Thorstein's sister
Kari - thrall owned by Ingeld
Ketil - Norseman, neighbor and friend of Thorstein
Ljot - Norseman of Tyrker's clan
Manton Bandolf - Annoure's fiancé
Nesbjörn - Ketil and Rethel's father
Nidhad - Norseman, one of Ingeld's crew
Njal - Thorstein's older brother
Oddkell - thrall on Garth's homestead
Olaf - neighbor of Thorstein, Dahlia's brother
Refr - a farmer living on the Shetland Islands
Rethel - Norseman, brother of Ketil
Rothgar - son of Walfgar and Asa
Sandey - daughter of Thyri and Njal
Skalagrim - thrall on Garth's homestead
Sturlee - Dahlia's brother
Thorstein - Norseman, son of Garth
Thyri - Njal's wife
Tola - one of Tyker's thralls
Tondbent - Brother Tondbent, monk at the monastery in Jarrow
Turgeis - the captain of a longship Thorstein's goes a-viking on
Volsung - Dahlia's father, his farmstead is on an island near Garth's farmstead
Walfgar - Thorstein's older cousin

Norse / Old English / English Glossary

a-viking - to travel by ship to trade or raid foreign ports
Aethelred - Anglo-Saxon king of Northumbria in 793
Aldeigjuborg - village in Northwestern Russia
amma - grandmother
Anglo-Saxon - Old English, Germanic language
Asgardhall - where the Norse god Odin lives
bairn - child
Bergen - ancient trading village in Norway
Bertran - Announre's brother's horse
Birka - area in Sweden where Ingeld is from
Bloodrun - the name of Rethel's sword
bróŏir - Norse word for brother
Bulgar - an ancient center-of-trade city on the Volga River in Russia
Celts - historical Celts were a tribal society in Europe
Daugava River - Name the Norsemen called the Dvina River in Russia
dóttir - Norse word for daughter
dragon ship - name given to the longship by the Norsemen's enemies
drakkar - Norse longship

Druids - religious leaders of Celts until the Celts converted to Christianity

Dvina River - flows southeast into the Baltic Sea; Norse called it Daugava River

einvagi - a duel often fought outside the law

faðir - Norse word for father

Fenrir - monstrous wolf of Norse mythology, son of the god Loki

Frey - Norse god of agriculture, harvest, love and marriage, and fertility

Freyja - Norse goddess, twin sister of Frey

Frigga - wife of Odin, Norse goddess of love, marriage and destiny

Futhark - 24-letter Norse alphabet

Grimmr - The name of Thorstein's sword, means fierce

Gunnar - Thorstein's horse

gunwale - the upper edge of a boat or ship's side

hangerock - Norse women's paneled over-dress

Hanna - Ketil's dead wife

Hedeby - trading town in late 700s on Baltic Sea, Jutland Peninsula

hudfat- two-person skin sleeping bag, often made of sheepskin

hvalr - Norseword for whale

Ilmen Lake - A Lake in Russia

iron lamp - bowl on a stickmade out of metal that burns fish oil

já - Norse word for yes

Jarl -title for a Norse chief

Jarlshof - Norse settlement in the Shetland Islands

Jarrow - village in Northumbria and monastery in Northumbria

jerkin - sleeveless jacket, often made of leather that Norsemen wore

Jutland - Now Denmark
Kaupang - ancient town in what is now Norway
Kolobrzeg - ancient Slav city on the Baltic Sea known for its salt mines
konungr - title for Norse tribal ruler
kross - cross
Lindisfarne - Monastic settlement on island off the northeast coast of England
longship - Viking ship
Manton Bandolf - Annoure's fiancé
matr - Norse word for meal
mead - an alcoholic drink of fermented honey and water
Mjölnir - name for the god Thor's hammer
móðir - Norse word for mother
nei - Norse for the word no
nabidth - alcoholic drink
nithigar - coward in Old Norse
Norge - Norwegian name for Norway
Norse - language of Norsemen, a primitive Nordic language
Norsemen - Member of ancient Scandinavian people; Northmen
Northumbria - ancient Anglo-Saxon kingdom on the coast of northern England
Northumbrian - People of Northumbria
Odin - Norse king of Asgard, god of war and death, sky, and wisdom
palfrey - a type of horse valued for riding in the Middle Ages
rune - an old Norse letter or inscription; important role in rituals
rune master - person who inscribed runes on swords to give them good luck in battle

Runic alphabet - 24-letter Norse alphabet written on rune stones; also known as Futhark
Rus - Swedish Vikings who came down the river were called Rus
saga - prose narrative recalling events or exploits in Norway
silver coins - these coins came from the east via the Russian trading routes
skald - wandering minstrel in Norge
Slav - people living along the east side of the Baltic Sea
sonr - Norse word for son
stern - rear of ship
steeringoar - an oversized oar to control the direction of the ship
Sumburgh head - a cliff in the Shetland Islands
Svantevit - main god of Slavs
svima - Norse word for swim
tarpaulin - covering put up on ships to keep out the rain
Thor - Norse god of Thunder and sea, carried a hammer, son of Odin
thrall - Norse slave
ting - Norse legal assembly
Tyrker - Norse war chief killed on the Jarrow raid
under-dress - Norse women wore a floor-length dress under their hangerock
Valhalla - the souls of Norse warriors slain in battle go to Vahalla
Valkyrie - celestial warrior maidens who welcome heroes to Valhalla
Varangian Sea - Norse name for the Baltic Sea
Varangian - Name given to the Norsemen by the Greeks and East Slavs
verr - Norse word for husband
vif - wife

Vind Oga - opening in the wall covered with thin animal hide to let in light

Volga River - largest river in Russia; was used as a trade route

Volkhov River - a Russian river

wimple - head covering worn by Anglo-Saxon women

yardarm - horizontal pole at the top of a sail

Table of Contents

Chapter 1

Attack on St. Paul's Church in Jarrow

Jarrow, Northumbria 794 A.D. (Northeast Coast of England)

ANNOURE TIGHTENED HER GRIP ON Bertran's reins and peered into the dark forest, uneasy to enter it alone. She knew this might be her only opportunity to explore the ancient oak grove and drew a deep breath of late summer air, inhaling the scent of dry leaves. Resolved, she kicked her heels into the horse's flanks and the brown palfrey trotted forward. Predawn light barely penetrated the thick canopy of leaves, making it hard to see as he wove his way through elms, Scots pines and silver birch.

An owl swooped by, startling Annoure, and wind moaned through the trees. She glanced around uneasily, missing her guardian's solid presence, though she'd purposely slipped out of the castle before he awakened. He'd never allow her to come here.

Before long she found the grove, a stand of massive oaks. She'd discovered it when riding with her brother Cedric. They both recognized it as an ancient place of worship for the now nearly-extinct Druids. Cedric said the place was evil and they should leave, but she'd felt drawn to it and decided to come back on her own.

Annoure slipped off Bertran, and clutched her jeweled Celtic cross. A guilty feeling tightened her stomach. Her father and the priests wouldn't approve of her fascination with the Druids. Her discomfort gradually disappeared as her attention became absorbed in her surroundings.

Enormous oaks towered overhead. Moss, twisted twigs, acorns and leaves covered the ground. An arcane power pulsed in the air. What ceremonies were performed here? She poured water from her flask onto the ground to honor the Celtic gods, half-expecting them to appear.

A trickling sound of running water led her to a brook that emptied into a pool. Energy swirled around the water. She knelt and gazed into its still surface.

At first she saw only her own reflection, but as she slid deeper into a trance-like state, the image of her grandmother appeared. The Druidess sat by a fire, wearing a blue gown trimmed in gold. Her black hair, highlighted by silver streaks, hung to her waist. She paused in her spinning and sat poised with her head cocked. Then her dark, intelligent eyes focused on Annoure.

"Be careful, Granddaughter."

"Of what?" Annoure whispered.

"The dragon."

Wind blew across the water, rippling its surface and the image disappeared.

"Grandmother, come back! What do you mean by *the dragon*?"

The fine hairs on the nape of Annoure's neck rose. She remembered her dreams of a man with flaxen-colored hair and vivid sea-blue eyes. Dragon tattoos wound around his powerful arms.

The wind increased in intensity and Annoure wrapped her cape more tightly around her slender body. She knew her grandmother's image wouldn't reappear in the now rough water.

Annoure spotted a vine-covered cave opening. She peered into its ink-black interior, wondering if Druids used it. When she stepped inside, a spider web stuck to her face. She grimaced and brushed it away, then took another step inside.

A chill rippled through Annoure as an invisible dark power beat against her. Then a small creature flew past her head. More creatures flapped by. Shrieking, she ran toward the entrance, realizing the creatures must be bats.

Her toe struck a hard object that rolled out of the cave. She followed it outside and discovered it was a human skull! She made the sign of the cross. Was the skull the remains of a sacrificed Druid enemy?

Lightning lit the sky, followed by a rumble of thunder. She lifted her skirts and ran to Bertran. When she tried to mount him, the horse jerked away.

"You feel the magic too, don't you, Bertran." She scratched the horse behind the ears. "We need to get home before the storm breaks." Annoure mounted the palfrey, made a clicking sound and the horse started forward.

The sky darkened rapidly as the clouds thickened. She shivered in the cool, damp air and pulled her wimple over her head as the horse trotted through the forest. A fallen tree lay in the path. Annoure guided him around it with the unsettled feeling she was being watched.

A fox ran in front of the palfrey, startling him and he reared. Annoure squeezed her knees against the horse's sides and tightened her grip on the reins as she struggled to stay on. The horse's hooves thundered back to the ground and she quickly brought him under control. She gave a short laugh, pleased that she was able to handle her brother's horse, even though he insisted Bertran was far too spirited for her to ride.

The horse cantered through the trees and soon reached the trail. Relieved to be out of the woods, Annoure guided Bertran along the path. She came to a hill overlooking the small River Don where it emptied into the much larger River Tyne. Movement on the Tyne caught her attention.

She gasped as the head of a dragon emerged from the heavy fog. When it drew closer, she realized it was just a carving on the prow of a ship. She recognized the design as a dragon ship. It was raised at the bow and stern, rode high on the water, and had a red-and-white sail that billowed in the wind. Four more ships soon appeared.

Annoure uneasily watched the ships sailing toward her. They must be coming to trade at the village of Jarrow, but why come so early while most villagers still slept?

The crew lowered the sail and began rowing. When they passed below her, she saw they wore helmets and armor. One warrior spotted her. He swung up his bow and fired an arrow. She ducked as it whistled over her back and struck the tree behind her.

Terrified, she kicked the horse's flanks and yelled, "Go, Bertran!" The horse stretched its long legs and raced down the path. *I must warn the villagers!* she thought.

When the village of Jarrow came into view, Annoure slowed the horse. Wattle-and-daub houses with thatched roofs perched along the shoreline of the River Don. Twisted stick fences enclosed gardens and farm animals. A rooster crowed, setting off a chorus of roosters. No one appeared to be up yet, so she urged the horse on and galloped toward the farthest edge of the village where St. Paul's church was located.

She crouched low on Bertran's back, clinging frantically as the wind blew her wimple onto her shoulders and whipped her hair out of its fastenings. The horse's hooves thundered along the ground and houses flew by in a blur. The horse galloped faster and faster, its muscular body heaving and sweating beneath her.

Soon the hundred-year-old stone church appeared, with its twin monasteries and the guesthouse, which had colored glass windows. She sailed through the herb and vegetable gardens on the south slope facing the Don. A few monks working in the terraced gardens glanced up with astonishment as she hurtled past, her horse's hooves kicking up dust. She rode straight to the Jarrow monastery and reined in Bertran. Sliding off, she rushed inside.

"Father Eian!" she called, bursting into the scriptorium, panting for breath.

Startled, Father Eian splashed ink on the elaborate page he laboriously worked on. He scowled in disapproval. "Look what you caused me to do, child!" he said in Frankish, the language of the nobility.

"Father, there are—"

"Calm down, Annoure. You're fifteen—a woman now—too old to be rushing around like a peasant child and why—"

She interrupted him. "Five dragon ships are rowing down the Don toward the village and church!"

His wrinkled face paled. "Have they come to trade?"

"No. One of the men shot an arrow at me. They could be the same men who ransacked Lindisfarne last winter. We need to ring the bell and warn the villagers."

Father Eian rose stiffly, a frown deepening the grooves of his forehead. He ran a hand through his white hair and stood hunched over, frail under his monk's robe.

Annoure wanted to urge him to move faster. The Norsemen would be upon them shortly!

A monk stepped into the room. "Excuse me for bothering you, Father Eian, but we were alarmed when we saw Lady Annoure galloping to the monastery."

"Ring the warning bell," Father Eian replied. "Norsemen are attacking. Gather everything of value and instruct the monks to carry what they can to safety."

The monk turned toward the doorway.

"Don't forget the books. The heathens will burn them or steal them for their jewels."

The priest lifted the large Bible from his desk. "Come, Lady Annoure, we'll save what we can."

They left the monastery as the warning bell began ringing. Once inside the church, Father Eian shuffled to the altar. He put the Bible, a wine chalice, silver candlesticks and other valuables into a soft leather bag and handed it to Annoure. He reverently lifted the chiseled-stone cross from the altar and hoisted it over his shoulder.

Loud male voices roared in the courtyard, accompanied by a horrendous banging sound. "Odin! Odin! Odin!"

Filled with dread, Annoure gazed out the window, transfixed by the horde of Norsemen who ran toward the monasteries, hammering swords against their shields.

"Hurry!" Father Eian exclaimed. "This way!" He slid through a narrow hidden passage near the altar.

Footsteps pounded up to the entrance of the nave. Annoure spun around and saw a ferocious Norseman at the door. His tall form darkened the chapel and his cape swirled around him, as if Satan himself had entered the church. A leather helmet covered his hair and he clutched a large broadsword and shield.

When their eyes locked, Annoure couldn't breathe and her legs wobbled. She felt like a rabbit cornered by a large dog.

He strode into the room followed by two more Norsemen. One swung a battle-axe and the other carried a bow nearly as tall as the length of his body. Annoure felt their bloodlust like a strong wind ripping into the quiet church.

She fled through the altar door, following the priest to the back of the church. They reached an outside door and together pushed it open. Footsteps pounded on the wooden floor behind her and Annoure glanced back. The tall Norseman was a mere four feet away! She leapt through the doorway and the heavy bag slammed against her legs.

Outside cool rainwater beat on her face and hair. She pursued the priest along the slippery cobblestone pathway leading through the church courtyard. The air was thick with smoke. Flames rose from burning buildings around her and the sound of shouts and weapons clanging against each other rang out.

Annoure sensed the Norseman behind her pressing close, then was jerked backward. She whipped her bag at him, breaking his hold. He lunged again and she tried to dodge him, but lost her balance and fell face forward with him on top of her. The wet ground soaked the front of her dress. She rolled onto her back and pounded her fists against his chest.

Father Eian hurried back and grabbed the Norseman's arm. The warrior's shorter comrade whipped out a knife and attacked the priest.

"No!" Annoure cried in horror as the Norseman plunged the blade into the priest's heart. The old man collapsed to the ground beside her. The warrior grabbed the cross and triumphantly held it over his head, a savage grin spreading across his face. His helmet formed a sinister mask with an iron strip over his nose and holes for his eyes.

A townsman rushed to Annoure's defense, swinging a rake. Her captor sprung to his feet and sliced his sword through the man's wooden rake handle and into his chest. The farmer backed away, screaming in agony. The warrior heaved the bag of relics over his shoulder and pulled Annoure upright. Around them, other Norsemen battled soldiers armed with swords and villagers armed with farm tools.

Annoure stumbled along beside her captor, numb with shock. As they passed the monastery of Wearmouth, butchered monks lay dead or dying, their spilt blood blending with the rain-soaked earth. A few feet away, a wounded boy moaned for water. His torso was slit from neck to waist. A wave of nausea swept through Annoure. She was sure the Norsemen were inhuman demons.

When they began torching farm sheds, Annoure breathed in the smoke and started coughing. Brother Daniel ran out of a burning hut covered in flames. A warrior fired an arrow and it pierced the monk's chest. Brother Daniel's eyes widened in shock and he collapsed to the ground.

"Brother Daniel!" Annoure cried. Screaming hysterically, she dug her feet into the ground and tried to pull her arm from the warrior's grip. The Norseman clamped a hand over her mouth—she felt trapped in a horrible nightmare.

Annoure's heart raced as she was pulled down an embankment to the dragon ships anchored on the shore of the River Don. *He's taking me with him!* she thought. *I have to escape!* The warrior pulled her across a gangplank and onto the ship. He brought her to the middle of the ship and said in Anglo-Saxon, "Stay."

After thrusting the leather bag of church relics into a trunk, he began helping other Norsemen load stolen goods onto the ship. The warriors pressed in around her as they stashed their booty.

Rain continued to beat down on Annoure. She looked around, desperate for a means to get away before the ship left land. A warrior hauled a boy to where she stood and dumped him on the floor. The child's body splashed in the rainwater that was collecting on the bottom of the ship and he began moaning. Blood flowed from a gash on his forehead.

"You're hurt!" Annoure exclaimed, squatting beside him. She put an arm under his thin shoulders and helped him sit, then used the hem of her skirt to wipe off the blood.

"The wound isn't too deep," she said to reassure him. "But you're going to have a bump the size of a goose egg. What's your name?"

"Cearl. Are they going to kill us?" he asked, shaking with fear.

"No, they already would have if they wanted us dead."

Another Norseman hauled Brother Tondbent over and left him with them. She'd always liked Brother Tondbent, a young monk with a gentle disposition, and was sad to see he was captured.

On shore, Norse comrades loaded the last two ships while fighting off townsmen and soldiers. A Northumbrian farmer leapt onto one of the ships and repeatedly swung his axe into the steeringoar. A Norsemen thrust his sword into the man's back.

Annoure's stomach churned at the sight. Nauseated, she rushed to the side of the ship and retched into the water.

"Annoure, are you all right?" Brother Tondbent asked. He addressed the young boy. "Cearl, untie me so I can help Lady Annoure."

Annoure shoved her hair away from her face and raised her aching head to look at the monk. "I'm fine, but Cearl's hurt." She moved to the monk and worked at the knots that bound his hands behind his back. Her fingers shook. *How many people were captured or killed?* she wondered. *Will I ever see my family again?*

An iron-helmeted warrior with a bushy rust-colored beard shouted orders. Galvanized into action, the warriors sat on trunks lining both sides of the ship and began rowing. Annoure counted more than a dozen rowers on each side and her heart sank as she realized her chance for freedom was rapidly slipping away. Their ship followed two others down the Don, heading toward the wide, storm-roughened River Tyne.

The sky grew darker overhead and the rain increased its intensity. Waves splashed over the side of the ship and water sloshed from port to starboard on the deck.

"What will they do to us?" Annoure asked Brother Tondbent in a strangled whisper. She shuddered as dread descended over her like a heavy shroud.

The monk put a comforting hand on her arm, his eyes filled with anguish. "We'll probably be sold as slaves. Let us pray to Christ our Lord for the strength to endure our fates." He knelt in the water with his head lowered and raised his hands in prayer.

"Slaves! Won't we be ransomed?"

"No one was ransomed from the raid on Lindisfarne."

Their ship was still being rowed, but the two ships further downriver had raised their sails. Annoure knew their ship would soon do the same. She stood, braced her legs for balance, then tugged off her wimple and cape. She placed the cape over the monk's shoulders and said, "May Christ protect you."

The ship was moving quickly away from land, but Annoure was sure she could still reach shore if she jumped off now. None of the Norsemen were paying attention to her. She sprung onto a trunk just behind a rower and vaulted over the side of the ship. A man shouted and grabbed for her skirt. The fabric slipped out of his hand as she fell toward the water.

Her body tingled when the cold, churning water closed in around her and she sank into its embrace. Her waterlogged wool dress dragged her down as she desperately paddled her way upwards. Upon reaching the surface, Annoure gasped for air. Water sprayed into her mouth and she choked and coughed.

The ship kept moving away. Bobbing up and down with the waves, she yanked off her water-soaked dress so it wouldn't drag her to a watery grave, then swam for shore in her shift.

Large waves tossed her about in the turbulent water and her arms and legs soon ached from the effort of swimming. Overcome with exhaustion and shaking with cold, she rolled onto her back and floated for a few moments. Then she started swimming again.

The shore was farther away than she realized and before long her strength began to ebb. A large wave engulfed her, pulling her under.

Don't let me die, Mother Mary! she thought in anguish as she fought her way to the surface.

Your Christian god can't help you, Grandmother whispered inwardly. *Draw on the power of the Druids.*

I don't know how. Help me, Grandmother!

Still caught deep in the dark, churning water, Annoure's ears ached and her lungs burned. Images came to mind of the blue-eyed young man from her dreams. He told her to fight for her life. She felt him reaching out to her.

Annoure clawed her way to the surface again, desperate for air.

Chapter 2

Thorstein

RAIN BEAT DOWN ON THORSTEIN as he rowed near the stern of the longship. His cousin Herjulf yelled, "The woman jumped overboard!"

Adrenaline shot through Thorstein, knowing the only female on board was the pretty little noblewoman he'd kidnapped. He sprang to his feet and scanned the churning water for her. Finally he caught sight of her swimming toward shore. He knew she'd never make it in such rough water. A large wave broke over her and she disappeared beneath its dark surface. Thorstein held his breath, waiting to see if she'd resurface.

"Bad luck, Thorstein. She was a rare beauty," Herjulf said, shoving a lock of red hair off his forehead.

The woman's head reappeared. Thorstein unbuckled his sword belt and dropped it to the floor.

"It's too dangerous to go after her!" Herjulf exclaimed.

"She'll drown if I don't." Thorstein threw off his cape, armor, jerkin and shirt.

"You'll drown if you do."

"I don't fear death." Thorstein removed his boots and stepped onto his trunk.

Herjulf grabbed his arm. "The woman is nothing to you."

"She belongs to me." Thorstein jerked his arm free and dove, slicing through the waves. The cold water instantly chilled him. He swam to the surface with powerful, steady strokes and drew a breath before looking for the woman. He spotted her treading water.

Thorstein began moving toward her, propelling easily through the water with muscles hardened from rowing and farm work. The violence of the waves hindered his progress and he realized the woman might drown before he reached her. He swam with strong strokes, pushing himself beyond his normal endurance.

Thorstein raised his head to be sure he was still on course, but didn't see her. He treaded water, twisting his head from side to side. The rain fell in sheets, nearly blinding him. At last, he located her dark head bobbing up and down on the waves.

Lightning zigzagged across the water and thunder boomed like a series of rolling drumbeats. *The god Thor must be angry to send such a storm,* he thought. *What have we done to cause such offense?*

Thorstein began swimming again. Soon his arms and legs screamed in pain and he feared they'd cramp up in the freezing water. He wanted to stop and rest, but didn't dare. The woman couldn't last much longer.

"Svima!" he yelled to her. Remembering she didn't understand Norse, he shouted, "Swim!" His voice was caught by the wind and tossed away. He'd almost reached her when she sank beneath the water and didn't resurface.

Thor's Hammer! I'll not lose her! Thorstein drew a deep breath and dove under, entering the world of the river. He no longer felt the rain pounding on him or heard the roaring wind. He kept his eyes open, but saw only churning water around him.

Swimming deeper, he peered through the dark water and spotted her hair fanned out around her head like seaweed. He dove down, grabbed her tresses and swam up, breaking the surface as he pulled the woman after him. He slid his arm under her chin to keep her nose and mouth out of the water.

She drew in a breath and began coughing and spitting up water. She kept choking up water until he thought she'd spewed out half the river, then she collapsed limply against him.

Now that Thorstein wasn't moving, he began to shake with cold. He treaded water, too worn out to do more than just keep them both afloat. The river felt as if talons were pulling them under. He kept one arm around her neck as she recovered from nearly drowning.

He looked around for the ship and spotted it a long way off moving swiftly toward them. He knew they'd come after him since he had two kinsmen and many neighbors and friends aboard the ship.

Thunder cracked loudly again, startling the frightened woman. She climbed on top of his head, pushing him underwater. He kicked back to the surface and tried to turn her in his arms. She fought him and he forcefully thrust her away, breaking her hold. He rolled her onto her back, put one arm under her chin and began swimming toward the ship.

The rain continued to beat down and large waves crashed over them from several directions. He realized he might die trying to save the girl. He redoubled his efforts, swimming as he fought a battle against the river. The water became the enemy—a force of furious, unlimited power.

Please Thor, spare our lives! Thorstein pleaded.

The ship drew close and Herjulf threw him a rope. Thorstein caught it and tied it around the woman's waist. His cousins, Herjulf and Walfgar, heaved on the rope and pulled her upward, then onto the deck as the ship bobbed and moved away. Thorstein fought to keep his head above water, his strength nearly depleted.

The men rowed close and Herjulf tossed the rope again. It landed a short distance from Thorstein and disappeared into the waves. The ship rocked away.

Drained of energy, Thorstein sank beneath the surface. His ears hurt and everything started to go black.

Then water splashed near him and Herjulf appeared. He grabbed Thorstein's arm and swam upward. Thorstein's head broke the surface and he gulped in blessed air.

Herjulf tied a rope around his waist and Thorstein held onto the soaking hemp strands as Walfgar and Ketil dragged both of them onto the ship. Thorstein collapsed on deck, too weak to move.

"You thickheaded ox," Herjulf scolded. "You almost drowned for some skinny Saxon thrall. You need to start thinking with your head, instead of with what's between your legs."

"I'm glad to see you're alive as well, cousin." Thorstein's eyes sought out the woman. She lay near him shivering in her thin shift, retching water. The monk squatted beside the woman and placed a cape over her shoulders.

Rain dripped off Walfgar's shoulder-length hair and braided beard as he handed Thorstein and Herjulf dry clothes, insisting they change into them. Thorstein tried to pull on the shirt, but shook so violently that Walfgar had to help him. Once Thorstein had changed into dry clothes, he began to warm up.

Walfgar handed him a woolen tunic. "This is for the woman. She must be frozen."

"Thank you." Thorstein took the tunic and turned to the woman. Her teeth chattered through blue lips as she sat huddled on the oak plank floor. He held out the tunic and said in Anglo-Saxon, "Put this on." He knew some of her language from trading and many Anglo-Saxon words were similar to Norse.

She grabbed the tunic and clutched it to her chest.

"I'm Thorstein." He pointed to himself and then pointed at her. "What's your name?"

"Annoure."

"Annoure," he repeated, liking the sound of her name. He pointed to the tunic. "Change into that."

She shook her head.

Thorstein looked at Walfgar, who knew more of the Anglo-Saxon language than he did. "Tell her to change into the tunic."

Walfgar spoke to the woman, but she shook her head. Thorstein frowned realizing he'd have to force her to change or she'd die of exposure. He glanced at the monk and Saxon boy who hovered protectively beside her and decided to get rid of them.

"Bail water," he said. He thrust wooden buckets at them.

They both went to the middle of the ship where rain and seawater had collected and scooped their buckets across the deck floor.

Thorstein spoke to Annoure in Anglo-Saxon. "Change."

She backed away from him.

"I won't hurt you." He shoved the cape off her shoulders, then grasped the bottom of her shift and pulled it upward. Her eyes widened in alarm and she fought him, pummeling her fists against his chest and scratching his cheek. He drew the wet garment over her head and tossed it onto the floor. She was naked except for her stockings. Thorstein enjoyed the brief view of her alluring body as she snatched up the tunic and pulled it over her head.

At the same time the priest rushed over shouting, "Don't touch her!" Herjulf grabbed the priest and held him back

"Give her a taste of your tool, Thorstein," Rethel yelled, thrusting his hips. More crew gathered around to watch the show.

Thorstein was glad the girl couldn't understand what Rethel said. She already looked terrified. The Saxon boy pushed his way through the men and stood guarding Annoure.

"Your little Saxon is full of fire," Herjulf said, a wide grin spreading across his face.

"Your cheek is bleeding, cousin." He released the monk who hurried to Annoure and stood protectively in front of her.

Thorstein wiped the blood off his cheek. She was indeed full of fire, but he'd rather it be spent in different ways than fighting him.

As the sails rose, Thorstein walked over to his neighbor Olaf who stood near the stern of the ship. Olaf navigated their route, but as head helmsmen it was Thorstein's responsibility to see that they stayed on course. At seventeen, he was young to be the head helmsman, but he'd been sailing since he was ten and learned quickly.

"It's dangerous being on the sea in this weather," Olaf said.

Before Thorstein could answer, Captain Turgeis said, "Keep away from the rocky shore." They sailed through the mouth of the river and entered the North Sea where violent waves hammered the ship, sending cascades of water over the sides.

Thorstein braced his feet for balance as the seventy-foot longship was tossed about like a toy. Overhead the yellow-and-black patterned sail billowed out.

A man shouted, "Look ashore!"

Thorstein turned to gaze at the mouth of the River Tyne just as one of their longships rolled over and sank beneath the waves. Some of the men swam to shore where soldiers and villagers struck them down with swords, axes, rakes and hoes. Blood pounded in Thorstein's temples at the sight of his comrades being slaughtered.

"Those Saxon pigs are butchering them!" Herjulf growled. "Let's go back!"

"Should we turn around?" Thorstein asked Captain Turgeis.

"Nei, one of our other ships is closer."

Norsemen on the nearby longship began pulling their comrades from the angry water.

A huge wave hit the ship Thorstein was on and he grabbed the gunwale as it pitched into a deep trough. The oak boards creaked with strain and water sprayed over him. Olaf struggled to hold the steeringoar in place and Thorstein grabbed on to keep it steady. A second wave hit with equal force and they rode it down into another deep trough and rode it up again. The ship flexed from the force of the water. Thorstein's heart pounded as if he's been running. Although the ship was designed to take much abuse at sea, waves of such size and force could capsize even the best ship if it was hit wrong. He watched uneasily as a double set of large waves swept toward shore. The first wave hit the remaining longship as the crew tried to help the men out of the water. The ship pitched to one side. A second wave pounded the drakkar and it snapped in two. It disappeared from view.

"Should we go back to help them?" Thorstein asked the captain.

Turgeis shook his head, his eyes filled with anguish. "In this storm, I fear our ship will sink if we try."

"They'll all die if we do nothing."

"I know," he said grimly.

Thorstein strained to see if any warriors were swimming to the shore. In the short time since the ship sunk, their own longship was carried further out to sea by gusty winds.

"By Odin's Ravens, it was an unlucky raid," Captain Turgeis growled, clenching his fists. "Tyrker the Courageous was killed in battle and now we've lost two drakkars and all the men aboard."

"Tyrker's dead!" Thorstein exclaimed, shifting his stance as the ship tipped steeply to the right.

"Já, he died with a sword in his hand and will go to Valhalla."

"He was a good head war chief," Thorstein said, saddened at the loss of such a great man. The sail flapped as the wind furiously pounded against it. "It's too dangerous to keep the sail up in this storm."

Captain Turgeis nodded, then shouted orders to the men. "Lower the sails! To your oars, men! We head out to sea." The men went to their places, grumbling about not going back to help their comrades whose ships had sunk.

Thorstein sat on his trunk, then lifted a long oar off the oar rack, fit it into a rowlock next to his trunk and began to row.

One of the men shouted, "Stroke! Stroke!" to keep them rowing in unison. Thorstein rowed hard, putting his distress about his lost comrades into each stroke. His chest tightened as he thought of the men's families who would never see them again.

Thorstein's calloused hands gripped the oar tightly as he continued rowing, contending with the cold seawater spraying in through the oar-hole.

"Thor is angry!" Edgtho Scar-Face yelled.

Rethel shouted above the wind. "It's because we have a Christian monk on board! Throw him overboard! He's brought us bad luck."

"If we don't, our boat will sink as the others did!" Edgtho yelled. "And we'll all die!"

The other men shouted to throw the monk overboard. Thorstein glanced toward the thin monk as shouts to get rid of him grew louder.

Several warriors seized the monk when he came to dump a bucket of water. Others gathered around. The monk's face turned ashen. He pressed his palms together and lowered his head in prayer.

What good did it do to pray? Thorstein wondered. Better to grab a sword and take a few men with you to assure yourself a place in Valhalla.

"No!" Annoure screamed, pushing her way through the men. Thorstein drew in his oar and headed after her. The crew could decide it was best to get rid off all Christians.

She grabbed Rethel's arm and tried to pull him away from the monk. Thorstein admired her fearless nature. She should be afraid for her own life.

Rethel tore his arm from Annoure's grasp, then he and his cousin Edgtho hurled the monk into the ocean. Rethel leaned over the side of the longship and laughed as the hapless monk disappeared beneath the waves.

The ship rolled sideways toward the sea, pitching Rethel off-balance and he nearly went overboard. Taking advantage of the moment, Annoure gave him a forceful shove.

Rethel flung his arms out as he grasped at air, then he plunged over the ship's side and fell into the water with a terrific splash. Thorstein reached Annoure a moment later, horrified at what she'd done.

By now Rethel was already a distance from the ship, bobbing up and down with the waves. Ketil threw him the end of a rope and, once he'd gotten a hold of it, Edgtho and Ketil began to pull. Thorstein joined them and they finally succeeded in hauling him back onboard.

Rethel lay on deck, catching his breath for a moment, then stood and roared, "I'm going to kill that Saxon witch!" His face was red-blotched with rage as he started for Annoure. She spun away, disappearing into the crowd of men gathered around them.

Thorstein stepped in front of Rethel to block his way. "Leave her be. It was an accident."

"It was no accident!" Rethel's nostrils flared and the veins in his neck stood out in vivid ridges. "She shoved me. I had to discard my grandfather's sword to keep from drowning. If I still had it, I'd cut her up piece by piece."

"We'll settle this later," Captain Turgeis said. "Get to the oars, men!" The crew returned to their places.

"This isn't over!" Rethel stomped away.

Captain Turgeis shot Thorstein an irritated look. "See that the woman doesn't cause any more problems."

"She won't." Thorstein lifted a coiled rope off a rack and crossed over to Annoure who huddled in a ball near the stern of the ship. His annoyance with her softened when he saw tears streaming down her face. Perhaps the monk was her friend. She didn't resist as he bound her wrists together.

Herjulf came over to him. "There's going to be trouble. Rethel wants revenge."

Thorstein tied Annoure to a wooden bar then stood. "You think I don't know that? She's made an enemy and I can't think of a man I want less for an enemy."

Herjulf smiled. "True enough, but I like her spirit."

Thorstein smiled back despite his misgivings. "A thrall needs to quickly learn her place or risk a beating—or worse."

"She won't take easily to being a thrall. I'd say she's a noblewoman from the finely woven dress she wore and her soft hands."

Annoure rose to her knees and retched over the side of the ship. Thorstein felt a wave of sympathy, remembering how sick the rough sea made him on his first voyage.

He looked for the shoreline. It would be easy to get off course with the sun masked by storm clouds. In clear weather they could reach the village of Bergen in five days. In this storm, the journey would be much longer and he didn't want to be out at sea for more days than they had food and water.

The horse-shaped weather vane showed the horse's head pointed west. He studied the swell. Using the vane and wind, he judged which way to adjust the steeringoar.

Turgeis ordered the men who weren't rowing to get something to eat. The remaining crew kept the ship on course. The waves became smaller and soon the rain lightened to a drizzle.

The men ate, then traded places with the rowers. Thorstein didn't leave his station to eat so Walfgar brought him dried fish and a flask of water.

"It should be safe to put the sail back up," Walfgar said. "The men are tired."

Thorstein nodded. "Já, ask the captain for permission."

When Olaf finally took over steering the ship. Thorstein took his sheepskin *hudfat* out of his trunk and went over to Annoure. She was pale with dark circles under her eyes and shaking with cold. After untying her, he handed her a flask of water. While she drank, he unrolled the sleeping bag and told her to get in it. She handed back the flask and slid inside the hudfat.

When evening came, Herjulf carried an iron lamp to the ship's stern. He put its rod into a hole, poured fish oil into the lamp's bowl and lit it with a flint lighter. His red hair glowed in the flicking flames.

The rain started up again. As it grew into a steady downpour, the men put a tarpaulin, tent-like cloth, over the center section of the ship. Once it was in place, the men rolled out their hudfats underneath and slept two to a bag.

Thorstein lifted Annoure, still in the hudfat, off the floor and carried her to an open spot beside Walfgar and Herjulf's hudfat. He removed his rain-soaked clothes before crawling into the hudfat beside her. It was warm from Annoure's body heat, and a welcome change from the rain and wind. He felt the whole length of her body beside him. Her tunic covered her torso, but her bare legs touched his. She tried to move away, but the bag wasn't large enough. He thought of how desirable she'd looked naked and wondered if his fatigue could be held off long enough to enjoy the enticing pleasures her body offered.

He'd rarely had to curb his desires. Thralls in his homeland were usually quite accommodating. This woman wouldn't be. He'd have to force her if he wanted her. A willing partner he could summon the energy for, but a fight didn't interest him, even if he could easily win.

Moreover, he felt compassion for the seasick, frightened girl.

When she'd jumped overboard, he'd instinctively dove after without thinking of the risk. She was special. From the moment he'd first saw her in the church with light shining upon her beautiful, fine-boned face, her thick, dark hair tumbling to her waist, he'd thought she was a celestial vision. She looked like the maiden he'd seen in his dreams, but when she'd run from him he knew she was flesh and blood.

His body wasn't listening to any arguments against taking her. He touched her cheek, amazed by the softness of her skin under his work-roughened hand. She trembled beneath his touch. She was young; it was likely she was still a maiden. He caressed one of her breasts, feeling the fullness of it through the rough cloth of her tunic.

She pushed his hand away and crawled out of the hudfat. Pulling on her cape, she went to a nearby bucket and threw up. *Still seasick,* he thought as he waited for her to return. Instead she stayed by the bucket. Annoyed, he rolled onto his side. Let her sleep in the cold if she preferred it to his company.

He started to doze off when he heard her cry out. Instantly alert, he scrambled out of his hudfat to see Rethel rip off her cape. She took a trembling step backward into Edgtho who stood behind her. Both men were tall and strongly built and she only came up to their shoulders.

"Leave her be!" Thorstein growled.

"Nei, it's only fair that she warms my frozen flesh since she's the one responsible for my chill," Rethel said. He grabbed the front of Annoure's tunic and jerked her to him. "Let me bury my sword in her."

A surge of rage sliced through Thorstein. "Let her go, Rethel," he said, his voice low and threatening.

Captain Turgeis appeared in the darkness. "Thorstein, I see your thrall is the source of an argument again. I warned you before about her."

"She's sick and merely got up to use the bucket when Rethel grabbed her."

Captain Turgeis fastened hard eyes on Rethel. "It's been a day filled with bad luck and I have no tolerance for troublemakers. Take a shift with Ketil and help navigate the ship since you're so full of energy. The sea is rough tonight and your bróðir will appreciate the help keeping on course."

"It's my right to punish her for what she did," Rethel said, not releasing Annoure. Thorstein clenched his right fist, wanting to smash it into Rethel's face.

"Let her go," Captain Turgeis said. "You know the rules. No feuding is allowed at sea. I command this ship and expect my orders to be followed." His hand grasped the hilt of his sword. "Hurt her and you'll cross swords with me." The two men stared at each other. Finally, Rethel flung the woman away and stalked off.

Annoure scrambled back to Thorstein's hudfat.

Captain Turgeis stared pensively after Rethel. "Keep her guarded." Thorstein nodded curtly, pursing his lips together in suppressed fury.

He crawled back in the hudfat and curled his body around hers, then rubbed her cold arms to warm them. This time she didn't push him away. He wondered what to do about Rethel and Edgtho. This wouldn't be the end of the matter. He'd have to keep a sharp eye on Annoure.

Chapter 3

The Voyage

ANNOURE LAY STIFFLY ON HER side, her back to Thorstein's chest, worried he'd rape her. Her stomach churned, but she had nothing more to throw up. As the Norseman's breathing gradually grew deep and regular, she realized he'd gone to sleep. Apprehensive about waking him, she didn't dare move his heavy arm off her shoulder.

Sleeping men in fur bags surrounded them on all sides. Rain pounded against the leather cloth stretched overhead and creaking boards complained beneath her. She shuddered. The ship seemed vulnerable and small on the rough, expansive sea.

Warm in the fleece-lined bag, Annoure closed her eyes and tried to rest. Immediately images from the raid appeared in her inner vision: the butchered boy moaning for water; Father Eian's throat slit; Brother Daniel hit by an arrow as he ran from a flaming hut; and Brother Tondbent hurled overboard. Tears filled her eyes.

"Please help me, Mother Mary," she whispered. Distress enfolded her like a spider wrapping its web around a hapless fly. She took several deep, calming breaths, fighting to control her despair. She wondered what would happen to her. Would she ever see her father and brothers again? Would she be ransomed or sold as a slave? Who were these people and where did they come from?

Unable to relax and sleep, she decided to try a technique Grandmother taught her. She put her attention on the center of her forehead where there was an opening to the dream worlds. As she continued to focus inwardly, the outer world disappeared and she found herself standing in the center of the sacred oak grove.

She felt a loving presence nearby that she couldn't see. When she placed her attention on the presence, it solidified into a blond haired man. She ran to him and he held her in his arms that were adorned with tattoos of dragons twisting up them. She stared into the deep, blue pools of his eyes and found herself floating in a vast sea.

Sometime later, voices awakened Annoure. When she opened her eyes, she found Thorstein's face inches from hers. His sea-blue eyes studied her. Startled for a moment, she didn't remember where she was. Then the memory of the events of the day before crashed in on her.

Thorstein reached out to touch her cheek and she shrank away. His hand froze in midair. He seemed uncertain about what to do and lowered his hand. He had a straight, well-formed nose, blond hair and the start of a light beard. He appeared to be not much older than she was.

Nearby other crewmembers rolled up the fur bags they'd slept in. The boat rocked back and forth on a much calmer sea than the night before despite the still-falling rain. Naked, Thorstein stood and made his way across the crowded deck to the side of the ship where he urinated into the water.

As Annoure sat up, the coarse wool tunic chafed her skin. She stared at Thorstein's well-built body when he returned to her. Twisting up his long, muscular arms and legs were exquisite tattoos of dragons and vines, reminding her of the tattooed Druids. He caught her staring as he drew closer and she quickly looked away, feeling her cheeks heat. *Didn't Thorstein know nudity was sinful?* Around her other Norsemen were in various stages of dress as they prepared for the day.

Thorstein pulled clothes out of a sheepskin-fur bag. He slid on linen breeches and covered them with tight-fitting woolen trousers tied with a drawstring. She watched the way he moved. He had the bearing of a person confident of who he was and his place in the world. She wondered why he seemed so familiar.

As he reached for his shirt, she looked closer at the dragon tattoo on his arm and a jolt of recognition shot through her. Her eyes flashed up to Thorstein's face. Their eyes met and held. His movements stilled. *He can't be the same man,* she thought in bewilderment. Her clean-shaven Druid friend wore a robe and spoke her tongue in her dreams. But this man's eyes were the same.

Annoure studied the artistic beauty of the tattooed dragon. It looked as proud and dangerous as he did. She followed the lines of the dragon to his gold armband, thinking of her grandmother's warning about the dragon.

Annoure met his gaze again. In his eyes she saw the same puzzlement she felt. He still hadn't moved, as if caught in the same spell that captured her. Mystical energy charged the air between them. *Who was he? A Norse barbarian—ruthless and wild—certainly, but something more, something deeper.* She looked away and the moment vanished. He pulled on his shirt and tunic, covering the dragons that adorned both his arms.

He sat down across from her and combed out his shoulder-length, golden hair. He handed her the comb and she examined it. It was made from an antler with an intricately carved reindeer on it. She shoved the comb through her snarled hair and tugged hard, trying to unknot the wind-blown strands.

The Norsemen took the comb from her and motioned for her to turn around. She flinched as he started combing her hair, working from the ends upward to free the tangles. Gradually she relaxed, surprised at his gentleness as he continued combing the long tresses that reached to her waist. When he was done, he slid the comb back into his bag. She turned to face him as she braided her hair into a coil and tied it with a strip of leather he gave her.

A young man with red hair and beard, a thin nose and freckled face sat down beside Thorstein. He carried a flask and a wooden bowl filled with salted meat and the reddish-orange fruit of a cloudberry plant.

He smiled at Annoure and pointed to himself. "Herjulf Redbeard."

"I'm Annoure."

He handed her the flask and she sniffed it. Satisfied that it was only water, she took a drink before handing it back. He held out the meat and she shook her head; her stomach was still not settled enough for food.

After eating, Thorstein wormed his way through the seated men to the stern of the ship and exchanged places with the helmsman. Annoure yawned and crawled back into the warm hudfat. Nearby, Herjulf started a game of backgammon with another Norsemen. The rain fell in a light but steady mist, lulling her back to sleep.

Sometime later, Annoure awoke and squinted her eyes against the bright summer sun reflecting off the sea. She sat up and saw that the tent-like covering had been taken down.

The boy Cearl came over and squatted beside her, holding the bucket he'd been bailing water with. He had a large bump on his forehead. Annoure wrinkled her nose. He smelled of farm animals and wore a filthy, tattered tunic.

"Do you think we're going to reach the edge of the earth and fall off?" he asked, his eyes round as plates.

Annoure uneasily scanned the vast sea; nothing but water was visible in all directions. "I've never been on a ship before," she said, returning her gaze to Cearl. "It's rather frightening, but I've heard the Norsemen are good sailors. They must know where the edge of the earth is."

"Where are they taking us?"

"I don't know. They come from a distant land."

"Do you think we're lost?" he asked, his face ashen.

Annoure shuddered. "I hope not. I'll ask Thorstein." She made her way between the seated men, large round shields, weapons and riggings, trying to keep her balance on the swaying deck.

Even the dragonhead, she'd seen on the front of the ship when the Norsemen attacked, had been brought aboard the crowded ship. She sensed someone watching her and glanced around to see the man called Rethel staring at her. His ugly, scar-faced accomplice, Edgtho, also looked at her with narrowed eyes and pursed lips.

She moved quickly over to Thorstein, who stood at the steeringoar talking to a young man with sad eyes and long, wind-blown hair.

"This is Ketil," Thorstein said to Annoure.

Ketil gave her an unfriendly glance before returning his attention to Thorstein.

"Ketil," Annoure repeated, feeling a tingling along her spine. Grief surrounded Ketil like a dark cloud. She tuned into his sadness saw an image of Ketil weeping beside the still figure of a young, dead woman. Her heart softened with compassion for him.

Before Annoure could ask Cearl's question, Thorstein turned the steeringoar over to Ketil and took Annoure's hand.

"Come." He led her back to where Herjulf sat.

In the evening the warriors unrolled their fur hudfats to retire for the night. Thorstein and Annoure sat near Herjulf who talked with two other men. Thorstein gestured to Herjulf's companion. "This is Walfgar." Walfgar looked a few years older than Thorstein and Herjulf. She was fascinated by his beard, which was plaited into many small braids.

"Herjulf and I are Thorstein's cousins," Walfgar said in Anglo-Saxon." I know some of the Northumbrian tongue since I traded there for several years. Norsemen settled the Shetland Islands north of your homeland. Our language is similar enough to yours that I can converse with your people when trading. You'll learn Norse quickly."

The knot in Annoure's stomach loosened at discovering she could converse with someone. Perhaps she could even learn enough of their language to convince Thorstein to ransom her. Mustering up her courage she asked, "Will you help me learn Norse?"

Walfgar studied her thoughtfully. "Perhaps, if it isn't too much trouble."

Cearl walked by with a bucket of water to dump, reminding Annoure of the boy's question. "Are we lost?" she asked.

Walfgar's brow wrinkled. "We were blown off course and lost sight of land to help guide us, but we can still find our way by the sun and stars."

"Where are we headed?"

"Across the North Sea to the village of Bergen in Hordaland, then back home to my family's farmstead," Walfgar said.

"Was St. Paul's Church the only place you raided?"

"Já."

"What will become of me and the boy?"

"Nobility are sometimes ransomed, but after such an unsuccessful raid I doubt we'll go back to ransom anyone. Booty from the raid will be divided up in Bergen. The chieftain and other merchants, who own the ships and funded the voyage, are paid first. Our war leader was killed and another captured, plus two ships went down—maybe more—it was a bad expedition. There won't be much booty to divide."

"You mean I could be given to some chief as payment for the voyage or compensation for the loss of those ships?'

He shrugged. "Já."

She shuddered, dismay flooding through her.

Concern clouded Thorstein's eyes. He and Walfgar exchanged a few words in Norse, then Walfgar said, "Thorstein would like to keep you as part of his booty, but it remains to be seen if he can."

Annoure leaned earnestly toward Walfgar. "Tell him I'm a valuable hostage. My father will pay a large ransom for my return."

Walfgar and Thorstein spoke again, finally Walfgar replied, "Thorstein doesn't want to ransom you."

Annoure stuck out her chin defiantly. "Tell him he doesn't have the right to keep me!"

"He has the right. You're lucky he rescued you when you jumped overboard. I wouldn't have. It's foolish to risk your life for a *thrall*."

"What's a thrall?"

"A slave."

"I'm a nobleman's daughter, not a slave," she hissed.

"You *were* a nobleman's *dóttir*; *now* you're a thrall." Walfgar said with a smug look on his face.

"Why was Brother Tondbent thrown overboard instead of selling him as a slave?" she asked, saddened as she thought of the monk.

"He was sacrificed to appease the angry gods."

"He was a good man." She wanted to say more, but held her tongue.

Walfgar spat on the floor. "The man was a Christian." He turned away, ending the conversation.

Annoure glowered at his back. Cearl squatted beside her on skinny legs. "What did you find out?"

"They're not sure where we are."

"What if we never find land?" Cearl said with grave eyes.

"We will. The stars will guide them."

Cearl's downturned mouth tightened and his eyes still showed trepidation. He scooped up water from the deck with his bucket and moved away.

When the sky grew dark, Thorstein stripped off his outer clothing before crawling into his hudfat. He gestured to her. "Come, Annoure."

She looked uneasily around at the men pressed in all around them, before joining him. Thorstein drew her close and kissed her. Annoure turned her face to the side and shoved her hands against his chest, trying to push him away. He kissed her cheek and ear, his beard rubbing against her delicate skin, and his hand slid onto her breast.

She jabbed her elbow into his stomach. He grunted and grabbed both her wrists. He held them over her head with one hand while keeping her body still with the weight of his. She tried to buck him off, but was crushed under his weight.

"No, Thorstein," she said, her voice a frightened whisper.

He stilled and she waited tensely for his next move. He shifted his weight onto his arms and she took a shaky breath, only to panic a moment later when he slid his fingers into her hair. He held her head so she couldn't turn away and kissed her again.

She bit his lip. He raised his head and scowled at her. Releasing her wrists, he slid his hand under her tunic and up her thigh. She grabbed his wrist, stopping his advance.

"No, please," she choked out. Tears sprang to her eyes and rolled down her cheeks. She struggled to hold them back, not wanting to reveal weakness, but her frayed emotions gave way and she began sobbing uncontrollably.

Thorstein brushed the tears on her cheek away with his thumb and moved off her. He drew her gently into his arms. She continued to weep with her face pressed against his chest, overwhelmed by all that had happened.

She tried to stop crying, but new tears flooded her eyes as she thought of how she was at his mercy and might never see her father or brothers again.

Gradually her heartache lessened and she sniffed back her tears. As she lay there, trying to collect herself, she noticed Thorstein held her in the curve of his arm, stroking her hair. She sniffed back more tears, feeling thickheaded. She'd thought Norsemen were ruthless animals, but Thorstein saved her life when she jumped overboard and now showed compassion for her plight.

Annoure rolled onto her back, dismayed that she'd allowed him to comfort her. She needed to be on guard against him. He was her enemy and would exploit any weakness. Gazing up at the vast night sky, she saw thousands of sparkling stars—the same stars that shone over her homeland. She wondered if she'd ever see the ancient trees and lush green hills of Northumbria again.

Chapter 4

Shetland Islands

THORSTEIN LEFT ANNOURE SLEEPING IN the hudfat to take a shift navigating the drakkar. Walfgar and Herjulf slept in the hudfat next to her's in case of more trouble with Rethel and Edgtho. Although they were both kin of his good friend Ketil, they were mean-spirited men who liked to cause trouble. As boys, Thorstein and Ketil had often suffered from their abuse.

Rethel rightfully blamed Annoure for losing his sword. It was his most valued possession and Thorstein doubted he had the means to replace it. A good sword could cost as much as a small farm. A new, untested sword might bend or break in a fight and wasn't as valuable as a sword passed down from a relative, which would be imbued with powers from the previous owner.

From his position at the stern, Thorstein studied the position of the stars, navigating their course. The salty breeze felt good on his face. He was grateful he survived the raid and subsequent storm.

His thoughts turned to Annoure. She looked much better today than she had the day before when she was still recovering from seasickness. Color had returned to her cheeks and she was alert to everything around her. She had asked Walfgar many questions and wanted to know the Norse name for everything on the ship.

Thorstein wondered if the booty he stole was enough to pay the chieftain so he could keep Annoure. His stomach tightened at the possibility of giving her up. He thought back to what was in the bag he'd taken from Annoure on the raid: a jeweled book, a chalice, silver dishes and candlesticks. He was lucky to obtain such wealth. Yet more than just riches motivated the chieftain to sponsor the raid. The barbaric Christian church was getting too powerful and becoming a threat to his people.

At dawn, Captain Turgeis approached Thorstein. "Have you seen land yet?"

Thorstein shook his head. "By my calculations, we should reach the Shetland Islands sometime today."

"Until we actually see land, it's best we continue to ration food and water." The captain scanned the sea. "I thought we'd see the other two ships by now."

"I hope they didn't capsize in the storm."

"They had good captains and were ahead of us. Most likely we were blown too far off course to catch up to them." Captain Turgeis nodded to Ketil, who came to relieve Thorstein of his post.

"I heard you tell the captain we might reach the Islands today," Ketil said, stretching.

"If the gods favor us."

Ketil's expression darkened grimly. "I'll be glad for the sight of land. I'd hate to be lost at sea." He changed the subject. "My bróðir is in a rage about your pretty Saxon. She made a fool of him in front of the other men and caused him to lose grandfather's sword."

"What will appease him?" Thorstein asked.

"I don't know. It's not easy to restore honor."

"True. I don't want him for an enemy. I'd rather our families had a strong bond between them. Kalsetini asked if you would be at the fall festival."

Ketil's eyes lit with pleasure. "Tell your sister I'll be there. Will you need help with the harvest?"

"Njal's in-laws usually help, but we can always use more men. It's a big task."

"I'll come after our crops are in." Ketil sighed heavily. "It never seemed fair to me that our older bróðirs inherit the family farms while we get nothing and must risk our lives at sea to make our fortune."

"I like the adventure of seeing new lands, though I'd rather go on a trading expedition than another raid."

"I don't want to go on another raid either. My little dóttirs will be orphans if I'm killed. I'd feel better if I had a mother for them."

"Kalsetini likes your dóttirs, but you've got to be willing to live again to marry her. You haven't been yourself since Hanna died. It's been two years, Ketil, time enough to move on."

"You don't know what it's like to lose a woman you love! You've never experienced such pain."

Thorstein knew he'd said too much. He and Ketil had been friends for a long time and he wanted Ketil to get over losing his wife. Since Hanna's death, Ketil was prone to melancholy and easily provoked to anger. Thorstein yawned. "I'd better get some sleep before the crew rises."

Thorstein awoke in the early afternoon and immediately looked for Annoure. She sat nearby watching Herjulf and Walfgar play backgammon.

After dressing, Thorstein joined Ketil, who pointed to a landmass in the distance. "We've reached the Shetland Islands."

Relief flowed through Thorstein. They'd made it! "We'll have to be on guard. The currents and tide are strong and treacherous here."

As they sailed closer, the cliffs along the coast and the green, nearly treeless land became visible. Thorstein recognized the high rocky spur of Sumburgh Head. The thunderous noise of hundreds of seabirds roosting in the cliffs greeted him.

After lowering the sails, they rowed to shore, landing in a natural harbor. Two sturdy, long houses built of wood, stone and turf stood near the ocean. Oxen, pigs and sheep roamed the yard. A barking dog ran up to the ship as they put out the gangplank. The stout farmer Refr walked to the rocky shoreline and heartily greeted Captain Turgeis as he stepped onto land.

"I'm glad to have company, Turgeis. This place gets lonely."

"Greetings, Refr. We're glad to be on land again and need drinking water."

Thorstein joined the captain. "Have you seen other ships from our expedition?"

"Nei, you're the first to land here."

Thorstein hoped the others had survived the storm. He gazed across the grass-covered land at the ancient stone ruins and wondered about the people who once lived here. This place was full of spirits.

He and Herjulf selected a place to camp for the night, setting up a tent that consisted of a large piece of leather held up by poles. After stowing his hudfat inside, Thorstein carried Annoure's cape to where she stood at the edge of the sea, looking out over the waves. Walfgar stood close by to guard her from Rethel.

A strong wind blew Annoure's long, dark hair. She looked small and forlorn in the men's clothes Thorstein had loaned her. She had to roll up the shirtsleeves at the wrists and the pant legs at the ankles to make the clothes fit her better.

Thorstein placed the cape over her shoulders. She turned and looked at him with a puzzled expression, surprised by his consideration. She said something in Anglo-Saxon and Walfgar translated. "She thanks you."

She spoke again and Walfgar interpreted, "She said this is a lonely, forbidding place."

Thorstein looked around at the few stubby trees and rocky shoreline. The wind blew endlessly with no tall trees to break its force. "Tell her there are vast forests, waterfalls and beautiful mountains where we live."

Walfgar translated then told Thorstein her reply. "She would rather go home. She misses her *faðir* and *bróðirs*."

Thorstein hadn't thought about her family before. He didn't like the idea of her yearning to return home to father and brothers. She probably loved her people just as he did his. For the first time it occurred to him that maybe it hadn't been right to abduct her just because he wanted her. He pushed the thought aside to ponder at another time. "What about her *móðir*?" he asked, wondering why she didn't mention her mother.

"Her móðir died when she was young."

Thorstein wished he could more easily converse with Annoure and get to know her. He decided to work harder at learning her language.

Annoure spoke again in Anglo-Saxon. "My betrothed and father will pay well for my return."

"Your betrothed?" Thorstein asked, to be sure he understood correctly.

"Yes, I'm engaged. Her mouth formed a tight line and he wondered if she was happy with the match. If marriages were like those in his land, a daughter had little to say about the man her father picked for her. But perhaps her expression just meant she was distressed that the marriage would never take place.

"Who is this man?" he asked.

"Sir Bandolf, a friend of King Aethelred and a man of wealth." She answered with Walfgar's assistance. "He has nearly grown sons."

Thorstein shifted his stance uneasily. She probably wanted a man of power and wealth and would be unhappy with a landless second son.

Thorstein took Annoure back to where he'd set up the tent and she paused to look at the painting of intertwined dragons on its side. They sat on a log before the campfire and Herjulf handed Annoure a bowl of hot stew. She took it without smiling and ate only a few bites.

Thorstein wondered what was wrong as he observed how rigidly she sat. Perhaps she was afraid he'd force himself on her now that they were on dry land. He felt badly about making her cry and had left her alone since then.

Annoure rose and disappeared into the tent. He was about to join her when the farmer Refr, Ketil and their neighbor Olaf came over with a flask of wine and settled comfortably around the fire.

After a few drinks, Ketil began to tell a story about a village of dwarfs that was known for making weapons. "The dwarfs grew very rich from their trade and had a hoard of gold and jewels." The firelight reflected off Ketil's thin nose. As Thorstein listened to the story, he wondered if Ketil was over the worst of his grief. It had been a long time since he'd shared in the storytelling. Maybe Ketil was ready to remarry. Kalsetini always liked him and was disappointed when he married Hanna, although Kalsetini was too young to marry at the time. Thorstein's attention drifted back to the story.

"The dwarfs' hoard was stolen by a fierce dragon. A small group of dwarfs, led by a brave dwarf named Egil, set off to get back their hoard. Egil had a magic cape that made him invisible when he put it on. When they reached the dragon's lair, Egil used the cloak to cover himself, then snuck up to the dragon and slew him as he slept."

In the morning, the crew filled their water barrels from the stream and purchased food from Refr before departing. Thorstein calculated it would take two or three days at sea to reach Bergen with fair weather. He was anxious to find out the fate of the other ships and eager to return home with Annoure before more trouble erupted from Rethel.

Chapter 5

Bergen

A FEW DAYS LATER, ANNOURE STOOD on the deck, enjoying the fresh, salty wind blowing on her face. She liked sailing now that the sea had calmed and her seasickness had subsided. Thorstein pointed to a fountain of water shooting up in the air. "*Hvair,*" he said.

"Hvalr," she repeated, eager to learn more of the Norse language so she wouldn't feel so lost among its people. Since Walfgar worked with her daily and there was little else to do during the long days at sea, she'd learned the rudiments of the language quickly.

When they sailed closer to where the water sprayed up, a creature's smooth, black back appeared above the surface of the water.

"Holy Mother Mary!" she exclaimed, sucking in her breath. It was bigger than the ship and could easily capsize them!

"It won't hurt us," Thorstein said, noticing her distress. "We hunt hvalrs for oil and meat."

Annoure realized *hvalr* referred to the sea animal, not shooting water. She kept her eyes on the sea when it disappeared, still worried.

"It must be dangerous to hunt. It's so big." She put her hands out wide.

"Say it in Norse."

She said it as best she could. He laughed and told her how to say it correctly.

"We trade the havr meat, oil and teeth," Thorstein said in Anglo-Saxon. His ability to speak her language was limited mostly to words that had to do with trading.

He pointed to a seagull and said in Norse, “Birds live near land.”

Her eyes lit up. “We’re near land?”

He pointed off in the distance. “Straight ahead.”

She stared in the direction he pointed and could make out a faint outline of mountains on the horizon.

Late in the day, they sailed into a narrow inlet surrounded by seven mountain peaks. Thorstein told her the inlet was called a fjord. The men lowered the sail as their ship approached a small coastal village nestled in the mountains.

Annoure saw women washing clothes and children playing along the shoreline. It was a comforting sight after living among dangerous warriors for so many days. The Norsemen moored their longship alongside two other drakkars.

“Are those your missing ships?” Annoure asked Thorstein, who cheerfully waved at the men on shore.

He smiled. “Já, it’s good to see they made it.” The men put the gangplank down and their comrades came over to greet them. Annoure uneasily stepped closer to Thorstein.

From his trunk, Thorstein handed the hudfat to Annoure, then strapped on his sword before picking up the bag of loot and supplies. When they stepped on land, Annoure felt the ground roll beneath her feet. She walked with her feet apart to keep her balance as she had at sea.

Herjulf Redbeard came up behind them. “You walk like a sailor,” he said, laughing.

“Good to be on land,” she said in Norse. She stared up at the snow-capped mountains and scattered waterfalls, enthralled by their rugged beauty.

Thorstein and his kin set up a tent in the Norsemen’s camp and stowed their hudfats and supplies inside. Afterwards Thorstein led Annoure to town.

“Bergen is a trading village,” he said in Anglo-Saxon. The crowded, busy streets were lined with houses, shops, a stable and food stalls. Sheep, dogs and cats ran loose.

Thorstein led Annoure to a dark, one-room shop and a pretty, plump woman approached them. “Ota, we need clothes and baths,” Thorstein said.

The woman cast a sharp look at Annoure, before smiling brightly at Thorstein and giving him a full kiss on the mouth. Annoure bristled as she studied the Norse woman. Ota was too familiar and bold with Thorstein. Annoure needed Thorstein's protection and didn't want his interest to wane.

Ota began speaking Norse so rapidly that Annoure couldn't understand her. Thorstein replied, speaking just as fast. He laughed at something Ota said and she boldly grinned back. Annoure gave up trying to follow the conversation and looked around.

A fire burned in the center stone hearth, making the room smoky and hot. Shelves along the walls were piled high with fabric, clothes, jewelry and other trading supplies. A large wooden tub sat in the corner.

The woman yelled to a boy who was putting wood on the fire. He picked up a bucket and ambled from the shop. The woman continued talking to Thorstein as he looked over clothing on a table. The boy returned with a full bucket of water and poured it into the wooden tub. He made several trips from the well, then added hot water from the cauldron over the fire pit.

Annoure looked at brooches on a table, appreciating the fine craftsmanship as the youth worked. Many brooches were fashioned in gold and silver and set with stones. She picked up an oval-shaped silver brooch with a dragon on it.

Thorstein handed her clothing and said in Anglo-Saxon, "Bathe, then dress." He handed her a brooch that matched the one in her hand.

Annoure sat on the chair beside the tub and took off her leather slippers, then washed her face and hands. Thorstein came over. "Nei, undress and get into the tub."

"The priests forbid regular bathing," she said. "It's bad."

"Bad? What's bad about bathing?"

Ota said in Norse, "I'll help her."

Thorstein scowled, looking frustrated as Ota drew a curtain in front of the tub. The tall, sturdy Norse woman grasped the hem of Annoure's shirt and tunic and pulled them over her head. Annoure slipped off the pants and quickly climbed into the tub, her cheeks burning with embarrassment.

The hot water felt good, but Annoure sizzled with indignation. Ota picked up a bar of soap and vigorously scrubbed her back.

"I can do it!" Annoure exclaimed, taking the soap from Ota. Aware that the woman couldn't understand her, Annoure began washing herself.

Ota dumped a bucket of warm water over her head and Annoure shrieked in surprise. Ota ignored her outburst and began enthusiastically scrubbing her hair with soap, then she poured another bucket of water over Annoure's head to rinse out the suds. Ready for it this time, Annoure squeezed her eyes shut. Once her hair was rinsed, Ota held out a drying cloth.

Annoure climbed out of the tub and wrapped the cloth around her body. Once she'd dried herself, Ota slipped a pleated under-dress over her head. The floor-length linen gown had long sleeves. Ota placed a woolen garment over the under-dress and fastened the shoulder straps with the two dragon brooches.

"This is a *hangerock*," Ota said, gesturing at the over garment. It consisted of two panels of woven green cloth that exposed the under-dress beneath it at the sleeves, sides and bottom. The garments were plain and the fabric coarser than what Annoure was accustomed to, but she was glad to be wearing women's clothes again.

Annoure put her slippers back on and tied the leather straps, still angry with Thorstein for making her bathe. She detested being ordered around by a pagan conqueror.

Ota pulled open the curtain. When Annoure stepped out, Thorstein looked her over appreciatively with smug satisfaction.

"Norse pig," she said, glaring at him.

Thorstein's eyes narrowed. "Christians are pigs. They are dirty and smelly." He stomped past her to the tub and jerked the curtain close.

Annoure stiffened, chagrined that Thorstein thought her people were pigs for not bathing. She regretted angering him after he'd been kind enough to buy her new clothes and brooches. Her nursemaid had told her many times a woman must learn to control her temper. It had gotten Annoure into trouble way too often.

Ota grinned, as if pleased by the tension between Annoure and Thorstein. The Norse woman handed Annoure a bone comb.

Annoure sat on a stool by the fire and began the tedious task of combing the snarls out of her waist-length hair. Finally it was free of tangles and fairly dry from the warmth of the fire. Ota knotted it on the back of Annoure's head, letting the rest hang down in a ponytail, and secured the knot with hairpins.

Thorstein emerged from his bath with damp hair and paid Ota with silver pieces weighed on a scale. He left the shop carrying a small bundle. Annoure hurried after him, nearly running to keep up with his long strides. Apparently his temper hadn't cooled.

They joined Thorstein's kin and friends by a campfire. Thorstein took a drinking horn from Walfgar and tossed down its contents in one long drink. He refilled it from the jug and drank more. The men stared at Annoure.

"You look like a Norsewoman," Walfgar said in Anglo-Saxon. "What's put Thorstein in such ill temper?"

"I displeased him."

Walfgar spoke to Thorstein in Norse and Thorstein replied in Anglo-Saxon, "I should sell her."

Walfgar and Herjulf both grinned, amused by his remark. Annoure found nothing to be amused about. Herjulf slapped Thorstein on the back and said something in Norse. She frowned, even more determined to learn the language.

Walfgar handed Thorstein a wooden bowl of stew. "Eat." He glanced at Annoure and said in Anglo-Saxon, "Fill yourself a bowl."

She shook her head, too distressed to eat, and worried that Thorstein might punish her for insulting him. She looked toward the ocean, longing to go home. She wondered where Cearl was; the boy always stuck close by on the ship. She missed her only Anglo-Saxon friend.

"Sit and eat," Herjulf said in a kind voice.

"I'm not hungry." Annoure wrapped her arms around her chest. She liked Herjulf. He was always friendly, good-natured and liked to entertain her with board games. Walfgar was older and more reserved. He seemed to merely tolerate her, though he was willing to pass the long hours at sea teaching her Norse. With Thorstein, everything was layered with dream memories and emotions, such as her anger at him for stealing her from her home and her growing attraction toward him.

While the men ate and drank, she looked around, uneasy at the prospect of being in a camp of drunken men. The Norsemen sat around the campfires, eating and talking. Someone moaned nearby. Annoure peered through the bushes and saw a couple mating on the ground. Shocked, she quickly turned away.

"Thorstein," she said wearily. He was listening to Walfgar and didn't seem hear her. "Thorstein," she said, speaking louder. "I'm tired."

Walfgar said something she didn't catch and Herjulf chuckled, looking lewdly at her. Thorstein rose. "I'll take you to the tent."

As they walked through the camp, Annoure was puzzled that the sun still hadn't set by now. Daylight was long in this land. In the distance, Annoure heard singing. Nearby two men argued in loud, angry voices. She followed Thorstein into the tent and stood with her hands clenched into fists. Thorstein removed his sheathed sword and drew her close. She only came up to his chin. He smelled clean and fresh from his bath and his hair was still slightly damp. She trembled, fearing that he was drunk and still angry with her.

He slid one hand onto her neck and with his thumb gently tilted her chin up so she faced him. Their eyes met and held. Her pulse quickened as he lowered his head and covered her mouth with his. She tried to push him away, but he held her firmly.

"You are beautiful, Annoure," he said in Anglo-Saxon.

She stared up at him, her throat constricting.

He pulled off his shirt and tunic. The candlelight cast gold and reddish tones across his broad, muscular chest. He stepped closer and she gasped as he picked her up and set her down on the furs.

"No, please!" she begged, knowing he wanted her.

He put his arms around her and kissed her again. She gave him a shove and scooted as far away from him as possible in the small tent. Then she drew up her knees and wrapped her arms around them.

"What's wrong?" he asked in Anglo-Saxon.

"You're not my husband."

"Your *Verr*!" he exclaimed saying husband in Norse. "Thor's Mjölnir! You're a thrall!"

She pursed her lips together.

"Please me or I'll sell you! Come here."

She shook her head.

His eyes flashed. "There are other willing women." He jerked on his shirt and tunic. "Ota will welcome me to her sleeping bench." He strode out of the tent.

Annoure scowled. *Ota! That fat hussy. What did he like about her?* Then she remembered his threat to sell her if she didn't please him and a rush of heat went through her. *What if Rethel bought her? She couldn't let that happen! She had to find Thorstein and convince him to ransom her.*

Annoure left the tent and headed toward Ota's shop. On the way she'd pass the campfire where Herjulf and Walfgar were. Perhaps Herjulf would help her find Thorstein.

Soon she spotted the campfire. Herjulf was still there—Thorstein sat beside him. She paused, feeling conflicted and not knowing what to do.

The scuff of a footstep sounded behind her. She spun around to see Rethel and Edgtho approaching. Rethel stopped in front of her. He gazed at her with a leering grin, reeking of mead. Annoure's mouth went dry. She was too frightened to move or cry out. Rethel pulled her roughly to him and captured her mouth in a bruising kiss. Annoure pounded her fists against his hard chest, twisted her mouth free and screamed, "Thorstein!"

Rethel backhanded her and she crumpled to the ground in a blaze of pain. He shoved up her dress and tried to pull her legs apart. Squeezing her thighs together, Annoure pushed her hands against his shoulders. He whipped out a large knife and held it to her throat pricking her skin. A trickle of blood oozed down her neck and terror froze her heart.

Chapter 6

The Fight

THORSTEIN SPRUNG TO HIS FEET when he heard Annoure scream his name. Quickly scanning the area, he spotted Rethel struggling with her on the ground; Edgtho stood nearby. Thorstein charged toward them. When he reached Annoure, he saw Rethel held a knife to her throat.

"Rethel!" Thorstein yelled.

Rethel looked up, whipping the knife away from Annoure toward him. Thorstein leapt, knocking Rethel off her. Rethel slashed his blade at Thorstein. He grabbed Rethel's wrist and slammed his hand against a rock, causing Rethel to drop the knife. Thorstein sprung to his feet and kicked the knife out of his reach.

Rethel rolled to his feet and yelled, "Edgtho, your sword!" As Edgtho handed him a sword, Thorstein reached for his—only to discover he'd left it in the tent.

"Thorstein, here!" Herjulf yelled, racing over to them. Herjulf thrust the hilt of his sword into Thorstein's hand just as Rethel swung his sword toward Thorstein.

Thorstein parried the forceful blow. "I don't want to fight you, Rethel!" he exclaimed. "Can't we resolve this peacefully?"

"Give me the woman if you're too cowardly to fight," Rethel yelled, his face distorted with rage.

"Nei, she's mine."

"Then you can die with her."

"I don't plan to die. You overrate your skills." Thorstein circled

Rethel as he spoke, looking for an opening.

Men gathered around them to watch the fight. Thorstein swung his sword toward Rethel. As the clang of metal hitting metal rang through the air Thorstein wished for a shield to protect the blade.

Ketil ran to where they fought and drew his sword. In response, Walfgar drew his.

Thorstein realized the conflict could easily turn into a bloodbath. "This is between me and Rethel," he yelled. "Stay out of it!"

Rethel attacked with renewed violence, pressing forward, forcing Thorstein back. Thorstein regretted having drunk so much earlier and eaten so little. It slowed his reflexes and made his movements clumsy. He swung his sword and Rethel met it with his. They broke apart and glared at one another.

Rethel beckoned Thorstein forward with his hand. "Come and get it, Thorstein. Tonight you go to Valhalla."

Thorstein leapt forward and their swords clashed once again. Thorstein felt the force of it reverberate through his thick shoulders and arms. He twisted his blade away and swung again. Rethel's lips contorted grotesquely as he charged Thorstein. They fought on, moving back and forth across the ground.

The crowd that had gathered formed a circle around them. Sweat poured down Thorstein's forehead and his arms shook with strain. He knew he was outmatched. An expert swordsman, Rethel seemed to grow in power as Thorstein began to wane. Rethel broke through his guard and Thorstein gasped in pain as the blade sliced into his shoulder. He took a staggering step backwards.

"I'll carve up your Saxon witch," Rethel yelled.

Thorstein went berserk at Rethel's words and struck repeated blows with his sword until Rethel began to weaken. Rethel's eyes revealed his uncertainty and he glanced down at the unfamiliar sword in his hand, his fearless confidence draining from him.

Rethel charged wildly at Thorstein who twisted to the right and plunged his sword into Rethel's side. Thorstein drew away and pulled out the blade, horrified to see it covered in blood almost to the hilt. Rethel tried to raise his sword, then collapsed onto the ground in a pool of blood.

Ketil squatted beside him, trying to stop the flow of blood with his hands. "Bróðir, you must live!"

"I was cursed by that witch." Rethel gasped. "She caused me to lose Bloodrun to the sea and now to lose my life." He took several labored breaths before whispering, "Avenge me." His head rolled back and he was gone.

Ketil held Rethel close to his chest, rocking back and forth. "Nei, don't die." The anguished words sounded as if they were ripped from his heart and tears dampened his cheeks. Ketil lowered Rethel to the ground and slowly rose, holding his blood-covered hands toward Thorstein. "He's dead!" he cried in agony. "You killed him! You killed my bróðir!"

"You'll pay for this," Edgtho said, grabbing his sword.

Though winded and breathing hard, Thorstein's fighting blood pounded. "It was a fair fight and Rethel started it. If you're not satisfied, I'll battle you both!" Thorstein tightened his grip on the sword. Walfgar stepped forward with his sword drawn and Herjulf pulled out his axe.

Edgtho trembled with rage, looking from Thorstein to Herjulf and Walfgar. "Now is not the time," he snarled. "But this is not over. I'll have my revenge!" He slid his sword back into its sheath, then knelt beside Rethel's body and bowed his head in grief.

As Thorstein handed the sword back to Herjulf, the realization hit him: he'd just killed his best friend's brother. Ketil would never forgive him. He wasn't sure he could forgive himself. If he'd drunk less, perhaps he could've just wounded Rethel. He drew Annoure close, grimacing at the pain the movement caused his injured shoulder. Annoure trembled in his arms. "Let's get out of here," he said, glancing from Walfgar to Herjulf. "They're angry enough to cause further trouble." Thorstein kept his arm around Annoure as they walked toward their tent.

"Edgtho will try to kill you, Thorstein," Herjulf said.

"I have no fear of him."

"You should. He is a better swordsman than you are."

"How is it you were without *Grimmr*?" Walfgar asked. "It's always at your side."

"I was upset and left the tent in haste."

"If I hadn't been here, he would have killed you," Herjulf said.

"Your faðir will be furious when he hears you killed one of our neighbor's sons over a thrall," Walfgar said, shaking his head in concern.

"I know the magnitude of what happened. This will probably be brought before the *ting*," Thorstein said, thinking of the legal assembly that settled disputes.

"It's not your fault," Herjulf said. "Rethel attacked Annoure."

"She's a thrall and has no rights," Walfgar said. "No good can come of this."

In the tent, Thorstein winced in pain as he sat on the furs. Annoure helped him remove his shirt, then pressed it against his bleeding wound. The fabric immediately reddened.

"Why did you leave the tent?" Thorstein asked her.

"Don't sell me." Her eyes were wide with worry, her face pale and drawn.

"He won't sell you," Walfgar said. "He wants you for himself."

"Keep your teeth together, Walfgar," Thorstein said, not wanting Annoure to know how much he wanted her.

Walfgar wiped blood from Thorstein's wound and examined it. "You'll live, though it's a deep cut." Walfgar handed him a flask and Thorstein took a drink, then handed the flask to Annoure. She took a drink and made a face as she realized it was strong wine, then passing it to Herjulf. When it came back to him, he drank again. The flask passed several more times as he talked about the fight with his kin. The pain in Thorstein's shoulder was already beginning to lessen from the alcohol.

"It could easily be you who lays dead right now. I still can't believe you left *Grimmr* in the tent." Walfgar put a folded cloth against the wound and told Annoure to hold it as he bound it in place with another piece of cloth. He had just tied the knot when Annoure crumpled onto the furs.

"Annoure!" Thorstein exclaimed. "What's wrong with her?"

"She fainted," Walfgar said. "She must not be used to tending wounds."

Herjulf knelt beside her. "She's coming around." He helped her sit up and she said something in Anglo-Saxon.

Walfgar translated. "Annoure said the blood made her light-headed. She apologizes for leaving the tent and is sorry you were wounded, Thorstein."

"Tell her it's my fault. I shouldn't have lost my temper and threatened to sell her." Thorstein closed his eyes, hoping the throbbing in his shoulder would lessen soon as Walfgar translated his words for Annoure.

Herjulf and Walfgar went back outside to enjoy the stories and companionship of the other warriors, promising to stay close in case there was more trouble.

Thorstein felt Annoure crawl into the hudfat beside him. He was glad to have her there. It had made his blood run cold when he saw Rethel holding a knife to her throat. One slice and she would have been lost to him forever. He'd have to keep her close until they reached the safety of his family farm.

Sleeping with her, but not making love, had tested his patience. For many days he thought of sharing pleasure with her once they reached land and was disappointed when she still refused him. He thought over their argument and realized he shouldn't have expected her to yield to his desires. She was a maiden, sheltered from men, reared to be chaste until she married. Sometimes Norsemen married women they captured on a raid. Annoure was a woman worthy of marriage. Yet she wouldn't bring him a dowry or brothers-in-law to help with the harvest or fight by his side.

"I was afraid Rethel would kill you," Annoure said in broken Norse.

"I am a skilled warrior."

"So was Rethel." She lightly traced the patterns of his arm tattoos. "I dreamed of you in Northumbria," she said.

He tensed, wondering if he understood her correctly. "I also dreamed."

"What did you dream of?" she asked.

"Of you, my sweet." He tried to shake off the feeling of mystery that sprang up between them, but it persisted.

"We dream-traveled together." Her eyes were full of wisdom beyond her years as she gazed at him and he felt a deep connection to her.

* * *

Annoure awoke with a pounding headache and a foul taste in her mouth. She regretted drinking so much wine. Thorstein still slept beside her. Herjulf and Walfgar had returned during the night and they also slept.

She gazed at Thorstein in the gray morning light, dismayed that she'd come to care for him. She ought to hate him for attacking her people and stealing her from home. Instead she felt a strange unwanted attraction to this handsome Norseman.

She was drawn to his courage, vitality and inner strength. He also fascinated her with his Norse beliefs and his willingness to face death at a moment's notice, whether at sea or in combat.

This attraction confused her. He was a pirate who robbed the church and killed with no conscience. He'd threatened to sell her and saw her as a thrall—spoils of a raid—to be used or discarded as it pleased him. Clearly he couldn't be trusted. Her Christian upbringing should have made him repugnant to her. Instead her Druid training seemed to take over and the Mother Goddess whispered, *It's right to want him. Your life is intertwined with his.*

Annoure slipped out of the hudfat, trying not to awaken Thorstein, and pulled on her hangerock. She stepped out of the tent and saw that the sun was rising. The camp was quiet for most of the men had celebrated late into the night.

She headed into the woods to relieve herself, then walked to the stream Thorstein had taken her to the day before. Since it was a warm day, she hadn't bothered to put on shoes. She washed her face and drank from the stream to get the awful taste of stale wine out of her mouth.

The sunlight danced on the clear, inviting water. She lifted the skirt of her dress and waded in, listening to the sound of babbling water and the birds singing. She relished being alone.

The peaceful setting was such a contrast to spending so many days on the ship with a crew of rowdy, treacherous men. The ship had seemed large until she was forced to live in its confined space. Moreover, the journey didn't allow for privacy or a chance to be alone to look for inner stillness, in keeping with the ancient, hidden Druid secrets her grandmother had imparted.

Back on shore, Annoure knelt and raised her hands in prayer. The Celtic cross hung heavy around her neck. Would she burn in hell for being attracted to a heathen enemy who participated in a raid on St. Paul's church? "Virgin Mother, please hear my confession. There is no priest to hear me and absolve my sins."

She paused, feeling a female presence. It was not the gentle Virgin Mary however; it was her strong grandmother's energy. The power of the Mother Goddess flowed through her. "Your Christian God will not serve you amongst the Norse," Grandmother said inwardly. "It's time to go deeper and embrace your Druid heritage. See with eyes other than your physical ones. Strengthen your inner awareness and perceptions. Embrace the gifts life offers, even if they are not the ones you asked for. Trust life to give you the experiences you need."

Annoure recognized truth in her grandmother's words. She stood and raised her arms in the air in worship, feeling Mother Earth beneath her feet and the warm sun on her face. The scent of tall pines permeated the air around her and the majestic mountains beyond rose high into the sky.

"Annoure!" a male voice called. She recognized the voice as Thorstein's.

"I'm here," she answered in Norse, annoyed that her solitude and moment of connection to Mother Earth was broken.

He burst through the bushes, carrying a sheathed sword; he wore only a pair of tight-fitting pants as if he'd left the tent in a hurry. The bandage on his shoulder had dried blood on it, reminding her that he was wounded on her account. His eyes narrowed and his jaw tightened at the sight of her. Grabbing her arm, he pulled her to him. "Why did you leave the tent?" he demanded in Anglo-Saxon.

"I wanted to," she replied in her own tongue.

"Don't ever leave the tent alone!" he said speaking a combination of Norse and Anglo-Saxon, gesturing with his free hand. "Didn't you learn anything last night?"

"You're hurting me."

He released her and said, "Do you understand? You're not to leave the tent by yourself!"

"Yes, I understand."

"See that you obey."

Irritated by his manner, she snapped, "I'm not a thrall! I'll do as I please."

"Annoure," he said earnestly. Concern for her welfare reflected in his eyes. "Edgtho is dangerous."

Annoure's temper faded. Thorstein was not trying to enslave her; he was worried about Edgtho finding her alone. She wished they could communicate better and stop quarreling. With so much to learn about the Norsemen's ways, she always seemed to be doing something wrong.

Despite her embarrassment with having to explain personal things, she said in Anglo-Saxon, “I needed to make water and I didn’t want to wake you since you were wounded.” She hoped he could understand the gist of what she said, even if he didn’t understand every word.

His stance relaxed. “Wake me next time,” he said in a calmer voice. “I was worried.” He held out his hand and when she took it, he smiled.

Chapter 7

Funeral Ceremony

THORSTEIN LED ANNOURE BACK TO camp where Walfgar and Herjulf sat by the cooking fire. Savoring the smell of hot food after so many days at sea, Thorstein dished up a bowl of porridge from the cauldron and handed it to Annoure. "You must be hungry," he said in Norse. "You didn't have anything to eat last night." He was still on edge after awakening and finding her gone. He'd feared she'd run away. After filling a bowl for himself, he sat down on a log beside her.

Herjulf handed Thorstein a drinking horn. "Have a cup of nabidth. Compliments of Tyrker the Courageous."

"We drink in honor of our dead war chief, Tyrker," Walfgar explained to Annoure in Anglo-Saxon. "He was killed during the raid on St. Paul's Church. For several days, we'll feast and drink while fine clothes are made for him. On the fourth day, we'll have the funeral ceremony. His family sold his possessions, except for what he'll take to Valhalla, and bought nabidth for all his men."

"What's Valhalla?" Annoure asked. Thorstein handed her the horn and she took a sip. Her pretty nose wrinkled at its strong taste.

"It's a place of gods where courageous warriors go when they're killed in battle," Walfgar said.

Herjulf frowned gloomily. "I heard that *all* his horses will be killed and sent with him. I think it's a waste to kill so many fine animals."

"He'll need them in the afterlife and it will keep his family from becoming too powerful," Walfgar said.

"Better to give the horses away," Herjulf said. "I'd rather have a horse than nabidth to remember Tyrker by."

Thorstein pulled his sword from its leather sheath and began cleaning the double-edged blade and silver hilt.

Annoure pointed to the letters on the blade. "What does it say?" she asked.

"*Grimmr*," Thorstein said, speaking slowly so she could understand. "It means fierce. The name gives it power."

Thorstein held up the sword and turned it so the light reflected off the steel blade. "I should have had Grimmr in the battle last night."

He lowered the sword uneasily as Ljot Flatnose, a warrior of Tyrker's house, approached. An old woman with snow-white hair and deep wrinkles on her shriveled face accompanied him.

"Who is the crone with Ljot?" Thorstein asked softly, feeling power surrounding her.

"She's the appointed Angel of Death for the funeral ceremony," Walfgar replied. "I wonder what they want."

Ljot and the crone stopped in front of them. "Tyrker the Courageous needs a woman to accompany his journey to Valhalla," Ljot said, puffing out his barrel chest. He gestured to Annoure. "The Angel of Death has chosen this thrall."

"Nei!" Thorstein exclaimed, tightening his hand on his sword hilt as he stood. "It's custom to use one of the war leader's own thralls for the ceremony."

The crone's eyes narrowed angrily. "I cast the stones and the oracle said she is the one to accompany him."

Thorstein stammered, "There must be a mistake. She is my woman." Annoure rose and he put his left arm protectively around her.

"There is no mistake."

"What exactly did the oracle say?" Herjulf asked, also standing.

"That a woman who is not from our land will make the journey with Tyrker," the Angel of Death said.

"Annoure is not the only woman from another land," Herjulf said.

"It's an honor to accompany a great warrior on his final journey," said the crone. "It is the only way a woman can get to Valhalla. Give her to me."

"A woman is never forced to perform the ceremony unless there are none willing," Thorstein said. "Tyrker was a great warrior, but we are all great warriors. Ask among his thralls before demanding mine."

"The oracle must be followed or you will be cursed!" spat the crone.

Thorstein broke into a sweat. His whole being rebelled at the idea of Annoure being sacrificed. "You can't have her! I'll fight for her if I have to!"

"We do not want a fight," Ljot said. "We'll ask among Tyrker's thralls. If none are willing, we'll return."

"Nei, this is the one!" the crone exclaimed.

Ljot Flatnose scowled. "A man was killed last night over this woman. Her value to Thorstein has already been demonstrated."

The crone glared furiously at Thorstein. "You made a poor choice. This will bring bad fortune on your house." She spat, spun around, and strode away with Ljot.

"By the gods, Thorstein!" Walfgar exclaimed. "No thrall is worth being cursed. I beg you to reconsider. Oracles should be followed."

"She is worth the trouble to me." He sheathed his sword and held Annoure close as he watched the Angel of Death and Ljot walk over to a group of Tyrker's thralls. Many Norsemen gathered around to watch the proceedings.

"Which of you will accompany Tyrker the Courageous on his journey to Valhalla?" Ljot asked the thralls.

For several moments, a tense silence ensued, then a trembling woman stepped forward. "I'm honored to share Tyrker's final journey."

"Where are you from?" the Angel of Death asked.

"I was born on Tyrker's farmstead."

"You are not the one." The crone scanned the other thralls. "The woman must be from another land."

Everyone's attention turned to a dark-skinned thrall. "Tola is from another land," Ljot said. Tola's eyes widened and she took a step backward.

"Where are you from?" the Angel of Death asked her.

"I was taken from across the Varangian Sea," Tola said, her voice breaking.

"She will fulfill the oracle," Ljot said.

Tola collapsed onto the ground and the other thralls gathered around her. The Angel of Death picked two women as attendants for Tola until the funeral.

"What's going on?" Annoure asked.

"Keep your teeth together," Thorstein replied sharply, releasing her.

"What did they want?"

"You," he said crossly, worried about angering the gods.

"You did what any man would do if his woman was chosen," Herjulf said. "The old hag shouldn't have asked for Annoure. Everyone in camp knows of Rethel's death by now. His cousin Edgtho probably suggested it for revenge."

Herjulf filled a drinking horn from a leather flask. "Have some nabidth. It will cheer you."

Thorstein slugged down the fiery drink.

A few days later, as Thorstein played backgammon with Herjulf, Tola walked over to a circle of men sitting nearby. She wore a finely made hangerock and gold bracelet. She glanced over to Thorstein, glaring at him murderously.

He winced, knowing the cost of Annoure's life was Tola's. Before long, Tola took a drink and began to sing vulgarly. Soon after, she disappeared into a tent with one of the men.

Walfgar said to Annoure in Anglo-Saxon, "Tola will mate with many of Tyrker's warriors to honor him. It's part of the ceremony."

"You mean she . . ." Annoure flushed.

Herjulf laughed, then took a swig of nabidth from his drinking horn.

Thorstein threw the bone die and moved one of the stone markers on the backgammon board. They played until Thorstein won the game. Herjulf paid him a silver coin and challenged him to a rematch. They made a bet and soon Thorstein became so engrossed in the new game that he was startled when a female voice said, "I come to you for my Master."

Thorstein looked up and saw Tola standing before him, eyes narrowed with suppressed fury.

He hesitated, suspicious of why she'd chosen him, then said the words of the ritual, "Tell Tyrker when you see him that I do this only for the love of him." His mind raced as he tried to think of a way to avoid participating in the ceremony, without being disrespectful to Tyrker and further angering the Angel of Death.

"My Master thanks you," Tola replied. She knelt down in front of him and put her hands on his thighs, leaning forward.

Annoure gave Tola a shove and she lost her balance and fell onto the ground.

With a scream, Tola leapt toward Annoure.

"You should be in the ceremony, not me! The crone chose you!" A knife flashed in Tola's hand.

Thorstein grabbed Tola and pulled her away from Annoure.

"Let me go!" Tola screamed. "I'll kill her! She's the one meant to die."

Tola slashed the knife toward Thorstein. He jerked back and the blade missed his chest by a hair's breadth. She sprang at Annoure, who spun out of the way, and the knife stabbed harmlessly into the ground. With a furious cry, Tola thrust the knife at Annoure again.

Herjulf grabbed Tola's arm and twisted it behind her back. "Drop the knife!"

"Let me go!" Tola yelled.

Herjulf gave her arm a jerk and the knife fell to the ground, but he didn't release her.

"I should kill her for trying to stab Annoure!" Thorstein yelled, seething with anger.

"Control your temper, cousin," Walfgar said. "Tola is to be treated with honor. Your little thrall will cost you your life if you offend all of Tyrker's family by killing Tola. Besides if she's dead, they will look for a new thrall to take her place."

"She attacked Annoure!"

"She'll join Tyrker in Valhalla soon enough."

"If the gods are willing," Thorstein said, breathing heavily. "I refuse to perform the ritual with her. You perform it, Herjulf."

Herjulf looked warily at Tola. "I don't think she wants to perform the ritual with me."

Tola savagely struggled to get away as Thorstein helped Annoure up. Thorstein and Annoure walked out of camp, heading toward the town of Bergen.

"Why did you shove Tola?" Thorstein asked in Norse.

"She had a knife," Annoure answered in Anglo-Saxon. Thorstein realized she always reverted to her native tongue when she was upset and was glad his command of her language was rapidly improving from conversing with her.

"She wanted to kill you," Annoure added. Her lips trembled and she twisted her hands together.

"Why do you care?" he asked.

"You saved my life several times." She looked down, then faced him again. "Please, Thorstein, I beg of you: ransom me. I don't belong here and I've only brought you trouble."

"Tomorrow we leave for my home. You'll be safe there," he replied, speaking slowly so she would understand.

She shook her head. "I want to go home. My father will pay for my return."

"It was decided at council that no one will be ransomed from this raid. It wouldn't be profitable to make the journey back. Besides, it's time for fall harvest. We'll all be returning to our farms." He frowned, knowing she wouldn't understand everything he said.

"What's to become of me?" Tears sprang to her eyes.

"I'm keeping you as my booty from the raid." There was enough treasure in the bag she'd carried to pay for his share of the voyage to Jarrow.

She brushed her tears away and turned from him, hiding her grief.

That evening Thorstein brought Annoure to the ocean where a longship was moored. A crowd of people gathered on the shore and Thorstein pushed his way through them to join his cousins.

Before long, four of Tyrker's male relatives walked by carrying Tyrker's body on a funeral bier. The corpse was in a sitting position, dressed in a tunic made for the funeral with his sword by his side. The men carried the body into a tent erected on the ship.

Next, a man brought a dog to the ship and one of Tyrker's men pulled out a knife. Annoure gasped and turned away as the man ritualistically slaughtered the dog and threw it on the ship. Thorstein realized the ceremony was distressing her and he drew her into his arms as two horses were led to the ship. One of the horses screamed shrilly just before its throat was cut.

She pressed her face into his chest, trembling. Two men butchered the horses, then the meat was carried onto the longship to provide food for Tyrker on his journey.

The setting sun cast brilliant colors across the sky as Tola walked through the crowd. She stopped at the shoreline near the Angel of Death. Annoure turned to see what was happening as two warriors lifted Tola into the air.

"Lo, there is my master who is sitting in Valhalla," Tola said, looking at the ship. "Tyrker the Courageous calls me, so bring me to him."

One of the men reached up and handed Tola a hen. She cut off its head, threw the head away and handed the hen's body back to the warrior, who threw it on the deck of the longship.

Tola took off her bracelets and handed them to the Angel of Death. The men lowered Tola and carried her onto the ship. Six men, all relatives or close friends of Tyrker, boarded the ship with shields and staves. Edgtho was among them. One handed Tola a horn containing nabidth.

She drank it and said, "With this, I take leave of those who are dear to me." Then she began to sing a wild, discordant song. The crone grabbed her by the hair and dragged her inside the tent. The warriors followed.

"What's going on?" Annoure asked.

Thorstein swallowed, uncomfortable answering her. "It's a ceremony to honor Tyrker, our war chief."

"Tola will go to Valhalla with Tyrker," Walfgar said in Anglo-Saxon.

Annoure's face drained of color.

"Don't explain in more detail, Walfgar. You've frightened her enough," Thorstein snapped, knowing it could easily have been Annoure who was about to be killed.

On land, several warriors began beating their staves against their shields. Despite the noise the warriors made, Tola's screams could still be heard.

Thorstein felt Annoure shaking and kissed the top of her head before looking back at the ship.

By the time the Angel of Death and warriors reappeared from the tent with fresh blood on their clothes, the sky had grown dark. The warriors raised the red-and-white striped sail and all but Tola disembarked.

Tyrker's brother walked naked onto the beach with a flaming torch. He walked backward toward the shoreline and threw the torch onto the longship.

Thorstein took Annoure's hand and led her to a roaring bonfire onshore. The heat from the fire prickled his hand as he reached for a small burning branch and handed it to her. The wind shifted and Thorstein breathed in smoke as he picked up another one for himself. Then they walked to the shoreline with the others and threw their burning branches onto the wood stacked on the longship.

Tyrker's brother untied the burning ship and it began drifting out to sea. Enthralled, Thorstein watched the sail catch fire. Red and orange flames leapt into the dark sky. He had never seen a war chief's funeral ceremony before and he thought it was a fine way to honor Tyrker the Courageous.

Chapter 8

Garth's Farmstead

EARLY THE NEXT MORNING, ANNOURE stood near the busy Bergen waterfront, keeping watch over the trunks and hudfats while Thorstein and his cousins brought their boat down to the sea. A flurry of activity surrounded her. Now that Tyrker's funeral was over, all the Norse warriors were leaving for their farmsteads.

Through the crowd she spotted the men coming toward her, carrying their boat. Thorstein was at the bow and Walfgar and Herjulf at the rear. They were in especially good spirits as they put the boat in the water and loaded it. All of them had bathed and dressed in clean clothes in anticipation of their homecoming.

Annoure sat on the narrow wood seat at the stern of the boat. Thorstein sat on the thwart facing her with his back to the bow. As the men rowed, she sadly watched Bergen fade away, knowing she was being taken even further from her home.

Before long, the men raised the sail and talked among themselves in Norse as the boat sailed across the water. They traveled past lush green valleys, snowcapped mountains and numerous waterfalls cascading down the cliffs surrounding the fjord.

As the day wore on, Annoure became uncomfortable sitting on the hard wooden seat in the hot afternoon sun. Finally they started down a long, narrow inlet of sea between two cliffs.

"This is the Hordaland fiord," Thorstein said. "My family's homestead is here."

"Will we reach it by tonight?" she asked.

"Já, if the wind keeps up."

Thorstein leaned forward and tucked the cross that hung around her neck under the neckline of her dress. "Keep your *kross* hidden."

"Why?"

"Faóir hates Christians and he's the head of the farm."

"Faóir?"

"Faóir means father. Here you must worship the Norse Gods for our land is harsh and they rule our lives."

"Why does your father hate Christians?"

With Walfgar's help, Thorstein explained, "Christians are weak and fearful of living. Your priests teach life is suffering and only death brings lasting happiness. We embraced life and death. If we die in battle, we go to Valhalla, Odin's palace in Asgard. In Valhalla, heroes fight one another all day and in the evening they recover from their wounds and have a huge feast with Odin."

"That sounds like an awful place."

"You're a Christian and a woman," Thorstein said. "You wouldn't understand."

Annoure found Thorstein's beliefs odd. "What gods do you worship?"

"Odin, the king of the gods, rules over battle and death," Walfgar said. "Thor, who Thorstein is named after, is the god of rain, thunder and wind. Frey is the god of farming and love."

"You worship the old gods," Annoure said. "The peasants in Northumbria still put out food for them."

"Then your land is one of many religions."

She squared her shoulders, proud of her country and answered in Anglo-Saxon. "Some still believe in the old gods, some the Celtic gods and others the Roman gods, though most are Christians now."

"Different people have different gods," Walfgar said ending the conversation as the men began to talk among themselves.

Annoure tuned out their voices as her thoughts drifted to her fiancé Manton Bandolf. She wondered if he was heartbroken by her disappearance or just sorry to lose her dowry. Manton had a stern manner, but he was intelligent, wealthy and well-educated. As his wife, she would have been a respected woman. She could read and speak

Frankish, Latin and Anglo-Saxon. She'd looked forward to debating ideas with him.

Yet truthfully, she doubted she'd be happy married to Manton. He was much older and his rank body odor and pudgy body repulsed her. She dreaded the thought of sharing his bed and had even contemplated running off to live with her Druidess grandmother.

The ship sailed past a series of small islands with rocky shorelines and twisted trees. The wind held out and by late afternoon Thorstein pointed toward land. "That's our farmstead."

As they drew closer, Annoure saw houses, outbuildings, sheds, a stable, an apple orchard and fields of grain that sloped to the sea. Beyond the fields were trees at the base of green, rolling mountains.

Before long, they pulled up to a wooden dock and Herjulf moored the boat by a boathouse. Thorstein stepped onto the dock and helped Annoure out. "Does your family own all this?" she asked.

"Já," he said proudly as he gazed at the fields. "The crops look ready to harvest."

Women, children and two men hurried to the shoreline to greet the travelers. One woman rushed over to Walfgar and he put down his hudfat and kissed her. She carried a redheaded baby in her arms and a young boy clung to the hem of her dress. A gentle expression softened Walfgar's features as he kissed the baby who pulled on his braided beard. Then he swung the boy into his arms.

"Rothgar, have you taken care of your móðir and sister while I was gone?"

"Já, Faóir."

"Is Walfgar married?" Annoure asked Thorstein. She had not thought of the Norsemen as family men loved by someone at home.

"Já, he has a vif and two bairns." She frowned in confusion and he said in Anglo-Saxon, "Wife and two children."

"Oh." Then she frowned. "Are *you* married?"

Thorstein grinned. "Nei, I don't have a vif."

Just then a pretty, young woman threw herself into his arms and he lifted her into the air, laughing. "It's good to see you, Kalsetini!"

"Did you bring me a gift?" she asked.

He pulled a silver bracelet from his pocket and handed it to her.

"Oh, it's lovely. Thank you!" She stood on her toes, kissed him on the check, and then slid the bracelet on her wrist. Her thick blond hair flowed down to her waist and was fastened back from her face with silver barrettes.

A tall, mature woman wearing a navy hangerock and a scarf on her head embraced Thorstein. "I'm glad you're safely home."

"So am I. Many didn't make it. We can speak of it later. There's much to tell." He handed her several bags.

She used the scissors that hung from a brooch on her hangerock to cut open the string that tied one of the bags closed. Her face lit up as she looked inside.

"Oh, you've brought us almonds." She opened a second bag and pulled out a piece of fabric. "And silk. Thank you, silk makes the best undergarments. Where did you get these wonderful gifts?"

"I traded for them in Bergen. They come from distant markets."

A broad-shouldered, stocky man strode up to Thorstein. His presence seemed to dominate everyone around him. "Welcome home, *sonr*."

"It's good to be back." Thorstein put his hand on the small of Annoure's back "This is Annoure. Annoure, this is my faðir and móðir, Garth and Freydis."

His father raised his bushy eyebrows, not replying.

"Welcome to our farmstead," his mother said.

"Thank you," Annoure replied in Norse, conscious of her Northumbria accent.

"She's foreign," his mother said, casting a questioningly look to Thorstein.

"Já, I captured her on the raid."

"She's a thrall then," Garth said. "Not worth our notice."

Annoure proudly lifted her chin, refusing to be cowed by him.

"Her faðir is a nobleman," Thorstein said.

"Her faðir is our enemy." Garth turned away and greeted Herjulf.

Frowning deeply, Thorstein lifted his trunk onto his shoulder.

A sandy-haired man whose round face resembled Thorstein's picked up a hudfat. "I see you managed to bring home more than cows and sheep this voyage. Any one can see why you abducted her, but what possessed you to present her to Faðir?"

Annoure tensed, not accustomed to being dismissed as a person of no importance.

“Annoure, this is my older bróðir, Njal,” Thorstein said. “And his vif, Thyri, and their sonr Brandi and dóttir Sandey.”

Annoure greeted Njal and Thyri, then the two blond children who looked to be about four and five years old.

Before they started for the house, Walfgar’s wife came over with the baby in her arms and her little boy beside her.

“Thyri,” she said to Njal’s wife. “Will you watch Astrid and Rothgar for me?” Her freckled cheeks were flushed with excitement. “Walfgar does not want them around for a while.”

Thyri grinned as she lifted the baby into her arms. “Já sure, Asa, I’ll watch them. You see to that randy verr of yours. You’ve been missing him for weeks.”

Asa’s face lit up. “Thank you.” She ran back to Walfgar, laughing. He put his arm around her and gave her a hardy kiss.

Annoure smiled forlornly at the couple, missing her own family and envying the Norse woman’s happiness. All the women wore well-made, bright colored clothes. The children looked healthy and were dressed in smaller versions of the same style clothing as their parents.

Brandi hugged Thorstein. Thorstein affectionately ran his hand through his nephew’s golden curls. “Should we go fishing tomorrow?”

“Já, and hunting, too!”

“We’ll go hunting when harvest is over.”

Everyone started walking toward the long houses and Annoure ambled after them, feeling much safer in the company of women and children than she’d felt among only warriors. She was glad she’d worked so hard to learn Norse and was grateful to Thorstein for buying her women’s clothing.

Thorstein stopped and studied the field. He looked happier and more relaxed than Annoure had ever seen him. “It looks like a bountiful crop.”

“The god Frey was good to us,” Njal said. “The wheat is ready to harvest and the rye, oats and barley will be ready soon.” He slapped his hand on Thorstein’s back. “It’s good to have you safely home, sonr.”

“It’s good to be back. I always miss the farm when I’m gone.”

Once they reached one of the houses, Thorstein turned back and smiled at Annoure, waiting for her to catch up. “This is the principal longhouse where I live with my parents, sister and Herjulf. It’s a fine, well-built house.”

The house had a sod roof and was made of upright timbers, standing side by side with the ends buried in the ground. A brown and white goat ate grass by the house.

"That's Loki," Thorstein said, following her gaze. "He's full of mischief."

Brandi ran to the door and held it open. Thorstein bent down to go through the opening and Annoure followed. It was only wide enough for one person to go through at a time. She tripped over the raised threshold and Thorstein grabbed her arm to steady her.

"Watch your step. The threshold is raised to keep snow out in the winter. The low door makes it easier to defend ourselves against our enemies."

"Do you get attacked often?" Annoure asked.

He shook his head. "Nei."

Annoure stepped onto a thick, wool rug placed in front of the door and looked around.

The single-room house seemed especially dark and cool after being in the warm sunlight. A smoky haze hung in the air. What a depressing place to live, Annoure thought as she waited for her eyes to adjust.

A woman, wearing a faded dress, tended the centrally located fireplace. Her hair was short, shorter than most of the men's. An iron kettle hung over it. Fragrant herbs, dried fish and pans were tied to the overhead rafters. Shields and weapons hung on hooks while skins and wool rugs covered the dirt floor. Sleeping benches with furs on them lined the two long walls and a trestle table stood between the sleeping benches.

A small opening cut in the exterior wall allowed light to shine on a standing loom. Colorful balls of yarn sat in a basket beside it and woven clothes hung on the walls. Annoure decided her first impression of the house was wrong. Despite being dark, it was cozy and well-kept. "I like the window," she said.

"It's called a Vind Oga," Thorstein said proudly. "Eye of the wind in Anglo-Saxon. Not many homes have them. It lets light in, but is covered with a thin, scraped animal hide to keep the wind out."

"It's a good name."

Thorstein set his trunk next to a sleeping bench. "We'll sleep here. Please remove our soiled clothes from the trunk so they can be washed."

He looked at the boy. “Come, Brandi. Let’s finish unloading the boat.” He kissed Annoure on the cheek, then took Brandi’s hand and left the house.

Annoure removed the musty clothes from the trunk. Beneath them she found the bundle Thorstein purchased at Ota’s shop in Bergen. Curious, she unfolded it and found a blue hangerock and linen underdress with narrow pleats. He’d probably purchased them for her, but hadn’t given them to her after she’d called him a pig. She sighed, regretting her angry words.

Next, she found the Bible Thorstein stole from the church. Most of the jewels on the cover were missing. She opened it and found the page where Father Eian had splashed ink when she’d interrupted to tell him about the Viking attack. As Annoure set the Bible back in the trunk, she shuddered, remembering that horrible day.

Near the bottom was Thorstein’s helmet and chest armor. Examining the armor more closely, she saw it was made of several layers of animal hide with bones sewn in. He wore it the day he raided her village. Fury coiled in her chest as she thought of the attack on the church. She didn’t want to live with these pirates. They were her enemies and everything about them was alien—their customs, homes and religion.

“Who are you?” the short-haired woman, asked, interrupting her thoughts.

“I’m Annoure. I was stolen from Jarrow.”

“Then you’re a thrall. I’m Hilda, head of the female thralls.”

“I am a free woman.” Annoure spoke sternly as she would at home when reprimanding one of her servants.

Hilda’s eyes flashed. “You’re a thrall now. As head thrall, I will assign your work.”

“Nei, Thorstein is my master, not you.”

Hilda crossed her arms and her eyes swept over Annoure from head to toe with contempt. “You’re his bed thrall?”

Annoure drew in a sharp breath. “Nei.”

“Then your hair needs to be cut short like the other female thralls.”

Annoure took a nervous step backward. Hilda was the first woman she’d ever seen with short hair. She hated the thought of being marked as a thrall by having her waist-length hair cut off.

“Come, I’ll show you where you’ll live.” Hilda headed to the door.

Annoure glanced at Thorstein's sleeping bench, realizing he intended to make her his bed thrall. Better to be an ordinary thrall than Thorstein's whore. She hurried after Hilda.

The pungent-smelling outbuilding was nothing more than a depressing den, eight-by-ten paces in size. No weavings adorned the walls and it had no eye of the wind to let light in. The only furnishings were a crudely made table and two benches on a dirt floor. When she walked further inside, she noticed a toddler napping on a fur.

Hilda said, "You'll sleep here. The men there." She pointed to the other side of the fire. She picked up scissors and told Annoure to turn around. Annoure's heart raced and she shook her head.

The toddler stirred and reached for Hilda crying, "Móðir."

Hilda turned to the child and smiled tenderly as she lifted him into her arms. "Your hair can wait."

The child resembled Thorstein with his beautiful blue eyes and blond hair. Annoure felt as if she were punched in the stomach as it occurred to her that perhaps the boy *was* Thorstein's.

Hilda pointed to a worn under-dress and hangerock hanging on a wall hook. "Put these on. There's work to be done."

"I have clothes."

"Do you want pig dung on your hangerock?"

Annoure reluctantly changed into the coarse under-dress, which chaffed her skin, then put the dingy hangerock over it. She felt more like a slave than she ever had with Thorstein. He'd called her a thrall more than once, but his eyes always conveyed that she was a desirable woman.

"Wash Thorstein's clothes." Hilda handed Annoure a bar of lye soap and told her there was a stream to wash them behind the principal house.

As Annoure knelt at the edge of the stream washing clothes, she wondered again if Hilda's child was Thorstein's. That would explain Hilda's hostility toward her. Once the clothes were clean, she hung them up to dry on a hemp rope strung between two nearby trees, then returned to the main house. Inside Kalsetini and his mother, Freydis, worked at the cooking fire. The rich aroma of spices, fresh-baked bread and cooking meat filled the air.

"Come help us with the second *matr*, Annoure," Freydis said.

Annoure realized matr must mean meal as she crossed to them.

"My dóttir will show you what to do."

Annoure smiled at Kalsetini, happy to discover she was Thorstein's sister and not a girlfriend. She needed Thorstein's protection in this alien world.

She helped Kalsetini put ale, veal, chicken, cheese, apples and bread on the table. She was surprised at the variety and abundance of food and hoped there would be enough to last all winter. Food was often scarce at home by late winter.

Annoure noticed the trestle table's wide legs had flowers and leaves carved on them. "It's a beautiful table," she said.

"Thorstein made it," Kalsetini said.

Just then Thorstein walked in with his brother Njal and their father. He smiled upon seeing Annoure, but as his eyes swept over her old clothing, his smile faded. She lowered her eyes, wondering if he was displeased with her for changing into them. She was uncertain as to her place here and from whom she was to take orders.

Thorstein and the rest of the family sat down at the table and began to eat. Annoure's mouth watered as she poured ale for Garth. The food smelled delicious especially after being on the longship where they ate mainly dried fish.

Garth asked about the raid. Herjulf told about invading the church and killing the monks, but he became more sober when he spoke of Tyrker the Courageous' death and two ships sinking.

Saddened at the memory of that day, Annoure returned to the outbuilding with Hilda. The thralls gathered around the table to eat. Annoure dished up some broth from the cooking pot hanging over the cooking fire and sat down with them. Hilda begrudgingly introduced the other woman at the table as Ginna and the two coarse-looking men as Oddkell and Skalagrim.

Ginna was a young woman with a plain face. Her short hair reminded Annoure that Hilda was going to cut *her* hair and she wondered if it would be done tonight. Annoure broke off a piece of flatbread from the loaf on the table and dipped it into her broth to make it soft enough to chew. She wished she'd grabbed an apple and piece of cheese from the main house.

After eating, Annoure sat on a fur with her arms curled around her bent legs as the thralls talked too rapidly in Norse for her to partake in the conversation. She felt terribly alone. Finally the thralls went to sleep and snoring soon filled the room.

Annoure began to pray silently to Mother Mary. She asked for strength to endure her fate and for help finding a way back home. Surely some day she would see her family again.

After removing her over dress, she crawled between the furs beside Ginna. Despite her exhaustion she lay awake, uncomfortable sleeping next to a woman she'd just met. As she thought of her father and brothers, tears began rolling down her cheeks. She put her fist over her mouth, not wanting anyone to hear her weeping.

Finally she dozed off only to be shaken awake sometime later. Groggy with sleep, she opened her eyes and saw Thorstein squatting beside her. The fire was low and the room had grown dark and cold.

"Why are you sleeping here?" he whispered. "I told you to sleep in my sleeping bench."

Still half-asleep, it took her a moment to translate the Norse words. "Hilda told me to sleep here," she whispered.

"Hilda's not your master."

Annoure sat up. Thorstein smelled of ale and she suspected he was drunk. "She told me she was in charge of the women and that she's going to cut off my hair."

"I don't want your beautiful hair cut off!" Thorstein exclaimed, sounding annoyed. "I'll tell her you're not a common thrall and to leave it alone. Come to the house with me."

"Nei, I won't be your bed thrall."

"It's not for you to decide."

"Do you plan to force me to sleep with you?"

"Nei, I'll not force you." They stared tensely at each other, then he stood. "Thor's hammer, you can be difficult!" He strode from the outbuilding.

Annoure curled up on her side, upset that they'd quarreled.

"I'll satisfy his lust if you won't." Hilda rose from her fur and left the building.

Annoure's heart constricted. So she was right; Hilda *was* his bed thrall.

After a restless night, Annoure glanced over and saw Hilda sleeping beside her child. She must have returned sometime during the night.

Annoure pulled on her hangerock and left the house to use the outhouse.

The early morning air was cold and she realized she needed to retrieve her cape from Thorstein's trunk when she had a chance. The outhouse was a small, wooden structure with a hole in the floor. After using it, she returned to the outbuilding and found everyone up and dressed.

Hilda ordered Ginna to take Annoure along for morning chores. Ginna led her to the woodpile and they picked up firewood and carried it to the principal house. Inside the family still slept since they had celebrated the men's safe return late into the night. At the hearth, Ginna showed Annoure how to feed small twigs to the coals to get the fire going. Once the fire had started, Annoure fetched her cape from Thorstein's trunk.

She and Ginna carried two buckets of food scraps to the strong-smelling pigpen and dumped the scraps into a trough. Then Annoure walked to the stream and filled a bucket with water to fill the water trough. It took many trips to fill the water troughs for the pigs, horses, oxen, sheep, cows and goats. After feeding and watering the larger animals, Annoure and Ginna brought water and grain to the chickens, ducks and geese. Once that was done, they gathered eggs.

In the barn, Ginna showed Annoure how to milk the cows and goats. As Ginna sat on a stool and milked a cream-colored goat, she said, "The goats are named after the gods. This one is called Freya." A brown-and-white goat butted against Ginna's back.

"That naughty one is Loki. He likes to butt you while you're milking the other goats. The black one climbing on the hay is Thor. They are my favorite animals because they have so much personality."

"I like the horses best," Annoure said, looking over at the black stallion with a white star on its forehead in a nearby stall. She wondered what had become of her brother's horse Bertran. She left him on the church grounds when she'd gone to warn the monks. It was likely the horse returned home of its own accord. She hoped so. Her brother Cedric deeply loved Bertran.

Ginna led her to the principal house, carrying the basket of eggs. "We have to prepare the family's first matr," Ginna said.

Annoure set out hard-boiled eggs, porridge, bread, butter and warm goat's milk. Thorstein and Garth came in from working the fields and began to eat.

Thorstein had shaved and Annoure stared at him, feeling her spine tingle. Without the beard, he looked like the druid man she'd dreamed of. He ignored her and, after a quick meal, returned to work. Annoure and Ginna ate what was left after everyone else had eaten, then washed the pots and wooden bowls.

Afterwards Annoure trudged to the fields with Ginna where the men cut wheat with long handled scythes. Ginna showed her how to put the sheaves together with the butt end down to form a shock of eight to ten sheaves. Then they tied the shock together with a piece of straw and put a sheaf on top to protect the wheat from wind and rain.

Ginna held up the sheaves and Annoure clumsily tied them together. She shed her cape, but was still hot from working under the bright sun. Soon her back hurt from bending over as they moved down the row to where Thorstein cut the wheat.

Thorstein squatted by Annoure. "Here, let me help you. It's done this way." He quickly tied up a neat sheaf.

"You make it look so easy," Annoure said. She felt tension between them and knew he was still annoyed with her for refusing to share his sleeping bench. Yet, she didn't intend to give into him. She stood up and pushed her hand against the small of her back. "By the gods, yours or mine, I'm tired."

He laughed good-naturedly. "Let's take a break." He reached out his hand and she smiled as she took it.

"You have a pretty smile," he said.

She smiled broader. "And what do you hope to attract with your honey-sweet words?"

"I've found what I want."

They walked over to the stream and sat in the shade.

"Have you ever worked in a field?" Thorstein asked, chewing on a piece of straw.

"Nei, I did the spinning and weaving." She leaned closer to him and touched his clean-shaven jawbone. "You look like you did in my dreams."

"Tell me more of your dreams." His voice was soft and husky.

"We went on journeys together." She could understand Norse pretty well, but couldn't speak the language as fluently. It frustrated her that she couldn't communicate with him better. "You were a Druid in my dream. A different lifetime."

"You believe we live more than once?"

"I don't know. Grandmother does," she said, searching for the right words in Norse. "The Celts believe people come back as people or animals. They even believe some people are shape-shifters and can change forms."

"We also have tales of changing shape. One story is about a man who changes into a dragon to protect his treasure."

"I doubt that a person could turn into a dragon. Do you think it's possible we knew each other in another life?"

Thorstein frowned. "It is not what our priests teach. They say we go to another world when we die where we stay until Ragnarok. That's the final battle between good and evil. We don't come back until a new world is created."

"Those are just stories."

Thorstein grunted and rose, not bothering to reply. "We better get back to work." He held out his hand and helped her up.

They worked for the rest of the afternoon, then Thorstein walked with Annoure back to the main house. "My back hurts and I'm so tired I could go to sleep right now," Annoure said. "Do you always work so hard?"

"Já, during harvest. We have to get all the grain in while the weather is good. We'll go back to work after we eat."

They washed their faces and hands at the well, then entered the house. As Annoure helped the other women set out food, the aroma of chicken and fresh bread made her stomach grumble. She was pleased when Thorstein insisted she eat with him. She sat down between Thorstein and Sandey, Thyri's little girl, who had helped Freydis prepare the meal.

She heaped her bowl with chicken, cheese, horseradish, blackberries and took a mug of goat's milk. It was the first good meal she'd had since being kidnapped from her home. She stuffed herself with all the delicious food and filled her bowl a second time.

Thorstein stared at the food heaped up in her bowl. "You must be hungry."

"We worked hard today," she said, spreading butter on a slice of still-warm bread.

"I thought you just didn't eat much."

“I’m used to better fare than what I’ve been offered up to now.”

Thorstein’s eyes met hers, catching the rebuke in her words. “We have plenty to eat on the farm.”

Thorstein returned to the field with little Brandi, who liked to follow his uncle around. Annoure stayed inside to help clean up after the meal before joining him. As she washed the dishes, she wondered what her father and brothers were doing at this moment and if they missed her as much as she missed them.

Chapter 9

Dahlia

A FEW DAYS LATER, THORSTEIN HEADED to the fields with Herjulf just as the sun rose over the mountains. He cut wheat while Herjulf tied bundles. He liked working in the fields, feeling the scythe in his hand, watching the wheat fall. Once this field was finished, they'd harvest the rye, oats, flax and barley.

He spotted Annoure feeding the pigs and paused in his work. He hadn't given any thought to what her place on the farm would be, but it bothered him to see her put to work like a common thrall.

She was a beautiful, educated nobleman's daughter, refined in speech and manner. He admired her pride, courage and spirit. Moreover, she was intelligent and interested in everything, evidenced by the way she easily learned his language and asked about his customs.

Herjulf took a drink from his flask then handed it to Thorstein and said, "Dahlia will arrive today with her kinsmen. Njal sailed to their farm yesterday to ask if they can help with harvest. They're willing since our crops are ready before theirs. We planted earlier last spring."

"It will be good to see Dahlia again," Thorstein replied, thinking just the opposite. He wasn't ready to see Dahlia because he wasn't sure what he wanted anymore. Before meeting Annoure, he'd planned to talk to Dahlia's father about a marriage contract.

Dahlia turned fifteen this summer and was old enough to marry. And he was almost eighteen, ready to start his own home. Moreover, he'd known her all his life since her family lived just across the fjord.

"Dahlia will be jealous of Annoure," Herjulf said, interrupting his thoughts. "Her bróðir Olaf probably told her how you risked your life to save Annoure from the raging river and about your battle with Rethel."

"What is there for Dahlia to be jealous of? Annoure is a thrall."

Herjulf grinned and his eyes twinkled. "Don't pretend indifference with me. I've seen the way you look at Annoure and noticed the connection between the two of you."

"Faðir expects me to marry Dahlia."

"I'm glad to hear it, for I like Annoure well enough to overlook her lack of kin," Herjulf teased.

Thorstein scowled, even though he knew his cousin was only jesting. "She's mine."

"Cousin, you can only have one woman." Herjulf went back to work, leaving Thorstein to fume.

Thorstein looked toward the ocean and saw several boats sailing toward the dock. "They're here," he said. He walked down to the shoreline where he greeted the neighbors. When he helped Dahlia out of the boat, she gave him a friendly hug. He noticed how fresh she smelled and how pretty she looked with her pink cheeks and braided blonde hair. Yet she didn't stir him the way Annoure did; she seemed like a common wildflower, not an exotic rose.

He turned from her and greeted her father, Volsung, and two husky brothers, Olaf and Sturlee. Together they walked to the principal house.

Inside Annoure prepared the morning meal while Thyri kneaded bread in a wooden trough and little Sandey set out plates. Thyri screamed with delight upon seeing her family and joyfully embraced them.

Hungry from working in the fields, Thorstein loaded up his plate with bread, eel, cabbage and eggs cooked in garlic. Dahlia sat beside him and asked questions about the raid on Northumbria. He was uncomfortably aware of Annoure's presence in the room as he answered her questions.

Dahlia pointed to Annoure and asked, "Is that the ugly little thrall you killed Rethel over?"

Annoure stiffened. Kalsetini paled and gasped, "You killed Rethel!"

"In a fair fight."

"But Rethel was our neighbor and Ketil is your friend! How could you kill his bróðir?"

"Rethel drew a sword on me. I had no choice."

Garth glowered at Thorstein. "What is this all about?"

"I was going to tell you, faóir," Thorstein said, cursing himself for not telling his family sooner and cursing his luck that it should come up now. "I tried to talk Rethel out of a fight, but he wouldn't listen to reason."

"Why did he want to fight?"

"He attacked Annoure and when I stopped him, he came at me with his sword. I had no choice but to defend myself."

"Thorstein speaks the truth," Olaf said. "I saw it myself. Thorstein wasn't even armed and Rethel would have cut him down as he stood if Herjulf hadn't tossed him a sword."

Garth's face turned a fiery red. "You attacked Rethel without even a weapon because of *her*—a thrall!" He stared intently at Annoure, as if seeing her for the first time, before his eyes switched back to Thorstein. "Why were you in camp without a sword?"

"I left the tent in haste and forgot it."

Garth shook his head, exasperated. "You know better than to be without your sword when in camp. To think my sonr was almost killed and no one bothered to tell me." He glared at Herjulf, who looked down at his plate. "It takes a visit from my neighbor for me to learn of this. Were there any other witnesses to this fight?"

"Já," Herjulf said. "Several men were there."

"Nesbjörn will want retribution," Dahlia's father Volsung said. "Thorstein will be called before the *ting* in the spring and be expected to pay tribute."

"He will be fortunate if Edgtho doesn't challenge him to a *holmgang*," Olaf said.

"What's a *ting* and *holmgang*?" Annoure asked Herjulf under her breath.

"*Ting* is a legal assembly. A *holmgang* is a duel," Herjulf whispered back.

Garth looked at Thorstein with a worried frown. "Edgtho's dangerous. You'll have to guard your back at public gatherings."

"There's more you should know," Thorstein said, deciding he'd better tell it all now and get it over with before his father found out from another source. "I also refused to give Annoure to the Angel of Death when the crone said the bones showed she was to accompany Tyrker to Valhalla."

Garth's red face turned purple. "What?" he thundered. "You risked offending the gods over *a thrall?"*

"The oracle said the woman was to be of foreign blood," Herjulf said. "A foreign woman among Tyrker's own thralls was sacrificed instead. It was for the best since she understood the ritual and performed it well."

"Do you claim to know more than the Angle of Death, Herjulf?" Garth growled as he stood. "Thorstein, come with me! I want a word with you." He stomped out of the house.

In the deadly quiet room, Thorstein's eyes met Announe's. He stood and Dahlia clasped his forearm. "I'm sorry, I didn't know you hadn't told your faóir."

"He had to find out sooner or later."

Thorstein joined his father outside and the two men walked in silence toward the wheat field. At last his father spoke. "Why didn't you tell me about this trouble?"

"I was going to after harvest."

"Are you saying you didn't think it was important enough to tell me immediately?"

"It was important enough, Faóir. I just delayed the unpleasantness."

"Never avoid your problems. Face them and deal with them directly. Why is your sister so angry with you?"

Troubled, Thorstein said, "Because she likes Ketil and hoped he'd ask you for a marriage contract."

Garth shook his head. "And now you have killed his bróðir, causing hatred between our families."

"Já, and I'm worried because Ketil was crazy with grief when his vif died. I fear his bróðir's death will make him crazy again. He and Edgtho nearly joined in the sword fight. Worse, Rethel's dying words to Ketil were to avenge his death."

"Ketil isn't the only one who can't understand your behavior. Why would you kill a neighbor over a thrall? You've always been strong-willed and spirited, yet it's been tempered by good judgment until now."

"I couldn't let him slay her." His father studied him intently. Thorstein broke into a sweat, realizing his father didn't see things the way he did.

"She's spoils from a raid and fighting a skilled warrior like Rethel over her was dangerous." His voice rose. "Defying the Angel of Death was even worse; you've risked angering the gods!"

Thorstein didn't try to defend his actions, knowing it would only lead to an argument. He couldn't make his father understand the protectiveness he felt toward Annoure or the dreams he'd had of her.

Garth stopped walking and turned to Thorstein. "You've let lust cloud your thinking. In the future you must show more responsibility. Enjoy your pretty Saxon while your loins burn for her, but don't let her mean too much to you. What you need is a vif. I thought you wanted to marry Dahlia. We can speak to Volsung while he's here, then draw up a marriage contract and settle on the bride price and dowry. It is a good match and will further strengthen the ties between our two farms. Olaf and Sturlee will be like bróðirs to you. When you go a-viking, you will need men around whom you can trust and whom will battle at your side. Dahlia can run your household while you are gone. She has family close by who can help her set up a home. What do you say to this marriage?"

Thorstein broke into a sweat. "I'm not ready to take a vif yet."

"I was already married and had a sonr by your age. You're enamored by this thrall. As long as she's here, you'll be content to not marry. We'll sell her at fall market."

"Nei! I'm not selling her!" Thorstein abruptly walked away from his father and strode over to the barn where he'd left his scythe. He tore off his shirt before heading to the field to work in the hot sun.

Dahlia came out of the house and joined him as he cut wheat. Free women rarely worked in the fields, but Dahlia said she liked taking a break from all the cooking. Even though he worked fast, seeking to take out his frustrations in hard labor, she kept an even pace with him in tying the wheat bundles. It would be so much easier if he did want Dahlia; unfortunately, since Annoure had entered his life, he was no longer attracted to her.

He always strived for his father's approval and respect. Even as a young child he never showed fear when his father was around or backed away from a challenge. He wanted his unyielding father to be proud of him. It dismayed Thorstein that his father thought him stupid and ruled by lust.

As the sun beat down on him, sweat poured down his tanned back and chest. He paused to wipe the moisture from his brow.

"Why didn't you ransom the thrall instead of bringing her home?"

Dahlia asked.

"It was a bad expedition. No one was ransomed."

His eyes swept over Dahlia. She was a practical, efficient girl who'd be an excellent wife and good mother for his future children. Moreover she was Norse, shared his religion and already had his father's approval.

"I think you kept Annoure because you wanted her for yourself."

"There's nothing wrong with a man owning thralls. Enough about Annoure. Tell me of your summer."

"Summer is always rather dull with you men all gone a-viking. I missed you." She smiled invitingly at him.

Chapter 10

Fall Harvest

ANNOURE GLARED AT DAHLIA, WHO harvested the ripened wheat alongside Thorstein. Wind blew through the girl's golden braids as she brushed chaff off her blue hangerock and laughed. The irritating, girlish sound made Annoure clench her teeth. Since Dahlia and her kin arrived several days ago, Dahlia was always near Thorstein—in the fields, at meals or around the evening fire where everyone gathered to tell stories.

Annoure's dislike of Dahlia had turned into a smoldering fire in the pit of her stomach after Ginna told her Thorstein was expected to offer the bride's price for Dahlia this fall. Why had Thorstein kidnapped *her* if he already planned to marry Dahlia? Annoure had been sure Thorstein genuinely cared for her; she'd felt certain something special existed between the two of them. Now she wondered if she was mistaken.

Annoure glanced in Thorstein's direction and caught him looking at her, which caused her chest to tighten and her breath to catch in her throat. She turned away and trudged toward the house to help Freydis prepare the evening meal. The Norse people only ate twice a day and she was hungry. When she entered the house, Freydis told her to gather the eggs.

At the chicken coop, she went from nest to nest, pushing chickens off and putting eggs into a basket. A loud whinny broke the silence, followed by hoofs pounding against wood.

She set down the basket and ran to the stable where she saw Thorstein's stallion Gunnar kicking the stall door. Something had obviously frightened the exquisite creature. As she hurried over to him, the familiar smell of horse and straw reminded her of home and her own horse.

"You don't like being penned up, do you, Gunnar?" she said in a soothing voice. The wild-eyed horse laid back his ears, but stopped kicking the door to watch her.

"You must long for freedom as I do. Do you want to run free in the mountains where no man can make you do his bidding? Shall we ride away together?" The horse snorted and tossed his head.

Annoure stepped inside the stall and the door thudded shut, startling her. She stood still, waiting to see how the powerful animal responded to her. The horse whinnied and stomped his front hooves. She reached hesitantly toward Gunnar and began stroking his heaving side. Then she moved her hand to the spot behind his ear where her brother's stallion, Bertran, liked to be scratched.

The door to the stable opened. As Thorstein and Dahlia entered, Annoure quickly squatted in front of the horse. "Gunnar seems to have quieted down," Thorstein said. "I wonder what upset him."

"Probably nothing more than a mouse," Dahlia replied. "It's nice and cool in here."

"As long as we're here I might as well sharpen my scythe."

Through a slot in the stall, Annoure saw Thorstein lift a whetstone off the wall.

"I've been wanting a chance to talk to you privately," Dahlia said.

"What about?" Thorstein asked as he began sharpening the large blade.

"Don't pretend to be ignorant!" Dahlia put her hands on her hips. "You know well enough. Last spring you said you were going to offer Faðir the bride's price for me with the booty you got from the raid."

Annoure felt sick. She strained to hear the rest of Dahlia's words. "Instead you've brought home a bed thrall that you're obviously besotted with."

"She's not my bed thrall and I'm not besotted with her."

"I've seen the way you look at her."

"You're imagining things." Thorstein kept sharpening.

"And you've been acting differently toward me. You used to want to be alone with me, but this visit you seem only interested in the harvest.

Put the scythe down and look at me. We've been friends since childhood. I want to know if you still care for me. Can't you at least be honest?"

Thorstein sighed deeply and set the tool against the wall. "You're making a fuss over nothing. Annoure's a thrall—not someone for you to be jealous of."

"You have feelings for this thrall."

"I desire her. It will pass."

"What if those feelings grow stronger instead?"

"They won't."

Dahlia stepped forward and placed her hands on his bare chest. "If you have need for a woman, marry me and I'll take care of your needs."

He drew her to him and kissed her. Dahlia's arms encircled his chest and he pushed her against the stable wall, moving his hips rhythmically against hers as the kiss deepened.

Annoure slumped against the wall of the stall, wishing for a way to sneak out of the stable without being seen. Thorstein's words stabbed like daggers into her heart: "Annoure's a thrall—not someone for you to be jealous of." How could she have been so wrong about his feelings? She was just bounty from a raid.

"We'd better get back to the fields," Annoure heard Thorstein say. "Your faðir will notice our absence."

Annoure looked back through the slot and saw Dahlia standing close to Thorstein. "Faðir wants us to marry," Dahlia said. "Offer him the bride price."

"You're still too young to get married."

"I'm nearly fifteen. I'm older than your móðir when she married."

"It was hard for my móðir to leave home so young and take on the responsibilities of a home. She was only thirteen when Njal was born. Let's get back to work." The door banged closed as they left the stable.

A lump formed in her throat and she fought back the urge to cry. Gunnar pushed his head against her; she rose and put her arms around his neck. Tears began to flow down her cheeks and her shoulders shook. She couldn't let herself break down. Besides, she'd be missed if she didn't return soon with the eggs, but her tears kept coming.

She denied being a slave, but hearing Thorstein speak of her as one suddenly made it true. Thorstein took her freedom, not because a mystical force brought them together, but merely by chance. He saw her in the church and desired her, the same as he desired the bag of riches she carried. Annoure wept harder, feeling alone and forsaken. Without Thorstein, she had nothing. Apparently although she'd grown to care for him, he cared nothing for her.

It was dark in the stable now and Annoure knew she'd be in trouble for not helping with dinner, but she no longer cared. These people and their harvest had nothing to do with her.

The stable door opened and a voice called out, "Annoure, are you here?"

She recognized Herjulf's voice and thought of not answering, but dreaded getting in even worse trouble. "I'm over here, Herjulf," she said, her voice a little nasal from crying. She sniffled and wiped the tears off her cheeks with her hands.

He crossed over to her and opened the stall door. "What are you doing in Gunnar's stall? He's only half-broken. Come out before he tramples you!"

She crept past Gunnar and moved out of the stall.

"Thorstein and I were looking for you. We were afraid you'd run away." He touched her chin and tilted her face up. "You've been crying."

New tears sprang to her eyes at his unexpected kindness. Herjulf put his arm around her. "What's wrong?"

"Please help me to find a way home. I'll give you this." She pulled off her ruby ring and thrust it at him. "And my father will pay you a large ransom."

He slid the ring back on her finger. "You will have to plead with Thorstein for your freedom. You belong to him."

"Thorstein doesn't care what happens to me."

"Já, he does. He's upset that you disappeared and is about to form a search party to hunt for you."

"Dahlia will make him forget me."

"So that's what this is about. It's Dahlia who should be worried, not you."

"I saw him kiss her."

Thorstein entered the stable and stopped when he saw them. "Annoure, what are you doing here?"

"She was quieting Gunnar," Herjulf said. "It's lucky she didn't get her skull kicked in."

Thorstein scowled. "Why didn't you tell me you'd found her?"

"I just got here." Herjulf released Annoure, who kept her head averted so Thorstein wouldn't see her red, swollen eyes.

"I'll let the others know she's safe," Herjulf said.

"Why were you gone so long, Annoure?" Thorstein asked.

"I . . . I have to get back to work." She hurried outside and ran to the outbuilding.

Inside she found Hilda putting her son to bed. Hilda stood when Annoure entered. "Where have you been?" she demanded.

Annoure took a step back, frightened by the menacing expression on the other woman's face. "In the stable."

"You think you're better than the rest of us and can do as you like, but you're a thrall, just like us. If you disappear again, you'll be beaten."

Hilda stepped forward and shoved Annoure into the wall. The back of Annoure's head hit the wall with a painful thud. She moaned, cradling her head in her hands.

"You'd better learn to follow orders," Hilda said. "Go to the main house and get to work."

Annoure fled to the well where she washed her tear-streaked face and dried it with her hangerock. She retrieved the basket of eggs from the chicken coop and brought them into the principal house then apologized to Freydis for her long absence. As Annoure cleared the table, her stomach cramped with pangs of hunger and the back of her head ached. She scraped the dinner scraps from the wooden plates into a bucket for the pigs.

Thorstein entered the house and sat down at the table with a bowl of food. Dahlia slipped onto the bench beside him. Annoure noticed he didn't eat much and nor did he laugh with the others as Olaf told jokes.

Once the dishes were washed, Annoure left the house. Not wanting to face Hilda, she ambled to the stream and sat on its bank. Dahlia's family had set up tents nearby and Annoure stared at them gloomily, glad they'd be leaving soon to harvest their own fields.

Annoure's thoughts turned to home. She wondered, as she had many times before, how her father and brothers reacted when they discovered she'd been abducted by the Norsemen. Initially her father would have been upset with her for having snuck out of the castle so early in the morning, but when that feeling faded she was sure he'd be greatly distressed. He loved her as did her brothers.

Or maybe he didn't know she was kidnapped and thought she'd run off to live with her grandmother. No, surely one of the monks or townsmen saw her at the church. As her thoughts spun, she watched the water rushing over the smooth rocks, finding some measure of peace in the sight and sound of it.

When the sky grew so dark she could no longer see the water, Annoure reasoned that Hilda must be asleep by now since the thralls always rose at dawn to begin the morning chores.

Annoure opened the door to the outbuilding and moved quietly toward her sleeping furs. Oddkell sat on a bench and gave her a leering grin, revealing several missing teeth. She walked uneasily by him and wrinkled her nose, wondering if he ever bathed. He caught her wrist. "Your fur is taken."

"Let me go!" She planted her feet and tried to twist her arm away. Nearby Ginna and Skalagrim were bumping around under the fur.

He pulled her closer. "Tonight you'll share my furs."

"No!" she exclaimed, reverting to Anglo-Saxon. "I'll never sleep with you. You're a vile, filthy dog!"

In one quick motion, he twisted her arm behind her back and hauled her onto his lap. He grabbed one of her breasts. "Come on, pretty. Don't put up a fuss. You'll enjoy it." She jabbed her elbow into his ribs and sprang from his lap. He grabbed her hangerock and dragged her back. "I like them feisty. A little rough doesn't bother me."

In panic, she sought the words in Norse. "Thorstein will kill you! He killed Rethel."

"He killed Rethel because of *you*!"

"Já. I'm Thorstein's!" Taking advantage of his uncertainty, she pulled her dress free and ran from the outbuilding. She burst into the principal house and scanned the dimly lit room for Thorstein. He sat near the center of the room by the hearth with Herjulf and Kalsetini. His parents were already in their sleeping bench a short distance away.

Thorstein rose, his eyes troubled. "Annoure, what's wrong?"

She ran to him and hurled herself into the safety of his arms, still feeling Oddkell's brutal hands on her. Thorstein's arms closed around her and he held her close.

"Let's sit by the fire," Thorstein said. They sat down on his sleeping bench and he put his arm around her. She cuddled next to him, comforted by his concern and the warmth of the fire.

"So, Annoure, have you come to end my cousin's suffering since he is too proud and stubborn to end it himself?" Herjulf said.

"What do you mean?" Kalsetini asked, as she carded wool.

"Thorstein has been in a bad mood since returning from a-viking because Annoure hasn't been sharing his sleeping bench."

Annoure felt heat rise to her face, realizing Herjulf must think she was no longer a maiden—that she'd already been satisfying Thorstein's lust on the ship. Now Kalsetini would think she was Thorstein's bed thrall was well.

Kalsetini scowled at Herjulf. "No woman would want to sleep with a man who kills his neighbors!"

"She would when he did it to save her life," Herjulf said.

Thorstein grunted. "Would you rather I let Rethel run his sword through me, Kalsetini?"

"Thorstein prefers sleeping with Hilda," Annoure interjected, pushing his arm off her shoulder in an attempt to restore her dignity. She was pleased to find her Norse had improved enough that she could follow the conversation.

"I never slept with Hilda!" Thorstein exclaimed.

"Were you so drunk you don't remember her coming to you our first night here?"

"She offered, but I refused, so she slept with Herjulf instead."

"He tells the truth of it," Herjulf said, grinning. "It was a most enjoyable night."

"Her child is Thorstein's," Annoure said, uncomfortable with the open discussion of reproduction.

"The child's not mine!" Thorstein said.

"Já, it is."

"Nei, it isn't, we're not married."

She narrowed her eyes. "It's still yours!"

"Babies have nothing to do with men. Only women have the mysterious power to make life."

"Oh, you're a stupid Norseman!"

Thorstein frowned. "I'm not stupid."

"Ignorant then. A woman can only have a child if she mates with a man."

"That's true," Kalsetini said. "It is alluded to in a story of the god Rig,"

"Which story do you refer to?" Herjulf asked.

"The story where Rig goes to the humble dwelling of a serf named Oldefar and his vif Oldema, then to the prosperous farm of Bedstefar and his vif Bedstemor, and last to the fine home of a noble named Far and his vif Mor. In each house, he stayed several days and shared the couple's sleeping bench. Nine months later each vif gave birth to Rig's child."

"Why, that just means the gods can give a woman a child, but mortal men can't," Herjulf said. "I have been with several women and none had a baby."

"It doesn't happen every time, but without a man a woman can't have a child." Annoure said.

"She might be right," Thorstein said. "Remember that time Volsung killed his bull because it almost ran its horns through Olaf when he was a boy?"

Herjulf nodded. "Já, he was a mean bull."

"After that his cows stopped having calves and giving milk, so he came over here and bought one of our male calves. He didn't have any calves of his own until that calf grew into a bull. But regardless, Hilda's child isn't mine since I never mated with her."

"Are you sure?" said Annoure.

"I would certainly know if I'd been with her or not."

"It's true; he never liked Hilda much," Herjulf said.

"Then perhaps you are his father," Annoure said.

Herjulf cocked any eyebrow, then grinned and puffed up his chest. "I like the idea that I created a child like the god Rig."

Thorstein frowned. "So what does all this have to do with why Annoure won't share my sleeping bench?"

"Because, my slow-witted bróðir," Kalsetini said. "Annoure is concerned that she will end up with a baby, but no verr."

"Is this true?" Thorstein asked Annoure.

"It's ah . . . not the only reason." She felt her cheeks coloring again. Why she did or didn't want to make love to Thorstein wasn't something she wanted to discuss with his family.

Herjulf stood, yawning. "I'm going to sleep. We have another long day tomorrow."

Thorstein turned to Annoure. "Let's go for a walk." He took Kalsetini's cape off a hook and placed it over her shoulders.

Outside, Thorstein cocked his head and took a deep breath as he gazed at the moonlight dancing on the ocean waves. "Ah, it's a warm, still night. I'm glad I'm not out at sea, waiting for a breeze."

She smiled. "Sailing is in your blood."

"Já, it's true. I love being at sea on a starlit night." He clasped her hand and started walking. "So now that we are alone, will you tell me what frightened you?"

Annoure shivered and held the cape more tightly around her body. "Oddkell tried to force me to share his furs."

Thorstein's eyes narrowed with fury. "By Thor's hammer, he won't do it again!" He spun around and strode toward the outbuilding.

She hurried after him and grabbed his arm. "Nei, tomorrow is soon enough to deal with Oddkell. We need to talk."

"I'd rather deal with Oddkell right now."

"Thorstein, he had no way of knowing I belong to you. How could he?"

"Everyone on the farm knows." He bunched his hands into fists and his jaw tensed. "If anyone touches you, they're accountable to me."

"Thorstein, I . . . Herjulf said I must ask you for my liberty. Please ransom me. My father will pay you in gold for my safe return, especially since I am still a maiden." She spoke in Norse, which she'd worked hard to learn so she could beg for her freedom.

Thorstein stiffened. "You're mine. I will never let you go."

"Never? Why? I am worth more ransomed than as a slave. With the gold you get for me, you could buy many thralls."

"I don't want many thralls. I want you."

"That's not what you told Dahlia."

"Dahlia? What's Dahlia got to do with this?" He paused, frowning. Then understanding entered his eyes. "I heard Gunnar causing a commotion and went to the stable, but by the time I got there he was quiet. Were you in the stall when I entered?"

She nodded and twisted her hands together, feeling the weight of her unhappiness pressing against her.

"You should have made your presence known." He shifted his stance. "You saw me kiss Dahlia, didn't you?"

"Já. Are you going to marry her?"

He glanced toward Dahlia's tent. "I'm not sure."

"If you marry her, I'll run away."

"There is no place to go." He swept his arm toward the mountains. "Beyond the farm is only wilderness and you wouldn't survive. Don't ever try it."

"I'd rather risk dying in the wilderness than living as a thrall. Return me to my father. Give me my freedom. You know in your heart it's not right to enslave me. We were friends in the dream worlds. I'm sure we were destined to meet in this world, but not so you could steal my freedom. You dishonor us both by keeping me here."

They reached the fjord and Thorstein looked across the water where moonlight lit the waves.

"There *is* mystery between us. I've remembered more and more of the dreams we've had together as the days pass. When I dreamed of you, I thought you were a celestial being. I never imagined I'd find you in this world. I lost my freedom the day we met." He gazed into her eyes, letting her see into his soul. "I should enjoy Dahlia's kisses. But when I kissed her, I found myself comparing her to you. I realized what I feel for her is pale compared to the burning desire I have for you. My sweet, I'm happiest when you are near." He brushed a strand of hair off her cheek and his touch made her tremble.

"When you smile or laugh, it brings me joy. When you weep, it makes my heart ache." He gazed at her intently. His sea-blue eyes had shifted to deep navy with the onset of evening. "Do you really want to go home? Have you no feelings for me?"

"It's not about my feelings for you. I want to be a free, honored vif someday, not a bed thrall."

"I haven't forced you to be my bed thrall."

"Nei, yet it is what you want."

"I've never made a secret of that. I want you in all ways."

"For how long, Norseman? A night, a week, a month perhaps?"

"My desire for you won't wane."

"You told Dahlia your feelings for me would pass."

He winced. "I wanted it to be true because it would make things so much easier, but I know deep within that my feelings won't go away."

"You just want me because I refused you and now I'm a challenge."

"If all I wanted from you was a night or two of passion, I would have taken you by now. I want more than your body. I want your heart."

"So you can break it when you marry Dahlia?"

He threw his hands in the air. "My family expects me to marry Dahlia."

"So you want me to risk my heart while you risk nothing, reveal nothing and offer nothing but the privilege of being your bedmate. How can I refuse such an offer?" She glared at him, wanting to smack his handsome, arrogant face.

"Your accusation is unfair." His words were soft, but underneath them she felt his anger. "I've risked so much for you." He raked his hand impatiently through his shoulder-length, blond hair. "Before I met you I planned to marry Dahlia—a match my faðir approves of. Faðir won't consent to me taking you for my vif because you are a Anglo-Saxon Christian who brings nothing to our family. If we marry without his permission, we can't stay on the farm and I don't know where we would go. Unfortunately, I'm not a man of wealth who can buy property and the only open land in Norge is covered with mountains and snow."

"So marry Dahlia and go back to your simple life! No one is stopping you."

"No one but you. Between us, there is fire and passion!"

"There seemed to be plenty of passion between you and Dahlia from where I sat in the stable."

He touched her cheek. "Annoure, when you disappeared this afternoon I was crazy with worry that something had happened to you. I love you. I've loved you since the first time I saw you standing in the chapel. Yet, among my people love is not a consideration when choosing a vif. But how can I settle for marrying someone I don't love after experiencing this amazing feeling I have for you?"

"You love me?" she gasped, wondering if it was possible.

"I love you more than my own life." He drew her to him and their lips met in a heated kiss that quickly deepened. Warmth flooded through Annoure and she found herself surrendering to him. She wrapped her arms around him, wanting and needing him, too.

They drew apart and gazed into each other's eyes. "Before the Mother Goddess, I claim you, Norseman, for my own," Annoure said, her voice sounding throaty and breathless. As she said the words, standing under the moon and tall trees, she felt like one of the pagan maidens given to a Druid on the night of the Beltane fires. The night seemed wild, full of mystery and Thorstein's nearness made her feel reckless and wanton. She felt her power and was aware of her innate sensuality and its effect on him.

"And I claim you for my own, Lady Annoure of Northumbria," Thorstein replied, sliding his fingers through her hair.

She pulled his head down to hers, welcoming his kisses and caresses. Her body throbbed as he held her so close that she could feel his heart beating against hers. She sensed a deep bond with him. He was her friend, lover, husband returned from another life to join with her. She thanked the Mother Goddess for letting her see who he truly was.

Thorstein slid the cape off her shoulders and she pulled away, quivering with uncertainty.

"Have I misunderstood you, my love?" he asked. "I don't want to force you to share pleasure with me. Our joining must only take place if both of us want to be one." He took her hands in his and gazed at her with love in his eyes. "Dear Annoure, I can't give you up. I will find a way to make you my vif. I swear to you, I will find a way."

Her heart sped up and she stepped closer to him. "Truly, you'll break off with Dahlia and marry me?"

"I want to spend my life with you."

"And I with thee. I love you, Thorstein. I know we have known each other in many lives and are brought together in this one because of the love that exists between us."

Their mouths met in a hungry kiss and the last of Annoure's reserve fell away. Thorstein's kisses increased in intensity and she felt her knees go weak as a curling desire grew deep inside her.

In one fluid motion, Thorstein slid her clothes over her head. She stood naked before him, feeling beautiful because of how he looked at her. The moonlight seemed to caress her pale skin and she felt her hair flowing down her bare shoulders and back.

"Surely, you are a celestial maiden," Thorstein said in a hushed voice. "By the gods, no earthly woman could be so lovely."

"I'm real. I will not disappear into the mist, my pagan lover."

She helped him pull off his shirt and tunic, admiring his thick muscular chest and arms. Her fingers lingered for a moment at the almost-healed shoulder wound he'd gotten when he saved her from Edgtho.

Her hands slid down to his waist and she untied his pants. His stomach was taut against her fingers. Annoure's hands shook and her movements were clumsy.

His nude body was as glorious as the first time she saw it aboard the ship when he arose naked from his hudfat like a proud god, completely comfortable with his body. His arms, chest and legs were tattooed with patterns of dragons, ravens and birds. Annoure found the tattoos fascinating and erotic. She drank in the sight of him, intoxicated by the vision as he gazed upon her.

She thought of her grandmother's warning, *beware the dragon.* The dragon brought change and her life had been torn apart. Yet the dragon ship also brought Thorstein and love. It brought her to this moment of trusting her life to a power greater than herself—trusting their love would be enough to find a way to happiness.

He captured her mouth with his as he'd already captured her heart. *Tonight I'll make him mine—heart, body and soul,* she thought, letting the tension build, thrilled at the sensation of her nude body against his. He pushed away her hair and kissed her neck and ear, sending chills through her.

Swinging her off her feet, he placed her on the cape. She smiled up at him. It felt right to be with him, to not to care about anything but this man and the passion between them. Time seemed to ripple and she saw him as her Druid lover—past and present merging into one.

All thoughts fled as her body warmed to his touch and she surrendered to the response building within her. She throbbed at the sweet torture his hands and mouth brought.

He moved on top of her saying, "I'll try not to hurt you." She gasped, as their bodies became one. He held still for a moment, gazing down at her. "Are you all right?"

Annoure smiled. "More than all right." She closed her eyes and tilted her head back. "I feel the magic between us." She exalted in the power and strength of him. She gasped again, this time with delight as he began to move.

I will never be the same, she thought. *Our lives are woven together in a fine mesh.* She felt his love surrounding and supporting her. She was renewed and fulfilled, for he'd made her his in a deeply profound and ancient way, just as she'd made him hers. Pleasure caught them up in its embrace and they were lost together in shared rapture.

Once the heat of passion passed, she became aware of the hard ground beneath her. A stick poked into her back and Thorstein's body felt heavy on hers. His body radiated a masculine aroma mixed with the scent of their lovemaking. Her own body was covered with a fine layer of perspiration. He rolled off and drew her near, so her cheek rested in the hollow of his shoulder. Thorstein covered her with the cape and she felt herself drifting off with the night sounds. It was an emotionally draining day. So much had happened.

She slid into the dream worlds in full consciousness and found herself standing beside Thorstein. "I kept my promise to find you," he said.

"Yes, my love. Our two worlds are united at last."

His eyes were troubled. "I see darkness ahead."

She looked up as a dragon flew across the sky, casting a shadow over both of them. Thorstein pulled out his sword. "I must kill the dragon before we can live in happiness. Stay here and protect our child." He placed his hand on her belly.

"Don't go. It's death that shadows you."

"Then I'll meet it as a warrior. I will return and find you again. I will always find you."

"Nei, Thorstein, don't go," she moaned.

"I'm right here, love," said Thorstein.

She opened her eyes to find him gazing down at her. "I dreamt of you," she whispered.

"Was it a good dream?"

"It was a warning about danger ahead."

He chuckled and slid on his pants. "It seems danger always lies ahead where you're concerned."

Announe pulled on her clothes and Thorstein lifted her into his arms. He carried her to the house and placed her on his sleeping bench. An ice-cold fear came over her and she began to shake. Thorstein removed his pants and lay beside her, gathering her to him. "I shouldn't have kept you outside in the cool night air for so long," he said.

"I shiver from fear, not the cold. I just had a vision that death searches for you."

"I do not fear death. I'll meet it as a warrior with a sword in my hand."

"Nei, you spoke the same words in my dream. There is more honor in living a life of worth than dying in battle."

"Death will not come this night. Go to sleep, sweetness. Morning will arrive soon enough. Think of the joy of our lovemaking—not of death."

Chapter 11

The Storm

THE NEXT MORNING, THORSTEIN AWAKENED when Herjulf shook his shoulder. "Get up, cousin. Do you plan to spend the day in bed while the rest of us work?"

Thorstein tightened his arm around Annoure. "Go away. I'm tired."

Herjulf laughed as he walked to the door. "I don't have any sympathy for you. A night of pleasure has its price. The men are already threshing, so hurry up."

Thorstein glanced around and realized the house was empty except for his mother who was preparing the first meal. His attention returned to Annoure. Thinking of the night before, he wished he had time to make love to her again. She opened her eyes and looked sleepily at him. "Is it time to get up?"

"I'm afraid so. Everyone else is already at work."

Her eyes widened in concern. "I should have already fed the animals." She started to sit up when Dahlia walked into the house and bristled upon seeing Annoure.

"So Thorstein Garthson, I see your denial about her being your bed thrall is a lie!" She stomped out of the house and slammed the door.

Freydis rounded on him. "Couldn't you have waited until Dahlia was gone before taking a thrall to your sleeping bench? Dahlia won't marry you if you have no consideration for her feelings."

"I'm not going to marry her." Thorstein sat up. Annoure scrambled out of bed and dressed quickly.

"You must. Your faðir expects you to."

Annoure flinched but Thorstein quickly replied, "I'm marrying Annoure."

"Garth won't approve of your marrying an Anglo-Saxon Christian!"

"Then I'll marry without his permission."

"You'll have to leave the farm if you marry against your faðir's wishes. Think on it, Thorstein. Don't be so impulsive. There's no open land. Where will you live?"

"I don't know," he said sullenly, drawing on his pants. He hoped his love for Annoure wouldn't cost him his home and family.

"Dahlia will bring a dowry of bed linens, a spinning wheel and farm animals." Freydis gestured at Annoure. "She will bring you nothing."

Annoure proudly raised her chin. "My father's wealthy. We can live in Northumbria in a much finer place than this."

"Your people will kill Thorstein if he goes to Northumbria," Freydis said. Then she turned to her son. "Marriage must be built on strong bonds between families. What good is it to marry your enemy?"

"I love Annoure."

His mother put her hands on her hips. "Love isn't a good enough reason to marry."

"I think it is."

"I see you're too smitten to think clearly, Thorstein." Freydis turned back to her work.

Thorstein jerked open his trunk and tugged out the pleated dress and hangerock he'd bought in Bergen. He handed them to Annoure, carefully addressing her in a much gentler voice than the one he used when arguing with his mother. "These are a gift for you. Please wear them today."

"They're lovely. Thank you." She ran her hand across the finely woven fabric. "But I can't work in these. I might ruin them."

"Dress as a free woman, so my family will see you as one."

He watched her change into the new outfit, mesmerized by her beauty and the grace of her movements. He realized he could never let her go, even if it meant losing everything else. "I'd better go help with harvest."

"And I better help Ginna with the milking." Annoure fastened her silver brooches on the new hangerock.

Thorstein smiled. "You look like a proper Norsewoman now." They left the house together. Outside, Thorstein kissed Annoure. Her eyes clouded and her pretty mouth curled downward. "Your mother hates me."

"She doesn't hate you. She just wants what's best for me."

"I'm sorry I've caused trouble between you and your family."

"It's not your fault. I'm the one who took you from your home."

"I love you."

"And I love you to distraction." He watched her walk to the outbuilding. Then he strode to where the men threshed wheat, wondering how to convince his stubborn father to let him marry Annoure.

At the wooden threshing platform, he tensed upon seeing Dahlia. Bright pink spots appeared on her cheeks when their eyes met. Her fresh, round face made her look young and innocent.

Feeling guilty, he picked up a flail and began to separate the wheat from the straw. Dahlia was a good friend. It wouldn't be easy to tell her he wasn't going to marry her.

Njal came to the platform leading an ox that pulled a two-wheeled cart full of wheat. Thorstein helped empty the cart, then continued threshing. After they separated the kernels from the straw, the women helped the men gather everything into baskets. Thorstein and Herjulf tossed one of the baskets repeatedly into the air. The chaff blew off in the wind, leaving kernels of wheat behind.

Once all the chaff was gone, Dahlia took the basket from Thorstein. He smiled at her, trying to ease the tension between them, but she didn't smiled back. Her mouth was drawn into a tight line as she poured the kernels into a barrel.

* * *

A few days later, Annoure stood on the dock, watching Thorstein sail away with his kin and Volsung's family to harvest their neighbor's crop. He still hadn't told Dahlia he wasn't going to marry her. Annoure worried that he might change his mind. Dahlia was a cheerful, fun loving girl and he'd known her all his life.

She trudged back to the principal house. It seemed especially cheerless and meager with Thorstein gone. Inside Annoure sat near the loom and began carding wool, enjoying the smell and feel of lanolin.

Once the task was completed, she began rolling the wool into roll logs to use for spinning.

Nearby, Freydis worked on the large loom. Annoure couldn't remember ever seeing her idle, taking time to relax or play a game. Freydis had been aloof ever since Thorstein said he planned to marry her.

Freydis wove yarn through the warp that was kept taut by free-hanging stone weights, then she beat the weft upward with a short sword-beater. The loom was different than the ones Annoure had woven on at home, but the weaving techniques were similar.

Once Annoure had made the roll logs, she spun wool at a distaff wheel, making a fine, even thread. The familiar task transported her to happier times when she'd spun in the evening while her father read aloud or her brothers talked about their adventures. *Would she ever see her family again?*

Annoure glanced at the trunk where Thorstein kept the Bible. It was locked, but once they were married, Norse custom dictated that he would give her the key. Then she could read the Bible at her leisure. Perhaps he'd even let her ride Gunnar. As she spun wool, she wished Thorstein were with her.

Annoure was so wrapped up in her thoughts that Freydis startled her when she said, "Thorstein loves his family and the farm. If you care for him, you won't make him give up everything for you."

"I'm a thrall. I don't have any control over Thorstein."

"You expect me to believe that! You've used your charms to bewitch him. Convince him to marry Dahlia."

Annoure's heart sunk at the thought of losing Thorstein to Dahlia.

Freydis continued as if Annoure had no feelings. "Dahlia will be the perfect vif for him. We've known Dahlia her whole life and are fond of her. Njal's vif Thyri will be especially disappointed if Thorstein and Dahlia don't marry. She and Dahlia are sisters. "

"And what is to become of me?"

Freydis frowned thoughtfully and tapped her foot. "We could probably find a second or third sonr on another farmstead willing to marry an Anglo-Saxon noblewoman, if we offer a small dowry."

"But I love Thorstein. I don't want to marry some other man."

"Be grateful I'm suggesting we find a verr for you. We could just sell you."

"You only offer to find me a verr because you know Thorstein will never agree to sell me!"

Freydis eyes narrowed. "You conniving bitch! I suppose you want to be ransomed, so you can return home."

"My fiancé won't want me now that I'm no longer a virgin. Christians put high importance on such things. My father would probably put me in a nunnery."

"Wouldn't you rather be at home in a nunnery than here?"

"Nei, I love Thorstein."

Freydis stood and began to pace the room. "You don't love him! He is merely your chance to be a vif instead of a thrall."

Annoure restrained herself making an angry retort as she continued to spin wool into thread. She didn't want to make an enemy of Thorstein's mother.

"You've brought us nothing but trouble," Freydis said. "Because of you the Angel of Death has cursed our family. This spring Thorstein will have to appear before the konungr and land-owning men at the legal *ting* and explain why he killed Rethel. If he's found guilty of murder, he will be an outlaw—and forced to live in the wilderness where he can be killed on sight."

A chill passed through Annoure. She hadn't realized Thorstein was in so much trouble.

"Most likely he'll just have to pay tribute to Rethel's family since it was a fair fight," Freydis continued. "The real danger is not from the ruling at the *ting* but from Edgtho, Rethel's cousin. He'll want revenge."

Annoure felt uneasy every time Edgtho's name came up. He was an angry, violent man. She was tempted to gaze into a still pool of water to see if Edgtho was in her future, but the Christian priests had forbidden the old ways.

* * *

Two weeks later as Annoure gathered squash in the garden, two boats sailed toward the dock. She dropped the vegetables and ran down to meet them. Thorstein leapt out of the boat and swept her into his arms. He kissed her and she returned the kiss, relieved his desire for her hadn't dampened. When Thorstein released her, she noticed his family gaping at them in astonishment.

"It's good to be home," Thorstein said to her. "How did things go while we were gone?"

"Your mother would like to marry me off to a neighbor or ransom me."

Thorstein glanced at his father who was getting out of the boat and whispered into her ear, "Faðir is in a rage because I told Dahlia I wasn't going to marry her."

Over the next few days the family worked in the field harvesting the rye. One afternoon, Annoure felt heaviness in the air and paused to look at the dark clouds rolling in the sky.

Thorstein followed her gaze. "We've got to get the last of the rye into shocks before it starts raining." He began to work faster and Annoure found it hard to keep pace.

The day was unusually sultry for fall. Annoure's dress and wool hangerock trapped the heat beside her skin and soon she was drenched in sweat.

Thorstein seemed unaffected by the weather and cheerfully whistled as he worked. She tied a group of sheaves together and stood up. Black spots swam before her eyes. She felt dizzy and then crumpled to the ground.

Annoure awoke to find Thorstein's worried face above her. "What happened?" she asked.

"You fainted. How do you feel?"

"Light-headed."

"I'd better bring you to the house." He lifted her up as if she weighed no more than a child and carried her across the field.

She squeezed her eyes closed and tried not to throw up. "Walk slower," she murmured. "I feel sick." She heard the door open and felt the coolness of the air inside the house. Thorstein set her on his sleeping bench.

"What's wrong with her?" Freydis asked, hurrying over to them.

"She fainted."

Freydis put her hand on Annoure's forehead, frowning pensively. "She doesn't have a fever, but she's pale." Her frown deepened. "Have you had your monthly bleeding, Annoure?"

Annoure flushed, embarrassed to be asked such an intimate question.

"I'm late."

"She's with child, not sick," Freydis said.

Annoure gasped. She hadn't connected not having a monthly flow to being pregnant.

A flood of emotions crossed Thorstein's face. "But . . . we . . . " he said sounding dismayed. He rubbed his temple. "Annoure said a woman can only get with child if she mates with a man. If that's true, this child is mine." The confusion cleared from his face. "No child of mine will be a faðirless thrall. Annoure and I must get married right away. I'll talk to faðir this evening after he comes in from harvest."

Freydis' eyes widened with alarm. "Garth won't give his consent!"

"He must."

"You know how difficult he can be."

"Then I'll marry her without his permission."

"Don't anger your faðir into disowning you."

"I'll make him understand."

"And if he doesn't?"

Thorstein's defiant expression changed to uncertainly. "I'm not sure what I'll do."

"We need you on the farm. There is more work now than we can do."

Thorstein pinched the bridge of his nose. "I know, I know. There must be a solution." He glanced toward the door. "I have return to the field to help with the harvest before it starts raining." Thorstein clasped Annoure's hand. "Will you be all right?"

"The sun just made me light-headed. I'm better now." Annoure tightened her grip on his hand, struggling to absorb the idea of being pregnant. She wanted to ask Thorstein how he felt about it. He might be annoyed that this new responsibility was thrust upon him with things so discordant between him and his parents."

"Rest for a while," he said. "Everything will work out."

She shook her head, full of anguish. "No, it won't."

He kissed her forehead. "I'll take care of you and the baby."

Thorstein left the house and Annoure rolled on her side and soon fell asleep. The sound of gleeful young voices awakened her. Nearby Freydis' grandchildren and their cousins played with carved figures of people, horses and other animals. The smell of food cooking filled the room and she surmised it must be nearly time for the evening meal. Annoure sat up, then quickly lowered her head as a wave of dizziness swept over her.

Freydis glanced at her and said, “You’re awake. Will you watch Astrid so Sandey can help me work?”

Annoure tried sitting up again and found the dizziness had passed. She took the baby from Sandey. *What would be like to have her own baby?* she wondered as she swayed Astrid in her arms. *Would her child be a boy or a girl?* After awhile Astrid fell asleep and Annoure set her on the sleeping bench, then sat on the floor with the two boys, Rothgar and Brandi.

“Would you like to learn to write letters?” she asked.

Brandi nodded eagerly.

Annoure wrote a letter *A* in the dirt and said, “This is ‘A.’” She then drew a *B*.

“Do you know how to read and write?” Freydis asked.

“Já, I know Anglo-Saxon and Latin.”

“Is that why you talk funny?” Rothgar asked.

She smiled. “I talk like the people of my country. My home is across the North Sea.”

“Where did you learn to read and write?” Freydis asked.

“My brothers’ tutor taught me.”

“Thorstein knows runes. He carves runes into wooden boxes to label what’s inside when he’s on trading voyages.”

“We make paper and write on it with ink. Thorstein has a Bible from the raid in his trunk. It has wonderful stories in it, like your sagas.”

Annoure drew the letter *C* in the dirt. Sandey set down her stirring spoon and squatted by Annoure. “Will you teach me, too?”

“Já, I’ll be glad to.”

Freydis looked up from where she sliced vegetables. “Sandey, come back and help with the cooking. You’ll have to learn another time.” Freydis peered at the writing. “There is magic power in words.”

“It seems mysterious because so few know to read and write, but it is a skill that can be learned,” Annoure said.

“Magic spells can be woven in runes.”

“Perhaps if a person believes it has power, it does. The real magic in writing is that a person can write down important things and others can read them, even years later. Their stories and thoughts won't be forgotten once they're written down."

Rothgar copied the letters she made, then said, "I can write, too! I can make magic."

Annoure laughed and clapped her hands. "Já, that is good." She looked at Freydis. "Do you need some help?"

Freydis gave her a tired smile and pushed a wayward strand of hair back under her scarf. "Já. I'm cooking for everyone on the farm. The other women are working in the fields to get the crop in before it rains. Could you cut the beef into chunks and put them in the kettle?"

Freydis looked at Rothgar and Brandi. "You boys have had enough of a break. Go gather some eggs."

Annoure began cutting up the meat on a wooden board.

Freydis sighed deeply, looking worried. "There's bound to be trouble when Thorstein asks for Garth's permission to marry you."

"Is there any chance Garth will give it?"

Freydis paused in her cutting and looked at Annoure. "More likely he and Thorstein will argue."

Before long the boys returned with the eggs. Soon after, some of the workers came in from the fields ate quickly and returned to work. Thorstein and his father arrived with the second group. Thorstein came over to where Annoure stood, stirring the stew. "You look better. How are you feeling?" he asked.

"Better—I took a nap." She dished up a bowl of steaming hot beef and vegetable soup for him. It smelled good so she picked a piece of meat out of his dish and popped it into her mouth. It was tender and well-seasoned.

"I'm afraid we won't finish the harvest before it begins to rain," Thorstein said, between bites. "Sit beside me."

Annoure sat down and picked a carrot out of his bowl. Thunder rumbled across the sky and Thorstein pushed the bowl over to her.

"You finish it. I'd better get back to work." Thorstein kissed her and left the house.

As Garth started toward the door, Freydis said, "Stay a moment, Garth. I have something to say to you."

Garth paused at the door, stroking his fingers through his bushy beard. "What is it? I'm in a hurry."

"Thorstein will ask to speak to you and I beg you to listen to him. He wants to marry Annoure."

"She's a thrall. He can't marry her."

Freydis held his gaze. "I don't want this match either, but if you don't agree to it, we'll lose a sonr. Thorstein will leave the farm with her. She's going to have his child."

"It is of no concern to me."

"The child will be your grandchild."

His thick eyebrows made a solid line across his forehead as he scowled. "The child will be a thrall, as she is."

"Annoure is educated. She can read and write Anglo-Saxon and Latin." Garth cocked an eyebrow and looked at Annoure with new interest.

Annoure's dug her fingernails into the palm of her hand.

"How is it you know Latin?"

"I learned it so I could read the Bible."

His eyes blazed murderously. "No sonr of mine will marry a Christian. Thorstein needs a strong Norse woman with kin to guard his back when a-viking, especially with this trouble between him and Nesbjörn's family. He'll marry Dahlia."

"He says he won't."

"It's not his choice if he wants to live here," Garth growled, his tone livid. "I won't have a Christian corrupting my farmstead with her beliefs, planting seeds of fear, sin and damnation. I'll sell her at market when we go to the trading camp to sell the fall crops. Thorstein will forget her soon enough, once he marries Dahlia."

He jerked open the door and stomped out before Freydis could reply. Annoure pressed her hands against her racing heart, terrified at the possibility of being sold.

"I won't corrupt your family," she said.

"You already have!" Freydis exclaimed. "There will be a fight tonight! Thorstein can be as bullheaded as his faðir." She wrung her hands together. "Why did you have to bring up the Bible? He was softening toward you when he heard you could read and write. Thorstein will be furious when Garth tells him he's going to sell you."

"Perhaps Thorstein will follow his father's wishes," Annoure said, beginning to tremble. "As you've told me so often, he loves his family and the farmstead."

"He loves his home," Freydis said, studying Annoure. "But does he love you more?"

The baby began to cry and Annoure picked her up, grateful for the distraction.

Shortly afterwards Asa and Thyri came into the house. "It's starting to rain," Asa said, lifting the baby from Annoure's arms. "Thanks for watching Astrid. Come, Rothgar, we need to get home before the rain gets worse."

Thyri called Sandey and Brandi to her and left with Asa. The patter of rain hitting the roof filled the small house with its sound.

Garth and Kalsetini dashed in, their hair wet and clothes soaked. When Garth saw Annoure, he yelled, "Get out of my house! I'll not have a Christian under my roof!"

Annoure rose from the table and Freydis clasped her arm. "Wait, Annoure. Garth, please reconsider. You haven't even talk to Thorstein. Try and reason with him. Don't make this a fight."

"Why do I care what Thorstein wants? *I* am the master here and I've decided to sell this thrall at fall market! If you hadn't spoiled Thorstein so badly, he wouldn't be so strong-willed."

"I didn't spoil him. He always works hard to please you."

Garth snorted. "Little Buliwyf's death made you too soft on him." His fierce eyes seared into Annoure. "Get out!"

She ran into the pouring rain and was soon drenched. Dark storm clouds covered the sky and a ferocious wind snatched at her hair and clothing. She frantically looked around, not knowing what to do or where to go. She couldn't let Garth sell her at market.

Her eyes lit on the forest—surely this was her only chance for escape. Through the driving rain she spotted Thorstein working alongside his brother. He hadn't noticed her yet.

Annoure sprinted to the stable and approached Gunnar's stall. The horse stuck his head over the stall door, looking for the apples and carrots she often brought him.

"I don't have anything today, Gunner." She led the horse out of his stall and used an inverted bucket to mount him. Once outside, Gunner trotted across the field, jumping over streams of rainwater cutting through it.

“Annoure, where are you going?” Thorstein shouted. She kicked her heels into Gunnar’s sides and the horse leapt forward. Soon they reached the shelter of trees with its canopy of colored leaves. She found a narrow trail and guided Gunnar along it.

Lightning crackled and thunder boomed overhead, frightening the stallion, and he broke into a run. Annoure crouched forward, clutching his mane and holding on tightly with her knees, afraid she’d lose her hold as tree branches whipped past, snapping threateningly at her arms and legs. *If she could make it to the mountains, she’d be free.*

Chapter 12

The Dream

ANNOURE HEARD THORSTEIN SHOUT HER name again as she rode Gunnar up the mountain trail. She urged the stallion to go faster. Hooves pounded on the trail behind her and she glanced over her shoulder. Through the pouring rain, she saw Thorstein racing toward her on horseback. Annoure kicked her heels into Gunnar's sides and the horse broke into a gallop.

A savage wind whipped through the woods and a branch crashed to the ground in front of her with a thundering boom. She screamed as Gunnar reared up and she lost her hold. She flew through the air and landed on the wet ground, the wind knocked out of her. Gunnar whinnied and trotted off. Annoure moaned and tried to rise, then slumped back to the ground.

Thorstein galloped up to her and leapt off. He squatted beside her. "Annoure, are you hurt?" He drew her to him and she pushed him away. "What's wrong?" he asked.

She glowered at him, panting for breath. "I hate your father and I hate you for bringing me here! You and your family are savage heathens!" She sprang up, but he grabbed her leg and pulled her back to the ground. They wrestled in the mud until he managed to capture her hands and hold them above her head.

"I would rather be dead than a thrall!" she gasped, unable to get enough air with his weight on her. "I won't be sold like a cow in the marketplace."

"I'd never sell you. What brought this on?" He moved off her.

She sat up, emotions flooding through her. "Your father sent me from the house because I'm Christian. He said he's going to sell me with the fall crop."

Thorstein's face flushed with indignation. "I won't allow him to sell you! We'll leave the farm together."

"There is no place for us to go," she shouted to be heard over the howling wind.

"We can live on the Shetland Islands."

An image of the bleak, barren islands in the North Sea flashed before her. "You can't leave your family and home for me. You love it here."

"I love you more!"

She stared at him through the heavy sheet of rain beating down on her nose, eyelashes and cheeks. The depth of his love for her shone in his eyes. She threw herself into his arms. Their mouths met in a heated kiss. When they drew apart, Annoure said, "I don't want you to have to leave your family for me."

"You are my family now and soon we will have a bairn. My bróðir inherits the farm anyway. What reason is there for me to stay?"

Thunder cracked overhead followed by the sound of more branches crashing to the ground. Thorstein looked around, worried. "We need to get out of this storm!"

Annoure froze in terror, watching a spiral of wind tear through the forest, uprooting trees. It was on a direct path toward them. Thorstein threw himself on top of her, shielding her body with his as a tree fell toward them. She screamed as branches and leaves hammered them. The ground vibrated and the sound of the tree smashing to the earth reverberated through the air.

Thorstein's body weight and the branches crushed Annoure into the wet ground.

"Thorstein! Thorstein, wake up!" she cried. Through her rising panic, she felt his heart beating against her chest and knew he was still alive. She needed to get help! She tried to slither out from under him, but discovered she was trapped. Surely, his brother and cousins would come looking for them, knowing they were out in this storm. She screamed for help until her throat grew raw, but no one came.

Annoure was terrified that Thorstein was badly hurt and they'd be trapped outside all night. In desperation, she focused within, going deeper and deeper. Gradually the outer world disappeared and she found herself sitting beside her grandmother near a warm fire. She smelled smoke and felt warmth radiating from the burning logs.

"Help will come," Grandmother said. The vision faded and a sense of peacefulness flow through Annoure.

The rain continued to fall, seeping through the leaves and dripping onto Thorstein's back. As she lay there, she regretted stealing Gunnar and leaving the farm. Her heedless act had led to her and Thorstein being trapped under this fallen tree. *When will I learn to think before I act?* she wondered.

Finally she heard the rhythmic thudding of horses' hooves. A man yelled, "Thorstein! Annoure! Where are you?"

"Herjulf, we're over here!" she shouted back, recognizing his voice.

"I can't see you."

"We're under the tree branches. Thorstein's hurt."

She heard branches cracking as Herjulf made his way through the fallen tree branches. "Keep talking so I can find you," he called out.

"We're here. Please hurry!" Through the canopy of leaves, Herjulf finally appeared above her.

"I see you. What's wrong with Thorstein?"

"He was knocked unconscious."

Herjulf struggled to lift a branch. When it wouldn't budge, he used a stout limb as a lever. The branch shifted only slightly.

"It's no use," he said at last. "I need to get help."

"Nei! Don't leave. I'm frightened."

"I'll be back as quick as I can." She heard him walk away and then the sound of his horse's hooves faded in the distance.

Annoure felt a stab of intense dread when he was gone. *What if he couldn't find them again and they died out here?*

It seemed like hours before Herjulf finally returned with his male kin. They used axes to clear away branches. Then Garth and Njal lifted Thorstein off Annoure and turned him onto his back. Annoure sat up and cradled Thorstein's head in her lap, leaning forward to shelter his face from the driving rain.

Garth knelt beside his son. "Is he alive?" he asked, his voice filled with anguish.

"Já, he still breathes," she said. Annoure felt the back of Thorstein's head and found a large, wet lump. When she drew her hand away, it was covered in blood.

The men made a crude sled for the horse to drag. Then Walfgar and Njal gently lifted Thorstein up and placed him on it. Garth led the horse down the path.

Annoure ached all over and was soaked to the skin. She slowly followed the men, too tired to keep up. By the time she reached the farmstead, the men had already brought Thorstein inside the main house.

She entered just as the men set Thorstein on his sleeping bench. Herjulf and Njal removed Thorstein's wet, dirty clothes and covered him with blankets.

"He's bruised and scratched, but his head injury is the only serious wound." Garth said, his face gray with concern.

Shivering with cold, Annoure anxiously squeezed her hands together, watching from a distance. She didn't dare go closer with Garth present.

"There is nothing more we can do tonight," Freydis said. Njal and Walfgar left the house and Kalsetini sat on the edge of Thorstein's sleeping bench, tears streaming down her face.

Garth noticed Annoure's presence and his face reddened. "You're the cause of all this!" he shouted. "The punishment for runaway thralls is a whipping." He grabbed her arm and pulled her across the room.

"Nei, Garth, she is with child," Freydis pleaded. "Don't whip her! Thorstein will never forgive you."

"Thorstein may never awaken because of her."

"It's partly your fault this happened. You sent her from the house."

"I ordered her from our home. I didn't tell her to run away. She must serve as an example to the other thralls."

"I wasn't running away," Annoure gasped.

"Silence, both of you!" Garth roared. Freydis uneasily bit her lip while Kalsetini looked on, stricken.

Garth yanked Annoure out of the house. A blast of wind and rain slammed against her. He dragged her to the stable, pulled her hangerock down to her waist and tore open the back of her under-dress.

As he tied her hands to a post she said, "Please don't whip me. I wasn't running away."

"You rode off on Gunnar, forcing Thorstein to go after you. If he dies, you will accompany him on his last journey!"

"I wasn't thinking. I panicked when you said you were going to sell me at market, but I would never leave Thorstein. I love him."

"Your so-called love is a curse!" He grabbed a short whip off the wall, shaking with rage.

Annoure's blood turned to ice as he walked toward her.

"My sonr lies as if dead because of you! Expect no mercy." He raised the whip.

She gritted her teeth, anticipating the pain and deciding the bastard wouldn't get the satisfaction of hearing her scream. The whip whistled through the air and slashed into her back.

Her body jerked from the intensity of the pain. The second lash landed like fire and she screamed with shock. The third time the lash bit, her legs gave out and she slid to her knees. Her world blacked out for a moment.

She awoke to excruciating pain. "Stop! Please, stop!" she begged, worried she might lose the baby.

"Nei, you've stolen my sonr."

"The gods brought Thorstein and me together."

The barn door banged opened as Njal and Herjulf barged in. "Faðir, stop!" Njal yelled, his voice vibrating with anger. "You can't do this!"

"She's a runaway thrall and must be punished."

"Nei, she's Thorstein's woman!" Njal untied her wrists and caught her as she swooned. She cried out as his arm pressed against her tender back, then wrapped her arms around his neck as he lifted her up. Hatred for Garth pounded through her.

"She'll never be his woman!" Garth shook with rage. "I'm selling her. She's a witch who's brought misfortune upon us."

"She's only a young, frightened woman," Njal said. "She didn't cause the tree to fall and hit Thorstein, nor did you when you drove her from the house. Fate controls our lives."

Herjulf took the whip from Garth's hand and hung it on the wall. "Go back to the house, Uncle. Thorstein will recover."

"Thorstein defied the Angel of Death for her," Garth muttered, sounding tired and defeated. "The gods are punishing us all. She should have been sacrificed."

"Nei," Herjulf said. "I was there. Thorstein loves her and would have fought to the death to save her. If he had, Walfgar and I would've fought at his side."

"Why would you fight for a thrall?"

"None of us see her as a thrall. She has rare spirit."

Njal carried Annoure from the barn into the stormy night. Moaning in pain, Annoure turned her face into the warmth of his thick shoulder as the rain beat on them. Njal's wife, Thyri, stood in the open doorway of their home, her eyes wide with concern as she ushered Njal inside. He carried Annoure to a sleeping bench and set her down so that she was sitting on the edge of it.

Herjulf followed them in. "How is she?"

"She'll be all right," Njal said. "I'm glad you came to fetch me."

"You're the only one Garth listens to."

Thyri told the men to turn around as she carefully pulled Annoure's clothes over her head. Annoure gasped in pain as the fabric slid against her open wounds, then she lay down on her stomach.

Thyri covered the lower half of Annoure's body with a wool blanket and put a damp cloth on her back. When the cloth touched her torn flesh, Annoure flinched, nearly fainting.

"I'm sorry," Thyri said. "I know it hurts, but it needs to be cleaned." Thyri washed off the blood. "Your back should heal without scarring. Garth held back from using his full strength."

"It felt like he was using his full strength. Thyri, I wasn't running away. I was upset and rode off without thinking."

"Hush, don't speak of it now. Garth's afraid Thorstein will die and you were the easiest target to take out his anger on." She covered Annoure's back lightly with a linen cloth. "Try to sleep."

"If Thorstein dies, Garth said I will accompany him on his last journey," Annoure said, feeling sick and scared at the memory.

"How dare he threaten you like that!" Thyri exclaimed. "He doesn't have the right. Njal is the oldest sonr and married, so he is head of the farm now. "

"Faðir still rules with an iron fist," Njal said.

"By law, the farm is yours," Thyri said. "It's time he turned it over to you."

"He will when he's ready," Herjulf said. "There's no pushing him. I'm going to check on Thorstein." He left the house.

Njal came over to Annoure and placed a cool hand on her shoulder. "You can live here as long as you like. Now try to sleep."

His voice reminded her so much of Thorstein's that tears sprang to her eyes. She wondered if she'd ever hear Thorstein's voice again. "Thank you for helping me," she said. He nodded and crossed over to his sleeping bench. Thyri turned off the oil lamp so the only light in the room came from the cracking fire in the hearth.

When Thyri spoke again, it was in a soft voice to Njal as she undressed. "Garth will never turn the farm over to you. He wants to control everything. It wasn't right for him to whip Annoure."

"He runs the farm better than I could," Njal replied in an equally hushed voice. "I'm still learning. It's because of him that the farm prospers; he works from dawn to dusk."

"I only say he had no right to whip Annoure." Thyri slid under the covers of their sleeping bench.

"Though his actions anger me as well, he had the right. She *is* a runaway thrall. He doesn't tolerate misbehavior and whipped me plenty of times when I was a boy."

"He never whipped you with a horse whip."

"True, he used a leather strap."

"He was a strict faóir. Mine wasn't so stern."

"Your faöir didn't have three free-spirited sonrs, two after Buliwyf died, always in some type of mischief or another. Thorstein was the worst. He took so many risks it became obvious that the gods favored him or he never would've survived childhood."

Annoure's interest peaked upon hearing about Thorstein as a boy, yet she was slipping fast into unconsciousness, escaping her emotional and physical pain.

In the dream worlds, she found herself sitting at a spinning wheel with Thorstein nearby, working on a cradle for their baby. Her belly was swollen with child and she felt the baby kicking.

"Your sonr is restless tonight," she said to Thorstein. The dream shifted and she was standing outside in winter. Red blood covered the snow and a man lay dead. She tried to see who it was, but her vision blurred. Then she saw Edgtho standing in front of her, his sword dripping blood.

Annoure jerked awake in a sweat and looked wildly around the unfamiliar room, trying to remember where she was. It was dark except for the embers glowing in the dying fire.

Thyri and Njal slept on a bench near the fire, and their two children, Brandi and Sandey, slept across from them on another bench. Everything came rushing back to her with terrible force and she felt an overwhelming urge to check on Thorstein.

She rose, suppressing a gasp when her back protested. Her still-damp clothes hung near the fire and she gingerly slipped them on and took several deep breaths, waiting for the agony to lessen.

When Annoure stepped outside, she discovered it had stopped raining. Cold water and mud oozed through her bare toes as she walked through puddles of standing rainwater. A dark form stood near the barn. She paused, waiting for her eyes to adjust in the darkness. Gradually the form took the shape of a horse. When she walked closer, she saw it was Gunnar. She stepped toward him and he pranced backward. "It's just me. I won't hurt you." He tossed his head.

"I know you are a wild animal, not some tame beast of burden." He pushed his head against her chest and she reached up, unfastened his halter and slipped it off. "Go. You're free. You don't belong here." He raised his head, watching her.

"Go on." She pointed toward the woods, then started walking toward the house. He followed behind her.

"I said go on. Claim your freedom before someone awakens and finds you. It will be light soon." He twitched his ears as if he understood, but didn't leave. She continued toward the house. The horse pushed his nose against her throbbing back and she cried out in pain. She turned toward him. "Don't you want your freedom?"

He whinnied and stamped his front hooves. Resigned, she led him to the stable and gave him oats. He needed a rubdown, but she didn't have the strength. One of the men would have to take care of him.

"Why did you return to the farm? You're no longer the untamed stallion Thorstein captured in the mountains." She sighed. "I guess we're both bound by our hearts."

She left the stable and went outside where dawn was breaking, turning the dark world into gray forms. Annoure unlatched the door to the principal house and peered inside. Assured that Garth and the others were still sleeping, she crept over to Thorstein. His cheek felt warm and relief spread through her. He was still alive.

She lay on the bench beside him and studied his beloved face.

"You will awaken, my love, but I worry that death follows you," she whispered. "Whose blood stained the fresh, white snow?" She meant to stay only a moment, but her eyes were heavy and her head thick.

An angry male voice jerked her back to consciousness. Garth towered over her with bunched fists. Dark energy radiated from him.

"What are you doing here?" he demanded. She scrambled off the sleeping bench, too upset to speak. "Didn't I tell you to stay out of my sight and away from Thorstein? If he dies, his blood will be on your hands!"

Annoure cowered before him, afraid of being struck.

Chapter 13

Faðir and Sonr (Father and Son)

TREMBLING BEFORE GARTH, ANNOURE SUDDENLY remembered her dream of Thorstein where he was fully recovered and making a cradle for their baby. She knew it was a true vision of the future. She drew instinctively upon the power of the Druids to give her strength to stand up to Garth. She rose to her full height and met Garth's fierce gaze, feeling a potent energy surrounding her. "Thorstein will awaken. I've seen it in a vision." She spoke with such clarity and force that the fire faded from Garth's eyes, replaced by hope.

Annoure crossed to the door in this new altered state. Freydis and Kalsetini stared at her, but she hardly noticed them. Energy still pulsed through her. She stepped outside and breathed the fresh air, aware of her grandmother's presence.

She entered Njal's house and found Thyri serving the first meal to Herjulf and her family. Annoure sat on a bench. The door opened and Kalsetini rushed in. "Is it true? Will Thorstein live?" she asked, her eyes glowing.

Annoure nodded. "Já, I saw him alive in my dream."

Kalsetini walked closer, her face intent. "What did you see?"

"Thorstein making a cradle for our baby. It was winter, but warm in the house."

"Can you see the future in your dreams?" Njal asked.

"Sometimes. This was a true dream—a sending."

"We all believe her," Kalsetini said. "Power surrounded her—it still does. She practically glows with it! Although the way she spoke sent shivers up my spine, her words gave me and my parents hope."

"It's the power of the Druids," Annoure said.

"Faðir has gone to pray at the shrine," Kalsetini said. "Móðir said you are to come to the house and stay with Thorstein."

Annoure's stomach turned to acid. "I don't think it's safe for me to go back. Garth could return at any time."

"Móðir wants you there. She thinks you have the power to save Thorstein. Even Faðir will not dare touch you now. He also felt the magical power radiating from you."

Thyri came over. "Annoure looks pale and faint. She should rest and not leave so soon."

"I'd rather be with Thorstein than rest." Annoure and Kalsetini went outside and Kalsetini pointed to where Garth knelt by the altar.

"Faóir is praying to the gods. He brought food as an offering and will plead with them to spare Thorstein's life." Kalsetini hummed a sad tune as they walked along.

Inside the main house, Annoure sat on the sleeping bench beside Thorstein, who looked as if he was sleeping. She kissed his cheek, wondering if he'd ever open his eyes again.

"I feel terrible for being so mean to Thorstein," Kalsetini said, her voice unsteady. "I don't really blame him for getting in a fight with Rethel. He was only trying to defend you."

"I'm sorry Rethel's death caused trouble for your family."

"I was upset with Thorstein because of Ketil. I've liked Ketil since I was a young girl, but he's seven years older and thought of me only as a child. When he married Hanna, I was heartbroken. They had two dóttirs and when the second one was a year old, Hanna became sick and died. Ketil was so gravely distraught that he barely ate or slept for months afterwards. When I saw him again, I barely recognized him. He'd lost weight and vitality, yet what changed most was his disposition. Gone was the sweet, fun-loving man I fell in love with. In his place was a moody, temperamental man. He rarely smiled or seemed content.

"Two years passed with him in such despair, but when I saw him last spring he was more himself and finally noticed I'd become a woman.

Since we were already friends, we grew close quickly. Now Rethel's death has spoiled everything. We can't marry with a death dividing our families."

Annoure recalled the first time she'd met Ketil; she'd seen a vision of him weeping beside a dead woman.

"Do you love Thorstein?" Kalsetini asked.

Annoure smiled. "Já, a powerful bond existed between us before we even met. Thorstein knew it on some level when he first saw me in the church, but I didn't know it until I realized he was the man I visited in my dreams. My grandmother is a Druidess. She says when two people recognize each other upon meeting for the first time, it's because they have known each other in previous lives."

"Do you believe you've lived before?"

Annoure looked at Thorstein. "Já, sometimes I dream about another life where I was a powerful Druidess. In this life, my father raised me Christian and forbade me to live with my grandmother, but she taught me things I haven't forgotten."

"What did she teach you?"

Annoure hesitated, wondering if it would be better to remain silent, but Kalsetini seemed sincere and it was good to have someone to talk to.

"She taught me how to look into a still pond to see visions; how to stare into flames to leave my body. She also taught me to understand messages from the gods and goddesses. She encouraged me to memorize many Celtic stories and the teachings of the Druids so they wouldn't be lost. The Druids memorize the history of their people."

"So do our skalds. Do you often see visions?"

"I rarely look into still water because the Christian priests say it's a sin and only witches use such powers."

Kalsetini thoughtfully tilted her head. "If you have visions that come true, why do you let the Christian priests scare you into believing your powers are evil?"

"What if they are right and I *do* burn in hell for eternity? Father Eian said the Druids are evil."

"Your grandmother doesn't sound evil."

"She's not—she's a healer."

"Among my people, women who practice magic are highly respected. Some make prophecies as you did. Others serve as the Angel of Death in religious ceremonies."

"Our people once respected wise women with power too, but now the church forbids magic."

Annoure was worried about Thorstein because he hadn't yet awakened, so she stayed with him for much of the day. When the power had flowed strongly through her, she was sure her dream was a true sending, but now that it faded, she was troubled.

Before the evening meal, Herjulf took Annoure to the shrines. As she knelt, the wounds on her back sent sharp needles of pain through her. She groaned softly.

Herjulf grasped her arm and steadied her. "I shouldn't have brought you here. You should be resting."

"I wanted to pray with you and learn more about your gods."

He nodded. Then he put some grains of wheat into a wooden bowl. "Odin, please accept our gift and spare Thorstein's life."

Annoure lowered her head and put her hands together in prayer. *Please, God, don't let Thorstein die,* she said inwardly.

"Thorstein and I were inseparable growing up," Herjulf said. "We explored the woods, went boating, played with wooden swords and dreamed of going a-viking. Thorstein always loved the sea."

He pointed to a wooden statue of a man holding a hammer. "That is the god Thor whom Thorstein is named after him. We pray to Thor for a bountiful harvest and good fortune.

"He is a huge being and has a red beard and hair like me. He rides the clouds in a chariot drawn by two sacred goats. The pounding of their hoofs and the rumble of the wheels are the thunder. He guards the universe with his mighty hammer, Mjölnir, against the menace of the evil giants who lurk just beyond the edge of the world."

Herjulf gestured to the statue of a nude man. "Next to Thor is the god Frey." Annoure flushed, noticing the statue's male part looked just like Thorstein's did when he wanted to couple with her. Herjulf continued, not noticing her discomfort.

"He has the power of fertility, prosperity and controls the rain and sunshine. We call upon him for fruitful harvests and blessed marriages. Beside him is his twin sister, Freya, whom Aunt Freydis is named after. She is the goddess of love, beauty and has magical healing powers."

Herjulf turned to the last two statues. "This is Odin, the king of the gods and his vif Frigga." The male statue was a one-eyed man with a raven on his shoulder and two wolves at his side.

"Odin rides an eight-legged horse. He is the god of battle and death and is wise and strong."

Annoure studied the gods, wondering if they were real beings with power.

Njal hurried over to them. "Thorstein has awakened and is asking for you, Annoure. Garth said you are to come quickly. He's afraid Thorstein will hurt himself trying to get up to look for you."

Annoure lifted her skirts and ran to the house, great joy giving her speed. The room was filled with Thorstein's kin, including the children. They'd gathered around his sleeping bench. They cleared a pathway for her and she walked over to Thorstein.

He smiled upon seeing her. She clasped his hand, feeling her throat constrict with emotion. "Thorstein, thank God you've awakened."

"Annoure, were you hurt when the tree fell on us?"

"Nei, your body shielded me. How are you feeling?"

He rubbed one of his hands against his forehead. "My head feels like Thor is pounding his hammer inside it. Hand me some clothes and help me dress. We must leave here and go live on the Shetland Islands."

"We can't leave until you are better."

"I'm well enough now." He moved to sit up. "My clothes."

Njal rested his hand on Thorstein's shoulder, pushing him back into a reclining position.

"Bróðir, it is too late in the season to sail there and set up a home before winter sets in. You and Annoure can live with Thyri and me until winter passes."

Herjulf stepped forward. "I'll go with you to the island in the summer. You'll need help building a home and planting crops."

"We leave now," Thorstein said. "I'll not stay another day where we're not welcome." He shoved Njal's hand away and sat up. All the color drained from his face and beads of sweat appeared on his forehead. "A bucket!" he gasped.

Herjulf grabbed one and thrust it at Thorstein, who retched into it, then lay back down.

"Rest, sonr," Freydis said. "There's no reason for you to be upset." She glanced at Garth. "Your faðir cares only that you get better. No one wants you and Annoure to leave."

"The girl can stay with you," Garth said in a choked voice. "There is no reason to go anywhere. Use all your strength to get well."

Thorstein closed his eyes and appeared to go back to sleep. No one moved. Finally Garth spoke. "It's not good that he woke up so weak and then threw up, especially after being unconscious for so long." He turned to Annoure, his eyes filled with anguish. "Stay beside Thorstein until he becomes strong again."

Annoure sat on the bench beside Thorstein, glad her beloved wanted to leave for the Shetland Islands. She didn't want to live on the same farmstead as Garth. Yet she felt love and concern for Thorstein radiating from his family gathered around the bed, including the little children. It would be hard for Thorstein to leave them.

* * *

Thorstein awoke with an excruciating headache. He opened his eyes and smiled when he saw Annoure curled beside him. "Good morning, sweetness," he said, tightening his arm around her slender body.

"Ouch!" she exclaimed. "Don't hold me so tightly."

He removed his arm. "What's wrong? Were you hurt when Gunnar threw you?"

She nodded, her eyes not meeting his.

"Is the baby all right?" He put his hand on her stomach.

She smiled. "I'm not even sure I'm with child. You mother just thought that might be why I fainted."

"Móðir is usually right about these things. She knew when Asa and Thyri were going to have a baby."

"How are you feeling?" She put her hand on his forehead.

"My head still hurts."

"Do you remember anything from when you were unconscious for so long?"

He thought back, trying to remember his dreams. "I was in a heavy fog, searching for you. When I awoke and you weren't here, I was worried."

"Your father wouldn't let me stay with you." She sat up. "I need to use the outhouse."

When she rose he noticed that her underdress had fine stitches down the back as if it had been mended. She drew her hangerock on with stiff movements and he could tell she was hurting more than she let on.

"Rest. I'll be back soon." She leaned over and kissed him. He put his hand gently on her back and she flinched, then hurried to the door, tensing as she walked past his father.

"You gave us quite a scare," Garth said, coming over to him.

"It's lucky I have a thick skull." Thorstein drew in a breath, remembering his Faðir's advice to face problems and deal with them directly. "Faðir, I want to marry Annoure. Please consent to our marriage."

"She's bad luck. Three times you've nearly died because of her. The first time, you almost drowned at sea; the second time Rethel almost killed you in a sword fight; now you nearly died when a tree fell on you."

Thorstein felt a chill go through him, wondering if Annoure *was* bad luck. He pushed the thought away and decided to confide in his faðir so he'd understand. "I dreamed of Annoure for years before I found her in the church."

Garth glanced uneasily toward the door. "She has powers. I've seen them. She came to see you the morning after you'd been injured. I said if you died, it would be on her hands. At first she looked frightened, but then I felt her gather power and she appeared taller somehow. She looked me directly in the eye and said, 'He will awaken' in a voice filled with her magic. Get rid of her. Sell her at fall market. She'll bring a good price."

Thorstein clenched his fists. "I'm not selling Annoure. A woman with powers is to be respected. Besides, she carries my child. We're going to be married."

Garth glowered. "She is a thrall and her child will also be a thrall. You have no responsibility for it."

"I already consider Annoure my vif though we have not yet taken marriage vows."

"I'll keep my word and let you keep her for the winter. Take her as your bed thrall since your blood runs hot for her. You'll tire of her by spring and be glad to sell her and settle down to marry Dahlia."

"I will never tire of Annoure. When spring comes, our child will be born and I'll be bound to her even more."

Garth's whole body became rigid. "I don't want bad luck in my house! Keep your bed thrall in the outbuilding with the other thralls!"

"We'll live with Njal if Annoure's not welcome here."

"Good! I'll be glad to be rid of you both!" Garth stormed out the door.

Thorstein rose unsteadily to his feet and began to dress. His head throbbed mercilessly.

"You shouldn't be up yet," Freydis said, startling him. He hadn't realized she was in the room. She stood by the loom where she'd been working the whole time.

"We're not welcome here," Thorstein said, pulling on his shirt.

"You're welcome, just not Annoure. She frightens Garth. She does have magic. I saw it, too."

"Norse priests, rune masters and crones have magic and you don't think they're evil."

"I don't think Annoure's evil. Garth just blames her for nearly causing your death. He loves you and wants what's best for you."

"I can't live with him any longer." Thorstein walked unsteadily out the door. When Annoure returned from the outhouse, she hurried over to him. He put his arm around her shoulders and leaned heavily against her small frame.

She grimaced, but didn't complain. "You shouldn't be out of bed."

"I can't stay in Faðir's house any longer. We'll go live with Njal until we are able leave for the Shetland Islands."

When Thorstein entered Njal's house, his brother quickly crossed over to him and helped him to a sleeping bench. Thorstein sank down, waiting for the dizziness to pass. "Can Annoure and I live here?"

"Já. I've been expecting you. I knew you wouldn't forgive Faðir."

Thorstein stared at Njal with a sicking feeling. "Forgive him? For what?"

"Whipping Annoure. Didn't she tell you?" Njal looked at Annoure, who lowered her eyes.

Thorstein trembled with fury. "By Odin's Raven! Why didn't you stop him?"

"I did as soon as Kalsetini told me."

"Why did he do it?"

“To punish her for running away. He treated her no differently than he would any other runaway thrall.”

“She’s not any other thrall. He knows I intend to marry her.”

Thorstein drew Annoure onto his lap and kissed the top of her head, careful not to touch her injured back. If anyone else but his faðir dared whip her, he’d kill them.

Chapter 14

Trading Camp

DURING THE NEXT WEEK ANNOURE spent most of her time in the house with Thorstein as they both recovered. Thorstein wouldn't let her do any outdoor work, so she helped with meals and weaving. Thyri and Njal were easy to live with and Annoure enjoyed their young children Brandi and Sandey.

She was sure she was with child now. Her breasts were tender and she was abnormally tired. She calculated she was almost a month pregnant and the baby would be born in early summer.

With the fall harvest over, the men hunted roe deer, bear, fox and mink. The meat was then salted for winter storage and the furs tanned. Once these tasks were completed, Thorstein, Herjulf and Walfgar prepared to visit a nearby trading camp to sell extra grain and furs. Asa and Kalsetini planned to accompany them so Thorstein invited Annoure to come along. She was eager to go because in Northumbria, jugglers and storytellers abounded in marketplaces. She assumed the trading camp would also be entertaining and a break from everyday chores.

They set out for the trading camp early one fall morning in a sailboat. The trees were now shades of scarlet, rust and gold. Annoure sat beside Kalsetini, across from Walfgar and Asa who held Astrid. She listened to the waves lapping against the sides of the ship and breathed in the cool salty air.

"My bróðir Danr will probably be at market," Asa said, her cheeks flushed with excitement. "You'll like him, Annoure. He's a lot of fun."

"I have two older brothers. They are also enjoyable to be around."

"You must miss them." Asa's eyes were full of sympathy.

“I do.” Annoure appreciated Asa’s understanding.

“Maybe Ketil will be there,” Kalsetini said, not interested in Annoure’s family. She pointed to a distant farmstead. “That’s where his family lives. During other harvests we’d help each other, but with the trouble between our families, he didn’t come this year.” She frowned unhappily. “If Ketil is there, his cousin Edgtho will be with him.” She looked at her brother who sat by the steeringoar. “You need to guard against Edgtho, Thorstein. He’ll want revenge for Rethel’s death, even though it was a fair fight.” She clasped his hand. “I shouldn’t blame you for what happened. I know you are not a man to fight without a reason and Rethel had a mean streak in him.”

Annoure’s spine tingled. “If we meet Edgtho, would he challenge you to a fight, Thorstein?”

“If he does, there’s nothing to worry about. I’m a better swordsman.”

Herjulf hooted. “I’ve seen Edgtho fight. He’s one of the best. You won’t beat him unless the gods decide to favor you.”

“You’re just jealous, cousin, because you don’t have a woman. Perhaps at camp you’ll find one to cool your blood.”

In the afternoon, they reached the small trading camp. As Herjulf and Thorstein put up a tent, their friends came over to greet them. Annoure recognized some of the men who’d been on the dragon ship returning to Norge after raiding St. Paul’s Church.

Once camp was set up, the small group set off for the marketplace. They browsed from vendor to vendor, passing baskets of fish, caged chickens, fabric and imported spices. Some merchants spread their goods out on blankets; others set up make-shift tables. The air was heavy with the smell of cooking pork and beef, and the sounds of people bartering.

Asa’s round face lit up with enthusiasm as she haggled with merchants over the cost of spices and salt. The men wandered off to look at other booths. Annoure stayed with the women. Asa balanced Astrid on her hip and examined a silk scarf while Kalsetini scanned the crowd for Ketil.

“I love the farm, but winters are long, dark and lonely,” Asa said to Annoure. “The houses seem especially small when you’re trapped inside. It is different for the men. They get away in the summer and hunt in the winter.” Her face suddenly broke into a dimpled smile and she squealed with delight, yelling, “Danr!”

The slender youth looked up and grinned when he saw his sister. He pushed his way through the crowd and embraced her and the baby. “Asa, you look well.”

“And you’ve grown tall, little bróðir!”

Danr kissed the baby, then kissed his sister’s cheek. His face was smooth—apparently he didn’t need to shave yet—and his pant legs and shirtsleeves were too short, as if he’d outgrown them over the summer. Moreover, he moved as if he hadn’t had time to get used to his new longer limbs.

“Danr, you must meet Annoure,” Asa said, drawing Annoure forward.

Danr’s eyes widened. “By Odin’s Raven, she’s a lovely girl.”

“She’s Thorstein’s, so you best take your eyes off her.”

Danr flushed a deep red. “I’m forgetting my manners. Where are you from?”

“Northumbria.”

Danr glanced at his sister. “Did Thorstein abduct her on a raid?”

“Já, on his last voyage. He plans to marry her.”

“I’ll go a-viking next year. Faðir’s given permission.” He tickled the baby under the chin.

“Astrid’s a pretty girl. Is she a good baby?”

“She smiles all the time.”

“Like her móðir. And how is little Rothgar?”

“As hearty as his Faðir.”

“Where is Walfgar? I’d like to find out about their latest voyage.”

She glanced around. “He was here a moment ago. I think he wandered off when we stopped at the spice table.”

Danr’s brow wrinkled. “Isn’t that your neighbor Edgtho coming toward us?”

Annoure felt like a dragger had been thrust into her belly. She spun around and saw that Edgtho was barely twelve feet away.

Asa paled and placed a hand on Annoure’s arm. “Já, that’s him. There are problems between our families. We’d best return to camp.”

“Do you see Ketil with him?” Kalsetini asked, straining to see through the crowd.

Asa pulled Annoure along. “Kalsetini, Ketil is our enemy now. Let’s go.”

They had taken only a few steps when Edgtho moved in front of them, blocking their way with his large body. A cruel light entered his eyes.

"Hello, Asa," he said, his voice frosty. "Why are you in such a hurry to get away from your neighbor?" His eyes lit on Annoure. "I see you've brought a thrall to market. I'd like to buy her."

Danr's hand went to the hilt of his sword, his eyes wide with alarm. "You are mistaken. There is no thrall here."

Edgtho leered at Annoure, making her skin crawl. "I'm not mistaken. This woman was taken on the raid at Jarrow. I'll give you a few silver coins for her."

"I'm not for sale," Annoure snapped, trying not to stare at the ugly scar that marred Edgtho's cheek.

"There's been enough trouble, Edgtho," Asa said. "Let us by." She tightened her grip on Annoure's arm.

Annoure's heart raced. Seeing Edgtho brought back the horrible memory of Rethel attacking her.

Edgtho's eyes narrowed as he glared at Annoure. "You should have been the one to go to Valhalla instead of Tola. Did Thorstein tell you how she was killed after each of us mated with her? Tyrker's brothers tightened a rope around her neck as the Angel of Death stabbed her in the ribs."

"How awful," Annoure gasped as a wave of nausea swept over her.

"Let us by, Edgtho," Danr said. "You have no quarrel with us."

"I have a quarrel with this one." Edgtho grabbed Annoure by the hair and jerked her to him. She cried out in pain.

Danr drew his sword. "Release her or be prepared to go to Valhalla."

Edgtho laughed, not bothering to pull out his sword. "I don't fight boys. Go back to your móðir. It's too soon for you to be without her."

"I said *let go of her*!" Danr grasped Edgtho's wrist. Edgtho twisted free and punched Danr in the nose, knocking the youth backward. Danr fell to the ground.

Edgtho sneered as Danr grabbed his sword and scrambled back up, blood pouring profusely from his nose. He charged at Edgtho. The older man swung the shield off his back and used it to block Danr's sword, then drew his sword and advanced on the youth.

"Stop!" Asa screamed.

Annoure yelled Thorstein's name, frantically looking for him in the crowd that had rapidly formed around them, cheering on the fight.

"I'll go find the men!" Kalsetini said, pushing her way between two bystanders.

Edgtho fought off Danr with his sword and shield, looking amused. "You shouldn't pull a sword on a grown man, boy." Edgtho's expression hardened as he began to counterattack with vengeance. As Danr blocked Edgtho's blows with his shield, he stumbled backward and bumped into a man standing behind him.

"Edgtho, stop it!" Asa yelled, over the wail of her crying baby.

Ignoring her, Edgtho continued to rain fierce blows on Danr until sweat poured down the youth's forehead and his arms began to shake. Edgtho slammed his heavy sword into Danr's and the youth's blade bent.

Annoure grabbed Edgtho's sword arm. "Leave him be! You've done enough harm." Edgtho swung out his arm and knocked Annoure to the ground, then advanced on Danr who had stepped on the end of his bent blade to try and straighten it.

"Spare him!" Asa screamed.

"Edgtho!" Thorstein thundered. Relief flooded through Annoure as the crowd parted to make way for Thorstein. Close behind him were Walfgar, Herjulf and Kalsetini. Thorstein's sword was drawn and ready. "Your fight is with me, not Danr!"

Walfgar's sword was also drawn. "Let me fight him! He insulted my vif and kinsman."

"I'll kill Thorstein and then you!" Edgtho yelled.

Annoure scrambled to her feet. "There's no need for fighting."

"Herjulf, take the women back to camp," Thorstein said, keeping his eyes on Edgtho.

Herjulf tried to draw Annoure away. "This is no place for a woman." She resisted him, intent on the fight.

Thorstein's eyes filled with determination as he faced his enemy. Edgtho held his shield defensively and thrust his sword at Thorstein, who blocked it easily with his own shield.

Annoure was so terrified something would happen to Thorstein that she couldn't tear her eyes away. Herjulf was equally enthralled and made no further attempt to draw her away. The two men were well-matched, though Edgtho was older and more experienced. Thorstein fought aggressively, trying to get past Edgtho's shield.

"Enough! Put down your swords!" a man's deep voice roared. A large, middle-aged man pushed his way through the crowd.

"End this fight at once. One kinsmen is enough to lose to fighting. Edgtho, we're here to trade. We'll settle this dispute at the *ting*—not now with another death."

Herjulf whispered in Annoure's ear, "That is Nesbjörn, Edgtho's uncle; Ketil's faðir."

Ketil stood next to his father, his face twisted in rage. "A fight is the only way to end this. Thorstein must die for killing Rethel."

"Nei, Ketil!" Kalsetini exclaimed. "There must be a better way." He started at the sound of her voice, noticing her for the first time. Some of the hatred drained from his face.

"I won't allow this to become a blood feud!" Nesbjörn said forcefully. "If Edgtho kills Thorstein, then Njal or Walfgar will challenge Edgtho to fight. There will be no end to it until all of you are dead."

"I will kill them all!" Edgtho yelled.

"Nei, put down your sword!" Nesbjörn ferocious eyes bore down on Edgtho, who shook with rage but slid his sword back into its sheath.

Thorstein followed suit. The crowd broke up, disappointed that the fighting was over.

"Thorstein Garthson, if you hadn't killed Rethel in a fair fight," Nesbjörn spat out, "I would kill you myself." Nesbjörn spun around and walked through the crowd with Ketil and Edgtho in his wake.

Walfgar thrust his sword into its sheath. "I would rather put an end to this feud. Edgtho won't let this rest until he's dead. Let me fight him when the time comes, Thorstein. I'm a more skilled swordsman than you are. I can kill him; you cannot."

"I fight my own battles," Thorstein said. He put his arm around Annoure and she felt the tension in his hard body. He looked at her, his eyes softening with concern. "Are you all right, Sweetness? I saw Edgtho knock you down."

"I'm just shaken. Edgtho nearly killed Danr and he's only a youth."

"I shouldn't have let you out of my sight. Let's go back to camp. It's best if you stay there the rest of the time we're here."

Annoure looked at Danr who held a bloodied cloth to his nose. "Is your nose broken, Danr?"

"I don't think so," he said in a nasal-sounding voice.

"Ketil looked at me with such rage," Kalsetini said, her face scrunched up like she might cry.

"His anger was for me, not you," Thorstein said.

"He has that wild look in his eyes just like he did when his vif Hanna died. Only this time he has someone to direct his anger at," Kalsetini said. "I'm afraid for you."

"We shouldn't have brought the women to market," Walfgar said, taking the fussy baby from his wife. "I never expected Edgtho to attack the women."

Back at camp, everyone gathered around the campfire. Annoure sat on the ground between Thorstein's legs, her back leaning against his chest. He kept one arm around her and was unusually quiet. He didn't participate in the conversation around them and only drank one cup of wine.

In contrast, Kalsetini drank heavily, laughing and flirting with the Norsemen who'd joined them. Danr also drank with the men, beaming at the praise he received for his bravery. Asa cleaned the blood from Danr's face, but couldn't do much to stop his lip and nose from swelling.

Despite Danr's daring, Annoure thought he seemed shaken by the fight. He was a youth, no different from the young men back home. Perhaps Thorstein was not so different from her countrymen either. She wondered if he was afraid when he faced Edgtho, knowing he could be killed. She glanced toward Herjulf and caught him watching her. He stared back, lifting his mug to her. He was drunk and in good spirits, enjoying his friends' company.

Thorstein took Annoure into the tent while the others were still in the midst of their merriment. He began kissing her as soon as they were alone. She clung to him as turbulent emotions raged within her. She didn't know how she could bear it if Thorstein were killed. The battle made her realize just how much she'd grown to love him.

They knelt down on a hudfat facing one another and Thorstein looked at her with devotion. "If killing Edgtho would keep you safe, I would kill him a thousand times over. Yet his family is large and killing him would only bring more of his family's wrath upon us."

"Killing is rarely the answer."

"I do not welcome death as I once did. You and our child are my responsibility now." He drew her close. "Annoure, love me as I love you." He began kissing her again as he lowered her onto the hudfat. She kissed him back, not wanting her newfound happiness to end.

In the morning when Annoure awakened, she felt sore from their night of uninhibited coupling. She moved gingerly, pulling on her clothes. Thorstein lay on the furs watching her with a grin. "You seem a bit stiff this morning."

She shot him an annoyed look. He sat up and slid a hand along her thigh. "I'm hungry."

She slapped his hand away. "Aren't you ever satisfied?"

"Já, for a few moments right after I've made love to you." He chuckled and dressed, fastening on his sword before leaving the tent. She followed him into the daylight.

Asa was braiding Walfgar's beard while Kalsetini and Herjulf played a game of chess. Herjulf said, "We've been waiting for you two to awaken. We're going to the shrines to ask for good fortune when we trade today."

Herjulf picked up a small squirming lamb. Asa lifted the baby into her arms and they started walking toward the shrine. Annoure held back and Thorstein glanced at her. "Hurry up."

"I'm not coming."

"You can't stay here alone."

"Are they going to kill that lamb?"

"Já, it's a sacrifice to the gods."

"God doesn't require live sacrifices."

"Our gods do." He looked at her impatiently. "They waited until we awoke. Let's not make them wait for us at the shrine as well." He grasped her hand and hurried after the others.

"Sacrifices are wrong whether an animal or human," Annoure said. "Edgtho told me how Tola was sacrificed. They would have ritualistically killed me instead of Tola, if you hadn't intervened."

Thorstein stopped walking and turned to look at her, his brow furrowed. "I'm sorry he told you how Tola died. It's a brutal ritual. It's supposed to be an honor for a thrall to accompany her master to Valhalla, but I don't see the honor in a death like that."

"I feel badly that Tola died so horribly in my place. Now I understand why she attacked us with the knife."

"Thorstein, are you coming?" Herjulf yelled from where the family stood by a stone altar.

"Nei!" Thorstein called back. "Say a prayer for me." He returned his attention to Annoure.

"You can partake in the sacrifice if you want," Annoure said. "I'll go back to camp alone." She heard the lamb baa-ing as if it knew it was about to die. Its cry stopped abruptly.

She glanced at the altar and saw Walfgar catching the lamb's blood in a bowl. Her legs wobbled and she felt herself sway.

Thorstein put his arm around her. "What's wrong?"

She leaned against him, waiting for the dizziness to pass. "The ground is tilting."

Thorstein took Annoure back to camp and she sat on a log. "The sight of blood never made me faint before," she said. "I've seen animals butchered many times on the farm."

"Not when you were with child."

When the others returned to camp, Walfgar said, "We need to finish trading before we leave. Herjulf, will you stay behind to guard the women?"

"Já, though I don't expect trouble. Nesbjörn will keep Edgtho in line."

Thorstein kissed Annoure. "We won't be long."

After the men left, Danr came to camp, his lip and nose crimson and puffy. Asa was eager to hear about her family and Danr gladly shared stories about the farmstead. Kalsetini was quiet, withdrawn and didn't join the conversation.

Annoure watched the baby while Asa cooked the lamb on a spit over the fire. When Astrid napped, Herjulf and Annoure played a game of chess. She was pleased to discover she'd become good enough at the game to make winning a challenge.

When Thorstein returned that afternoon, he sat down on the log next to Annoure. He gave her a charming grin, his blue eyes lit with anticipation.

"I brought you a present." He took her left hand and slid a silver ring on her middle finger. The ring had an amber stone and fit perfectly.

"It's exquisite!" She put her arms around his neck and kissed him.

"Let us see it," Kalsetini said. Annoure held out her hand and Kalsetini and Asa both leaned close to admire the ring. "Amber is good luck," Asa said.

Thorstein pulled out his leather pouch and poured out a pile of silver coins. "I did well trading today."

"Did you get all that from trading wheat and furs?" Annoure asked.

Thorstein's arm froze. "Nei, I had something else of value to trade."

"What else?" she asked suspiciously, wondering if he'd traded something from the raid.

"Aren't you going to tell her, Thorstein?" Herjulf asked. A wide grin spread across his face, as if he enjoyed his cousin's discomfort.

"There's nothing to hide. I traded the book I stole on the raid. The jewels on it were valuable."

"But that book was the Bible—a sacred book!" Annoure exclaimed. "You shouldn't have traded it for silver and jewelry. Father Eian spent years carefully copying each word from an old Bible into elaborate script and decorating it with colored ink. It told all the stories about Christ's teachings."

"I didn't know the book was important to you," Thorstein said, crestfallen. "We need the money to start a new life on the Shetland Islands."

"I wanted to share the stories with you." Tears sprang to her eyes. "It was my only connection to home and my former life there."

"Garth won't allow you to share stories from the Bible," Walfgar said dismissively, gathering up their supplies. "He considers the Christian teachings poison that would corrupt his family. Let's break up camp and start home. You women pack and we'll carry everything down to the boat."

Annoure went into the tent and pulled her cross necklace out from under the neckline of her tunic. She'd worn the necklace hidden at Thorstein's urging, but now it felt as if she hid a part of herself.

Kalsetini and Asa followed her into the tent. Asa set down the baby and began packing supplies. "Annoure, among our people wealth is worn in the form of jewelry," Asa said as she worked. "Thorstein gave you the ring because he wanted everyone to know he's a man of wealth and you are of value to him. Don't be upset with him."

"I'm not really. It just makes me realize how different he and I are."

Norse people don't even have books, she thought. *How could Thorstein know the Bible had value to me? He hardly knows what reading is, having only read short verses on rune stones.*

"Did you notice how hurt Thorstein looked?" Kalsetini asked, shoving her long, thick hair over her shoulder. "He meant the ring as an engagement gift." She stared dreamily off into space. "I wish Ketil would give me a ring."

"Garth will find you a verr soon enough," Asa said. "You'll discover men and the babies that follow are a lot of work. Enjoy your freedom while you have it."

The women carried everything outside and Herjulf and Walfgar took down the tent. Then Annoure hauled Thorstein's hudfat to the ship.

Thorstein stood alone on the shoreline, studying the wind and waves. She climbed aboard the boat, still irritated with him for selling the Bible, even though she knew she should be grateful for the ring instead.

Chapter 15

Grandmother

ON THE WAY BACK TO the farm, the boat sailed over the sunlit waves. The air was crisp with the coming of winter and a strong wind blew against their backs. As Thorstein steered the boat, he pondered Annoure's distress about selling the book. He hadn't known it was valuable to her. Maybe she thought it was a holy relic, like one of the statues of the Norse gods.

Saxon women were hard to understand. If he married Dahlia, he wouldn't have this problem. Nor would he have to leave his family and the farm to live on a remote, windblown Shetland Island. Annoure sometimes acted like a pampered, spoiled child. Would she be happy raising a family in a modest house where she had to do all the chores? Would he be happy with such a strong-willed, difficult woman?

He gazed over at her. The wind blew through her long hair and the sun shone on her exquisite face and he realized it was her fire and spirit that drew him to her. If she were browbeaten, he would probably lose interest in her. Moreover, with Dahlia he'd never have the deep connection he had with Annoure.

Her jeweled cross glittered in the sunlight. He suspected she was displaying it openly to defy him. He decided against saying anything about it; in the mood she was in, she'd probably hit him with an oar. If his faðir saw the cross he'd be furious, but then things couldn't get much worse with Faðir anyway. He'd have to tell his faðir about the fight with Edgtho. At that thought, he regretted even more bringing Annoure to the trading camp.

By the time they arrived home, the sun had set. In Njal's house, everyone was already asleep and the only light came from burning logs in the hearth. When Thorstein and Annoure lay on their sleeping bench, he sensed her melancholy and put his arm around her, drawing her against him, sheltering her small body with his.

* * *

Annoure awoke early the next morning with a stomachache. She lay still, but the rumbling in her belly grew worse. Afraid she'd be sick, she rushed from the house and hurried across the cold ground in bare feet. She knelt near the stream as her body broke into a sweat, then she heaved the contents in her stomach onto the cold, damp ground.

For a few moments she felt better, then the sickness rolled through her again and she retched a second time. Afterwards she dipped her hand in the cool water and rinsed out her mouth. The little goat Loki came running up to her and butted against her side. "Leave me alone, Loki. I feel terrible."

A stick snapped and she looked up to see Thorstein approaching. He draped a cape over her shoulders. "Are you all right?" he asked, eyeing the mess on the ground.

"No, I must have eaten something bad."

"More likely it's morning sickness. When Asa was pregnant she got sick in the morning, but only for the first few months."

"I hope this isn't going to be a daily experience."

He scooped her into his arms. "I'd better get you back to the sleeping bench. Next time use a bucket so you don't risk getting a cold."

"I can walk."

"Your feet are bare." He carried her inside and tucked her under the furs on the sleeping bench, then built up the fire.

"I have to help Ginna with the animals."

"Nei, rest. You're with child."

A few hours later, Annoure felt better and ate a light meal. It was Saturday, the day when everyone in the household took their weekly bath and sometimes a sauna in the bathhouse as well. Annoure had gotten used to the custom of regular bathing. It felt good to be clean and not itching from lice or fleas. Moreover, she liked it when Thorstein came to her, smelling fresh from his bath.

She couldn't imagine going back to bathing only twice a year, as her people did. The Christian belief about nudity and bathing being sinful no longer made sense to her.

The water in the tub would be dirty by the time it was her turn to use it, so Annoure decided to bathe in the stream instead. At a place hidden by bushes, she undressed and waded into the chilly rushing water. She plunged her head under, then scrubbed her hair with soap and rinsed it. Back on shore, she dried off with a linen cloth, noticing her stomach was still flat.

Thyri said it might be another month before she started to show. Annoure pulled on clean clothing, wondering if Thorstein would still find her attractive when she was large with child.

Annoure sat on the shoreline, breathing in the scent of wild roses, as she watched the wispy clouds lit with streaks of purple and orange. She drew her knees up and wrapped her arms around them, feeling contemplative. On the edge of her consciousness, she sensed Grandmother trying to reach her. The feeling grew so strong that she found a place on the bank where the stream was still, perfect for gazing into.

At first she couldn't quiet her mind, but finally she moved into a deep meditative state. Grandmother's face soon appeared in the sparkling surface of the water. "I've been searching for you, Annoure. It's been a long time since you've come to me. You need to start using your powers to reach me more often." Grandmother paused, frowning. "I see you are with child."

Annoure's eyes widened, surprised her grandmother knew. "I'm carrying Thorstein's baby, but I'm uneasy because we aren't married. His father forbids it."

"Marriage is not important. A child is always a blessing from the Mother Goddess. He will have Druid blood and be strong with the Sight."

"Marriage is important so that I can be free and no longer a thrall."

"You are already free. True freedom is a state of being and does not depend on your outer circumstances. You have Druid blood and create your own path."

"I didn't choose to be stolen from my home!"

"Before being reborn, you chose to be reunited with Thorstein. I'm watching over you. Do not be afraid, no matter what happens. Through your trials, you will receive training and grow into your full powers."

The vision faded. "Grandmother, come back, please. I need you."

Her mind whirled as it often did after talking to her grandmother, whose ideas were so different from the priests. Annoure worried if she would go to hell for eternity if she didn't follow the teachings of Christ. Yet, perhaps the priests were wrong.

The Druids she knew were men to be revered. They were spiritual leaders, diplomats, healers, musicians and teachers. She sighed, sad that so few Druids were left in her homeland. The early Romans, and later the Christians, persecuted and killed most of them.

As she sat pondering, a vision of another time flashed before her. She stood next to a powerful Druid in a sacred oak grove where they'd come to worship. Gathered around them were a tribe of Celts from a nearby village. The Celts had red-painted cheeks and lemon-bleached blond hair and colorful clothing.

She gazed into the eyes of the man beside her, feeling the great love between them and knew he was Thorstein. He spoke to the people about their ancient history and of future prophecies.

The vision disappeared and Annoure looked around the forest surrounding her, sensing this life wasn't as real as the one she was just in. *Was Grandmother right?* Had she chosen to be with Thorstein again? She smiled thinking of him. She'd happily spend her life with Thorstein rather than old Bandolf, the noble her father had pledged her to.

The next day Thyri handed Annoure an iron kettle with a broken handle and told her to get it fixed. As Annoure drew near the blacksmith outbuilding, she heard the repeated pounding of a hammer against metal. She entered the dimly lit room and was hit with a blast of heat from a center fire. It took a few moments for her eyes to adjust to the dim light.

Herjulf stood over an anvil, pounding a piece of metal. He wore a leather apron and his rolled-up shirtsleeves exposed his thick, muscular arms. He glistened with sweat as he worked steadily, the firelight playing on his red beard and hair.

As if sensing her presence, he looked up and his startling blue eyes met hers. He smiled at her, his hammer raised in the air, ready to strike again. "Annoure, what a pleasant surprise! What brings you here?"

"Thyri wants the kettle handle fixed."

"Bring it over." He took the kettle from her and examined the handle.

Annoure looked at the hoe he worked on. "I didn't know you were a blacksmith. I thought Walfgar was the only one."

"Faðir taught us both. I make farm tools and shoe the horses."

"Why do you work in such a dark room? An Eye of the Wind would allow light in."

"Dim light is needed to see if the steel is tempered properly."

Thorstein entered the shop, leading Gunnar. He paused a moment as his eyes adjusted to the lack of light. "Gunnar needs a new shoe."

"A day for work," Herjulf said. "Annoure just brought me a kettle to fix." He crossed to the stallion and lifted up one of his hoofs. "His shoes are worn. I'll work on him this afternoon."

"Good, I'll need Gunnar tomorrow when we leave to round up the reindeer." Thorstein and Annoure left together, walking down the path toward the house. "Are you feeling better today?" he asked.

"Já, much better. Thorstein, I think we've known each other in many lives and planned to find each other in this one."

"I've never heard of such a thing. What makes you think that?"

"Grandmother told me in a vision." Annoure described the vision in detail and Thorstein told her about dreams he'd had that were similar to her vision. There was more to Thorstein than she'd first thought. He, too, had important dreams he'd never shared until she revealed some of her inner experiences. Perhaps Grandmother was right and she and Thorstein were meant to be together in this life. She felt magic between them.

Later that day when she returned to the house after watering the animals, she heard the sound of sword fighting. It brought back memories of the fight at the monastery and her heart leapt to her throat. She walked cautiously toward the sound to see what was going on.

Just ahead Thorstein and Herjulf sparred. Njal and Walfgar stood nearby, watching with obvious enjoyment. She gazed at them uneasily. Neither man wore armor and either one of them could be injured.

Both men fought with skill, yet her eyes kept returning to Thorstein. His movements and sword strokes were sure and smooth. Even to an untrained eye, Thorstein was a better fighter than his cousin. She watched mesmerized as the fight continued. Their sword practice was like a beautiful dance. It reminded her of two stallions she'd once seen fighting. It had both frightened and thrilled her.

She watched the way Thorstein's arm and chest muscles flexed and hardened. His bare chest and arms glistened with sweat despite the coolness of the air. The sight of him aroused her; heat rose to her face and her pulse quickened.

Thorstein sprang forward slamming his sword into Herjulf's shield. The sound of the men's panting breaths filled the air. Herjulf swung his sword into Thorstein's and the fight continued. Finally Thorstein got past Herjulf's guard and brought the point of his blade to Herjulf's chest. "Yield," Thorstein said. His eyes locked with Herjulf's. When Herjulf didn't reply, Thorstein drew back his sword. "Do you wish to keep fighting then?"

Walfgar stepped forward with a sword in hand. "Nei, the next fight is mine." His sword swung out and Thorstein's shield met it.

"You are too reckless," Walfgar said, as he continued to fight. "You leave yourself open and only think of attack when you should be equally concerned with defending yourself. You fight well, but on instinct. You need to fight with your mind. Watch your opponent's eyes to anticipate his next move and observe his fighting style. You must fight each man differently. Edgtho is a skilled, strong opponent, yet you need to be equally concerned about Ketil. Because of your past friendship with him, you might hesitate when you should deliver the deathblow."

Annoure slipped away unseen by the men. Walfgar's seriousness with the training alarmed and frightened her. She remembered the hatred and rage radiating from Edgtho and Ketil. The ferocity she saw in these Norsemen was unlike anything she had seen in the sheltered life she'd led in Northumbria.

The following morning, Annoure buttered a slice of flatbread and ate it with a glass of goat's milk. She found that ever since becoming pregnant, she was always hungry.

Thorstein came over to her. "Please pack me some food. I'll be gone a few days. We're bringing in the herd of reindeer so we can feed them over the winter." He gathered up supplies while Annoure put dried meat, bread and fruit into a leather satchel.

After Thorstein kissed her goodbye, she watched him ride into the woods with Herjulf, Njal and Walfgar. Loneliness engulfed her. What would become of her and the baby if something happened to Thorstein?

* * *

Several days later, thundering hooves brought Annoure outside. Walfgar jumped off his horse and held the corral gate open while Thorstein, Njal and Herjulf drove in a herd of majestic creatures with large antlers and brown fur. The reindeer raced gracefully around the corral, looking for a way to escape.

Annoure climbed up on the wooden fence and watched Thorstein work, enjoying how well he rode and handled his horse. The diversity of his skills never failed to amaze her. Once the gate was shut, Thorstein cantered over to Annoure, lifted her off the post, and set her in front of him on Gunnar. "I missed you," he said. His mouth covered hers in a kiss that left her breathless.

"I'm glad you're back. It's lonely when you're not here."

"You'll be sick of me before winter is out."

Garth walked up to them. "It's a fine herd, Thorstein. It looks like many calves were born this summer."

Thorstein tensed. "They're healthy. Food was plentiful this year." The strain between Thorstein and his father was obvious. Thorstein was still angry over Garth whipping her. She was angry too, but she understood that Garth had been terrified his beloved son might die and that was what lay behind his actions. Thorstein rode over to the barn and reined in Gunnar.

"I've been wanting to thank you for the ring," Annoure said. "I love the amber stone."

"I didn't mean to cause you pain by selling the book. I traded it for silver coins so we can leave the farm and marry."

"I'm sorry I got so upset. I know your intentions were good, but I wanted to share the Bible with you. It has many stories like the sagas your people love." He frowned, looking confused so she continued, "You carve on a stone to tell of a man's deeds. We write entire sagas in books. I realize now you couldn't have known how valuable the Bible was to me."

His fingers caressed her cheek, then he brushed a loose strand of hair off her face. "I'm sorry for not talking to you first. I could have sold the jewels and kept the book."

"I'm sorry I lost my temper. I love you in this world and in the dreams worlds." She kissed him and he kissed her back with heated passion.

Chapter 16

Winter in Hordaland

THE WINTER WIND BLASTED ANNOURE as she stepped out of the house. She drew her wool shawl tightly around her swollen belly and walked along the worn pathway in the deep snow, breathing the fresh air. Her leather boots crunched the ice and her cheeks tingled in the cold air. The eggs needed gathering and although Thorstein offered to do it, she wanted to escape the dim, smoky house. The short winter days were depressing. It was dark when she awakened and dark long before the evening meal.

She paused to look at the mountains, majestic with bright sunlight sparkling on the snow-covered peaks. She realized how much she would miss this land when she and Thorstein left for the Shetland Islands. She'd miss Thorstein's family as well. Thyri had befriended her like an older sister and eased her fears about childbirth. Good-natured Asa brought her children over every day and filled the house with laughter as the four children played together. And Kalsetini began to confide in her, sharing concerns about someday being given in marriage to a man she didn't love.

Off in the distance, Annoure noticed a man riding toward the farmstead. As he drew closer, she saw he had a thick beard and wore a wool cape, layered in snow. She hurried back to the house calling, "Thorstein, a traveler is coming."

Thorstein appeared on the doorstep and grinned broadly. "It is Erik the skald."

"How did he get here?"

"He came through the mountain pass from Nesbjörn's farmstead."

Erik rode up and dismounted.

"It's good to see you, Erik," Thorstein said, embracing him and pounding on his back. "You must have had quite a time journeying through the mountains this time of year."

"It was a challenge worthy of a saga."

"This is Annoure." Thorstein put his hand on the small of her back. "Annoure, meet our skald, Erik."

Annoure stared at Erik. She felt he was an old friend, yet she knew they'd never met. Neither she nor Erik moved. Wisdom and depth shone in Erik's eyes and his essence reminded her of the Druids.

"Erik, I'll take care of your horse," Thorstein said, not noticing the intensity between Annoure and his friend. "Annoure, will you take Erik to the house to see my parents?"

"I'll be glad to," she said as he led the horse toward the barn.

"The gods told me I must cross the mountain pass and I wondered why," Erik said. "Meeting you, I now understand. Our lives are linked."

A tingling sensation went up Annoure's spine. Kalsetini rushed out of the house, shouted "Erik!" and the moment was broken. Kalsetini ran through the snow and threw herself into his arms. "I'm so glad to see you. The winter has grown long and we all need a distraction. I hope you've brought new songs and stories."

He chuckled. "Fair Kalsetini, you could make a skald give up his wanderlust if he had you to come home to at night. If I didn't know how good Ketil is with a sword, I'd beg your faðir for your hand in marriage."

Kalsetini's smile faded and Erik quickly amended his words. "I'm sorry, for a moment I forgot the trouble between Ketil and Thorstein."

"How is Ketil?" she asked, walking toward the house with Erik and Annoure.

"He mourns the loss of his bróðir with an intensity that is unnatural," Erik replied. "He reminds me of a wolf cub I once found crying for its dead móðir. I tried to care for it, but it wouldn't take cow's milk or the love I gave, so it soon died. It's painful to see Ketil's distress and it grieves me to see Edgtho taking advantage of his despair, poisoning him with thoughts of revenge. I fear for Thorstein's life."

Annoure tensed at Erik's words. They reached the main house and went inside.

"What news do you bring?" Freydis asked, greeting him with a kiss on the cheek.

"Let the man have a drink and relax before he shares his travels," Garth said, from where he sat by the fireplace. "Welcome to our home. Join me by the fire and warm yourself."

Erik sat on a bench across from Garth. He pulled a lyre from his leather bag, carefully examining the harp-like instrument. "I worry when I travel with her in such cold weather, but she looks fine." His love for the lyre shone in his eyes. He set it down and reached toward the warmth of the fire. His well-formed hands had long, graceful fingers.

Asa came into the house carrying Astrid in her arms and Walfgar followed with their *sonr* Rothgar. "We heard you were here, Erik," Asa said, smiling happily. "Will you play us something on your lyre?"

"I will sing songs that will make you weep and tell you many colorful tales once I have rested. The snow is deep in the mountain passes and the journey is treacherous." His voice flowed like music.

Asa brought Erik a cup of mead. "Have you seen my family this winter, Erik?"

"Já. They all do well."

Erik enraptured Annoure. He glowed like a bright star in the middle of the dreary winter. He was not as old as she first thought, perhaps in his late twenties. His appearance wasn't striking; he was of average looks and modest in height and build in this land of tall men. But something about his countenance made him stand out. She sensed he was a man of depth and integrity.

News of Erik's arrival spread quickly and more family members packed into the principal house, eager for a distraction from the routine of everyday life. The women set out food and everyone sat at the table. As they began to eat, Erik shared information about relatives and friends on other farmsteads.

In the days that followed, Annoure heard many sagas of battles and daring deeds. She came to realize how much the Norse people valued courage. To them, it was an honor to die in battle. Life was short and difficult in this harsh land. Erik also played his lyre and sang. He had a wonderful, melodic voice that touched Annoure's heart.

One evening at Njal's home, Walfgar brought out a pan flute and Njal a recorder and they accompanied Erik. The older children danced and Asa laughed and bounced Astrid on her knee. Then Kalsetini and Erik began to sing together. Kalsetini's voice was clear and a peaceful expression settled over her young face. When the song was over, they passed wine around. Annoure leaned contentedly against Thorstein's shoulder, enjoying the fun.

Wolves began howling in the distance. Freydis put another log on the fire and the children drew closer to the light given off by the leaping flames.

"The end of the world is called Ragnarok," Erik said. The firelight danced eerily off his face. "When it comes, there will be a great battle between good and evil. The gods will fight terrible monsters and giants. Fenrir, the monstrous wolf, will gobble up Odin, the king of the gods. Our beloved Thor will fight the world serpent and kill it with his hammer and then die of the serpent's poison. The wolves howl tonight to remind us of Ragnarok, last battle when all the gods and men will die and there'll be an end to heaven and earth."

"Will there ever be men or gods again?" Brandi asked. The boy's eyes were wide with worry. "Is that the end forever?"

"The prophecies say the earth will rise out of the sea and a man and woman who survive the destruction will start the human race all over again. The gods and goddesses will come back with their wisdom and Asgard will form again. This new heaven and earth will be filled with goodness."

"Tell us the story of Prince Sigurd," Sandey said.

Erik smiled at Njal's daughter. "I'll tell you the story about the time Sigurd killed a dragon. The story begins before Sigurd was born. A man named Kreidmar had a fabulous treasure that the gods Odin, Hoenir and Loki helped him take from a dwarf. His sonr, Fafnir, became greedy for the gold and murdered Kreidmar to gain possession of the treasure.

"Once Fafnir had the gold, he could think of nothing else but how to protect it. He decided to change himself into a huge, fire-breathing dragon so he could guard his treasure in a lair."

Annoure loved listening to Erik's stories of bravery, love, betrayal, greed and magical creatures. They helped her understand Thorstein and his people. When Erik finished the saga, Annoure said, "We also have tales about warriors and dragons."

"You will have to share your stories with me while I'm here. If you'd like, tomorrow I will start teaching you the Futhark. Garth asked me to give you lessons."

Annoure was surprised that Garth wanted her to learn the Norse written language. She thought he just wanted to get rid of her.

Early the next morning, Erik arrived at Njal's home. Annoure and Erik sat on the dirt floor and he drew the letters of an ancient alphabet. Sandey and Brandi joined them, not wanting to miss anything. "The sixteen letters of the Futhark are all made with straight lines," Erik said, "so they're easier to carve."

"Several look similar to the Anglo-Saxon alphabet," Annoure said, "such as the letters P, R, I, and B."

Brandi copied the letters in the dirt, but Sandey got bored and started playing with her doll.

Erik pronounced each letter for Annoure. Many of them sounded different in Norse than in Anglo-Saxon. "We carve runes into wooden chests to label trade goods," Erik said. "And we chisel runes into stones to tell of a man's deeds after he dies."

"In Northumbria, we have books."

"Já, I have seen your books. Here you can make money naming things and putting good luck spells on them."

Annoure and Erik spent many hours together every day as he taught her their written language. Her ability to speak Norse fluently also improved.

One evening after dinner, Annoure sat with Thorstein and Erik near the fire. "Erik, you remind me of the Druids," Annoure said, her hand clasped in Thorstein's.

"The Celtic holy men. Why them?"

"Because they used to travel from village to village, sharing stories of their people. They memorized poems and the history of their people as you do. Most of the Druids are gone now. The Anglos, Saxons and Celts have become Christian."

"You said once that your grandmother was a Druidess," Thorstein said.

Annoure stared into the fire and an image of Grandmother appeared.

She felt power in the room and glanced at Erik. He stared back with penetrating, thoughtful eyes. “My mother was the daughter of a Druidess,” Annoure said. “She and my father fell in love and wanted to marry. At first, Grandmother wouldn’t consent to the marriage because my mother was destined to become a Druidess. There are so few left to carry on the teachings. On greater reflection, Grandmother decided since my father was a powerful man who knew the king, the marriage would be beneficial. My mother could help protect the Celts who still worshipped in the old ways.

“An agreement was made: in exchange for letting mother marry, instead of becoming a Druidess, my parents were to give their first girl child to the Druids to be raised as a Druidess. The child would be given to Grandmother on her fifth birthday. My father readily agreed. I’ve been told my mother was a rare beauty with inner strength and self-possession that came from her Druid training. I think my father would have agreed to any price.

“In the early years my parents were happy and mother gave birth to two healthy sons. But after that three babies died at birth. Mother was heartbroken and grew very weak. Grandmother insisted she keep trying to have another child because of the promised girl-child. Mother finally gave birth to me. She never recovered her health and died when I was a year old.

“Grandmother came to claim me when I was five. But by then my father loved me too much to give me up. My nurse told me I looked exactly like my mother, even at that young age and he cherished me as he had her. Grandmother didn’t have the power to force him to honor his promise. I remember them arguing. She told him misfortune would come from a broken promise.

“My father said he didn’t want any child of his raised as a pagan away from the world. He was a man of honor and so he compromised by agreeing to let Grandmother visit me if she didn’t teach me the ways of the Druids. He even let me stay with her a few times, accompanied by one of my brothers and a bodyguard. He didn’t intend to lose me to the Druids. He had plans of his own to use me to strengthen his allegiance with King Aethelred.”

“So, fair Annoure,” Erik said, “while you profess to be a Christian, in your heart you are a Celtic Druidess with furious warrior blood of your own.”

"Nei! I'm not a Druidess."

Thorstein looked from Annoure to Erik in surprise.

"You deny it," Erik said, "but I feel your powers. They're undeveloped but they are there. The Druids must have taught you something of their ways. I wondered how it is that you are literate and speak with wisdom beyond your years. You have the spirit and bearing of a young Druidess, not the bearing of a submissive Christian daughter."

Annoure stared into his kind eyes, uneasy at his words. Today his hair and beard seemed especially unruly. He was a Norseman of unusual inner strength with the intelligence of an initiate of the old gods. It frightened her because she knew his words were true. The power of the Druids fascinated, yet scared her because Father Eian had spoken so strongly against them.

"Grandmother told me spells that no Christian woman should know, but I have rarely used them."

"What powers have you used?"

"I learned to use water or fire to contact Grandmother and my dreams and visions reveal things about people or about the future."

Thorstein stared at her mystified. He recovered himself and said, "So you preach about your Christian God while you have abilities like the Angel of Death."

"Christians have visions, too. My vision doesn't make me like a Druidess or an Angel of Death."

"You had a sending from a Druidess," Erik said. "That is not the same as a vision a Christian might have. Are you afraid of your powers?"

Annoure looked down, not answering. Erik didn't press her further. Instead he picked up his lyre and began to sing. His beautiful melodious voice was rich and the music he brought forth from the lyre was pure. She closed her eyes, listening to the captivating music. It carried her back to a time when she sat and listened to a Druid bard as he sang tales of magic and other worlds.

She'd felt so much peace when she was with Grandmother. The Druidess seemed so serene, but Annoure had sensed beneath the serenity was power and magic that wasn't always used for good. If she hadn't been afraid of that power, she might have run away from home and become a Druidess. She hid behind Christianity even though she knew there were mysteries, ways of seeing and traveling in the other worlds that the Christians knew nothing about.

As the skald finished his piece, Annoure realized tears were streaming down her cheeks. "I love to hear you sing, Erik. Yours is a rare talent."

Thorstein stared at her with a puzzled expression. He accepted without question the stories of gods, goddesses and heroes. She wondered if he ever spent time thinking about things beyond the everyday struggle to survive. She loved him for his strength and courage, for his loyalty to her and his family and for his spirit of adventure on land and at sea. Yet she appreciated being able to talk of mystical things with Erik.

That night, Annoure slept poorly, thinking about her conversation with Erik. Were the beliefs of the Druids as evil as the Christian priests taught? Or were kernels of truth in them that she was afraid to look at? Was she pushing her Christian religion on Thorstein when she knew that other, perhaps higher, truths existed? She rose early while everyone still slept and built up the fire. Erik, who slept on a bearskin by the fire, woke and their eyes met.

"You look pensive this morning," he said softly. His voice was as rich and melodic when he spoke as when he sang.

"I've been thinking about what you said last night. Can we talk?"

"Let's talk outside where we'll have some privacy." He dressed while she slid on her boots and cape, then they stepped into the cold winter day.

Although it was morning, it was still dark and the wind had a bite to it. Snowflakes landed on them as they walked along the path. Annoure stopped under an enormous oak tree and put her gloved hands on its rough bark. She felt energy, life and ancient wisdom as its strength flowed into her. Finally she turned and faced the skald.

"If I were a Druidess, this grove of trees, the ground beneath me and the sky above would be my sanctuary, not the stone walls of a church. The Druids taught me things the Christian priests would say are of the devil's making. I believed the priests, but in this world where there are no Christian priests, I look through the dark mists alone. What am I to believe, Erik?"

"I don't know. I am a humble skald," he said. "I was taught the Norse sagas, which I sing or recite around a campfire. The stories are a way to explain the mystery of creation and life, and to explain the sun, moon and thunder. These stories are passed from one generation to the next until it's hard to know what is truth and what isn't."

She leaned back against the oak tree. "Christians believe there is one God who sent his only son here to suffer for our sins. The priests say they are intermediaries between God and man. I know this isn't so. I have my own experiences." The wind whipped up the corner of her cape. "I don't know if you can help me. You are of a different world than the two I was already torn between before coming here."

"The answers are in you, Annoure, not outside of yourself. You will not get answers from me, the priests, or even from the Druids. From each, you will get hints of truth and pieces to help you unlock the ancient mysteries of life. You will only know truth from experience, from what life teaches you, from your dreams, visions and travels into the other worlds. If I said to you, this is truth and that is not, you would not believe me. You would not accept it any more than you accepted what the priests and Druids taught you.

"I will say this much. Following the Druid practice of having power over others will not bring happiness. Your heart must be pure, your desire for truth must be for a good reason or you will be burned and torn asunder by this power. You will lose the purity and beauty surrounding you that draws others to you."

"Is there more you can share? A kernel of truth you've discovered in your wanderings or perhaps in the stories you've memorized?"

"I've learned there is more than what we see on the surface. Gaze upon the sea." He pointed at the fjord. "What do you see?"

"I see the sea is ever-changing as the waves rise up and down and I see the trees reflected in its surface."

"What about what lies beneath the sea — the rocks, seaweed, fish and hvalrs? Have you thought about what is not apparent on the surface?" He stared pensively at the water, not saying anything further.

"What else, skald?" she asked, touching his arm, knowing there was more she needed to learn from him to make sense of the world.

He looked at her smiling. "You are like a greedy child begging for sweets. Your hunger for truth is just as great."

"Greater. A child's craving for sweets is easily satisfied whereas mine grows within me ever stronger."

"Does Thorstein know or even suspect what kind of woman you are? Does he see that you're not just a pretty young woman to give him children and keep him warm at night? Does he know you're not a woman he can carve as a piece of wood to his northern ways? I suspect he does and is drawn to you as a ship is drawn to harbor during a storm at sea.

"I'll tell you this much. You are not your body, which will someday perish. The part of you that is immortal leaves your body in dreams and will leave your body permanently upon death. Whether you choose to call this inner world heaven or Valhalla, it makes no difference. There may be one God or power that created us, but there are also lesser gods and rulers who watch over our world. They are deities with human emotions, not the creator of life. Some lesser gods are good and some are evil, so be careful when you travel in their worlds."

His piercing eyes searched hers. She felt exposed before him as he seemed to be looking inside her. Although it was not an outer sensation, she wrapped her cape tighter around her body.

"Your lips are turning blue. It will upset Thorstein if you get sick. He loves you well. Don't try to control him or remake him into something he's not. He was reared to be a Norsemen warrior who has no fear of death. Will you try to make him lose his daring for fear of hell and eternal damnation?"

"The teachings of Christ can bring comfort."

"For some." His gaze returned to the sea. "I'm moving on today."

"I wish you could stay longer. I'll be sorry to see you go," Annoure said, heavyhearted that he was leaving. She'd miss his friendship and music. "When will we see you again?"

"I'll be at the spring festival and the legal *ting*."

Annoure tensed at the mention of the *ting*, reminded of Ketil and Edgtho's thirst for revenge. She felt a strong premonition of danger pressing in on her.

Chapter 17

Spring Festival

THE DAY OF THE SPRING festival was warm and sunny. Thorstein helped Annoure into the boat. Moving awkwardly because of her large belly, she made it to the wooden seat and sat next to Asa, who held Astrid. The family divided into two boats, then sailed across the fjord to the Volsung farmstead. Annoure looked forward to seeing Erik again, but not Dahlia.

They soon landed on the rocky shoreline alongside many other boats. The farm consisted of several long houses, sheds and a barn on the edge of the sea. Beyond it were mountains. Their fields were much smaller than Garth's because so much of the island was too rocky to farm.

Olaf came down to the shore and after greeting them showed where to set up tents. Many neighbors had gathered and brought baskets of food for the evening feast. The children played tag and board-and-dice games. The women shared news after the long winter months. The men and older boys participated in a variety of contests that went on all day.

Thorstein joined the sparring matches, fighting with a sword and shield. Annoure watched from the sidelines and cheered every time he won. He had sparred with his cousins all winter and vastly improved his skill. After fencing, he participated in a spear-throwing contest and then a horse race.

Herjulf and Walfgar entered a wrestling competition and Njal a swimming competition. After the sports events, the men sacrificed two lambs to the Norse gods and said prayers, asking for good weather and successful crops. As Annoure helped the women roast mutton over an outdoor fire, the aroma of smoke and cooking meat filled the air.

Singing and storytelling accompanied the evening meal. Wine flowed freely as the men told stories of past bravery and jested of their close calls with death.

Later in the evening, Annoure sat on a log near the bonfire with Astrid on her knees while Asa and Walfgar participated in circle dances. The heat of the fire warmed Annoure and the smell of smoke made her eyes water when the wind blew it in her direction. Thorstein was also dancing, but Annoure felt too large with child to join him. She looked for him in the circle and was annoyed to see him with Dahlia.

Erik played his lyre nearby and was joined by a few men who played drums, panpipes and horns. After several songs, Erik took a drink from his mug then asked Annoure, "Have you been working on the Futhark?"

"Já, I can label chests and name swords now, but I don't have magic to give the swords good luck."

Erik's intense eyes studied her. "You have your own magic. I've thought often about the conversations we had last winter. Have you found some peace reconciling your gifts with your Christian upbringing?"

"A little." She rocked the fussy baby in her arms. "I've come to think of my 'gifts' as a blessing and started to question some ideas the Christian priests taught me. Yet I still believe in one creator. The old gods seem to be merely stories to help us understand things we can't explain."

"It's good you're thinking for yourself and not accepting everything you're told. You need to embrace your gifts. I've seen darkness in your future and you will need them."

Annoure shivered. She would have liked to question him further, but Asa and Walfgar appeared. Asa laughed as she lifted Astrid out of Annoure's arms.

"How are you, little one?" she asked, kissing the baby's round cheek. "It's time for you to nurse and go to bed."

Njal and Thyri also came over. Then the mothers headed toward the tent with their children. Njal took out his recorder and Walfgar his small pan flute and they joined the other musicians.

Thorstein walked over with Kalsetini. He drank a cup of mead and asked, "Do you want to dance, Annoure?"

"Nei, I would look like a fool. The baby will be born in less than six weeks."

Kalsetini linked her arm in Thorstein's. "See, I told you Annoure doesn't want to dance." She dragged her brother back to the circle. Annoure tapped her foot in time to the music, wishing her baby were already born so she could dance. The evening had a feeling of wildness and excitement. She watched the men playing their instruments for a while, then looked back at the dancers. Once more, Thorstein was dancing beside Dahlia in the circle. Dahlia looked especially pretty with her rosy cheeks and trim figure.

Annoure felt fat, unattractive and graceless. If she and Thorstein were married, she'd be proud to carry his child. Unwed, she was merely his bed thrall. It irritated her that Thorstein was still free to take Dahlia for a wife if he chose. After several more dances, Thorstein and Dahlia came to the fire. Thorstein poured himself another cup of wine and took a long drink. Dahlia took the cup from him and swallowed the rest. She filled it back up and handed it to Thorstein. He smiled at her and she leaned into him, giggling.

"It's too bad you can't join the fun," Dahlia said to Annoure. "Thorstein is a fine dancer."

"So I've noticed," Annoure said, annoyed at Dahlia's familiarity with Thorstein. She stood awkwardly and pushed her hand against the small of her back to ease some of the stiffness. "Let's retire, Thorstein. I'm tired."

"You go without me." He smiled cheerfully. "I want to celebrate a while longer. I haven't seen my friends all winter."

"It's getting cold."

"I'm hot from dancing. I'll join you later."

Annoure wanted to insist he come with her, but it didn't seem right. He'd been cooped up all winter. She was about to walk away when Dahlia said, "Where are you going a-viking this year?"

"A-viking!" Annoure exclaimed. "You're going a-viking?"

Thorstein's smile faded. "Já, I always go a-viking in the summer."

"I thought we were going to the Shetland Islands," she said, uncomfortably aware that Dahlia was listening to their interchange with interest.

"We can't leave until the baby is at least four or five months old. Infants die easily."

"When are you going a-viking?"

He glanced at the sea then back at her. “In about a month. After planting and the *ting*.”

“In a month! But that means you’ll be gone when our baby is born.”

“I know. I’m sorry, but Móðir and Thyri will help with the birth.”

Annoure’s mouth went dry. “But I want you there.” Then another thought occurred to her. ”Do you plan to raid my people again?”

Thorstein crossed his arms. “I doubt we’ll raid Northumbria again after last year’s losses. More likely we’ll go on a trading expedition.”

“We’ll discuss this later,” Annoure said, not wanting to air the matter any further in front of Dahlia. She strode briskly to the tent. *Why hadn’t Thorstein told her he was leaving for the summer?* Once in the tent, she removed her clothes before climbing into the hudfat. She lay on the hard, uncomfortable ground, worried that Thorstein could be killed on a raid or drowned at sea.

The sound of laughter and singing floated in through the fabric of the tent. Annoure realized the festivities would go on for a long time. No sense waiting for Thorstein to join her, she might as well get some sleep.

Sometime later, she awakened to feel Thorstein’s cold body sliding into the hudfat beside her. “Were you dancing with Dahlia all this time or did you enjoy her in other ways?” she asked still annoyed with him.

“I’m drunk and tired, woman. Now is not a good time to start a fight.”

“You Norsemen like to get drunk and have adventures while your women stay home.”

“Have you been lying here letting your anger build the whole time I’ve been at the festival?” He put an arm around her and pulled close so that her back was to his chest.

“Nei, I’ve been sleeping. Why didn’t you tell me you were going a-viking?”

“It didn’t occur to me. You know I’m a second sonr and must make a living trading.”

“But last fall you were all set to leave for the Shetland Islands,” she said.

“I was upset and not thinking clearly. Obviously, we couldn’t leave with winter approaching and no silver to buy land. And now we can’t leave with you about to have a baby. Besides I still don’t have enough silver.”

"What about the silver coins you received from selling the Bible?"

"I'll need those to pay fines at the *ting* for killing Rethel."

"But I want to get married before the baby is born." She knew she sounded pouty, but couldn't help it.

"I know, love, but we have to wait until I've saved enough for us to start a new life together."

"I don't want to wait," she said sullenly.

"I don't want to wait either." He kissed her cheek.

"Would you rather marry Dahlia?"

"Nei, she's just a friend. I love you."

"Do you find me unattractive now?"

"Nei, it's good to see a woman swell with life, especially when it's your child she carries." He put his hand on her stomach. "How is my sonr tonight?"

"He is awake and kicking." She guided his hand to where the infant's foot pressed against her womb.

"He's a healthy boy."

"Or girl. Thorstein, do you have to go?"

"Já, now speak of it no more." His hand moved to her breast and he whispered into her ear. "Make love to me."

"I'm huge. You can't really want me."

He pressed hips against her to prove he did. "You're beautiful and I want you as much as ever. You needn't be jealous of other women, sweet love. I have no desire to share pleasure with anyone but you. My love grows stronger with each passing day." He rolled her onto her back and began kissing her, his tongue delving into her mouth. He tasted of wine and his hair smelled of smoke from the fire. She felt the strength of his need for her and it convinced her that her jealousy was groundless.

He moved on his side behind her again, kissing the nape of her neck and fondling her breasts, his hips against hers. She felt a dark shadow crossing over their happiness and clutched his hand. Thorstein was the center of her life and she couldn't bear the thought of anything happening to him.

Annoure and Thorstein didn't speak again of him going a-viking during the planting of the flax and rye fields. Thorstein and the men worked long hours harrowing and plowing the fields with a moldshare plough.

By the end of May, it was nearly time for Thorstein and other family members to leave for the *ting*. Afterwards, Walfgar, Thorstein and Herjulf would go a-viking and the others would return home.

Annoure resigned herself to not going along for the baby would soon be born and she would be uncomfortable traveling and sleeping in a tent. She packed supplies for Thorstein as he sat by the fire sharpening his sword, *Grimmr*. He'd hunted all winter for furs to trade and they were stacked in a pile near him. As Annoure worked she heard Njal telling Sandey and Brandi stories.

"I'm worried about the *ting*," Annoure said, placing Thorstein's pants in a hudfat.

"Don't be. It was a fair fight; I'll just have to pay a fine."

She looked up at him. "I don't want you to go a-viking. Will you reconsider and not go this summer? I want you here with me."

"We need silver so we can buy land and get married."

"At least promise me you won't raid Northumbria."

He was silent for a moment, then he nodded. "I'll find a ship that's going on a trading voyage."

Annoure stuffed his tunic into the hudfat, then picked up his animal-hide vest armor. It didn't look strong enough to keep a sword from piercing him. A vision flashed before her: blood covered Thorstein's vest armor and she felt the shadow of death. She swayed unsteadily and dropped the armor.

Thorstein sprang up and grabbed her. "Annoure! Are you all right?" He helped her sit down. "You look faint."

"I had a vision." She tried to shake it off, but still felt its power. "It frightened me," she whispered.

"What was your vision?"

She shook her head. "I . . . I'd rather not speak of it. I don't want to give it power."

She put her hand on Thorstein's cheek. He was superstitious and would think the vision was foreshadowing his death, but it could be someone else's blood covering the armor. She snuggled into the safety of his arms, deeply worried she might never see him again and their child might never know its father.

Thorstein rubbed the small of her back. "Let me share the burden of your vision."

"Nei, love, it is mine to bear alone." She leaned her head in the small curve of his shoulder. He would be gone for months. She would miss him as though part of herself was missing.

"What will happen to me and our child if you never return?" Annoure asked.

"I'll return."

"What if there's a violent storm and you drown at sea?"

"Was that your vision?"

She shook her head. "Nei, I'm just worried."

"You will always have a home with Njal and Thyri."

"I want to go back to Northumbria if you don't return."

"I'll ask Herjulf to see that you get safely home if something happens to me, though it might be better to raise our child here. He'll have a hard life as a bastard in Northumbria."

"I'm frightened."

"I'm going to return, Annoure."

"I wish you were going to be here when I have the baby. Women often die in childbirth."

"You're not going to die. Móðir delivered all of Thyri and Asa's babies safely into the world."

He kissed the top of her head. "I wish I could be here as well. I worry about you too. You're so small and first births are usually the hardest. Besides, I'm eager to meet my sonr."

"It could be a dóttir."

"I will welcome a sonr or a dóttir."

Early the next morning, Annoure awoke to an empty house. She dressed quickly and hurried to the shoreline where Thorstein and his family loaded supplies into the boats. She hung back, watching and listening to their laughter. They were jovial about the journey while she felt bereft of joy. *Whose blood was on Thorstein's armor? For whom did death await?*

Thorstein walked over to her. "It's chilly. Go back to the house and get a cape."

"Be careful, Thorstein."

"I will. Take care of yourself and our baby."

She embraced him, her swollen belly keeping her from getting as close to him as she'd like. "Oh God, I can't bear it. I miss you already."

"In a few months I'll be back and we'll be married. I promise." His mouth covered hers and the warmth of his love washed over her.

She watched him get into the boat. Dread that she might never see him again tugged painfully at her heart.

Chapter 18

The Ting

THE SALTY MORNING BREEZE RUFFLED Thorstein's hair as he and Herjulf walked through the busy port of Bergen. People were here from all over Hordaland for the *ting*.

When they reached the marketplace, venders hawked their wares and a crowd cheered two combatants in a sparring match.

Thorstein had left home two days earlier with misgivings. He didn't like leaving Annoure when she was about to have their baby and her anguish at his departure pulled at his heart. He hoped to have a successful spring trading voyage so he could return home in the middle of summer.

Thorstein and Herjulf left the village and followed a trail up the side of a mountain to a plateau where the legal assembly took place. His body tensed as they entered the clearing where landowners gathered annually to settle disputes. Thorstein scanned the raucous crowd and finally spotted his family. He and Herjulf waded through the crowd until they reached his father. As a landowner, Garth had a vote on major decisions brought before the chieftain. Freydis smiled uneasily at Thorstein as Njal, Kalsetini and Walfgar greeted him.

Garth put his hand on Thorstein's shoulder. "Nesbjörn's grievance will be one of the first heard since it concerns the loss of a sonr."

Thorstein nodded. The tension between him and his father had lessened over the winter. Now it was superseded by the strong family bond that drew them together in this time of trouble.

The *konungr,* Dylan, who ruled the tribal community, walked into the clearing with a priest and three earls. His wrinkled face was surrounded by white hair and he wore a heavy gold necklace, fur cloak and patterned tunic. The priest and earls also wore finely-made tunics with furs draped over their shoulders.

The konungr banged his sword against his shield and puffed out his barrel chest. The assembly quieted and landowners stepped forward to form a rough circle. Thorstein broke into a sweat when he spotted Nesbjörn, flanked on either side by Edgtho and Ketil.

The priest said a prayer, asking the god Odin for wisdom and the proceedings began. The first complaint was brought before the konungr and the council. After it was discussed and testimony was given, it was voted on. The second complaint followed the same procedure and then Nesbjörn was called.

"I have a grievance I would like heard by the assembly," he said.

"You have permission to speak, Nesbjörn Hardhitter," the konungr said.

"I am here on behalf of my sonr Rethel. He was killed by Thorstein Garthson and I demand that Thorstein be banished from this land."

A hum of voices immediately arose.

"Quiet!" Dylan yelled in a deep voice that carried across the crowd. "That is a serious accusation, Nesbjörn. Explain the circumstances of your sonr's death."

Nesbjörn related the events leading up to Rethel's death, slanting the facts to sound as if Thorstein slaughtered Rethel without just cause.

The konungr turned toward Garth and his kin. "Thorstein Garthson, step forward."

Thorstein walked over to the chieftain, fuming at Nesbjörn's inaccurate relating of the events.

"Thorstein, what do you have to say in response to Nesbjörn's accusations?" Dylan asked.

"At camp Rethel attacked my betrothed, Annoure. I heard her scream and ran to her defense. Rethel held a knife to her throat and was about to kill her. We fought over his knife and I managed to disarm him, but then he drew a sword on me. I was unarmed and Rethel would have gutted me like a Saxon enemy, but for Herjulf, who lent me his sword. Rethel died in a fair fight. I am sorry he's dead, but he drew a sword on me and I had no choice but to defend myself and Annoure."

Dylan looked over at Thorstein's family. "Is Annoure here to speak in her own defense?"

"Annoure is too heavy with child to make the journey," Thorstein replied.

The konungr turned to Herjulf. "Does Thorstein speak the truth?"

"Já. We heard Annoure scream and ran to her defense. Thorstein was weaponless, but disarmed Rethel of his knife. Rethel then drew his sword. If I hadn't been there to give Thorstein my sword, Rethel would have killed him. Many others witnessed the battle as well."

"Nesbjörn stated that the woman is a Saxon thrall," Dylan said. "Why would Thorstein defend her?"

"She was a noblewoman not a thrall and Thorstein intended to marry her," Herjulf said.

The konungr nodded thoughtfully.

"On the longship, the Saxon thrall pushed Rethel overboard, causing him to lose his sword!" Edgtho yelled. "He had the right to avenge the loss of his sword!" He drew his sword and advanced on Thorstein. Two of his kinsmen grabbed his arms and held him back.

"Put away your sword!" Dylan demanded, glaring at Edgtho. "We are here to hear the case. If there's to be a duel or *holmgang,* it will be decided by the council."

Ignoring the konungr, Thorstein shouted at Edgtho, "How could a fifteen-year-old girl push a strongly built man of Rethel's size overboard?" Thorstein clutched the handle of his sheathed sword, feeling the veins pulse in his neck.

"I saw her shove him!" Edgtho yelled back.

"This is a peaceful assemblage," Dylan said. "Edgtho, sheathe your sword or I'll have you removed."

Edgtho angrily thrust his sword back in its sheath, then Dylan addressed him, "Did you see the fight between Thorstein and Rethel?"

"Já."

"Did Rethel die in battle and earn a place in Valhalla?"

"Thorstein deserves to be banished for killing him."

"Answer my question," the konungr's voice rang with authority.

"Rethel died fighting," Edgtho said begrudgingly.

"How many men saw this fight?" Dylan asked, looking over the men gathered around him. Several men raised their hands.

"Was it a fair sword fight?"

He looked at each of the men in turn and each said "Já."

"Is there anyone else who wishes to bear testimony?"

"I do," Garth said. "Thorstein is a respected, honorable man. He was given the responsibility of navigator at a young age, whereas we all know Rethel was a troublemaker. He was mean-spirited, quick-tempered and enjoyed fighting. At the *ting* last year, he paid tribute to Harald for killing his *sonr*. The loss of a warrior is always unfortunate, but it was a fair fight with kin as witnesses."

The konungr nodded to acknowledge his words, then looked at Thorstein. "In the days before a funeral, there's lots of drinking and warriors get into fights. When two men fight with swords, both face the possibility of being wounded or killed. If their kinsmen and friends don't stop them, then they're agreeing to let the warriors settle their disagreement in this violent manner. If one man dies, it is not a crime for which banishment is deserved, but an honorable way to settle disputes. However, Nesbjörn lost a sonr who had value to him and tribute should be paid. Do you agree with this decision?" The konungr looked at the landowner men and women. Most of them lifted their swords and slammed them repeatedly against their shields to show agreement.

When it was quiet again, Dylan said, "Thorstein Garthson, you will pay tribute to Nesbjörn Hardhitter for the loss of a sonr."

"The Saxon thrall should die!" Edgtho shouted. "Our war chief Tyrker the Courageous was killed on the raid and the Angel of Death read the bones to see who should accompany him to Valhalla. The bones read the Saxon should be sacrificed, but Thorstein refused to let the Angel of Death have her."

"Do any of Tyrker's kin give formal complaint?" the konungr asked. He brushed a fly off his large jowls as he scanned the assembly.

The Angel of Death stepped forward. "I give complaint. Thorstein angered the gods. The bones told me a woman of foreign blood was to be sacrificed. I knew they referred to the female thrall Thorstein stole from Northumbria. She was part of the booty from the raid where Tyrker was killed. But when I tried to follow the sacred wisdom of the bones, Thorstein refused to give her to me. The winter was long and cold and many starved because of this."

"What do you have to say in your defense, Thorstein?" Dylan asked.

Thorstein drew in a sharp breath, catching a whiff of his own anxiety-ridden sweat. He hadn't expected this accusation. "Winter was no worse than usual and I doubt anyone starved for last summer's crops were bountiful. A man is never asked to give up the woman he intends to marry as a sacrifice to his war chief. The bones merely said a foreign woman was to be killed. A woman from Tyrker's own thralls ended up being the one to die with her master. She was the one the bones referred to."

"Do you claim to know more than the Angel of Death?"

Thorstein shook his head. "Nei, but it's custom to pick a woman from among a war chief's own thralls."

"Do you understand the importance of reading the bones and doing what they say, Thorstein?"

"Já."

"Do you realize by angering the gods you endanger all our people?" Dylan demanded.

"The gods were not angered. The only one offended was the old crone."

The konungr's eyes narrowed and his face darkened like clouds blacken the sky before a thunderstorm. "She is the Angel of Death. She has magic powers and serves our people."

"The Angel of Death knew Annoure was mine," Thorstein said. "Everyone in camp knew Rethel and I battled over her the night before. No man here would give his woman to the Angel of Death for sacrifice."

The women in the crowd started whispering to one another in agreement.

Freydis stepped forward. "Thorstein's right. A captured woman is considered a free woman if one of the Norsemen plan to marry her." She shook her fist. "Since when has it been acceptable to sacrifice a free woman?"

"Did you know of the swordfight between Thorstein and Rethel?" the konungr asked the Angel of Death.

"Já, but I did not question the oracle."

"Why were the bones consulted? It is not the usual way."

"Edgtho and Ketil paid me to read the bones."

A murmur of voices rose again. Several women yelled out against a free woman being used as a sacrifice.

Dylan looked at Thorstein. "This is a religious matter and will not be voted on. As the head priest of Hordaland, I will decide."

He paused thoughtfully and Thorstein's heart pounded in his chest, waiting for the verdict.

Finally the konungr spoke.

"Thorstein had a rightful claim to the woman since he planned to marry her. Yet the Angel of Death's magical powers can't be ignored. Thorstein Garthson, you will pay a tribute to the temple. If I ever hear of you going against the oracle of bones again, I will see that you are exiled from this land. Do you, Thorstein Garthson, agree to pay tribute to the temple and to Nesbjörn?"

"I will do all that is asked."

"Then the matter is settled." Dylan stated the amount of the tribute Thorstein was to pay, then told him to rejoin his kinsmen.

Thorstein returned to where his family stood, badly shaken. He wondered if he had angered the gods and worried that any future storms and droughts would be blamed on him.

Edgtho and Ketil stormed over to Thorstein.

"This is not over!" Edgtho yelled.

Ketil's face twisted with grief and anger. "You killed my bróðir!" he exclaimed and slammed his fist into Thorstein's jaw.

Thorstein staggered back from the blow, his jaw ablaze with pain. Nesbjörn pulled Ketil away from Thorstein and Njal grabbed Thorstein's arm as he moved to retaliate.

"Control your anger, bróðir," Njal said.

"Rethel tried to kill Annoure!" Thorstein yelled. "He deserved what he got."

Kalsetini moved between them and said, "No more bloodshed!"

"Nesbjörn! Garth!" the konungr shouted, "Control your sonrs unless you want to settle things with a *holmgang.*"

Thorstein lowered his clenched fists, still shaking with rage. He took several deep breaths, repressing his desire to slug Ketil back—he didn't want to fight Ketil in a duel to the death. Ketil was a good friend and his pain was understandable. He loved his brother. Rethel was a skilled warrior and a brave man in battle. A dead man was no good to anyone; Rethel should not have died that night.

Thorstein took another deep breath, then said, "Ketil, I'm sorry Rethel is dead. I wish things had not gone as they did."

Nesbjörn spat on the ground. “I curse your family and any sonrs you shall have.” He looked at the Chieftain. “I accept the tribute. I don’t want to risk losing another sonr or a nephew in a holmgang.”

Thorstein left the *ting* with his family, then he and his father walked to the rocky shoreline. “Thank you for speaking up for me,” Thorstein said.

“Edgtho was trying to make it sound as if you committed a crime, when in truth Rethel attacked you when you were weaponless. I’m sure Edgtho paid the Angel of Death to pick Annoure as the sacrifice for revenge. The tributes you were given are unusually high.”

Thorstein clenched and unclenched his fists. “I don’t have enough silver to pay the fines.” He cleared his throat. “Can I borrow some and pay you back after I go a-viking?” He had hoped for smaller tributes. With this new debt, he had no choice but to go a-viking for the whole summer.

“You dare to ask me for a loan after announcing to the assembly that Annoure is your betrothed when I forbade you to marry her?”

“I won’t marry her until I’ve earned enough to leave the farm and start a new life on my own.”

“With those fines, you won’t have enough silver to leave home this fall.” His expression softened. “Perhaps I’ve been too stubborn concerning Annoure. You’ve proven that your feelings for her aren’t just an infatuation and Erik the skald said she would make a worthy vif. He said she easily learned the runes and could someday be a powerful crone.”

“I didn’t know Erik spoke to you about Annoure.”

“It was a private conversation. The strain between you and I bothered him. Erik also made me see that eventually you’ll take Annoure and leave the farm if I don’t bless the marriage. I don’t want you to leave. Your place is on the family farm. Marry the woman if she’s what you want.”

Relief flooded through Thorstein. “Thank you for giving your consent.”

“One more thing.” Garth cleared his throat. “I apologize for whipping Annoure. It’s the usual punishment for a runaway thrall, but I should have been lenient. She was yours and with child. Unfortunately, I blamed her for your injury and my judgment was clouded with concern that you wouldn't awaken."

"It's Annoure you should apologize to."

Garth's jaw hardened and his face flushed. "I won't apologize to a runaway thrall." His coloring gradually returned to normal and then he sighed. "I suppose I must or my new dóttir-in-law will hate me and turn my future grandchild against me." He paused and a sparkle came into his eyes. "I like her spirit, Thorstein. Erik says she's more of a Druidess than a Christian. I'll lend you silver for the fines. We need you on the farm, *sonr*."

Thorstein stayed at camp with Herjulf and Walfgar when the rest of his family returned home a few days later. In the evening, he sat alone at the campfire, mulling over Rethel's death. If he'd been sober, perhaps he could have defeated Rethel without killing him, but drunk it was all he could do to stay alive. Death could come quickly and easily to a man whose reflexes were slow from drinking. He regretted Rethel's death and regretted losing his friendship with Ketil. He hoped Ketil would eventually accept what happened, though he knew Edgtho never would. Edgtho was dangerous and cunning; he would look for revenge. Thorstein picked up another branch and put it on the fire. He watched the flames leap into the air and within the smoke he saw a glimpse of Annoure's face.

Erik walked over to the fire and sat on a log across from Thorstein. "I've been looking for you. You shouldn't be alone. Edgtho and Ketil are still angry and likely to cause trouble."

"I'm on my guard."

"Is this how you keep on guard? Brooding alone, staring into the fire? Edgtho or Ketil could sneak up and kill you."

"I have my sword with me. Erik, thank you for talking to Faðir.

He's finally given his consent for me to marry Annoure." He sighed heavily. "I wish I didn't have to leave her for the summer. She'll have the baby soon and I'd like to be there when it's born."

"It's a hard lot to be a second or third sonr. I am no better off than you. My bróðir has a prosperous farm and I make my way traveling from place to place, singing for my supper."

"Where are you off to now?"

"To the trading village of Hedeby. It's a busy place this time of year with plenty of people who'll pay a skald for his songs."

Thorstein looked up and put his hand to his sword hilt as he heard someone approaching the fire through the darkness. Herjulf appeared in the firelight. "I just found out that Ketil and Edgtho left with their kin. I can't make any sense of it. They always come a-viking."

Thorstein shivered uneasily, certain Ketil and Edgtho must be up to something.

Chapter 19

Revenge

ANNOURE AWOKE WITH A START, unsure why. She felt a tingling along her spine and sat up on the sleeping bench, listening. Inside the room was quiet for Njal and his family still slept.

Outside the wind howled and a branch repeatedly hit the side of the house. She wondered if the branch was what had disturbed her sleep. Since Thorstein had left, she slept uneasily and the feeling of danger never left her.

Annoure rolled onto her side, so large with child that it was hard to get comfortable. She tried to fall back asleep but the baby shifted positions and she suddenly felt the need to make water. These days there wasn't room for anything but the baby in her large belly.

Reluctantly she slipped her feet out from under the warm furs and onto the cold floor and crossed to the door in her linen under-dress. The sun was just starting to come up and the gray forms of nearby houses began to take on color as she hurried to the outhouse.

When she started back to the house, she spotted dark figures approaching from the shoreline. As they drew closer, she recognized Edgtho and Ketil. She drew in a sharp breath as icy terror pumped through her veins. She glanced toward Njal's house, wondering if she could reach it before the men reached her.

"That's her! The gods are in our favor!" Ketil exclaimed. The men split up so one was between her and Njal's house and the other blocked her way to Garth's.

Annoure took a stumbling step backwards, knowing she was trapped. Edgtho strode forward until he was a few feet in front of her. "We've decided to take justice into our own hands," he said, his eyes filled with malice. "Thorstein should have been made an outlaw at the *ting*. We won't accept silver for Rethel's life."

Annoure opened her mouth to scream, but the sound caught in her throat. Edgtho smiled sadistically and drew out his sword. "I should carve out your heart where you stand." The tip of his sword cut through her under-dress and pricked her left breast. Inwardly she cried, *Don't kill me and my baby.*

"Thorstein can't protect you now." The tip of his sword lowered to her belly. "I see you're carrying his bastard. This makes our revenge all the sweeter."

When he grabbed her arm, she finally found her voice and screamed, "Njal, Njal, help me!" She tried to break away from Edgtho, continuing to scream. He twisted her arm behind her back and clamped a hand over her mouth. She bit his finger. He drew his hand back and she screamed again.

"Keep quiet or I'll kill you!" Edgtho growled. The panic his words evoked, caused her scream to die in her throat. He bound her wrists together in front of her just as Njal barged out of the house, a sword held ready. Ketil leapt at him with his own sword extended and the two men began to battle.

"Ketil, kill him quickly before the others awaken!" Edgtho yelled.

Njal fought furiously, forcing Ketil backward. Edgtho joined the fight, rushing Njal from the side.

Annoure screamed. "Njal, watch out!"

Njal thrust his sword toward Edgtho, lowering it at the last moment to slice across Edgtho's upper arm. Blood appeared on Edgtho's sleeve. Ketil swept his sword toward Njal who blocked it and countered the attack.

The door of Njal's house flew open and Brandi ran out followed by Thyri and Sandey. "Brandi, stop!" Thyri screamed. Brandi sprinted ahead of his mother, brandishing his wooden sword, yelling, "Daddy!" He thrust his wooden sword at Edgtho.

In a blind rage, Edgtho spun away from Njal and slammed his sword into the child's head. Brandi dropped like a doll to the ground.

Annoure cried, “Oh God!” She rushed to the child and squatted beside him.

Njal let out a savage cry and leapt at Edgtho, who swung his sword up to meet this new attack. The two swords clashed with a violence that caused both men to stagger. Njal fought with renewed strength, meeting a thrust from Ketil’s sword, then another from Edgtho.

Stunned, Annoure touched the uninjured side of Brandi’s head. His soft cheek was warm and he looked as if he was just asleep, but when she turned his head she saw the other side was covered in blood from a gash that ran from his nose to his ear. A wave of nausea rolled through her and she broke into a sweat; then she retched onto the ground.

Thyri almost reached her and Brandi when Njal shouted, “Take Sandey and get back into the house! Now!”

Tears streamed down Thyri’s face. “Nei, my child. I must help Brandi.”

“Go, I can’t hold them off much longer!”

Thyri snatched up Sandey and tore back to the house.

Njal slammed his sword toward Ketil, who blocked it with his shield, then swung his sword toward Njal. Edgtho rushed Njal from the other side. Getting by his guard, Edgtho thrust his sword into Njal’s stomach and twisted. Annoure staggered to her feet and started to run, supporting her large belly with her hands.

Edgtho overtook her and grabbed her by the hair. “You’re not going anywhere.” He shouted to Ketil. “Kill Thyri and her child. They can identify us!” Thyri stood in the threshold of her home, clutching her daughter and sobbing.

“Nei, you said there wouldn’t be any killing.”

“Then bring them along and we’ll sell them as well.”

Ketil started for the house and Thyri yelled, “Garth! Garth, come quickly!” She ran into the house with Sandey and slammed the door. Edgtho dragged Annoure to their boat. He released her to untie it and she fell on her hands and knees, breathing heavily. Edgtho pushed the boat further into the water.

Ketil arrived a moment later. “Thyri bolted the door and there was no time to break in. Garth’s coming.”

Annoure looked back toward the farmstead and saw Garth charging toward the boat, his sword drawn.

"Put the woman in the boat while I hold him off," Ketil said, raising his sword. The sound of steel hitting steel rang out as Garth's sword met Ketil's. Edgtho drew out his knife and hurled it toward Garth. It sank into his chest and Garth staggered backwards. Ketil slammed the broadside of his sword into Garth's temple and he fell to the ground.

Ketil carried Annoure into the water and deposited her into the bottom of the boat. Then he climbed into the front of the boat and Edgtho climbed in back. The men picked up oars and began rowing with strong, steady strokes that cut rapidly through the water.

Annoure's chest tightened as she watched the family homestead disappear from view. Everything seemed surreal. She felt in a fog, and was unable to organize her thoughts. She couldn't fathom that Edgtho had struck down a defenseless child. The Norsemen were truly a terrible, barbaric race. Yet why hadn't these men, who were so filled with revenge and bloodlust, killed her as well?

Thorstein would be grief-stricken when he returned home from a-viking and found three members of his family dead and his future wife kidnapped. She wiped away the tears that streamed down her cheeks, but they were just replaced by new tears.

The men rowed hard in silence until they were well away from the farmstead, then they raised the sail of the small vessel. Wind filled the square fabric and blew them forward.

"You shouldn't have killed Njal's boy," Ketil said in a voice filled with anguish.

"It's better that he's dead, so he won't grow up to avenge his Faðir," Edgtho said. He took off his tunic and looked at the sword wound Njal had given him on his upper arm.

"If you have no care for the life of a child, think of us. We'll be banished at the next *ting* for killing a defenseless child."

"We should've burned Thyri's house and killed her and the child rather than leave witnesses."

"I don't want to be part of killing women and children."

Ketil glanced at Annoure and their eyes held for a moment. She saw compassion in his thin face that she hadn't seen in Edgtho. Ketil's gaze returned to his cousin. "We can't return home. Where should we go after selling the woman?"

Annoure shuddered with horror at the thought of being sold into slavery.

"I don't know," Edgtho said, wrapping a cloth around his wound. "I have to think on it, Ketil. It wasn't meant to happen this way. I only wanted the woman and no one was supposed to see us. I struck down the boy without seeing he was only a child with a wooden sword. I merely acted on instinct, only aware that someone was coming up behind me. The council at the *ting* is to blame for this. If they'd banished Thorstein, none of this would've happened."

* * *

Thorstein sat at a campfire with Herjulf and Walfgar. He'd signed up to go on a trading voyage that would sail to Kaupang, a Norge town, then journey south. Trading suited him fine; he'd lost his fearless attitude toward death. Annoure, and soon their baby, depended on him. She didn't have her family to help her if he died, so his life had more value than ever before.

As he gazed at the rabbit roasting over the fire, his thoughts turned to Edgtho and Ketil. The news that they had returned home with their family gnawed at him. *They always went a-viking. Why not this year?* He was also uneasy about Annoure. Her anxiety about giving birth would make it hard for her. What if she or the baby died in childbirth?

"What's troubling you, Thorstein?" Herjulf asked, interrupting his thoughts. "You been on edge all day."

"I'm worried about Annoure. I don't like leaving her when she's so close to term."

"She'll be fine and you need the silver and other goods trading brings," Walfgar said. "I enjoy getting away from the farm for the summer and visiting new lands. And I know wanderlust is in your blood as much as it's in mine."

"I like travel well enough, but this summer I'd rather stay at home to be there when Annoure gives birth. Both your children were born in the winter months when you were home."

Walfgar's brow wrinkled sympathetically and he nodded. "True, it would have been hard to leave Asa when she was large with child. She needed my help to bring in wood, tend the animals, and do other chores. Moreover, she slept a lot and cried easily."

"Was she better once the child was born?"

Walfgar shrugged. "Not at first. New babies are a lot of work. They're not like a colt. They're completely helpless. They cry and want to be fed all the time—both day and night."

"Maybe I should return home."

"You're the navigator and we need you on the voyage. Besides babies are a mystery to us men, but women know what to do. And you can't help with the birth—you'd only be in the way."

"What if she dies in childbirth?"

"Thorstein, she's young and healthy," Walfgar said. "What has brought on this worry?"

"I had a nightmare last night that something terrible happened."

"What was your nightmare?" Herjulf asked, staring intently at Thorstein.

"I was home searching for Annoure in a dark fog and couldn't find her anywhere. There was a feeling of great sadness and everyone was grieving. I asked who died, but no one could see me, so they didn't tell me."

"It's a bad omen to have such a dream before going a-viking," Herjulf said. "We should make a sacrifice to the gods."

Chapter 20

Voyage on North Sea

IN THE SMALL BOAT, ANNOURE shivered in her thin under-dress. The wind was cold and waves sprayed over the side. Her thoughts were frayed and disjointed. She couldn't get the images of little Brandi's bloodied face, Njal's torn-open stomach, or Garth's crumpled body out of her mind. Despair rose within her as she wondered if she would ever see Thorstein again. It might well be fall before he even knew she'd been abducted. How would he find her after all that time? Grief overwhelmed her and tears gathered again. Finally she fell into an exhausted sleep, escaping from her pain.

When she awoke, the sun was high in the sky. Its heat felt warm on her chilled body and dried her under-dress. Ketil untied her wrists and gave her some dried fish and water. The smell of the fish made her stomach curl, but she took a drink of water and managed to hold it down.

Edgtho glared at her. "This is all your fault!" His hard, menacing eyes made her skin crawl. "You seduced Rethel with your beauty then called for Thorstein instead of submitting to him as any other thrall would have done. Tonight, I'll make you wish you had spread your legs for him."

"Leave her be," Ketil said sharply.

"Nei, she's my quarry." Edgtho pulled out a flask and took a drink. "Have some mead, cousin. You're too sullen. Here's to our new lives in banishment."

He tossed the flask to Ketil, but his cousin just threw it back. "Not even the taste of mead will sweeten the memory of what we did today."

"Why did you come along if you had no thirst for revenge?"

"You said no one would be killed."

"You knew the risk existed or did you think we could steal the woman from her home without anyone noticing?"

"I was caught up in my grief. I thought of nothing but Rethel's death and my hatred for Thorstein."

Edgtho laughed and took another drink. "I'm sorry you lost your taste for revenge because mine still runs strong."

By the time the sun dipped in the sky, the exposed skin on Annoure's face and arms was burnt and she ached all over from sitting in the cramped boat. The men lowered the sails and rowed to the rocky shoreline. Edgtho jumped into the water and pulled the boat onto the bank.

Ketil climbed out and helped Annoure from the boat. She made her way across the ground barefoot, avoiding the rocks and sticks. As she entered the dense woods to relieve herself, Edgtho shouted to her to return quickly or he'd come after her. She tensed at the sound of his harsh voice. As much as she wanted to escape, she knew she couldn't survive—pregnant with no supplies. When she rejoined the men, they'd set up a tent.

"Gather firewood," Edgtho said, glancing at her, "and stay within my sight." He drank mead as she gathered driftwood. She paused a moment to listen to the sound of waves crashing on the shoreline, thinking of Thorstein, then carried the wood over to where Ketil attempted to start a fire with a flint. The evening had grown dark and cool. Finally a flame flickered and Ketil fed it small twigs until the fire burned brightly.

Ketil took some food from a bag and said, "Have something to eat, Annoure." He handed her some dried berries and a piece of dried fish. "You must be starving. You haven't eaten all day."

Annoure ate some berries, knowing she had to stay strong for the baby, but her stomach was still too upset to eat fish.

Edgtho touched her hair and she jerked away from him. "All winter I've thought of burying my shaft into Thorstein's woman. Your screams will bring Rethel joy in Valhalla."

Annoure's eyes widened with alarm.

"She's too big with child to rape," Ketil said.

"I'll take her as a dog takes a bitch."

Ketil's eyes flickered to Annoure's across the fire. She silently pleaded with him for help. His distaste of Edgtho's words gave her hope, yet he seemed dominated by his older cousin.

"Do as you like, but I won't help you," Ketil said. "I won't tempt the wrath of the god Frey by raping a pregnant woman."

"What do you mean?"

"Frey's mysterious power gives women the ability to have children. You risk angering him by defiling a woman who is ripe with one."

"She's Christian. Frey won't care what we do to her."

"Now that she's Thorstein's betrothed, the Norse gods control her fate," Ketil snapped with an angry edge to his voice.

Annoure glanced from Ketil to Edgtho, feeling the tension between the two men mounting.

"I'm not afraid of Frey." Edgtho grabbed the front of Annoure's under-dress, tearing it open to expose her breasts.

"Nei!" Annoure clasped her under-dress closed. "Ketil, please. I beg of you, help me!"

"He won't interfere." Edgtho smiled tauntingly. "No one will help you. You are mine now."

"Nei! Thorstein will find me and kill you!"

"Thorstein is a-viking and doesn't even know your fate. By the time he returns, he'll never be able to find you." She sprang to her feet and Edgtho grabbed her ankle. She lost her balance and fell to the ground, wincing as sharp rocks cut into the palms of her hands and knees.

Edgtho pushed her under-dress up to her waist, holding her still by her hair as he unfastened his pants.

"Stop it!" Ketil growled. "Your thirst for revenge has done enough harm to Thorstein. We are more than even. He lost a Faðir, bróðir and nephew on this day due to our bloodlust. We took his pregnant woman and are selling her into slavery. It is enough. Revenge becomes wrongdoing when there is no end to it!"

"It is not enough! It won't be enough until Thorstein and all of his kin are dead. I will take my anger out on his woman and if you interfere, I will take it out on you!"

"Let her go and take it out on me then because I'll not stand by and watch you rape her." Ketil grabbed Edgtho's upper arm and yanked him away from Annoure. Edgtho slammed his fist into Ketil's chin. The two men fell to the ground, wrestling.

Annoure scrambled to her feet and ran into the dense woods as the fight continued. Before long she heard the men coming after her. She ran faster, wincing in pain as rocks cut into her feet and branches snapped at her face and arms. Her under-dress caught on thorns and she ripped it free to keep going. Soon her breath came in ragged, painful gasps and her heart felt as if it would burst, but terror drove her on.

One of the men grabbed her from behind and she felt his hard body through the thin fabric of her under-dress. She gasped for breath, so weak she couldn't stand on her own. As Edgtho came into view, she realized that Ketil was the one who held her. In the dark, she couldn't read Edgtho's expression. "Bring her back to camp and tie her up," he said, then turned and headed back.

"Come with me," Ketil said, releasing her.

She sank onto the ground and hung her head, clutching her stomach and panting for breath. "I can't. I hurt everywhere."

He didn't reply, but just stood there, waiting for her to recover.

In the distance, the *whoo-whoo* of an owl sounded. Finally, Ketil drew her up and put an arm around her. "Come, I'll help you."

She limped through the woods, leaning heavily against him.

"What's wrong?" he asked.

"I'm not wearing shoes and have cut my feet."

"Ah, I'll have to carry you then." He lifted her into his arms, despite her protests. "You're hardly bigger than a child. How old are you?"

"Sixteen."

"I suppose Thorstein told the truth of it when he said you were still a maiden when Rethel attacked you."

"He spoke the truth. I was fifteen then and a nobleman's daughter."

At camp, Ketil helped her inside the tent. Edgtho came in behind them and handed Ketil a rope. "Tie her up!"

Ketil tied her wrists in front of her body, then bound her ankles. "They aren't too tight, are they?"

"What difference does it make," Edgtho snapped. "I should have known you'd feel pity for the woman."

"She reminds me of my Hanna when she was large with child."

"Well, she's not your dead vif. She's our enemy."

Ketil handed Annoure a bearskin and crawled into the hudfat with his cousin. She wrapped herself in the coarse fur; her movements hampered by being bound. She shook uncontrollably with trepidation. She sensed a cruelness and anger in Edgtho she'd never faced before.

Despite her fear, Annoure awkwardly untied the rope binding her ankles. Then she tried to untie her wrists using her teeth, but only succeeded in rubbing her skin raw. She realized it was hopeless and tried to rest. Sleep wouldn't come and soon she had to pee. She left the tent and stepped into the cool night air.

She heard the rustle of the tent flap behind her and her heart leapt to her throat. "Where are you going?" a male voice said. She swung around and was relieved to see Ketil standing there.

"I have to make water."

"You already did."

She flushed, embarrassed that she had to explain her needs to him. "I'm big with child and have to make water more often."

"Don't run off," he said, looking at her in the marginal light the moon provided.

She started to move away and he clasped her arm. "Do it here. I have no wish to chase after you in the dark."

"My feet are so badly cut I can hardly walk. Besides, where would I go without food or clothing, not even shoes? Allow me a little dignity." She limped a short way from him and squatted down.

Back in the tent, she rolled up in the fur, trying to get warm. She couldn't sleep for a long time, but finally drifted off.

It seemed as if she had just fallen asleep when Edgtho kicked her awake. "Get up."

They broke camp in the pale dawn light and packed the boat. When Annoure waded into the sea, the salt water stung the cuts on her feet. Ketil came over and helped her climb into the boat. "Please untie me, Ketil," she said once she was seated in the middle of the boat.

Ketil glanced at his cousin, then untied her wrists. She rubbed her rope burns as the men began rowing out to sea. Water lapped against the side of the boat. "Where are we going?" Annoure asked Ketil, her teeth chattering in the cool morning air.

"To Hedeby. It's the center of trade on the Jutland Peninsula."

"Is that where you're selling me?"

Ketil looked away, as if embarrassed by her question. "Já."

"How long will the journey take?"

"A little more than a week if the weather is good."

"Don't talk to her, Ketil," Edgtho snapped. "She's a thrall and not worth your attention."

"I don't see any reason to make this trip unpleasant by not passing the time in conversation." Ketil looked back at Annoure. "When is your baby due?"

"What concern is that to us?" Edgtho asked.

"If the child might be born on our journey, it's good to know ahead of time." Ketil looked expectantly at Annoure.

"I'm not sure," Annoure replied. "Any day now."

Ketil took a tunic out of his hudfat and handed it to her. "Put this on. It gets cold at sea."

She slid it over her ripped under-dress, grateful for the protection from the elements and for Ketil's unexpected kindness.

* * *

About to leave on the trading voyage, Thorstein, Herjulf and Walfgar approached the gangplank of their longship. Thorstein hesitated getting on the ship; he couldn't shake the nightmare he'd had and was concerned that Annoure was in danger. "I expected Edgtho and Ketil to try to take revenge on me while we were a-viking," he said. "But since they aren't here, I'm concerned now they might be planning some kind of revenge on our families instead."

"I'm sure Njal and your Faðir will be on guard," Herjulf replied.

"I think I should return home."

Walfgar raised his reddish eyebrows. "The captain won't like it. You're signed on as head navigator."

"I know, but I can't shake this feeling that something's wrong. I can't go on this voyage."

"Then do what you must," Herjulf said.

* * *

Several days later Thorstein rode up to his family farmstead at dusk, praying his concerns were unfounded. He had made the journey home on horseback, using a newly purchased horse. It had been a difficult journey across glaciers and through narrow, icy mountain passes. He'd ridden long hours and looked forward to sleeping in his own bed.

He dismounted at the barn and put the horse in a stall, then headed to Njal's house. When he went inside, he saw Thyri and Sandey sitting on a bench. Thyri's hair was uncombed and her clothes soiled. Sandey was sucking her thumb, something she hadn't done since she was a baby. Thyri ran over to him crying, "Thorstein! You're home." She went into his arms and began weeping.

He put his arms around her. "What's wrong? Where's Annoure?" He glanced anxiously around the room with his heart in his throat.

"Gone. Edgtho and Ketil took her and killed . . ." Sobs racked her body and she couldn't continue.

His heart froze. "Killed who?" He clasped her arms and looked into her eyes.

Sandey had followed her mother over to Thorstein and now clung to her skirt, crying, "Móðir, móðir."

Ignoring the child, Thyri replied, "They killed Njal and Brandi!"

"Nei, they wouldn't dare be so bold! Tell me it is not so."

Her face hardened. "It's true. Avenge me, Thorstein. Kill them both. My bróðirs went after them, but found no trace. You won't give up so easily."

"Did they leave by land or by sea?"

"By sea."

"I'll go to their homestead. Someone will know where they've gone." He started for the door.

"Wait! There's more to tell."

He paused, his head pounding. "What worse grief could you give me than what I've already received?"

"Garth was stabbed and is gravely ill."

"I will cut out their hearts and burn their homes to the ground!" He dashed out of the house and ran toward the shore where the boats were kept, intent on leaving immediately.

Thyri raced after him. “Wait, Thorstein!” She caught up to him as he was untying one of the boats. “Don’t go off in a rage or you will be killed as well.”

“My death does not matter.”

“Thorstein, Annoure’s alive! They took her with them. You must bring her safely home.”

“All the more reason to leave at once. Every moment I delay lessens my chance of picking up their trail”

“Já, but not tonight. Look at me, Thorstein!” She tugged on his arm.

He turned to her, reluctant to let her convince him. He needed to give action to the turbulent rage and sorrow coursing through him.

Thyri looked him in the eye. “I want them dead as much as you, but the attack happened several days ago. If you leave now, like this, I fear you will meet your death. You need supplies and rest from your long journey home. My bróðirs should accompany you on this undertaking. Alone and unprepared, you are no match for them.”

“Has the baby been born yet?”

“Nei.”

He drew a deep breath and looked up at the mountains. He needed to think clearly, but his thoughts wouldn’t order themselves. He heard her words, but nothing of what she said fully reached him from the moment she said Annoure was captured and Njal and Brandi were dead. He felt as if something inside of him had snapped. “I can’t wait. I must go now.”

“First, you must see your faðir.”

She pulled him toward his parent’s house and he let her lead him. Sandey, who had followed them to the docks, walked toward them crying pitifully.

Thyri picked her up and Thorstein continued alone. When he stepped over the threshold of his parent’s home, the familiar smell of herbs immediately surrounded him. He looked around the dimly lit house and saw his father resting on his sleeping bench with his mother and Kalsetini sitting near him.

His mother hurried crossed the room and kissed his cheek. “My sonr! My sonr! The gods have brought you back to us.”

Kalsetini moved into his arms. “How could Ketil do such terrible things?" she asked, tears filling her eyes. "He is not the man I thought he was."

"I don't know. The man *I* knew wouldn't kill a child. How is Faðir?"

"He was badly wounded. It will do him good to see you."

Thorstein went to Garth's sleeping bench. His father's face was ashen with dark circles under his eyes and his head was wrapped in a bandage.

"Hello Faóir," Thorstein said, agonized by his father's wasted appearance.

"How is it you're back?" Garth asked in a rasping voice.

"When Edgtho and Ketil left for home after the *ting* instead of going a-viking, I became suspicious."

"They are the lowest of men and have no honor," Garth growled, sounding more like his old self. "Did Herjulf and Walfgar return home with you?"

"Nei, I'm alone."

"I'm glad you're here. You're needed to run the farm. It's your responsibility now. You must see that everyone on the farm has food to eat this winter."

"I can't stay. I have to find Annoure and avenge my kinsmen's deaths."

"You must face the truth, sonr. Edgtho and Ketil blame Annoure for Rethel's death and have probably killed her by now. We will seek justice at the *ting* next spring."

"They would have killed her immediately if they wanted her dead. Perhaps they want her for a thrall or plan to sell her. Regardless, I will find her and my enemies will taste my sword. This is too terrible a deed to leave to the justice of the war chief and council."

"You killed Rethel over Annoure and now your bróðir and nephew are dead because of her." Garth paused for a moment, gasping for air. "She is only a woman of foreign blood. Let the killing end here. If you are killed or if you succeed in killing Edgtho and Ketil, the feud will only continue."

"Rethel died in a fair fight. The crimes against our family are far greater. I will have Annoure back or all of Edgtho's kinsmen will die."

"And will you do this alone?"

"Já."

“Freydis, give your sonr a cup of wine, then take him to Njal and Brandi’s graves. Let him look at death before he seeks to find his own.”

Thorstein drank the strong-tasting wine, then followed his mother to the family gravesite situated at the foot of the mountain. Two new graves, one large and one small, lay side-by-side.

“They were buried together,” Freydis said.

Thorstein sank down on his knees and tears blurred his vision. The reality of their deaths overwhelmed him. His levelheaded older brother should not have died. Njal was supposed to run the farm and take their father’s place.

He felt the weight of his new responsibilities. The women and children depended upon him to provide for the clan, but he planned to go after Annoure. With his father wounded, Njal dead, and his cousins a-viking, there wouldn’t be any kinsmen left to run the farm. His mother would need to take charge and perhaps one of Thyri’s brothers could help out for the summer.

Thorstein hardly noticed when his mother left him to grieve privately. He cried aloud “Njal, why did you and little Brandi have to die? How could they kill a helpless child?”

He mourned at the gravesite late into the night. Finally his mother returned and urged him to come inside. “You need to eat, Thorstein, and sit beside your Faðir. He’s dying.”

“Is there nothing we can do to save him?” he asked, sorrow filling him anew.

She shook her head. “It’s hard to watch him die. He was always such a strong man. What will I do without him?”

Thorstein drew her into his arms and held her. He had no words to comfort his mother and felt overwhelmed by the horror of what happened. He’d left home with a future full of promise and returned to find death and loss.

They went inside and he ate a small meal without tasting it. His father slept and Thorstein sat by his sleeping bench, thinking of his childhood. His father had taught him everything he knew: how to farm, hunt, fish, sail, tame wild horses, survive in the wilderness, and build furniture. He had been angry with his father for whipping Annoure, but now he wished he hadn’t wasted the last winter of his father’s life estranged from him.

Sometime during the night he staggered over to a bench and fell into a deep, dreamless sleep. He woke late, groggy and thickheaded. He spent the day preparing for his journey, getting things in order on the farm, and sitting beside his father.

That evening Freydis and Kalsetini helped him pack supplies. "Annoure and the baby will need clothes," said Kalsetini. She stuffed their things into the bottom of a hudfat, then put a change of clothes for Thorstein on top.

"Thank you. I wouldn't have thought to pack anything for them," Thorstein said.

Kalsetini looked up from her packing. "When are you leaving?"

"I'll sleep a few hours, then leave in the middle of the night so I can reach Nesbjörn's farm before sunrise and find someone alone to question," Thorstein said.

"Please reconsider," Freydis said. "I don't see how you can find Edgtho and Ketil. But if you do succeed in finding them, what chance do you have against two men? They fought your bróðir without honor, two to one."

"I must do whatever I can to save Annoure and my unborn child."

Tears filled his mother's eyes. "I can't bear to lose you. You're my last sonr. My heart was ripped open when Buliwyf died as a child and now it's ripped open again with Njal and Brandi's deaths. I don't see how I will go on if you die as well. A móðir should never have to outlive her children and grandchildren."

"I don't mean to cause you more pain, Móðir," he said drawing her close. "But I have to find and rescue Annoure. She is my beloved."

"Please don't go. I beg you." She put her head against his shoulder and cried softly.

"I have to, Móðir. Please try and understand."

She continued to weep and he was greatly distressed, never having seen her so upset before. But finally she stepped away from him and wiped away her tears with the edge of her hangerock. "Go say goodbye to your faðir."

"Will you be all right?"

Kalsetini put her arm around her mother. "We can run the farm over the summer. Bring back Annoure."

Thorstein kissed his sister on the cheek, then walked over to his father's sleeping bench.

"I see you're leaving," Garth said weakly, his breathing labored.

"I have to find Annoure."

"I know. Some things a man just has to do. I want Edgtho and Ketil dead too. And I know your love for Annoure drives you to find her as long as there's a chance she's still alive."

"I hate leaving you and móðir. I know I'm needed here."

"Freydis can manage the farm as well as any man and Herjulf and Walfgar will be home for fall harvest." Garth coughed and specks of blood appeared on his beard. "I'm proud of the man you've become, Thorstein. You have rare courage."

Garth was quiet for a moment, resting with his eyes closed. Thorstein thought he'd gone to sleep, but then he opened his eyes and said, "I've been a fortunate man. I've had a family and a farm. I pass on the farm to you. Keep it strong."

"I will. Goodbye, Father." As Thorstein said the words, he realized with a sinking feeling this was the last time he'd see his father alive. He hated having to choose between his love for Annoure and his dying father. His father deserved a dutiful son who would sit beside him in his final hours.

Chapter 21

Journey to Nesbjörn's Farmstead

THORSTEIN SAILED HIS SMALL BOAT through the dark, rugged fjord by the light of the moon. The sun was beginning to rise when he finally reached the Nesbjörn farmstead. After landing on the rocky shoreline, he crossed the planted fields to the barn. Inside, the smell of hay and manure was strong. Several cows raised their heads and looked at him; one mooed in response. He waited behind the door for someone to come in to do the milking.

It wasn't long before a woman entered the barn. He grabbed her as she came through the doorway and clapped a hand over her mouth, then kicked the door shut. She dropped her milk buckets and jabbed an elbow into his stomach. He gasped in pain, but didn't let go. "Don't be frightened. I'm Thorstein of the Garth Farmstead. I've come here many times to help with harvest or hunt with Ketil." He felt her relax some. "If I remove my hand, do you promise not to scream?"

She nodded and he slowly withdrew his hand. She turned to face him, pushing a snarled clump of hair off her dirty face, watching him warily. Her clothes were the rough clothes of a thrall.

"Are Edgtho or Ketil here?" Thorstein asked.

"Nei, they went to the *ting* and didn't return."

"Do you know why they went to the *ting*?"

She twisted her hands together. "You killed Rethel and they wanted retribution."

"After the *ting,* they came to my farmstead and stole my betrothed. In the process they killed my bróðir and nephew and fatally wounded my faðir. I implore you to help me. Do you know anything that might shed light on where they took her?"

"Don't kill me," she pleaded, trembling.

"I'm not going to hurt you. What do you know?"

"Edgtho will beat me if he finds out I talked to you."

"He's not here. As soon as you tell me, I'll be gone as well."

She closed her eyes a moment then looked up at him. "I wasn't sorry when I heard Rethel was dead. He was a cruel man and my life is easier since his death. Edgtho is just as mean-hearted. Find him and kill him, but you must promise not to hurt Ketil."

He grabbed her by the shoulders. "Where are they?"

"I don't know exactly. They returned here after the *ting*. Edgtho was in a rage and I overheard him talking to Ketil one evening. Their plan was to kidnap the Saxon and sell her in Hedeby. Edgtho was in a violent mood. He beat me, then forced himself on me."

Thorstein frowned. He'd never given much thought to the difficult life of a thrall until he'd abducted Annoure. The thrall untied the string at the neck of her dress and pulled it down to show him bruises on her white shoulders and breasts. "See what he did?"

She started laughing hysterically. "He'll know I told you. He'll kill me! He'll kill me, but I don't care. It's better than this life I lead! I should drown myself in the sea!"

She started rocking back and forth. Thorstein wondered if she was demented. "Edgtho will use your woman badly. You will not want her back, even if you find her."

"Keep your voice down." Thorstein glanced at the door. "Is anyone apt to come to the barn?"

"If I don't return with the morning milk, they'll come here and beat me."

He tied her dress back up, feeling sorry for her. She'd be pretty if her face was clean and her hair properly brushed. "If the gods favor me, Edgtho won't ever hurt you again. Compose yourself while I do the milking."

He milked the cows, then carried two full buckets to the door. "Will you help me?" he asked.

"Why should I?"

"I can rid you of Edgtho. If you have any compassion, you won't want an innocent, pregnant girl sold into slavery."

"What do you want me to do?" she asked, her voice hesitant.

"Return to the house with these buckets and pretend we never met."

"I'll do it, but not because of Edgtho or your woman. I'll do it because you are a good man."

"Tell me if anyone is out there."

She took the milk buckets from him and stepped through the door. "No one is about yet. Go quickly."

He hurried out of the barn and ran across the field, not trusting the thrall. Even if she said nothing, her fearful face would be revealing.

Back on the water, he raised the sail and thought over the information the thrall had given him. Edgtho and Ketil were taking Annoure to Hedeby and had left several days ago, so they would almost be there by now. Thus he had no chance of catching up to them. And if she was sold in Hedeby, what chance did he have of finding her?

By Odin's Ravens, I wished I hadn't left Annoure, he thought, knowing her journey would be terrible in Edgtho's hands. *But how could I foresee that the fight with Rethel would lead to a blood feud?*

* * *

Annoure felt nauseated in the small boat on the Øresund strait. At first she thought it was just seasickness from the choppy water, but as the hours slipped by and the pain increased, she realized she was in labor. The idea of giving birth at sea frightened her.

She wondered why the men didn't pull to shore and wait for the incoming storm to pass. The boat leaned dangerously on its side, so Edgtho and Ketil moved to the other side to keep it from flipping. Edgtho yelled for her to join them and she quickly obeyed. Ketil adjusted the sail and the ship leveled out.

The journey had taken longer than expected because the boat had hit rocks, gashing a hole in the bottom that needed repairing.

Ketil had been quiet all day. They were near Hedeby and Annoure knew he was having second thoughts about selling her into slavery. During their days of journeying together, they had become friends of sorts. Edgtho's anger hadn't abated and only Ketil's presence kept her from being abused. She leaned over and clutched the gunwale of the boat as a particularly strong contraction caught her in its power.

"Annoure, what's wrong?" Ketil asked.

She looked up at him when the pain was over. "The baby is coming."

His eyes clouded with concern. "How soon?"

"I don't know. I've never had a baby before."

Ketil shouted to Edgtho over the wind. "The storm grows worse! Let's find a place to spend the night!"

"I want to reach Hedeby and spend the night with a woman and a flask of mead."

"It's too far! We'll never reach it before the storm hits. Even now we risk ripping the sail. It should be lowered."

"We'll stop when I say so!" Edgtho turned toward the front of the ship.

Ketil started lowering the sail.

"What are you doing?" Edgtho shouted.

"I have no wish to die! If we continue, we row!" Ketil shouted back.

The wind snapped the rope out of Ketil's hand and Edgtho moved to help him. They worked together to lower the sail. Rain began to fall and Edgtho cursed as he began to row. "Head for that cove," Edgtho yelled.

Ketil took up his oars and together they fought the wind and waves as they rowed toward shore. As the boat bobbed up and down, large waves continually sprayed in.

Annoure felt a tensing across her swollen belly as new contraction came over her. She gritted her teeth until the contraction passed, praying they'd reach land safely.

"Rocks!" Edgtho yelled. Using his oar as a pole, he shoved the boat away from the boulder. The side scraped against the edge of it, the boat jerked and Annoure fell sidewise. Righting herself, she saw rocks protruding up above the surface of the water—just waiting to tear out the boat's bottom again.

Rain began pouring down in torrents and the waves grew large and violent. Annoure held onto the bench, afraid of being tossed overboard. Pain came over her again and she wished with all of her being that she was with Thorstein.

Suddenly a vision of him appeared. He stood under the branch of a large spruce tree, looking at the violent sea. Rain poured down on him and soaked his clothes. The vision faded, but it was so vivid she knew it was a sending and not her imagination.

Finally the men brought the boat safely to shore and pulled it onto dry land. Ketil helped Annoure disembark, then he and his cousin put up the tent. Annoure unloaded supplies from the boat with rain pounding heavily upon her. Overhead a flash of lightning lit the sky followed by a boom of thunder that caused her to jump.

Once the boat was unloaded, Annoure crawled inside the tent with the two men and pulled the bearskin over her shoulders. Her hands were numb with cold. A particularly strong contraction came over her and she clutched her abdomen, moaning.

"Come lie down, Annoure," Ketil said, setting out a fur.

"What's wrong with her?" Edgtho asked.

"She's in labor. The baby is ready to be born."

"Babies always choose the worst possible time to come." Edgtho's voice was gruff, yet his face softened a little. He pulled out some dried fish and began eating, taking no further interest.

Annoure removed her wet tunic. Beneath it, her under-dress was fairly dry. The evening passed slowly while the men ate and played backgammon. Her contractions grew in intensity and became more frequent. She dreaded having a child with no experienced woman there to help.

As the rain continued pounding on the tent, water seeped under the sides and flowed across the ground. Annoure moved closer to the center of the tent.

When it grew dark, Edgtho crawled into the hudfat and Ketil asked how she was doing before joining his cousin.

"The pain is bearable," she replied, already exhausted.

"Are the contractions nearly continuous yet?"

"Nei. There is space between."

"Then it will be hours yet before the baby comes. I'm going to get some sleep. Wake me when it's time."

She heard him moving around, then all was quiet and dark in the tent. Outside the waves beat against the rocks and periodically flashes of lightning lit up the tent and thunder roared.

Annoure knew almost nothing about birthing. Her body no longer seemed to be her own as the contractions became worse. Pain built up within her like waves on the shore: building in intensity, cresting at the height, then washing away in brief periods of stillness. In between the pangs, she had time to fortify herself for the next onslaught.

The hours dragged by and she felt alone, caught up in some terrible nightmare that would surely kill her before dawn. The combination of pain and fright became more than she could endure. Annoure began to weep, wishing she could die so this suffering would end.

She became aware of movement beside her and a soft, calm voice said, "Annoure, are you crying? I didn't mean to sleep so long."

Ketil put his hand on her shoulder and began to rub it gently. She sat up and threw her arms around him, seeking relief from her fear and agony. He held her close as she wept. "I'm going to die, Ketil. I'm going to die and my baby will never see life."

"Nei, Annoure, birthing is a natural process. You mustn't be afraid and fight it. Haven't you ever been to a birthing?"

She shook her head. "I was raised in a house of men." She tensed as another contraction overtook her and she twisted his shirt in her fist.

"Relax and breathe deeply. Think of your beautiful child who will soon be born. The pain will pass; stay in control until it does. Giving birth is a normal part of life. See even now the pain eases."

Her dread passed with the contraction; she was not alone. Ketil's arms were strong and comforting. She wasn't going to die and her child would be born soon. Ketil told her to drink and pressed a flask against her lips. She drank and found it was wine, not water as she expected. It was warming and relaxed her.

Ketil helped her lay down on her side then rubbed her back. "Have *you* ever been at a birthing?" she asked.

"Not at a woman's, but I helped calves, colts and lambs into the world. It is not much different."

Another pain caught her in its power and she clasped Ketil's hand, holding on tightly until it passed. "Stay with me; don't go back to sleep. I'll die if I'm left to suffer alone in the dark."

"I'll stay beside you, dearest." He continued to rub her back, easing some of her discomfort. "I just needed to rest for a while. I was tired from rowing against the wind."

"Tell me a tale."

He cocked his head as if pondering which one to share, then said, "I'll tell you one of the goddess Freyja. She rides a chariot drawn by two large cats and weeps tears of red gold. One day a giant stole Thor's hammer, Mjölnir. Thor went to Freyja and suggested she marry the giant so he could get his hammer back. She flew into a rage at this proposition." Ketil laughed. "Thor should have known better than to suggest such a thing."

"Did Thor ever get his hammer back?"

"Já, he and his wolf had to fight the giant for it. It was a fearsome battle, but Thor won and retrieved his hammer. While he was gone from heaven no thunder could be heard even in the worst of storms. That reminds me of another tale.

"Once when the god Frey was looking across the worlds, he saw the giantess Gerd. Upon gazing at her lovely countenance, he fell in love with her. When he came home, he didn't speak and wouldn't drink or sleep. His faðir sent his messenger Skinnir to Frey to find out what was wrong."

Annoure squeezed his hand and gasped, "Keep talking." She no longer followed the story, but it was comforting to hear his calming voice. She hoped her child would be born soon.

After awhile she said between contractions, "The pains grow closer together now."

"That's good. It won't be much longer now. Listen the rain's stopped and it's starting to lighten up. It'll be easier to deliver your baby in the early morning light."

"Oh-h! It hurts so much!" She clutched his hand, digging in her fingers and screamed. Edgtho sat up and swore a string of Norse curses as he left the tent. Ketil wiped her sweaty forehead with a dry cloth and gave her a drink.

"You must let me see if the baby is ready to be born," Ketil said, uncovering her legs.

Mortified, Annoure shook her head. "Please leave. I must give birth alone."

He smiled with compassion. "You are a brave woman, but you have never been to a birthing and won't know what to do. What you have yet to endure is the hardest part, though it will last but a short time."

He gently pushed her bent knees apart. Another contraction overtook her and she gave in to the need to push. "I see the top of its head!" Ketil exclaimed. "It will come out soon."

Ketil stayed close and encouraged her. The baby was determined to be born and her body seemed to know what to do, although she didn't. As the sun rose, the baby's head came out. Ketil held it with one hand and with the next push he eased out its shoulders and pulled out the infant. He placed it on Annoure's chest, pulled open her torn underdress and set its mouth to her nipple. "Come on little one, suckle," he said. It latched on and began to nurse contentedly.

Annoure gazed at the child in wonder. It was a perfectly formed, healthy boy with a head of fine blond hair. Ketil covered her and the baby with the bearskin. She wished Thorstein were beside her instead of Ketil. He should be the one sharing this sacred moment with her.

Her stomach tightened in pain. "What's wrong?" she exclaimed. "It hurts again."

"You have to push out the sack your baby was in. It will be much easier than pushing out a baby."

Once the afterbirth slid out, Ketil left to bury it outside. When he returned, he crawled into his hudfat to sleep. Annoure ached all over and the ground felt especially hard beneath her. She lay awake thinking about Ketil. There was much good in him, though it was overshadowed by anger and grief.

Annoure remembered the first time she'd met Ketil. She'd seen an image of him weeping beside a woman who died. Thorstein said Ketil's wife died. The image must have been of her. "Ketil, are you still awake?"

"Já." He looked at her from his hudfat, which was only an arm's length away.

"You seem comfortable around childbirth and a woman carrying a child. Do you have children?'

"Two dóttirs." His face contorted with sadness. "My vif Hanna became ill and died when the youngest was a baby. I miss Hanna. The best part of me died when she died." He was silent for a while, then he said, "It's good to be around a woman again. You remind me a little of sweet Hanna. You have a gentleness about you as she did."

"Will you take your children with you if you are banished?"

"The life of a banished man is not one to share with his children. They are better off in the care of my kin."

"They must miss you. Perhaps if you return me and my child safely to our home, you will not be banished."

"Two men and a boy are dead. There will be just punishment for such an act of violence. The council made its decision and Thorstein paid his tribute. It should have ended there, but it didn't because Edgtho wanted revenge and I was crazy with grief. I let him talk me into kidnapping you. No one was to die and I didn't know you were a good-natured, virtuous woman with child. I thought you were a whore or witch who seduced my bróðir and caused his death. I realize now you wouldn't have done that, but in a military camp there are only whores and thralls, whom freely give their bodies for a man's pleasure.

"Rethel was loud and overbearing, but he wasn't a bad man and he was my bróðir. We went fishing and hunting when we were children. Later he helped me bury my vif and grieved beside me. His death was a great loss to me."

Annoure heard the love and despair in his voice and said nothing further. She'd seen only the terrible side of Rethel, but there was another side as well.

She awoke to the sound of Edgtho and Ketil arguing. Ketil lay beside her and Edgtho squatted at the tent opening in the rain. "We leave today," Edgtho said.

"Nei, it is too soon for Annoure and the baby to travel."

"What does it matter? We are taking her to Hedeby to sell. What difference does it make if she dies on the way?"

"There's been enough blood on my hands. You've had your revenge."

"Nei, my thirst for revenge won't be satisfied until Thorstein is dead."

"If you don't have any compassion for the woman, have some for me. I was up most of the night delivering the baby into this world."

"I have no compassion for a fool. You had no reason to stay up with her."

"Fool or no, I'm not getting up. I'm tired from yesterday's difficult journey and will not travel today. I've followed your every decision on this journey. Now you can bend to my will and wait a day to move on."

"I want to get to Hedeby. Once there, you can sleep as long as you like."

"It still storms. Go to Hedeby if you must and come back when you are feeling less mean-spirited."

"Very well. I'll pick you up on my return *after* I've sold the woman."

"Nei, she stays with me!"

"You're enraptured with her. Her beauty blinds you to what she is. Need I remind you it is because of her that Rethel is dead and we will be banished?"

"Rethel is dead because he tried to take what wasn't his and we'll be banished because of our thirst for revenge. Leave me to rest. It's enough that I can't return home to be with my dóttirs and kin because of you, without being forced into journeying to Hedeby in such foul weather."

Edgtho left, grumbling to himself.

The baby began to cry and Annoure put him to her breast. Ketil gazed at her and the child with a warm expression. "Did you hear all that was said?"

"Some of it. Your voices woke me."

"I'm sorry. How are you feeling?"

"I ache and I'm tired. Thank you for giving me a day to rest." She wrapped the baby in a fur and went back to sleep.

In the afternoon the baby started crying and wouldn't quiet no matter what she did. Ketil and Edgtho played backgammon in the tent because it was raining again.

"Perhaps he has pains in his belly," Ketil said.

Annoure tried to get him to nurse. He sucked a moment then started screaming again, his legs drawn up to his stomach. Annoure worried something was seriously wrong. She put him over her shoulder and rocked back and forth, patting him on the back as she listened to the sound of rain pelting the tent.

"I swear by hell's serpents, if you don't shut that baby up, I'll throw him into the sea!" Edgtho roared.

The baby stopped crying for a moment startled by his loud voice, then started screaming. Annoure desperately tried to comfort him, feeling waves of anger rolling through the small tent. She was near tears herself. She'd never taken care of a newborn infant and didn't know how to quiet him. She wished it would stop raining so she could walk him outside, away from Edgtho.

"Threatening Annoure isn't helping things," Ketil said.

"Do you think he's sick?" Annoure asked, a lump forming in her throat.

"Nei, sometimes babies just cry for no apparent reason."

Annoure wasn't comforted. What chance did her tiny baby have of surviving in the wilderness? She placed him on his stomach on her lap and rubbed his back. He continued to scream. His cries were giving her a headache and she saw that even Ketil was getting edgy.

Edgtho dumped over the backgammon board. "I can't stand that noise!" He snatched child from her and took him from the tent. "I'll throw him to Thor, the god of the storms!"

"Nei!" Annoure screamed, scrambling out of the tent. Ketil was faster and had already set off after Edgtho.

Through a sheet of rain, she saw Ketil grab Edgtho's arm. "Give me the child, cousin!" Ketil demanded.

"A slave child is of no value. There's little chance he will live. Why not end his life now before it really begins?"

"I brought the baby into the world. He won't be killed while I'm here to defend him."

The child's lusty cries continued to pierce the air. Ketil tried to hold Edgtho back as he stepped to the water's edge.

"Have you turned traitor?" Edgtho asked. "Have you decided to keep the woman for yourself instead of selling her?"

"I agreed to help you kidnap her and bring her to Hedeby to sell and I will keep my word, but I want no part of killing a baby."

"It's done commonly enough when food is scarce or a child unwanted."

"Please, I beg you. Spare my baby's life," Annoure pleaded, kneeling down at Edgtho's feet. "He is innocent in all this."

"He is the child of my enemy and so is my enemy as well." Edgtho tried to shake off Ketil's hold.

"Give me the child," Ketil demanded.

Edgtho tore free and pivoted around, hurling the infant into the water. Ketil dove in after the baby, snatching it up as it sank beneath the waves.

Annoure screamed hysterically as she waded into the water. When she reached Ketil, she took the baby from him. The baby was no longer wailing and she feared he was dead.

The infant coughed up water and began crying weakly. She carried him to the tent and held his cold body between her bare breasts to warm him. Ketil built a fire near the opening of the tent where it was protected from the rain by a large fir tree.

"Hush, little one, daddy will come and rescue us. You must live." She wept as she rocked him in her arms and shook with cold.

Ketil wrapped the bearskin around her and the baby. "I apologize for Edgtho's behavior." He glanced in the direction Edgtho had gone after throwing the child into the water. "There's so much anger in him. Do you think the baby will live?"

"What do you care? We are both to be sold as thralls. How can you plan to sell me and still pretend you care what happens to me and my baby? The man who buys me could be worse than Edgtho. He can keep me as a pleasure thrall or work me to death in the fields. If my son lives, he can be taken from me once he is weaned and sold to another farmstead. Don't pretend to be my friend—you are part of this. It is not only Edgtho who is to blame if I'm sold as a thrall."

"You are right to chastise and hate me for my part in this. The gods know I hate myself for what I've done and for what I am about to do."

"Then don't sell me and the baby!"

"The gods have already decided your fate," Ketil said, his pleasant face distorted in anguish. "There's nothing I can do." He reached through the tent opening and put another wet log on the fire. It crackled and hissed.

The child fell asleep in her arms. Ketil gave her a linen cloth to wrap the baby in and one of his tunics for her to wear. Annoure swaddled the baby and set him on the hudfat, then pulled off her wet under-dress and put on the tunic. Her heart was filled with anguish that her child might die from Edgtho's violent treatment of him.

After changing, she lay beside her son and fell asleep. When she awoke, it was warm in the tent. The sun shone through the doorway and cast rays of light over her and the baby. Annoure carried the infant outside where Ketil sat alone by the fire.

"My baby needs to be baptized. He could die and I want to be sure he'll go to heaven. Do you have a gold coin and a bowl?"

"I only have a silver coin."

"It will do."

He handed her a silver coin and the bowl he'd just eaten from. She rinsed the bowl out at the shore, then filled it with water.

"Are you a priestess?" he asked.

"Nei." Yet as she started the ceremony she felt the power of the Goddess flow through her. Everything seemed to disappear but the child and the fire. She passed the child over the flames three times and then walked around the fire three times.

"The number three is sacred to Celts," she explained to Ketil. "It represents earth, sea and sky." She gazed at the child. "You were born for a special reason. You will grow wise in the old ways and understand the new ways." She placed the coin in the bowl of water. "I put this coin in the bowl so you will have wealth."

Then she dipped her hand in water and drew a cross on his forehead. "In Christ's name, I welcome you back into the world and make nine wishes for you. May you have wisdom, happiness, health, freedom, prosperity, courage, honesty, virtue and compassion. I name you Ban Thorsteinson."

Now that the ceremony was complete, she looked at Ketil. "I need to clean myself. Do you have any soap?"

"Já." He looked through his pack and handed her a rough-cut bar. Carrying Ban, Annoure walked down the shoreline until she was out of view of the camp, then set the child down. She pulled off her tunic before wading into the cold water, which lapped gently around her legs. She kept going until it was up to her hips, then washed the dried blood off her thighs. She heard a noise and looked toward the shore. Ketil stood by a tree and was watching her, desire evident in his eyes. She moved deeper into the cold water, squatting down to cover her breasts.

"Go away, Ketil, so I can get out of the water."

"I've seen you before."

"You've seen me give birth. This is different."

"Já, this is different. You look like a goddess." He glanced back toward camp. "Edgtho said to check on you. He thinks you might run away."

"I am too weak to run away with an infant and I have no wish to try to survive in the woods without food or shelter. My Thorstein will come and rescue me and I intend to be alive when he does."

Ketil's eyes narrowed. "You will never see Thorstein again."

"I will! He will not stop searching until he finds me."

"Then he will search for you until he dies of old age." Ketil turned and strode away. She hurried from the water, pulled the tunic over her wet body, then checked on her sleeping child. Reassured that he slept peacefully, she washed the blood and dirt from her under-dress and hung it on a tree limb to dry.

Afterwards she gathered moss. She was determined to do all she could to meet the baby's needs. Somehow they both had to survive until Thorstein found them.

Chapter 22

Hedeby

THE NEXT DAY, ANNOURE SAT on the floor of the small boat with Ban in her arms. A sharp wind blew against her cheeks and tangled her hair. She felt thickheaded and her head throbbed from lack of sleep. The baby had kept waking up during the night and she was quick to quiet him, worried about disturbing Edgtho.

Her hand trembled as she clutched the gunwale of the boat. She saw houses and shops in the distance and knew they must be near Hedeby where she was to be sold into slavery. She wondered if she could convince Ketil to let her go. He seemed distressed about Thorstein's kin being killed during her kidnapping. Perhaps she could appeal to his higher nature. She scanned the Varangian Sea, still hoping Thorstein was on the way to rescue her and Ban.

As they drew closer, Annoure saw women washing clothes at the shoreline and a boy herding a flock of sheep. They sailed to the wharf where many boats were moored. Ketil tied the boat to a post, then helped Annoure out. A strong wind whipped up the edge of the cape Annoure wore and she tucked Ban under the woolen garment.

The men carried supplies to shore and set up their tent near some other tents. When they finished, Edgtho said, "Let's sell the woman and be done with it."

Annoure cringed and her eyes flashed to Ketil whose shoulders had stiffened. "Tomorrow is soon enough," Ketil said. "She'll fetch a better price rested and in new clothes."

"You don't want to sell her, do you?" Edgtho demanded.

"Nei, but I will." Ketil took some dried fish out of a sealskin bag. "Do you want something to eat?"

"I'm sick of dried fish," Edgtho replied. "I'll eat in town, then get drunk and find a woman for the night."

Once Edgtho left, Annoure let out her breath. She always felt on edge in his presence.

"I'm sick of fish as well," Ketil said, tossing it down. "Are you strong enough to walk to town?"

She shook her head and her eyes filled with tears. "I don't feel well. I hardly slept last night and need to rest."

Ketil's eyes lit with compassion. "Why don't you sleep in the tent for a while?"

Annoure wiped the tears off her cheeks, embarrassed to be so emotional and went into the tent. She removed the cape and tunic. Wearing only her under-dress, she fell asleep nursing Ban.

Annoure was startled awake as someone entered the tent. She opened her eyes and gasped upon seeing Edgtho.

"Where's Ketil?" he asked. His words were slurred and she smelled wine on his breath.

"I don't know." She sat up, feeling the chill of dread shoot through her.

He smiled sadistically. "It was foolish of him to leave you unprotected."

She backed into the side of the tent. "Go away. I'm sure he's close by and it will anger him if you hurt me."

"What do I care about Ketil's ire?" His cheeks flushed a fiery red, as if he'd been in the sun too long. "I'm in charge." He grabbed one of her legs and dragged her toward him, causing her under-dress to slide up to her waist.

"Ketil, help me!" she screamed, kicking Edgtho with her free leg. "Ketil!"

Edgtho shoved her onto her back and forced her thighs apart. "Submit or I'll beat you until you can't move."

Annoure pressed her hands against his shoulders, trying to push him off.

Ketil thrust open the tent flap. "Let her be, Edgtho!"

Edgtho glowered at Ketil. "You want her, too. Why don't we both enjoy her body before we sell her?"

"There are willing women in town. We don't need to abuse this one. We've done her enough harm already and will do her worse tomorrow when we sell her. Let that be enough to satisfy your need for revenge." Ketil dropped his bundle, grabbed the back of his cousin's tunic and pulled him from the tent.

Shaking, Annoure lifted up the crying baby and rocked him until he quieted. She could hear the men arguing outside the tent. Her heart raced with distress, afraid their argument would lead to a fight that Ketil would lose.

She picked up the bundle Ketil dropped and discovered it was a coarsely woven hangerock. The smell of lanolin rose from the wool fabric. Folded inside the hangerock was a linen under-dress, socks, soft leather shoes, a baby gown and small blanket. She quickly changed the baby and herself into the new clothes, then wrapped him in the blanket and drew on the cape. The shouting had stopped, so she peered out from the tent flap.

"He's gone," Ketil said. "Don't be frightened."

Annoure carried the baby into the sunlight. Ketil drew her and the infant into the circle of his arms. Her eyes overflowed with tears at his tenderness.

"I apologize for leaving you alone," Ketil said. "I didn't expect Edgtho to return so soon." He kissed her forehead. "Are you all right?"

She nodded and stepped away from him. "He just scared me."

"We need to talk."

Annoure looked up at him, meeting his intense gaze while trying to control her emotions. His melancholy eyes were filled with affection. She noticed he'd washed and combed his dark hair and looked quite attractive.

He cleared his throat and uncomfortably shifted his stance. "I have come to care for you, Annoure. More than care for you . . . when I saw Edgtho attacking you, I wanted to kill him." He clasped her free hand in his. "I love you, Annoure, and want you for my vif. Will you come with me and share in my banishment? We can find a place to make our home."

Annoure drew in a sharp breath, so surprised she didn't know how to answer him. She'd realized he felt protective of her, but it had never occurred to her that he might want to marry her. "I . . . I thought—well, I thought you and Kalsetini . . ." she stammered. She let the words trail off, realizing he could never marry Kalsetini now. Sorrow and regret flashed across his face at the mention of Kalsetini.

"And what of Edgtho?" Annoure continued, wondering how to salvage the situation. She couldn't afford to lose Ketil's friendship. "He will never agree to our marrying."

"Edgtho has nothing to say about who I choose to marry."

"Edgtho would go berserk if you took me for a vif."

"I'll convince him it's a perfect revenge on Thorstein. If you marry me, then Thorstein can never have you."

She couldn't breathe, knowing she couldn't betray Thorstein even to save herself and little Ban from slavery. But would Thorstein ever find her? "I care for you and I'm grateful that you helped bring Ban into the world and saved him from drowning, but I made vows to Thorstein that can't be broken."

Ketil's eyes flashed in anger. "Thorstein stole you from your home and kept you as a pleasure thrall. He never married you. You don't owe him any loyalty. Marry me and you'll be a free woman."

"Ketil, please try to understand. Thorstein wanted to marry me, but his father refused to give him permission. Thorstein and I were going to leave the farm together. I'm an honorable woman and the mother to Thorstein's child. I can't speak words of affection to you." Even as she spoke, Annoure knew for her child's sake she should let Ketil woo her. Their fate was in his hands.

Ketil's eyes revealed his deep inner pain. "I need you, Annoure; I'll raise Ban as my own. I've been miserable since Hanna died. Rethel's death drove me into even deeper despair. I kidnapped you because I wanted to punish you for his death, but now it seems I've been given a second chance for happiness. I feel like I've awakened from a dense fog to find there's still the possibility of joy in the world." He led her into the tent, then lifted the sleeping baby from her arms and gently placed him on a fur. Ketil drew her to him and she tensed as his mouth descended over hers. His lips were warm and his beard soft against her cheeks and chin.

Not wanting to anger him, Annoure fought the urge to shove him away. She needed to delay being sold so Thorstein could find her. *Thorstein, I'm sorry,* she thought as the kiss deepened. Ketil's hand slid under her cape and covered her breast. Then he sat on the hudfat and drew her down beside him. He began kissing her again while his hand unfastened the brooch holding her cape on.

"Nei, please, it is too soon!" she cried. "The baby is only two days old. My body needs time to heal."

He put her hand on his taut stomach. "Then give me pleasure in other ways."

She jerked her hand away, covered her face with her hands and began to cry. "I can't. I would rather be a thrall than betray Thorstein in such a way."

He grasped her by the upper arms and shook her roughly. "Do you love him?"

Tears rolled unheeded down her cheeks. "Já, I love him." She switched to Anglo-Saxon. "Virgin Mother, help me and my child."

"Speak so I can understand what you're saying!" Ketil demanded.

"All is lost. All is lost," she moaned in her native tongue, continuing to weep.

"Seductress! If you'd rather be a thrall than a vif, I'll give you your wish."

"Nei, we're friends!" she exclaimed in Norse. "Don't do this!"

He grabbed Ban off the fur and shoved the baby into her arms, then roughly pulled her from the tent. He headed toward town, dragging her with him.

"Where are we going?" she asked, trying to twist her arm from his grasp.

"To a slave dealer. You and your child can drown at sea for all I care."

"Nei, please, don't sell us."

He jerked her forward and she nearly lost her balance. "You're tainted. I should have listened to Edgtho. You are a seducer of men and the sooner you are gone from my sight, the better."

"Ketil, I like you. I truly do. You are kind and good to me, but I love Thorstein. Surely you can't believe that makes me evil. I never led you to believe I didn't love him." She tried again to pull free.

He stopped. His lips contorted grotesquely and his eyes looked wild.

"Resist me and I'll kill you right here. Because of you, my bróðir is dead and I will be banished at the next *ting*. You are a proud noblewoman, aren't you? Too good to share your body with my bróðir and now too good to share it with me! Once you find out what it's like to be a thrall, you'll wish you hadn't been so proud."

"Ketil, don't sell me! I beg of you. Show mercy. You are a good man. You had a vif. Would you want her sold into slavery?"

"Your pleas fall on deaf ears. I am no longer under your spell." He yanked her forward again.

Finally he stopped in front of a wooden house and pounded on the door.

Annoure dried her tears on her sleeve and stood rigidly beside him with her chin held high. Her nostrils flared as she glared at Ketil in hatred. His cruel actions seemed all the worse after his former kindness.

A man yelled from the house. "What's your business?"

"I want to speak to the thrall dealer, Ingeld the Much Traveled. I have a woman to sell."

The door opened to reveal a stocky man wearing a thick gold necklace. "I'm Ingeld," he said in a commanding voice. He looked at Annoure, absentmindedly rubbing a mole on his large nose. His braided beard reminded her of Walfgar, but he had a hardened look about him that Walfgar didn't have. "Bring the woman into the light so I can see her."

Ketil clasped Annoure's upper arm and pulled her inside. "She's fine merchandise and will bring a good price at a foreign market."

"What's that in her arms?" Ingeld leaned closer to peer at Ban who was almost completely covered by the blanket. Annoure smelled garlic on his breath and his sweaty body reeked. "A baby!" the slave dealer exclaimed. "It lowers her value. Virgins bring a higher price."

"It heightens her value. It proves she can have children. It's a boy who will grow to be a strong man."

"It will take many years and a lot of food before he is strong enough to be of use."

Annoure swallowed, letting none of her horror show. "I am a free woman stolen from my home," she said. "Ketil has no right to sell me!"

"Quiet!" Ingeld snarled. "I don't care about your plight."

"You'll be in trouble with the law for buying me."

"Another word and I'll cut out your tongue."

She gasped and took an uncertain step backward on shaky legs.

Ketil grabbed her chin and held her head so she faced the light of the lamp. "Look at her! She has the unearthly beauty of one of Odin's celestial warrior maidens. She will sell easily."

"She looks sickly and I doubt she'll survive the long voyage to market. It's expensive to buy slaves who die on the journey."

"She's just recovering from childbirth. The infant is only two days old."

"It will die on the trip, better to cast it into the sea tonight."

"He is a healthy baby. He will survive and if he doesn't, it matters not since you aren't paying for him. Do you want her or not? I haven't time to haggle. There are other slave dealers if you're not interested."

They dickered over the price, then Ingeld weighed gold coins on a scale and gave them to Ketil.

"It is done," Ketil said.

Annoure grabbed his arm. "Please don't do this."

He looked at her with tortured eyes and opened his mouth to speak, but then clamped it shut.

The slave dealer lifted an iron collar off a hook on the wall and Annoure felt a wave of dizziness spread through her. *This can't be happening.* Ingeld snapped the cold band around her neck and her composure crumbled. "Ketil, if you care for me at all, you'll spare me from this," she cried.

Ketil turned a sickening shade of green, then fled the house.

"The man has no stomach for dealing in thralls," Ingeld said, his voice flat and expressionless. He hooked a chain to her neckband. "Come, you will sleep back here."

Annoure swayed, nearly dropping the baby. He took her into a smoky backroom and Annoure's nose wrinkled at the smell of urine and filth. Five women sat on the floor. Ingeld led her to a mat and fastened the end of the chain to a bracket on the wall.

Annoure sunk onto a straw pallet with the baby in her arms, struggling to accept what happened. How could a man who only two nights earlier had helped deliver her baby into the world now sell her for a few gold coins, as if she was no more than a cow or reindeer? He said he wanted her for a wife, but what man would do this to a woman he cared for? And how would Thorstein ever find her now? She lay down and held Ban close as she began to sob brokenly.

She wept for a long time, but finally her tears were spent. She wiped her nose on her sleeve and focused her attention on Grandmother. *What is to become of me, Grandmother? I've been sold into slavery.* At first she didn't hear anything, but as she moved deeper into a contemplative state, the room faded away and Grandmother spoke to her. *Freedom comes from within. It can't be taken from you.* Her voice was no more than a soft whisper in Annoure's mind, like the sound of a gentle breeze through the trees.

After a while one of the women crawled over to her and put a kindly hand on Annoure's shoulder. "You must be strong. Only the strong survive. I am Fitela. I've been a thrall a long time and will teach you."

"I don't want to be a thrall."

"No one does. Let me see your baby." Fitela lifted the child into her arms. Her comely face softened as she gazed at Ban, then she held the child against her large bosom. "He is a bonny baby. What's his name?"

"I named him Ban after my grandfather, but it is a Saxon name and his father might not approve. He was born the night of the terrible storm."

"It no longer matters what his father might want. We will call him Ban the Strong-hearted since he survived the storm."

The other four women gathered as close as their chains would allow and introduced themselves as Bergthora, Gerd, Iona and Kari. Annoure repeated the names silently, trying to remember them all. They all looked young and she could feel all of the women's distress at their plight. The olive-skinned woman with raven-black hair named Bergthora, asked to hold Ban.

Annoure wanted to take the baby back from Fitela and keep him to herself, but could see no reason not to let Bergthora enjoy holding him for a moment. He had a way of giving comfort. "He's not used to anyone but me. Give him back if he starts to cry."

Bergthora took the baby from Fitela. "He's precious. You must do all you can to help him survive the trip. Take straw from our pallets to put around his bottom and when on the ship, shelter him from the wind under your cloak. I have seen babies much older than him die at sea."

Annoure shuddered, hearing the truth in Bergthora's words.

Chapter 23

Voyage on Varangian Sea (Baltic Sea)

ON THE THIRD MORNING, INGELD and two Norse warriors came into the backroom and ordered the women to rise. Annoure stood with Ban in her arms, relieved to be leaving the dark, foul-smelling place where they'd been held. During her time there, they'd been given water and a small meal twice a day, but never allowed outside.

Ingeld unhooked Annoure's iron chain from the wall bracket and fasten her to Bergthora on one side and Fitela on the other. Once all six women were chained together, they were taken outside. Squinting in the bright sunlight, Annoure stumbled, causing her neckband to jerk painfully against her throat.

She and the others were led down to the wharf on the Varangian Sea where Ingeld's men loaded a cargo ship with trade goods. The baby began to fuss and Annoure swayed back and forth to calm him. A feeling of hopelessness crashed down upon her as she realized leaving Hedeby meant she was being taken further from Thorstein.

Just then the sound of a lyre caught her attention. She listened more closely and heard a man singing to the accompaniment of the melodious instrument. The voice sounded like Erik the skald. She looked around and spotted him singing as he strolled along the wharf.

"Erik!" she shouted.

His eyes widened with amazement upon seeing her and he hurried over. They embraced, pressing Ban between their bodies. “Annoure, you’ve had your baby, but what happened? Why are you chained up?”

“Edgtho and Ketil stole me from the farmstead.” Her throat constricted and she found it difficult to continue. “Erik, they killed little Brandi and Njal when they came to my defense. Then they killed Garth at the wharf when he tried to stop them from taking me away. Ketil sold me and my baby into slavery. Please help me.”

His brow wrinkled. “I feared they would seek revenge, but I thought it would be an attack on Thorstein, not you.”

“I overheard Ingeld the Much Traveled say he was taking us to Bulgur. Find Thorstein and tell him.”

“To Bulgur! By Thor’s hammer, that’s a long journey from here.” He walked over to Ingeld and pointed at Annoure. “What do you want for that woman with a baby?”

“She is not for sale.”

“They are all for sale.”

“You can’t afford her, skald. Be off with you.”

Erik pulled out his coin purse. “I have silver coins.”

“She is worth much more.”

“She is sick and will die before you reach Bulgur. Better take what you can get for her now.”

“I paid more than that for her.”

“She belongs to Thorstein Garthson and was stolen from her home. Let her go or he will come seeking revenge.”

Ingeld whipped out a knife and held it to Erik’s face. “Don’t threaten me, skald!” His men came up on either side of Erik. “Teach him what happens to men who interfere with my business.”

Two of the men seized Erik’s arms. Erik struggled to free himself as a third man slammed his fists repeatedly into his face and stomach.

“Nei! Stop it! Stop!” Annoure screamed. She started forward, but was halted abruptly by the neckband that chained her to the other women. The men finally released Erik and he fell to the ground, blood running from his swollen nose. His broken lyre lay beside him. He tried to rise and they kicked him several times in the back and ribs.

When the men stepped away, Annoure was terrified they’d killed him. “Erik! Erik! Are you alive?” Annoure cried.

He groaned and rose to his knees, then spit blood. “I live . . . I swear

I'll find Thorstein and come in search of you!" He leaned over, holding his stomach, his face puffed and bloody.

"Come, Annoure," Fitela said. "The skald can't help now." She took Annoure's arm and tugged her gently along with the other women. They were taken down a wooden dock and led across a gangplank onto the ship. Annoure felt like her heart was breaking as images of Erik's beating kept replaying in her mind. She held the baby close as she sat on the floor of the cargo hold. A thin man missing two front teeth unlocked the chain attached to her neckband. Once all the women were unlocked, he handed each of them a fur to sleep on.

Before long the men cast off. Soon wind filled the raised square sail and the ship soared across the Varangian Sea.

Annoure closed her eyes and imagined she was home with Thorstein. She pictured him lifting her onto his lap and kissing her. Her distress eased as she envisioned his arms around her. Inwardly she felt his love wash over her and she knew they were still connected. Their love for one another would lead him to her.

Later in the day, the sky blackened and the wind began to howl. The air was heavy with moisture and Annoure felt a storm coming. Before long the sea became rough and large waves tossed the ship around like a toy boat. Savage wind beat against the sail.

Rain began pouring down. Annoure slid the baby under her cape and drew the hood over her head. The men put a tarpaulin over the center of the ship and the six women huddled together for warmth beneath it. As the violent rocking of the ship grew worse Bergthora and Iona grew seasick. They both retched repeatedly on the deck and the smell of vomit made Annoure gag.

"We're all going to die!" Fitela exclaimed, shaking with terror, her eyes large.

"Nei, the ship is well built and made to stand up in storms," Annoure said, putting a comforting hand on Fitela's arm.

The baby began crying and Annoure opened the slit in the front of her under-dress and put him to her breast. As he nursed, she stroked the soft fuzz on the top of his head and gazed down at his round face with tiny perfectly formed features and at his small hands and feet.

By nightfall the sea grew calmer, though it continued to rain. The men set out their hudfats. Some came over to the women to pick one for the night. Annoure kept her head low so her tangled hair hid her face. She didn't want any of the men noticing her; her fair looks were a curse among these Norsemen.

One of the men grabbed Annoure's arm and hauled her to her feet. "Come with me."

Fitela laughed huskily and stood. "Let me keep you warm. She has a newborn baby at her breast."

The warrior let go of Annoure. "Come then, I much prefer a willing partner."

"Thank you, Fitela," Annoure said softly, feeling guilty about Fitela taking her place in the man's hudfat. She sank back down to her fur. It took a long time for her to relax enough to sleep, but she finally slipped into the dream worlds.

Thorstein waited there for her, looking just as he had earlier in the day when she imagined being with him. He drew her into the shelter of his arms. As she gazed at him, he changed into the form he'd taken in the dream worlds when she lived in Northumbria.

"I found you once," he said. "I'll find you again." The dream felt more real, the colors more vibrant and her senses more alert than when she was awake. She felt detached from her current troubles. It was as if they were not as important as the love that existed between her and Thorstein—a love that extended beyond the physical world.

Annoure awoke with a sense of deep inner peace that vanished when she realized the ship was rocking wildly back and forth and a hard rain pounded the tarpaulin. Although the sky was still dark, she thought it was probably morning.

Peering past the edge of the tarpaulin, she saw black storm clouds rolling in on a furious wind. The sea boiled like a witch's brew and large waves crashed and broke over the sides of the ship. The deck was covered in water. Some of the women scooped it up with buckets and dumped it over the side.

A loud bang of thunder cracked, startling Ban and he began to cry. She lifted him into her arms.

"I see you've finally awakened," Fitela said. "You slept well into the morning."

"I awaken several times during the night to feed and comfort little Ban." Annoure yawned, then smiled, remembering her dream.

"I dreamed of Ban's father." Her stomach rumbled and she said, "I'm starving. Did I miss first meal?"

"Já, I saved something for you." Fitela handed her a piece of salted beef jerky.

Another boom of thunder sounded overhead and Fitela gazed at the sky. "The storm is worse than it was yesterday. Nidhad told me we're going to take shelter at Arkona on the island of Rügen. It's a Slav settlement. Ingeld dislikes going there because they charge a large tribute."

Annoure stopped chewing on the jerky and asked, "Who's Nidhad?"

"He's the man whose hudfat I shared last night."

"I don't like the Slavs," Bergthora said, moving closer to join their conversation. "But I'll be glad to be on dry land."

"The Slavs are men just like our Norsemen," Fitela replied. "They all want the same thing from a woman." Kari and Iona laughed.

"Thank you, Fitela, for sparing me from Nidhad," Annoure said. "It must have been terrible for you."

"A thrall learns not to be bothered by a man satisfying his lust with her. Nidhad is young and his hudfat was a warm place to spend the night."

"I will never accept being used by a man!" Annoure exclaimed.

"Look, there's land!" Bergthora said, interrupting their conversation. She pointed toward a landmass off in the distance.

"Thank Mother Mary," Annoure said. "Ban needs to get out of this storm."

"As do I," Fitela said, nervously looking at the large waves.

The men sailed the ship to a large wharf and docked. Once the ship was secure, Nidhad chained the women together by their neck collars. Rain hammered down on Annoure who held Ban under her cape and carried her sleeping fur. She walked with the others to an earth rampart. Beside it stood a tall tower, which was the entrance to Arkona.

Ingeld pounded on the gate and yelled, "We come to trade." A guard opened the door and the crew and female thralls were admitted inside. They headed down a wet, wooden platform, flanked by rows of block log houses on both sides. Each straw-roofed house shared its sidewalls with the house on either side. Finally, they came to open ground.

After the men put up a tent, the women went inside. Annoure was glad to be out of the rain that pattered on its leather sides. She spread her fur on the damp ground and rocked Ban, hoping he was warm enough.

After a while Ingeld entered the tent. He'd trimmed his beard and changed into a finely made jerkin and a jeweled sword hung at his side. He scanned the women, then his gaze rested on Annoure. He unlocked the band around her neck.

"Come with me." She rose with Ban in her arms.

"Leave the baby."

Her stomach clenched. "Nei, please, don't sell me without my child."

"I'm not selling you here, but in Bulgar where I can get a better price."

Annoure kissed the baby on the forehead and handed him to Fitela. "Take care of him for me."

"I will."

Annoure pulled up the hood on her cape and followed Ingeld out of the tent. She hated to leave Ban—she'd never been separated from him before and was concerned Ingeld had lied about his plans to sell her. The cold rain hit against her cheeks and nose as they walked to the crowded marketplace.

"Norsemen, Slavs, Arabs and Prussians come here to trade," Ingeld said as they passed booths selling jewelry, clothing, pottery, baskets, food and weapons. Ingeld stopped at a booth and held a blue kaftan up to Annoure. "This will fit you." The floor-length garment was made of silk and had long sleeves. Ingeld dickered with the merchant over the price, then went to another booth and purchased hair ornaments and a necklace. He handed them to her and kept walking.

"What am I to do with these?" she asked.

"We are going to pay tribute to the priest. I want him to see that I am a prosperous man with valuable thralls."

Ingeld led her inside a small log building and she immediately felt heat radiating from a blazing fire in the hearth. Wisps of smoke rose from the flames and escaped through a hole under the gable. Ingeld ordered Annoure to bathe and change into the new clothes he just purchased. Then he sat down at a table and ordered a drink.

A serving woman gave Annoure soap and a linen cloth then led her to a tub of water located behind a curtain on one side of the room. Annoure sat in the cool, gray-colored water and scrubbed herself with soap, noticing her belly was still round from her recent pregnancy.

She dried herself with the linen cloth before putting on the kaftan, hair ornaments and necklace. Once dressed, she stepped out from behind the curtain and crossed over to Ingeld. He looked up from his cup of mead and nodded. "I suspected you'd be a beauty once you'd bathed and dressed properly. Where are you from?"

"Northumbria."

"Then you were captured on a raid and are not a Norseman's woman as the skald claimed."

"Erik spoke the truth. I'm betrothed to Thorstein Garthson and he will rescue me!"

"He might try, but he'll never find you. What's your name?"

"Annoure."

"Come, Annoure, let's go to the temple. Arkona is the religious center of Rügen Island and the priest there is very powerful." He placed the cape over her shoulders and she drew up the hood as they stepped into the rain. They hurried along the wooden platform to the many-towered temple, the largest building in town.

Inside, Annoure glanced around the room, which glowed with golden candlelight. Large columns supported the high ceiling and statues stood near the outer walls. Annoure stared at a seven-headed wooden statue dressed in armor with a helmet on each head.

"That's one of their gods," Ingeld said. As they walked by a three-headed god Ingeld continued talking. "The Slav's have a god for fertility, sky, fire and war. And that is a statue of a demon." He pointed to a statue of a crouched creature with large claws and teeth. "Ah, there's the head priest," Ingeld said, gesturing toward a purple-robed man with a long beard. Behind him was an enormous statue that stood twice as tall as the priest; each of its heads faced a different direction.

"The idol is Svantevit, the main god the Slavs worship. He holds a fertility horn, which the priest fills with wine each year to foresee the crops of the next season. Grain is stored in the temple in case of a bad harvest during the next summer. The priest is a crafty man. He gets one-third of all captured booty and every man and woman must give silver to the idol."

Ingeld led her over to the priest and a robed assistant stepped forward. "What's your business here?"

"I'm Ingeld the Much Traveled. I come from Hedeby with my crew on a trading expedition. We stopped in Arkona because of the storm."

The assistant translated what Ingeld said in Slavic to the priest, who nodded. Ingeld continued, "I came to the temple to pay tribute to Svantevit." Ingeld pulled a coin bag off his belt. The assistant translated his words for the priest and took the bag.

The priest answered Ingeld in Slav, which was also translated by his assistant. "Ingeld the Much Traveled, the high priest says you and your men are welcome to stay and trade."

The high priest turned powerful eyes on Annoure and she took an uneasy step backward, worried that he might want her as part of Ingeld's tribute. The priest spoke again and the assistant said, "The high priest says if all your merchandise is of as high quality as this thrall, you will get many customers."

"Thank him for letting us stay," Ingeld said to the assistant. "Tell him we'll leave when the weather clears. We have a long distance yet to travel."

Annoure wiped her sweaty palms on her kaftan as Ingeld led her from the temple. When they reached camp, Annoure hurried inside the tent and clasped the sleeping baby to her heart. The other five women all looked at her. "Did Ingeld buy you those clothes and jewelry?" Fitela asked.

"Já, he wanted the priest to know he had valuable thralls."

Fitela frowned deeply. "I can't protect you from Ingeld."

Tension spread across Annoure's shoulders. "I know."

At dusk a warrior entered the tent. "Annoure, come with me. Ingeld wants to speak with you."

She stood with Ban in her arms. The warrior instructed, "Leave the baby here."

"I'll watch him," Gerd said. The round-faced girl reached for the infant. Annoure's hands shook as she handed Ban to her.

Annoure avoided the puddles the best she could as she followed the warrior through the drizzle to a tent with drawings of serpents on the exterior. She entered the tent and found Ingeld alone inside.

"Sit," he said, gesturing to a large pillow. After removed her wet cape, Annoure walked across the thick furs that covered the ground and warily sat on a pillow across from him.

“Share my meal,” Ingeld said. “There’s plenty.”

Roasted pork, fresh bread, figs, grapes and onions lay on a tray in front of Ingeld. As Annoure breathed in the delicious aromas, her stomach rumbled. She hadn’t had a good meal since she was kidnapped from the farmstead.

She heaped food onto a wooden plate and bit into a grape. Its sweet juice exploded in her mouth. They both ate in silence, finally Ingeld asked. “How is it you were sold into slavery?”

She finished chewing before answering. “I was taken from my home for revenge.”

“Didn’t anyone try to stop your captures?”

“Three were killed trying to save me.”

“How old is your child?”

“He’s a week old.”

“Then you’re still bleeding.”

She nodded, her appetite disappearing. The way Norsemen openly discussed intimate things always disconcerted her.

“It is bad luck to couple with a woman who’s bleeding. I’ll wait.”

The tension eased from her shoulders. “Tell me about these Arabs you’re going to sell us to.”

“Most Arab have dark skin and black hair. They consider white skin the color of slaves and non-Arabs. They dress in kaftans, as you are currently dressed, and often wear turbans on their heads because it’s hot where they’re from. They speak Arabic and believe in Islam. Their god is Allah, whose prophet is Muhammad. Many of their tribes are nomadic.”

Her stomach turned at the thought of being sold to these strange foreigners. She nibbled on a fig, which now seemed tasteless, then asked, “I heard we are headed to Bulgar. Where is Bulgar?”

“It’s a long distance from here. We’ll travel down the Dvina River to a large river called the Volga. From there we’ll travel down the Volga until we reach Bulgar, which is a meeting place for Norsemen, Slavs and Arab merchants.”

“How far have you traveled?”

“I’ve been as far as Constantinople. We traveled down the Dnieper River then across the Black Sea. But usually I just go as far as Bulgar where we trade thralls, furs, pottery, honey, arrows and amber. Arab merchants want our thralls and furs the most. I've heard a marten skin traded on the Volga for a green glass bead or small amount of silver will sell in Arab markets for a thousand times what it was purchased for."

Annoure wondered if the same was true for thralls.

* * *

Ingeld and his men spent the next day trading in Arkona. That night Ingeld's crew again selected a companion for the night from among the thralls, but they left Annoure alone and she uneasily realized that Ingeld had marked her for his own.

Early the following morning, they broke camp and returned to their ship. The weather was good and the wind strong, so they sailed all the next day and slept onboard that night.

Late the next day, Annoure was standing on the portside of the ship, rocking Ban in her arms, when she spotted a harbor.

"What town is that?" Annoure asked Ingeld who was close by.

"That's Kolobrzeg, a trading settlement where we're stopping next. It has a large harbor and a salt mine. Merchants travel great distances to trade for salt. The settlement is protected by a rampart and soldiers."

Annoure noticed the fortress was surrounded by fields of grain. Beyond the fields was a dense forest.

"There's a war going on, so Slavs build their homes inside fortresses," Ingeld continued. "The Slavs are always fighting amongst themselves: neighbor against neighbor, tribe against tribe, and kingdom against kingdom. When they aren't fighting each other, they fight the Varangian and Finnish tribes. This land is cultivated by farmer-warriors who band together for safety."

Once they had arrived in Kolobrzeg, they left the ship and crossed a bridge that spanned the moat surrounding the fortress. Ingeld walked beside Annoure, explaining that the community had over a thousand residents plus many merchants who were there for trade.

Annoure left Ban with Fitela and accompanied Ingeld to market wearing her silk kaftan as she had done before. She suspected Ingeld thought of her as riches to be displayed—as he did the thick gold chain around his neck—to show he was a prosperous man.

Ingeld purchased sable, ermine, fox furs, deerskins, beaver and goat pelts, which his men carried back to camp. Once his purchases were made, Ingeld strolled through the marketplace, leading Annoure past tables of pottery, jewelry and clothing. He stopped at a silversmith's booth where finely made earrings, cloak clasps and pendants were displayed.

Ingeld bought a pair of earrings and fastened them on Annoure's ears. "These are exquisite enough to enhance your beauty, Annoure. My patience wears thin waiting for you. Are you still unclean?"

"Já. It would be unlucky to touch me," Annoure said. She intended to use his superstition to her advantage for as long as possible.

On the way back to camp, Annoure saw three women on an auction block and she empathized with their misfortune. Annoure glanced at Ingeld, her stomach tightening. She knew she couldn't put him off forever.

Chapter 24

Retribution

AFTER LEAVING KETIL AND EDGTHO'S farmstead, Thorstein traveled long days at sea, hoping to find Annoure before she disappeared into foreign lands. He journeyed alone because Thyri's brothers had gone a-viking and weren't available to accompany him.

For safety, he sailed close to shore and spent the nights on land. A favorable wind and the long hours of daylight allowed him to travel sixteen to eighteen hours a day, and he covered a great distance quickly.

One day at sea, the sky turned black and rain began to pour, blurring his vision. His hair and beard soon became soaked and the cool rainwater crept below the neckline of his tunic, trickling down his back. The water churned and the small boat plunged and rose on the swells of enormous waves.

Thorstein untied the ropes that held up the sail and lowered it before rowing to shore. As he approached land, waves pulled the boat forward, nearly capsizing it. Thorstein jumped into the water up to his waist and pulled the boat safely between some large rocks.

After setting up his tent under a sheltering pine tree, he crawled inside and stripped off his soaked clothing. That night a howling wind battered the tent, loud thunder cracked repeatedly and waves pounded the rocky shoreline.

The next morning Thorstein stood under the pine boughs for shelter from the rain, debating the risk of continuing before the storm let up. Large, white-cap waves made the sea unsafe for a small boat. He laid out dried fish and prayed to Thor for an end to the storm so he could continue his travels.

It was late afternoon before the storm let up and allowed him to leave his forest refuge and venture back into the sea.

A day's journey from Hedeby, he spotted a small Norse boat on the shoreline and a tent set up at the edge of the woods. He glanced at the sky and estimated that there was less than an hour left of sunlight. As much as he wanted to get to Hedeby and find Annoure, he decided to join these travelers for the night and enjoy the company of his own people after so many days alone at sea. As he tied his boat next to theirs, he heard a branch snap and turned. He gasped upon seeing Edgtho step out of the forest with an armful of firewood. Thorstein's heart began to pound furiously, as if Thor was beating his hammer against it.

Edgtho dropped the branches and drew his sword from his sheath. Thorstein also drew his sword. Anger rolled through him. "Edgtho! So this is *your* camp!" He glanced at the tent. "Where is Annoure?"

Edgtho smiled sadistically. "Sold into slavery."

"Where did you sell her?" Thorstein asked, warily approaching Edgtho.

"In Hedeby." The two men circled each other.

"Where's Ketil?"

"Nearby." His eyes narrowed. "But I won't need his help to kill you."

Thorstein tightened his grip on his sword, glad for the opportunity to avenge his family. He measured his opponent. Edgtho looked confident; this was his kind of fight and he was used to winning.

All at once, Edgtho swung his heavy sword toward Thorstein and the fight was on. Their swords crashed together as steel met steel and sparks flew. Thorstein jumped back to disengage and then parried another blow, and yet another, as Edgtho's sword whipped narrowly past his ear.

Thorstein leapt forward and they met chest-to-chest with their swords locked. Thorstein strained to repel Edgtho's blade. He finally broke away and staggered back. Edgtho was a large man and a renowned fighter. Edgtho feinted to the left, then spun around and thrust his sword into Thorstein's chest. The blade hit Thorstein's armor with force, piercing his skin. Thorstein staggered backward, his chest throbbing.

"Annoure's skin is as smooth as silk," Edgtho taunted. "She trembled like a bitch in heat when I stroked her thighs."

"More likely she trembled with fear!" Thorstein attacked with renewed vigor, thinking of the frightened thrall he'd questioned on Edgtho's farm. By Odin's Raven, he'd kill Edgtho or die trying.

He forced Edgtho back. They fought from one side of the campsite to the other, neither giving ground. Thorstein moved past thought, all that existed was just this fight, the test of one man's skill and strength against the other. Thorstein had sparred so often with his kin over the winter that now he fought on instinct, ignoring the sweat pouring down his temples and his own heavy breathing.

"Annoure is probably dead by now—she had a difficult childbirth," Edgtho said.

Thorstein faltered in alarm and Edgtho leapt forward, slicing a gash across his forehead.

Thorstein sliced his sword upward and blocked the next thrust. "Did the baby survive?" he choked out, concerned for his child as well.

"Já, but you won't live to see it."

Thorstein ignored the stinging head wound and metallic smell of blood that dripped into his eyes as he concentrated on the battle. The fight took them into the woods where the setting sun made it difficult to see.

"You're a dead man, Thorstein," Edgtho yelled, panting for breath. He attacked with several powerful strokes that sent Thorstein's sword flying out of his hand. It landed on the ground a short distant away.

Edgtho swung his blade toward Thorstein's throat. "This is for Rethel."

Thorstein leapt backward and dodged behind a tree. Edgtho came after him. Thorstein dropped to the ground and grabbed his sword. He rolled onto his back and swung it upward as Edgtho came at him. The sword plunged into Edgtho's belly beneath his armor and continued up into his heart.

Edgtho collapsed to the ground, clutching the wound, then lay still. Thorstein rose and pulled his bloodied sword out of Edgtho's lifeless body. He heard a cry of rage and turned to face Ketil, who came rushing through the trees toward him, sword in hand. A new fight was on before Thorstein had time to recover from the first one.

Steel crashed repeatedly against steel until Thorstein was staggering.

Blood seeped from the cut on his forehead and chest. “We must talk, Ketil,” he gasped.

“It is too late for talk!” Ketil roared. ”You killed Rethel and Edgtho.”

“Both men died in a fair fight. You and Edgtho killed Njal two on one, slaughtered an innocent child armed only with a wooden sword, and mortally wounded my faðir. Then you a stole a helpless woman from her home.”

“She’s an evil witch.”

“Nei, she’s a good woman.”

“She bewitched you.” Ketil leapt forward and Thorstein was hard pressed to defend himself. They were fighting in near darkness now and Thorstein kept backing up, moving the fight to the beach where it wasn’t so dark.

At the campsite Ketil continued to force Thorstein backward until he fought in knee-deep water. He bumped into the side of one of the boats and couldn’t retreat any further. He took a stand, knowing he was losing. Exhausted from fighting, Thorstein’s breath came in ragged pants. Their swords clashed again and again. Thorstein’s sword was nicked in several places and he was concerned it would break from so much abuse. He wished for his shield.

Finally Ketil began to slow his attack and stagger as if he was exhausted as well. Raising his sword with trembling arms, Thorstein kept fighting, using the last of his strength to force Ketil onto the shore.

“Please, I beg you, Ketil. Tell me who you sold Annoure to so I can find her.” Thorstein wove back and forth, barely able to stand, let alone counter Ketil’s attack.

“You’ll never find her or your sonr!” Ketil spit. His sword pierced Thorstein’s armor and sliced into his side. Thorstein went down on his knees.

“I have a sonr?” he gasped.

“Já, a sonr you will never know.” Ketil swung his sword toward Thorstein’s neck.

Thorstein crumpled to the ground and blackness swallowed him. He found himself out of his body, rising up to a place filled with light and love. A warrior maiden appeared and he was sure she was a Valkyrie come to take him to Valhalla. He was drawn to her shimmering light. As he moved closer, ecstasy flowed through him.

"There is so much more for you to learn in this life," she said gently. "Think of those you love."

He immediately thought of Annoure and knew he couldn't go with the Valkyrie.

Thorstein groaned when he came to, not sure if he was still alive. But surely if he was dead, he wouldn't be in so much agony. The last thing he remembered was Ketil's sword sweeping toward him. His side felt sticky with blood and he feared he was bleeding to death.

From his prone position, he saw Ketil carry Edgtho's body to his boat and place him inside. Ketil put sticks and branches around his cousin's body.

"Nei, my boat," Thorstein choked out, realizing Ketil meant to burn it.

Ignoring Thorstein, Ketil used a piece of flint against a rock to make a spark and get a fire started. Once the fire was established, he carried a burning branch to the boat.

He stood naked in the moonlight, looking down at his cousin, then he lit the kindling and pushed the boat out to sea. The branches burst into flame as the boat floated away. Thorstein watched helplessly as the angry red and yellow flames climb up the sail, lighting the night sky. Without his boat, Thorstein realized, he had no way of rescuing Annoure. He slipped back into unconsciousness.

Thorstein awoke early in the morning in terrible pain. He still lay where he'd fallen; the water lapped at his feet. Nearby Ketil sat on a boulder, staring at the sea.

Thorstein closed his eyes. It took too much effort to keep them open. When he woke again, he felt a little stronger. Ketil still hadn't moved. After a while, Ketil glanced at him. Seeing he was awake, Ketil came over. "So you're still alive."

"Já," Thorstein said in weak voice.

Ketil squatted down and pulled up Thorstein's tunic. Thorstein cried out as sharp needles of pain shot through him. "It's a bad wound," Ketil said. "I doubt you'll see another dawn."

"It doesn't matter if my Annoure is dead." Great sorrow settled around him like a thick fog.

"She's not dead, merely sold into slavery."

"Edgtho said Annoure had a hard childbirth and was probably dead by now."

"First babies never come easily, but she and the child were alive and well enough when I left them."

Hope swelled in Thorstein's breast.

"Have you no thought for yourself?" Ketil asked. "Why don't you ask me to help you?"

"I don't expect help from you. You want me dead."

"Last night I did." Ketil sighed deeply and his eyes became clouded. "I have thought all night of this feud between our families and realize I acted without honor. I blamed you for Rethel's death when it was a fair fight. You paid tribute to my faðir and it should've ended there. But my heart grew black in the winter and I acted out of hatred. I am ashamed for what I've done, so I've decided to help you in your quest to find Annoure."

"I don't want your help," Thorstein said, sullenly.

"You don't have any choice." Ketil grabbed Thorstein by his shoulders and started to drag him into the tent.

"By Thor's Hammer, Ketil, have mercy!" Thorstein exclaimed as he was hauled over a sharp rock. A trail of blood followed him into the tent. Once inside, Ketil stripped off Thorstein's shirt and chest armor and washed the cut in his side with seawater. Thorstein swore a string of oaths as the saltwater stung his wound.

"You are weaker than a woman," Ketil said, continuing to wash away the blood.

Ashamed, Thorstein clenched his jaw and gritted his teeth together. Ketil wrapped a linen cloth around his torso, then washed blood off his forehead and bound his head injury. He lost consciousness as Ketil covered him with a fur.

Sometime later he awoke to the smell of cooking meat. Ketil entered the tent carrying a wooden bowl. "I shot a deer yesterday when I was hunting and made a broth for you," Ketil said.

Thorstein looked at Ketil with cold hatred, not wanting to accept his help. "I swore to Njal's vif Thyri that I'd kill you."

"You won't be able to do that unless you're alive, so you'd better eat." Ketil held the bowl to Thorstein's lips, but he wouldn't open his mouth, though his stomach contracted uncomfortably at the scent of cooked venison. "You're a fool!" Ketil exclaimed. "Will you lie here and die out of pride and spite? Annoure needs your help. Will you desert her?"

“I have no way to help her. You destroyed my boat.” The agony of despair ripped through him at the thought of being unable to rescue her.

Ketil was silent for awhile as if pondering this problem. At last he said, “I told you I will help you with your quest. When you are strong enough, we can sail to Hedeby and buy her back.”

“You kidnapped and sold her! Why would you now buy her back?”

“I have my reasons.”

“Why should I trust you?”

“If I wanted you dead all I’d have to do is leave you here.”

“I’ll trust my fate to the gods rather than accept your help.”

“You’re a stubborn fool!” Ketil packed up his supplies and carried them out of the tent.

Thorstein struggled to a sitting position. His head began spinning and his side throbbed. He cursed the gods as he tried to rise.

Ketil came back into the tent for more supplies and paused upon seeing Thorstein.

“You are in no condition to sit up.” Ketil sighed and closed his eyes a moment, then opened them again. “I’m sorry for the death of your kinsmen—no one was supposed to die. Will you stop being so proud and let me help?”

“You killed my bróðir, faðir, nephew and sold Annoure and child into slavery. Why would I accept your help?”

“Edgtho killed the boy by accident, not realizing he was only a child. He’s also the one who killed your bróðir and threw a knife into your faðir. He’s paid for his wrongdoing with his life. As for me, I am equally guilty for attacking your family, but my crime against Annoure is what keeps me awake at night. For her, I will do what I can to save you.”

Ketil left the tent. Thorstein collapsed back onto the furs, cursing his weakness, the gods and Ketil. Then he thought of Annoure and how he’d felt her near him one night when it was raining so badly he couldn’t travel. She believed in him and counted on him to rescue her and the baby. Could he put aside the terrible rage boiling inside him and accept Ketil’s help for Annoure’s sake? He sensed Ketil wasn’t telling him something—some other reason he wanted to help besides guilt. Thorstein drifted off to sleep, thinking of Annoure.

He found himself bound to a rock in the middle of the sea. A serpent slithered over and bit him. He felt its poison spreading throughout his body as he struggled against the ropes. Then the mist surrounding the rock parted and he saw Annoure standing on a boat with his child in her arms. She reached out to him as the boat sailed away. "Annoure!" he cried, as a great anguish rolled through him.

Thorstein awoke with a jerk, drenched in sweat.

Ketil knelt beside him. "You cried out in your sleep."

"We must leave immediately! The longer we wait the less chance we have of finding Annoure."

Thorstein tried sitting up, but Ketil put a restraining hand on his chest. "You're too weak. Your wound will start bleeding again if you don't let it heal."

"There is no time to heal."

Ketil moved aside. "Then go after her."

Thorstein pushed himself to a sitting position and the world began to spin. He lowered his head for a moment, then tried standing. He collapsed on the hudfat. "Please help me to the boat, Ketil."

"You will be dead before nightfall if I do. Rest. We'll find Annoure when you're stronger."

"I must find her as quickly as possible and return home. I'm the eldest sonr now and the farm is my responsibility. My móðir and the other women are alone there for the summer."

"Thorstein, I nearly killed you! Worry about yourself instead of the farm, your kin and Annoure."

Ketil picked up the broth. "Eat and recover your strength. If the gods are merciful, you may yet live." He shoved a fur behind Thorstein's back and helped him drink the now cool broth.

The next day, Thorstein awoke to find Ketil watching him. "I see the gods have let you live yet another day. Why they would favor a mean cuss like you is beyond my understanding," Ketil said, looking pleased. "Perhaps you will live after all. I didn't think you would. How do you feel?"

"Weaker than a newborn baby."

Ketil checked the wound in Thorstein's side and then left the tent. He came back a little while later with a steaming cloth he held on the end of a stick.

"I boiled the cloth. It will keep your wound from turning bad." Ketil squeezed out the cloth, then placed it on Thorstein's side. Thorstein drew in a sharp breath as heat seared his wound.

On the third day, Ketil broke camp and helped Thorstein to the boat. An uneasy truce had formed between them. They sailed to Hedeby, reaching it in the afternoon.

Inside the bustling town, Ketil led Thorstein to the house where he had sold Annoure to Ingeld the Much Traveled. A new merchant was there who didn't know anything about Ingeld.

Thorstein and Ketil left the merchant, not knowing how to find Annoure. Discouraged, they went to a crowded inn that reeked of mead and greasy food. They found a crude wooden table where they could discuss where to search next over dinner and sat down.

"If only we'd gotten here before Ingeld left," Thorstein groaned. Sensing someone approaching, he turned and saw Erik. The skald had a black eye, bruised cheek, and moved stiffly, as if in discomfort. "Erik, well met, but what happened to you? Have you been in a fight?" Thorstein asked. He leaned against the back of the booth too weak to stand and greet his friend properly.

"I could ask the same of you. You look near death." Erik's eyes went to Ketil's and his body tensed.

"Sit down and we'll share our misfortunes," Thorstein said.

"I don't like the company you keep."

"I haven't much choice."

"Then you don't know what harm Ketil has done to you."

Thorstein stood unsteadily. "Do you know something of Annoure?"

Erik drew his sword and held it threateningly at Ketil. "Though I'm not a fighting man, I have forsaken my lyre and taken up the sword because of what you've done. I promised Annoure I would find Thorstein and bring him to her."

The inn became quiet. Everyone watched them.

"Erik, lower the sword!" Thorstein ordered. "It serves no purpose to threaten Ketil."

"I challenge you to a duel," Erik said to Ketil. "Outside!"

Ketil didn't show any fear of the skald. "Erik the skald: a man of words, not swords. I won't battle you, for if I did you would die an early death. I have enough blood on my conscience without adding yours and I would miss your songs and tales of the gods."

"Erik, your bravery does you honor," Thorstein said, clasping his sleeve. "But tell me of Annoure!"

"You should be the one calling him out, not me. If you but knew, you would tell me to run him through where he sits."

Thorstein grabbed Erik's shoulder, forcing him backward a few steps. "Did you see Annoure? Delay your answer no longer." The movement caused a sharp spasm in Thorstein's side. A fuzzy grayness clouded his vision and he felt his knees give out.

Ketil sprang up and grabbed Thorstein as he started to fall. "Thorstein!"

Erik grabbed Thorstein's other arm and together they lowered him to the bench.

"What's wrong with him?" Erik asked Ketil. "Why is his head bandaged?"

"He was wounded in two different sword fights."

"Tell me of Annoure," Thorstein said weakly.

"I saw Annoure and your baby here in Hedeby a few days ago," Erik said.

Thorstein closed his eyes, waiting for the brutal pain to ease. Once it faded to a bearable level, he looked at Erik. "Where did you see her?"

Erik sheathed his sword and sat next to Thorstein. "She was boarding a ship headed to Bulgar."

"Bulgar? I have heard of Bulgar in sagas. Where is it?"

"It's a distant trading town in the land of the Rus. You reach it by sailing across the Varangian Sea, then through a series of rivers." He glanced scornfully at Ketil. "So why are you traveling with this scum who killed your kin and stole Annoure?"

Thorstein briefly told Erik all that had transpired and how he came to be traveling with Ketil. "So you see, I am in the unusual position of owing my life to a man who has wronged me. Moreover, I still need him and his boat to help rescue Annoure and my child."

The barmaid came over and Erik ordered some food before resuming the conversation. "I understand now why you're traveling with Ketil, yet it puzzles me as to why he wants to help you. All he wanted before was revenge."

"You'll have to ask him."

Erik looked across the table at Ketil. "Why are you helping Thorstein? It makes no sense."

"I have my reasons."

"I would sooner sleep with a poisonous serpent than travel with you," Eric said. "You've proven yourself to be a man without honor."

"Set off without me if you don't like my company, but I have a boat and silver coins, and I offer both freely."

"I've already accepted your help, Ketil," Thorstein said. "Stop quarreling." He looked at Erik. "How it is that your face is so abused?"

"I angered the slave dealer, Ingeld the Much Traveled, by saying you would come after him in revenge. His men beat me and stole the silver coins I offered for Annoure. He also broke my lyre, so I'm without the means to earn a living. I planned to work my way north on a trading ship and from there journey to your home. But we are well met here in Hedeby. I will come with you to rescue Annoure and your child."

"We should leave tonight," Thorstein said.

"We'll leave tomorrow after we buy supplies and get a good night's sleep," Ketil said.

Thorstein pressed the heel of his hand against his aching forehead. By the gods, he hated the delay. Every day that passed meant it would be harder to find Annoure.

Chapter 25

Inner Doorways

AFTER SAILING EAST THROUGH THE Gulf of Finland to the Neva River, Ingeld and his men tacked the ship upstream against the current. But when they reached the rapids, the wind turned against them so they decided to camp for the night, setting up tents on the mossy floor of a pine and spruce forest.

Annoure sat beside the evening fire with the five other women. She'd been feeling despondent for days, apprehensive about Thorstein's ability to find her. His life force felt weak and her connection to him was faint.

One of the warriors approached her. "Ingeld sends for you."

Annoure's throat constricted as she hugged the baby to her chest.

"I'll watch Ban for you," Fitela said, reaching for him.

"I can't go to Ingeld." Annoure looked around for a means of escape.

"A thrall's life is not her own," Fitela said softly, taking the baby from her. "Give Ingeld what he wants and he won't hurt you."

Annoure stood on wobbly legs and followed the large Norseman to Ingeld's tent. She paused at the entrance, gathering her courage, then entered. The light from an iron lamp eerily lit the mole on Ingeld's large nose.

Annoure sat on the furs, trying to control her trembling and hoping he only wanted to talk.

"You know why you're here," he said.

Her throat tightened, making a reply impossible.

"I've waited patiently for you to recover from childbirth. I am not a cruel master. I expect you to show your gratitude by pleasing me."

"I'm still not fully recovered."

"You've had two weeks—it's enough time." He took a drink from his flask then held it out to her. When she shook her head, he put the cap on and set it aside. "Come here."

"Never!" she said, reverting to Anglo-Saxon. She pulled open the tent flap and saw a warrior posted outside.

Ingeld smiled cruelly. "Didn't your previous master teach you to be an obedient thrall?"

"I was never a thrall to him."

"Then I'm the one who'll have to soften you for your future Arab master. Be submissive and I will be gentle. Fight me and you'll regret it."

Ingeld touched her tender, milk-engorged breast and she shoved his hand away. He hit her across the face with the back of his hand, sending her sprawling onto the furs, then knelt between her thighs and shoved up her hangerock and under-dress. "Don't fight me!" Ingeld growled. "It's a battle you can't win!"

"Go to hell!"

His mouth descended over hers in a rough, bruising kiss and his thick beard scraped her face. She bit his lip and tried to twist away.

He grabbed her around the neck and pressed his thumbs against her windpipe. She desperately yanked on his wrists, trying to loosen his hold. She couldn't breathe. Flashes of light appeared before her eyes, then she passed out.

She returned to consciousness, feeling weak and vulnerable. Ingeld helped her sit up and put a flask to her lips. She swallowed a mouthful of fiery brew. He pulled her close and when she cried, "Nei!" he forced his tongue into her open mouth. His hand moved under the bottom of her under-dress and she thrust her knee up toward his groin. He twisted to the side and her knee hit harmlessly against his thigh.

"Try that again and I'll kill you!"

"I'd rather be dead than raped by you."

He frowned pensively. "You are worth nothing to me dead and you won't sell for a good price bruised from repeated beatings. What do you want? New brooches, a necklace?"

She glared at him contemptuously.

"I see by your expression that none of those things interests you. What do you care about?" Then he smiled triumphantly. "Your baby?"

She glanced toward his sword.

"Undress or I will bash your baby's head against a tree."

Annoure lunged for the sword and Ingeld grabbed her before she could pull it from its sheath.

"Would you try to kill me?" Ingeld demanded.

"I'll kill anyone who threatens Ban."

"I should kill you and your baby! You're more trouble than you're worth."

She swallowed hard as the blood drained from her face. "Let him live. He's just a baby."

"Please me and I'll see that both of you survive the dangerous journey to Bulgar." He released her. "Undress or I'll cast the baby into the sea!"

Annoure's hands slowly reached toward her shoulders. She pulled her hangerock over her head and stood before him clad only in an under-dress. Ingeld handed her the flask and she took a swallow. It burned as it ran down her raw throat and she coughed. She drank another swig to dull her senses.

Ingeld removed his clothing, revealing a torso and legs covered with thick hair and tattoos. Several scars crisscrossed his muscular shoulders and chest.

"Take off the gown."

She picked up the flask and had another drink.

"Come, pretty, do as you're told. Shall I help you?" He slid the under-dress over her head, then his gaze devoured the curves of her naked body. He lowered her onto the furs and moved on top of her.

She gasped in pain when he entered her, feeling as if she was being ripped open. His large, thick body violently hammered against hers, each thrust renewing her agony. She squeezed her eyes shut, hating the smell of his sweating body. *I'll endure this for my baby,* she thought. *I'm not my body. I'm not my body. He can't touch the essence of who I am.*

Shifting her attention from what was happening, she thought of Thorstein's loving, gentle hands and the tenderness in his eyes when he looked at her.

After what seemed an eternity, Ingeld finally satisfied his lust. He lay still, breathing heavily, his weight a further burden upon her. She stared at the flame of the iron lamp, wishing for the power of her Druidess grandmother. As she continued to gaze into the flame, she slid into a trance. A vision appeared of Thorstein riding toward her on horseback. She ran to him and he scooped her up and set her in front of him on the horse.

At that moment, Ingeld rolled off, breaking her trance. "No tears?" he asked.

"Would it give you satisfaction to see me weep?"

"Nei, I only wonder at it. How old are you?"

"Sixteen."

"You're young to be so strong. Go back to your baby. I'm done with you for tonight. Next time I desire you, spread your legs more willingly and I won't hurt you."

Annoure's body ached as she dressed. When she left the tent, the guard was no longer posted by the entrance so she walked to the shore of the wide Neva River. The night was humid and stars filled the sky.

She slid off her hangerock, then lifted up the hem of her under-dress and waded into the cold water. She rinsed blood from her thighs, scrubbing vigorously to wash away the smell and taste of Ingeld and the horror of what happened.

She waded out further, trying to keep her balance on the rocks with her soft leather shoes. Perhaps hidden whirlpools and eddies would pull her under and she could drown and get away from all this. The river seemed to call to her. It would be easy, just float with the currents until she sank. She waded out further until the river swept her away, pulling her into its deep waters. Panicking, she realized Ban would die without her. She started swimming toward shore, but the weight of her now waterlogged under-dress made it hard. The river continued to carry her downstream where boulders lined the shore. She searched frantically for a place to climb out.

Swimming over to a high bank, Annoure grabbed a tree root and tried to pull herself up. Her hand slipped from the root and she was swept even further downstream. She desperately grasped a bush. The bush broke away and the river sucked her under. She was bashed and scraped against rocks on the bottom as she fought for the surface. Her ears ached and her chest burned. *So this is what it is to die,* she thought, surrendering her will to God. A calm tranquility flowed through her. Images of people she loved most flashed through her head: Thorstein, her baby, Grandmother, Father and her two brothers.

Just when she thought it was all over, the river suddenly released its hold and she was able to swim to the surface. Choking and gasping, she drew in a breath of fresh air. She swam weakly to a nearby sloping bank and crawled onto the sand.

She lay there shivering with cold and staring at the stars. *Why had God spared her from drowning?* Then it occurred to her that perhaps the freedom she sought was inside herself, not outside.

Although she doubted she would ever see Thorstein again, she had his son to live for. She'd teach Ban about the quiet place within himself, just as Grandmother had taught her. She'd help him find that place beyond thought and emotion, where he could be still and find his inner core of strength.

The words of the Druidess came back to her. "Experiences do not happen to us by mere chance. We are meant to learn from them. We are born time after time, life after life, surrounded by some of the same familiar faces. Hurting each other, learning from each other, until we gradually begin to understand the higher purpose behind it all."

Grandmother, what am I to believe? The Christian priests say you are evil. They deny the existence of the old gods who have been worshipped for longer than even the Druids can remember. Maybe there's nothing after we die. Maybe we are as easily extinguished as a candle. She feared being nothing after she died. Then a long forgotten memory arose.

She'd just turned five and her nursemaid brought her to see Grandmother for the first time. She thought Grandmother was beautiful with her knowing eyes, kind smile and flowing dark hair.

"The child looks just like her mother!" Grandmother exclaimed. "It both brightens and tears at my heart to see her." Grandmother sat down and lifted Annoure onto her lap. "I want you to come live with me, Annoure. If you're raised by your father, the Christian priests will fill you with their lies. There's a world inside you and I will teach you to explore it." Grandmother touched the center of Annoure's forehead and light flooded her inner vision, accompanied by a soft humming sound. It was as if a window inside her head opened.

Father entered the room just then and snatched Annoure off Grandmother's lap. "What are you doing here, sorceress?"

"I have come for the child," Grandmother said. "It is her fifth birthday."

Her father's arms tightened possessively around Annoure. "No, she will grow up with those who love her and not be shut away from the world."

"I will love her and raise her as my own daughter was raised."

"Your world is gone. Annoure will live in this world."

"Our world still exists for those who can see it. Let her be one of us. She has the Sight as her mother did."

"Breanna chose the life of a wife and mother, not the life of a priestess. I want that for Annoure as well."

"You caused Breanna to break her vows. It tore her apart to be caught between two worlds and she died because of it."

"Breanna died because she kept trying to have a female child to satisfy the unholy agreement she made with you when we married," Father replied. "Each time a baby died, a piece of her died until all the joy was gone from her. I won't let you take the child to satisfy your goddess."

Magic swirled around the Druidess and suddenly she appeared much taller. Annoure was alarmed and clasped her arms around her father's neck.

"I should curse you and your kin for not honoring the bargain we made," Grandmother said in voice that radiated power. Her face softened. "Yet I see my granddaughter loves you, so for her sake I won't. This much I ask. Let me come here once a year to spend time with Annoure and her brothers."

"Out of respect for Breanna, I will let you visit the children, *if* you don't confuse them with talk of the Sight and your gods and goddesses. They are being raised Christian."

Now lying on the shore of the Neva River, Annoure focused on the center of her forehead where her grandmother had touched her so long ago. She gazed deeper inwardly until her awareness of the outer world faded. Light streamed through the inner doorway and she soared out of her body toward the heavens. Her heart opened as a new sense of freedom filled her. She felt the presence of a celestial being nearby and knew she was loved. She felt at one with the stars, dancing and laughing as she sailed among them.

I'm not my body at all, she thought. *It is but a sheath I will discard someday. Perhaps I can stay in this inner world and never return.*

But then she thought of leaving Ban and Thorstein and her heart contracted. *How could she leave them?* She moved swiftly back through space and, unable to stop herself, slid back into her body.

Annoure opened her eyes, then rose and followed the river back toward camp. The wooded bank was hard to traverse and it took a long time to reach the place where she'd left her hangerock. She picked it up and moved toward the tents. Partway there she heard Ban's lusty cries and her breasts started leaking milk in response. She hurried to the tent.

Fitela rocked the crying baby while the other women slept. Shaking with cold, Annoure removed her wet under-dress.

"How did you get wet?" Fitela asked, as Annoure pulled on her kaftan.

Annoure took the baby from her. He eagerly searched for a nipple and began to nurse. Once he was quiet, Annoure answered. "I went to the river to clean myself of Ingeld's filth. I would have drown myself, but for my son." She nuzzled the soft peach fuzz on top of his head, breathing in his sweet scent. Love filled her. He was her life now, her reason to keep fighting, to keep living.

A worried frown creased Fitela's forehead. "You have to accept what can't be changed. It's natural for a man to want a woman for the night. They haven't beaten us. It isn't so terrible to be a thrall."

Annoure's hair swung in front of her face as she looked down. Fitela was right to reproach her. She'd even suffered in Annoure's place and never once complained or cried afterwards.

Fitela embraced her. "I don't mean to be unkind. You weren't always a thrall and aren't used to this life. Was it bad?"

Annoure nodded. "He choked me and it was painful when he forced himself on me."

"It sometimes hurts the first time you have sex after having a baby."

"Have you had a baby?"

"Já, but he was born with no life in his tiny body. My arms have felt empty ever since." She sighed and her lovely face clouded over. "Sometimes when I hold Ban, I pretend he's mine. I wonder if my son would have been so bonny a child."

Annoure switched Ban to her other breast and gazed down at his tiny fists, feeling furiously protective of him. After a while she said, "I feel so dirty and ashamed. In the end I submitted to Ingeld because he threatened to kill Ban if I didn't."

"Don't think about it."

Annoure burped Ban on her shoulder, then curled up on the fur with the infant beside her.

Fitela blew out the candle and said, "Somehow you must find strength to endure Ingeld's attention. It gets easier and, with some men, it is even a pleasure. At home, my master favored me. He bought me gifts and gave me coins. I was saving up to buy my freedom."

"What happened? How is it you were sold?"

"My master went off a-viking and his jealous vif sold me. He will be angry when he returns. Yet he likes his vif well enough and she has given him four bairns. He'll accept what can't be changed."

"What bad luck to be sold before you could buy your freedom." Annoure listened to the comforting sound of Ban breathing, then added, softly, "I'm sorry about your baby."

Chapter 26

Lake Neva (Now Lake Ladoga in Russia)

ANNOURE TOOK A BITE OF freshly caught perch, then swatted at the cloud of mosquitoes swarming around her and Ban. Unbearable heat caused sweat to gather under her iron neckband and it dripped down her back and throat. She hoped it would cool off once the sun set.

That morning they had reached Lake Neva and sailed along its southern side where pine, alders and willow trees grew along the shoreline. The lake was so large it looked like the sea. In the late afternoon, they had finally reached the Volkhov River and sailed upstream to the Norse settlement of Aldeigjuborg. There they had set up camp.

Whining mosquitoes swarmed around Annoure and the baby, and bit their exposed skin. She brushed them off and rushed into the tent with Ban. The insects followed them inside the stifling interior. In desperation, she shoved the infant into her hudfat and crawled in beside him.

Fitela entered the tent, carrying an iron lamp.

"Shut the flap, Fitela!" Annoure exclaimed. "You're letting more bugs in."

"The smoke from the lamp will help keep them away."

Unable to stand the smoldering heat inside the hudfat, Annoure climbed out and carried Ban closer to the smelly oil lamp. She felt a sting on her ankle and slapped the mosquito, leaving a circle of blood.

Annoure started squishing the mosquitoes on the interior cloth walls. "This place is miserable. Why would anyone build a village here?"

"Nidhad told me the Rus built it here to guard the Volkhov River. They can control trade with the Finns and Slavs from here."

"Who are the Rus?"

"Norsemen from Ingeld's homeland are called Rus."

"Are we going to stay here a few days to trade so Thorstein can catch up with us?" Annoure asked.

"How can you still believe he will find you?"

"I dreamed he's searching for me."

"Your dreams don't mean anything. He's probably off a-viking and doesn't even know you were stolen. Nidhad didn't say anything about staying to trade. Why don't you ask Ingeld?"

"I prefer to avoid him."

"Your life would be easier if you tried to please him."

"He's a thrall dealer. Why would I want to please him?"

"To get things from him: better food, pretty jewelry and clothes. He's a powerful, rich man."

"I don't want anything from him."

"You want information. Right now he's making arrangements to get boats to travel the rest the way to Bulgar. Our ship is too big for the smaller rivers."

"I'm sick of traveling." Annoure lay on her fur and said inwardly, *Thorstein, please hurry, I'm being taken to Bulgar.* She fell asleep thinking of him.

When she awoke in the morning, the tent was empty. Ban began to cry and she nursed him. He'd been fretful and his face was covered with red welts. His skin felt warm next to her body and she wondered if he was sick. After putting fresh moss under his bottom, she wrapped him in a blanket to protect him from mosquitoes and carried him outside. Ingeld sat on the ground near the tent and Annoure immediately felt uneasy.

Bergthora handed Ingeld a wooden bowl of water. He washed his face and hands, spit in the bowl, and then began to comb his beard and hair. Annoure passed by him quickly. She loathed his cruel face and hairy body covered with battle scars.

Bergthora coughed as she passed the bowl from Ingeld to Nidhad.

Since the women wouldn't get the bowl until all the men had used it, Annoure preferred to wash her face in the river. She tied Ban to her chest with a shawl and left the fortress. After washing, she went into the woods to search for fresh moss.

Before long, she heard Bergthora calling her name. She shoved another clump of moss into her bag and walked out of the forest. Bergthora lifted her skirts and ran toward her. "Ingeld is angry you left camp by yourself." She began coughing and couldn't continue.

"Are you all right?" Annoure noticed how thin Bergthora had gotten and her complexion had taken on an unhealthy pallor.

"I just have a sore throat. There are robbers along the river who attack merchants and steal their trade goods and thralls."

Annoure uneasily scanned the area, then followed Bergthora to the shoreline where Ingeld and his men loaded supplies into three boats carved out of large tree trunks. Rus traders loaded up four additional boats nearby.

"Don't go wandering off again, Annoure," Ingeld said when he spotted her. "It's dangerous. For the rest of the journey to Bulgar, we're joining up with other Norsemen traders. Robbers are less likely to attack a large group."

He held the boat steady as she climbed in. Ingeld, three crewmen and Bergthora got in the boat after her. The remaining crewmen and four other thralls divided themselves between the last two boats.

Ingeld ordered Bergthora to row with the men.

"Let me do it," Annoure said. "Bergthora's not well."

She handed the baby to Bergthora and lowered the oars into the water, watching the men to figure out how to row.

All morning they moved steadily upstream against the current and through a wooded land. Annoure's arms ached and blisters had formed on her palms.

In the afternoon, the roar of rapids grew louder until finally Ingeld ordered his crew to head to shore. The men hauled the boats out of the water, flipped them over their heads and started walking down a worn pathway.

Annoure tied Ban to her chest, picked up a hudfat full of trade goods and followed behind Ingeld who carried a drawn sword. He moved warily and kept scanning the woods.

"We're vulnerable to attack when the men carry the boats," Ingeld said. "Stay close. Many Norsemen who come here to trade never return home."

Annoure moved nearer to Ingeld and tried to keep up with his long strides. They hadn't gone far when Ban began to cry. Annoure sang to quiet him, but he didn't calm down.

"Quiet the baby before he draws all the thieves in the area to us!" Ingeld exclaimed. "I'm going to scout for signs of them." He disappeared into the woods.

Annoure sat down on a log and began nursing Ban, wondering if he was sick from the insect bites. The other women and the rest of the crew walked by. Before long she and the baby were alone. After Ban was content, she continued down the path, following the course of the river. Soon she came upon a moose and her calf chomping grass in the trail. The enormous mother moose snorted at her.

Annoure slid behind a pine tree, her heart racing with panic. The moose crashed into the woods and her calf followed. Branches cracked under their hooves as they tramped away. Annoure returned cautiously to the trail and continued after the others. She finally caught up to the group as they loaded up the boats.

Bergthora had another coughing spell as she started to hand Ingeld a hudfat. "Where were you?" she asked Annoure once she'd recovered. "We were beginning to worry."

"I stopped to nurse the baby."

"You should have stayed with us."

"Ban's crying put us all in danger. I had to quiet him." She put her hand on Bergthora's shoulder. "You look exhausted."

The young woman's hair hung in greasy clumps, her nose was red and dripping and her eyes had dark circles under them.

Bergthora shrugged with a sad frown on her face. "It's a difficult journey."

That evening Ingeld told Annoure to join him in his tent as he did nearly every night. She handed Ban to Gerd and reluctantly followed him. It never did any good to refuse; he just became angry and more violent. Annoure dreaded nightfall.

Once in his tent, Ingeld drank from a flask of beer he'd gotten in Aldeigjuborg as he boasted of fighting robbers during his past travels.

His narrative turned to telling her about his hometown, Birka. It had become a fast-growing, prosperous trading town.

Annoure took several sips from the flask and her uneasiness mounted as Ingeld became drunker and drunker. Once the flask was empty, he pulled her close and kissed her. She suppressed the urge to shove him away, not wanting to be beaten again.

He lowered her onto her back and shoved up her skirts. She bit her lip and turned her head away, squeezing her eyes shut as he lowered his hairy body over hers.

She shifted her attention off what was happening by thinking of her baby and how much she loved him. In her mind's eye, she saw Ban's large blue eyes, fine hair and little nose. She imagined Thorstein's joy when he finally got to see his son.

Ingeld grabbed her hair in his fist and kissed her again as he continued to thrust into her. She hated having to submit to him. She wished she had Grandmother's Druidess powers. Grandmother would never allow herself to be abused by a man.

With a satisfied grunt, Ingeld rolled off and soon began snoring.

"Pig!" Annoure snarled under her breath. She left the tent and cleaned herself at the river. A longing for Thorstein engulfed her. It seemed unlikely that he'd ever find her. Even if he made it all the way to Lake Neva, how could he survive alone in these dangerous lands? And how would he rescue her from Ingeld and his men if he did find her? Was she kidding herself to believe her vision of him was real and she would be saved? Were she and Ban destined to spend their lives as thralls?

She wondered if she dared run away with Ban. They were camped at the edge of an enormous pine-tree forest. It would be easy to disappear into its depths, but she doubted she and Ban could survive more than a few days alone in the forest. Brown bears, boars and wolves lived in the area. It was better to stay with Ingeld and his men for now.

She knelt down at the swampy shoreline, still thinking of Grandmother. Every night after leaving Ingeld's tent, she had tried unsuccessfully to contact her. She stared into the water and focused all her attention on seeing Grandmother's image. The water rippled gently, but no face appeared. She sat back, curling her hands into fists. What was she doing wrong?

A thought sprang into her mind. Perhaps she was pushing against a door that opened inwardly. She took several deeps breaths and tried to relax. Love filled her as she thought of the happy times she spent with Grandmother, learning about the ancient mysteries. The horror of being with Ingeld dissolved as she became more centered and serene. Soon the woods and chirping of birds faded away. She felt a shift, then Grandmother's face appeared in the surface of the river.

"I've been waiting for you to reach me," Grandmother said. "Don't forget your training and who you are. Use your power, Annoure."

"I don't have any power. I'm a thrall."

"That's an illusion. The essence of who you are can't be enslaved. The power I'm talking about is the ability to perceive things beyond this world, to glimpse the future and have visions. Your strength comes from within."

"What good does it do me to have these abilities?"

"They give you strength and courage. And they show you that you are *not* your physical body. You are like a wave on the ocean, afraid to crash into the rocky shoreline. But when it crashes, it becomes water and realizes it always was water."

"I wish I'd run away to become a Druidess."

"It was not your destiny. Before being born, you pledged to find Thorstein. He is from your past."

"I don't know if I'll ever see him again. The reason why I didn't become a Druidess was because I was afraid of the power I felt in you."

"I am only a channel for the power you feel radiating from me. It gives me protection. I don't try to control it or use it to control others. I have something for you."

A Celtic sword appeared in her hand. She handed it to Annoure. It felt heavy and Annoure realized she was no longer looking at Grandmother's image in the river. Rather Grandmother was standing in front of her, as if they were in a dream together.

"When someone attacks you, hold the sword in front of you and trust it to protect you."

Annoure held it in front of her, feeling its protective energy surrounding her.

The inner experience faded and Annoure became aware of her surroundings in the physical world once more. The sword was gone and so was Grandmother's image in the water.

Annoure went to the tent and took Ban from Gerd. She nursed him then tried to sleep, but Kari's snoring and Bergthora's coughing kept her awake late into the night. Finally she fell asleep and dreamed she was with Thorstein beside a mist-covered lake. She heard a hauntingly beautiful song and turned toward the sound.

Erik the skald stepped toward her from the haze. Beside him was the faint image of another man. As the vision became clear, she was startled to see it was Ketil. *What's he doing with Thorstein and Erik?* The men faded away into the thick fog, leaving her question unanswered.

The next day when Annoure looked at the mist-covered river, the memory of her dream returned. She wondered what the dream meant and why she saw Erik and Ketil with Thorstein.

Annoure joined the men and rowed the boat because Bergthora was still too sick to help. She didn't mind rowing now that her arms had grown stronger and she was better at it. They reached Lake Ilmen and sailed across the small body of water. On the south shore of the lake they entered another narrow river.

In the afternoon, Bergthora slept in the cramped space on the bottom of the boat with the baby beside her.

Ingeld steered the boat so it stayed near the shoreline where the current wasn't as strong. At times fallen trees hung over the bank and they had to maneuver around them. The river grew narrower until at last they reached another portage. The men carried the boats and the women toted supplies as they walked the trail toward the headwaters of the Volga River. The women split up Bergthora's share of the supplies. Even without the burden of carrying anything, the sick woman kept stopping to rest. Her face was flushed with fever and her coughing grew worse.

This portage lasted longer than the previous one and they spent the night along the trail.

In the morning, Annoure was jolted awake by Fitela's cry of alarm. "What's wrong?" she asked. Fitela and Iona sat beside Bergthora who looked as if she was still sleeping. Annoure moved closer and gasped. "She's dead!"

"At least she won't suffer anymore," Fitela said.

Annoure's chest constricted as she and Fitela held each other and wept. Bergthora was only fifteen—too young to die. She was one of the first women to befriend Annoure and help take care of Ban. Annoure wondered if she could have done anything to prevent Bergthora's death. She closed her eyes and prayed for the gods to guide Bergthora on her inner journey.

Gerd and Kari entered the tent after spending the night with two of Ingeld's men. The both began to cry when they saw that Bergthora had died.

"Perhaps she is the lucky one," Gerd said. "At least she won't be sold to Arabs."

Nidhad placed Bergthora in a dried-up streambed and the women covered her with rocks so animals wouldn't eat the corpse. Annoure said a tearful prayer for Bergthora's safe journey to the other worlds, not knowing what gods Bergthora worshipped.

Once the informal ceremony was over, Ingeld ordered the men and thralls to break camp and continue the portage. Disheartened, Annoure trudged beside Fitela, wondering if anyone else would die before they reached Bulgar.

The group arrived at the shoreline of the Volga River in the evening and set up camp. Afterward Annoure sat on the riverbank with Ban in her arms. She guessed they'd been traveling about four weeks. If she was right, it was the beginning of July and Ban was a little over a month old. As she gazed at him, he stared intently back. He was awake for much longer periods of time now and was more alert.

Ingeld came over to her and cleared his throat. "I'm sorry about Bergthora. I know she was your friend and friends are hard to lose. I've seen a lot of death and am used to it. But you're young and I know you must be hurting."

Annoure felt tears gather at his unexpected sympathy.

"The rest of the journey to Bulgar will be easier," Ingeld continued. "We'll be traveling with the current."

"How much further is it?"

"About seven hundred miles."

"Seven hundred miles!" She gasped. "That's such a long way. Will there be any more portages?"

"Nei, the Volga is a large river that goes all the way to the Caspian Sea."

"How long will it take to get to Bulgar?"

His brow creased. "If the wind stays in our favor, a few weeks. I plan to get there and back to Birka before it turns cold. In winter this land is covered with snow and the river freezes."

He scratched his beard absently. "Your journey will be different since I'm selling you to the Arabs. They'll take you far south to live in a much warmer land. It will take a couple of months to travel there by caravan."

Anxiety clutched at Annoure's heart like a raven's claw. What if the Arabs wanted her but not Ban? She held him closer and kissed his soft cheek.

Over the next few days, the weather grew hotter and drier with a constant wind. The terrain changed as well. On one side of the river, the bank rose sharply to forested hills. The other side sloped gradually to meet expanses of treeless land. The men kept constant guard against robbers and the warring Slav and Finn tribes.

Annoure often thought about Bergthora, missing her company during the long days on the boat. She also missed Thorstein and wondered if her vision of him coming for her was a true one. She often dreamt of him and the dreams seemed to be a link between them, as they had been before they'd met in Northumbria.

One evening after a long day of travel, Annoure sat by the river with Ban lying on a fur beside her. A strong breeze gave her some relief from the heat.

Ingeld walked over and tossed a wooden comb on her lap. "Comb your hair and wash your face."

She scowled at him. "I don't care how I look."

He grabbed her hair, pulling her up by it. "I paid a lot for you because of your beauty. Now I think I was cheated."

She tugged her thick hair out of his grasp. "How do you expect me to look pretty in the wilderness?"

"You could bathe in the river and wash your clothes. Clean yourself before you come to my tent tonight."

"I don't care if I please you or not!"

He grabbed her upper arms and shook her. "You're a thrall and must try to please me. I'm your master."

"I'm not a thrall! I'm a Northumbrian lady and Thorstein will rescue me. You'll burn in hell for how you've treated me!"

Red spots blotched Ingeld's cheeks and Annoure realized she'd gone too far. He swung her off her feet and threw her off the riverbank. Annoure screamed as she flew through the air. She hit the cool water and sank in its depths. Sputtering to the surface, she saw everyone gathered at the riverbank, staring down at her.

Annoure swam toward shore and stood up when she touched the bottom.

"There now you won't smell so badly," Ingeld said with a smug look, his arms crossed.

Incensed, Annoure slammed the flat of her hand against the surface of the river and sprayed him with water. The women gasped and the men glanced uneasily at Ingeld. Annoure was beyond caring what he thought. It was his fault Bergthora was dead. She was tired of being intimidated by him, traveling day after endless day, worrying about being sold to Arabs.

"I should drown you for that!" Ingeld exclaimed.

"What . . . and lose all the gold you traded for me!"

"You don't think I will?"

She put her hands on her hips and glared defiantly at him. "I know you will if it pleases you, but I don't care. I don't care if I die right here or am sold to some Arabs. It makes no difference to me."

"What about your child? He will die without you."

"Leave him out of this! This is between you and me." She looked at the others. "What are you staring at?" She splashed them with water.

Ingeld looked at his drenched men with a startled expression for a moment, and then started to laugh. The others joined him. "The woman's got spirit," he said, still chortling. "I'm glad it's not broken. This heat's put us all in a bad temper. I'm going for a swim." He stripped off his soiled clothes and dove into the water. Many of the men joined him.

Annoure removed her hangerock and, wearing only her under-dress, used the bar of soap Fitela handed her to wash her hair and scrub layers of grime off her arms and legs. Last she washed her hangerock. She climbed back up on the bank, feeling refreshed, and sat near Ban who'd fallen asleep. As she looked at the baby she regretted the angry words she'd shouted at Ingeld. It was dangerous to challenge him when he had so much control over their lives.

Fitela picked up the comb and began to draw it through Annoure's waist-length, tangled hair. Fitela's own short hair never needed much attention. She'd told Annoure her previous owner's wife cut it off so everyone would know she was a thrall.

As much trouble as her hair was to manage, Annoure was glad Ingeld hadn't chopped it off. He hadn't done it out of consideration for her, but because he thought the Arabs would pay more for her if she had long hair.

"You mustn't anger Ingeld," Fitela said. "He's your only chance to avoid being sold to Arabs. You captivate him. When you're clean and dressed in your kaftan, you're beautiful. You don't seem to realize what power that gives you. You could convince him to take you to his farmstead instead of selling you." Fitela plaited Annoure's hair into two braids and tied the ends with a rag.

"I hate him. I'd rather be sold to Arabs than be his pleasure thrall."

"Think on it at least. The Norsemen aren't bad masters; we know nothing of the Arabs."

Ingeld tugged on his pants and came over to them. "Come to the tent with me, Annoure."

Annoure narrowed her eyes in contempt, then reached for Ban.

"Leave the baby with Fitela," he said.

Annoure reluctantly left Ban and followed Ingeld, so upset her hands trembled. The regret she felt at challenging him began to fade with each step. *I am the granddaughter of a Druidess! I can't let Ingeld intimidate me. He* wants *me to be afraid because it makes him feel powerful when I cower before him. I'll never ask to be taken to his farmstead! Never!* She stepped into the tent and sat down on a fur as Ingeld lit his iron lamp.

"You are a passionate woman," he said. "But your passion would be better spent pleasing me. Why do you keep fighting me when it only makes matters worse?"

She put her fist against her heart. "I will never see myself as a thrall."

"But you are one. Undress."

"Nei." Rage tightened her chest and she felt the power of the Mother Goddess surging through her.

Ingeld hands tightened into fists. "Undress now."

Annoure glowered at Ingeld and imagined she held the Celtic sword

Grandmother had given her. A current of energy pulsed through her, vanquishing any remaining trepidation. "I curse you Ingeld the Much Traveled! May darkness and death follow you." She spoke the words with conviction, knowing they were true.

Uncertainty entered Ingeld's eyes and Annoure sensed his unease. His superstitious fear filled the air between them. "Touch me again and I swear by the god Frey that your manhood will shrivel up and you'll never be able to be with a woman again."

"Witch! I'll kill your baby."

"If you hurt him, I'll call on the god Thor to create such a storm that you and all your men will drown at sea."

Ingeld knocked her backward, then pulled up her wet under-dress. He came down on top of her and attempted to invade her, but was too flaccid.

She laughed at him. "You've lost your hold on me." She knew it was true; he was superstitious and believed her curse.

He slapped her across the mouth and she tasted blood on her lips where her teeth cut into them. Ingeld kept trying to thrust into her with no success. Finally he gave up and yelled, "Get out of my sight, witch!"

Annoure pulled down her still damp under-dress and left. Once away from Ingeld, she began to shake as the power flowing through her drained away. She felt weak and her injured lip and cheek began to swell.

She hurried to her tent, gathered her fur and a bag of food, then lifted the sleeping baby into her arms, intent on escape. She peeked out of the tent, looking for the guard. He stood a short distance away with his back to her. The forest was close by. She could disappear into the tall pines and never be found. Grandmother's voice whispered in her head, *"Not tonight. Wait. The time will come."*

She hesitated, wondering if it was Grandmother or the wind. The guard turned and looked at her. She ducked into the tent, taking deep breaths to still her racing heart.

Chapter 27

The Wrong Route

THORSTEIN, ERIK AND KETIL SAILED east on the Varangian Sea, traveling long daylight hours in fair and foul weather. When the wind died down, Thorstein took his turn rowing; the workout had gradually built up his strength.

"Let's camp early," Thorstein said one evening, fed up with the drizzle that had kept them wet for days. "We're short of food and the sea is an inhospitable mistress."

Ketil and Erik agreed so they headed to land and set up camp in the rain. Then Thorstein and Ketil picked up their bows and quivers of arrows and went into the woods to hunt. After hiking deep inland, Thorstein spotted several black grouse. He signaled Ketil and they slipped quietly behind a bush, readying their bows and arrows. They shot at the grouse through an opening in the leaves and killed two before the others scattered.

"We'll eat well tonight," Thorstein said, picking up one of the grouse.

"Perhaps our luck's changed." Ketil held out his arms. "I think even the drizzle has quit."

"Some sun tomorrow would be a welcome change."

Back at camp they dressed and roasted the grouse over a fire Erik built.

After eating, Thorstein felt refreshed. "I need to get my strength and skills back. Ketil, will you spar with me?" As soon as he suggested it, he broke into a sweat. Last time he'd crossed swords with Ketil he almost died.

“You won’t be a challenge. You still move stiffly from your wound. Spar with Erik. You two are more fairly matched.”

Erik sprang to his feet, drawing his sword and advancing on Ketil. “I’ll still that boastful tongue of yours if you insult me again. My faðir put a sword in my hand as soon as I could walk. He wanted me to be a warrior and I’ve not forgotten what I learned.” He sliced his sword through the air, making it sing.

Ketil continued to lean against a log, looking relaxed from his meal. “I didn’t mean to start a quarrel. You’ve certainly become quick-tempered since trading your lyre for a sword.”

“And whose fault is that?”

“We’re all quick-tempered from traveling in such foul weather,” Thorstein intervened.

“We can’t travel at a slow pace if we’re to have any chance of rescuing Annoure,” Erik said, glaring at Ketil. “I hate traveling with the man who sold her into slavery.”

“Enough, Erik,” Thorstein said, though he too disliked traveling with Ketil. But what choice did they have? He stood and began to stretch, wincing at the sharp pulling sensation it caused his injured side. Once he felt limbered up he said, “Let’s have a little sword play, Erik.”

He and Erik began to spar with sword and shield, using little force until they warmed up. Thorstein soon discovered Erik *was* an experienced swordsman. As the match grew more intense, Thorstein became out of breath and was unable to keep pace with his opponent.

“Enough. You need rest,” Erik said, lowering his sword. “We should practice every day until you are strong again.”

Thorstein leaned over, waiting for his breath to return to normal. ”Thor’s Thunder, I feel like an old man,” he gasped. ”You’re as good as you boasted, Erik. Your faðir taught you well.”

“It’s only because you’re still recovering from a bad wound that you think I’m good.”

Ketil stood. “Come, Erik, let’s test our skills against one another, then I’ll spar with Thorstein.”

Thorstein looked uneasily from one man to the other. If the match turned ugly, Ketil was sure to win. A vigorous battle ensued. Thorstein studied the two men’s fighting styles as their swords thundered repeatedly against each other’s shields.

Finally Ketil got his sword past Erik's guard and pressed the point of it to the skald's chest.

"You'd be dead if I had a mind to kill you. Insult me again and I'll leave you and Thorstein here without the means to rescue Annoure. She was abducted and sold as part of a blood feud. And that's the way of it." Ketil drew back his sword and turned to Thorstein. "Draw your blade if you're as filled with anger as Erik; this is your chance to vent it."

A wave of resentment flooded through Thorstein as he started to fight. Ketil was the cause of all his suffering. Before long Thorstein's side hurt as the newly healed skin and muscle stretched and his arm began to ache as he and Ketil slammed their swords into each other's shields. Thorstein pulled back and they circled one another.

"Why are you helping me find Annoure?" Thorstein asked.

Ketil faltered. "I'll give you the truth though I doubt you'll believe it. I felt terrible remorse after I sold her and the baby into slavery."

"Why would you feel remorse? That's what you set out to do."

"During the voyage I got to know and respect her."

"Then why did you sell her?" Thorstein swung his sword at Ketil who blocked it with his shield.

"I went berserk when Annoure refused to marry me."

"She's my woman!" Thorstein's arm shook as he continued to press his sword against Ketil's shield.

"You never married her."

Thorstein felt the veins in his neck pulse. "Do you still want her?"

"Nei, I just want to right my wrong."

Thorstein lowered his sword and sat on a nearby log, too tired to keep fighting. He was sure Ketil wasn't telling him everything. Perhaps Annoure willingly gave herself to Ketil in the hopes of winning her freedom and he betrayed her instead. Or maybe Ketil forced himself on her and felt guilty. If Annoure willingly shared pleasure with Ketil, he wasn't sure he could forgive her. If Ketil took her by force, he'd kill him.

They sailed near shore over the next few days, watching for the islands that marked the entrance to the Gulf of Riga. A Norse trader in Hedeby had drawn a crude map in the dirt to show them the land formations along the coast and how to find the route Ingeld might have taken to Bulgar.

Finally they found the Gulf of Riga and the small trading settlement, they were told about, by the Daugava River and landed their ship. They decided the best way to get information was to visit the tavern.

Thorstein stepped onto the dirt floor of the dimly lit structure and inhaled the rich smell of beer. The one-room tavern was nearly empty except for a few Rus gathered around a crude wooden table. Thorstein and his two companions bought beers and joined them.

Thorstein took a swig of his beer, savoring its full taste, then said, "Has anyone here seen Ingeld the Much Traveled? I was told he would stop here on his way to Bulgar."

"Why are you trying to find him?" a young man asked, looking suspicious and rubbing peeling skin off his red nose.

"He has something of mine."

The young man nodded. "He's not one to easily relinquish what he's acquired." He called to the bar tender. "This man wants to know if Ingeld the Much Traveled has come this way."

"I haven't seen him this year," the bar tender said. "If he's headed to Bulgar, he probably went to the Gulf of Finland and took the Volkhov River to the Volga. That's a shorter portage than the portage from the Daugava River to the Volga."

An anxious feeling surged inside Thorstein. *They'd taken the wrong route! How would they ever catch up to Ingeld before he reached Bulgar?*

"Where is the Gulf of Finland?" Erik asked, looking as crestfallen as Thorstein felt.

"About two days journey north if you have a strong wind at your back. Once you reach the gulf, keep the shoreline on your right and in another three days you'll reach the mouth of the river Neva."

"What do we do from there?" Thorstein asked, wondering how he and his companions would ever find their way through the vast connection of water systems.

"My friend, it's dangerous to travel through this wild land. The Slavs are always at war. But if you still wish to continue, the Neva River will take you to Lake Ladoga. Travel along the southern side of the lake to the Volkhov River. From there travel to the Norse settlement of Aldeigjuborg. Once you're in Aldeigjuborg you can join up with a larger group of Norsemen for protection and travel the rest of the way to Bulgar with them."

"We appreciate your help with the route." Thorstein slugged down the rest of his beer then said to Erik and Ketil. "Let's go."

"Nei," Ketil said. "Sit. Eat. We'll leave at dawn after a good night's sleep."

* * *

Ingeld and his party of men and thralls had been traveling down the Volga River with the other Norsemen for over two weeks when Annoure spotted a tall, round tower on the distant shoreline. She and Ban rode in the first boat with Fitela, Ingeld, Nidhad and two other Norsemen. The sail was up, catching a good wind, so no one had to row.

"That's Bulgar you see ahead," said Nidhad, pointing to shore. As their boat sailed closer, other brick buildings came into view. Annoure marveled at the size of the city. It was the largest place they'd visited on their journey. Numerous boats lined the riverbank and people worked in vast fields surrounding the city.

Although Annoure was apprehensive about being sold to Arabs, it would be a relief to get away from Ingeld. He'd become increasingly hostile toward her and she worried he might kill her or the baby. He'd told his men she was a witch and they became antagonistic toward her as well. Even Iona, Kari and Gerd nervously avoided her. Only Fitela and Nidhad were still friendly.

Once they landed, Nidhad chained the five women together and led them down a pathway toward the stone city walls. On the way, they passed a round brick building with one door and a small window. Its shape was unlike any structure Annoure had seen before and she wondered what it was used for.

At the gate to the city, Ingeld paid tribute to the guards, who allowed them to enter. The city smells and noises offended Annoure's senses. Smoke and aromas from cooking fires blended with the stench of garbage and human and animal waste. Horse-drawn carts pounded the stone streets and people in foreign dress hurried by, speaking to each other in unfamiliar tongues. While two-story stone buildings rose high overhead.

Several dogs raced toward them and started barking. Annoure held Ban tighter, hoping they wouldn't attack.

The group passed through a crowded marketplace where traders had spread their furs, spices, swords and honey on colorful blankets on the ground. Some of the traders were Rus while others had dark skin and wore long robes and turbans on their heads.

Finally they came to the edge of town where the Norse traders were all camped. Ingeld's men put up their tents, then Nidhad brought the women inside one of them, still chained together.

When night came, Annoure lay on her back. She was unable to move without the chain on her neckband pulling against Fitela's neckband on one side and Gerd's on the other. As she lay there, she wondered what would happen to her and Ban. "Are you still awake, Fitela?" she whispered.

"Já."

"What do you think the Arabs are like?"

"I don't know."

"I'm afraid."

"Afraid? Why, Annoure? You have Ingeld and all his men convinced you're a witch."

"But I'm not. What if the Arabs want me, but not my baby?"

"Then you'll survive without him. The gods determine our fate and we must accept it."

Annoure drew Ban against her side as a lump filled her throat. "I'd rather die than be separated from Ban." She inwardly focused on Thorstein. *Please find me. I'm in Bulgar about to be sold.*

The next morning, Ingeld unchained the women and removed their neckbands. Then Nidhad gave them a bowl of water and a comb.

Ingeld handed Annoure and Fitela silk kaftans and ordered the two women to put them on after they cleaned themselves. He gave the other three woman kaftans of lesser quality and left.

"Why are your kaftans finer than ours, Fitela?" Iona asked.

"Fitela and Annoure have always been favored," Kari said, splashing water on her face.

"Annoure is no longer in Ingeld's favor now that she cursed him. Are you really a witch?" Gerd asked.

Annoure shook her head. "No, I'm not a witch. I cursed him so he'd leave me alone."

"It makes no difference now," Iona said. "We're all about to be sold."

After letting the other women use the water, Annoure washed her neck, glad to be free of the awful neckband. Once she'd cleaned herself, she slid on the kaftan, noticing how soft the fabric felt against her skin.

Fitela was combing her long hair when Nidhad entered the tent again, his eyes filled with excitement. "A caravan of nearly a thousand Arabs has arrived in Bulgar. Ingeld says we'll be able to get high prices for all our thralls and trade goods."

"Fitela has been good to you on this long journey," Annoure said. "Why don't you keep her instead of selling her?"

His face crumpled. "I haven't any gold to buy her with. I'm only a hired crewman."

That afternoon, Annoure sat in the tent, bouncing Ban on her lap. He smiled up at her, gurgling. He was much stronger now and could hold up his head for short periods of time. She lay down on a fur with Ban and nursed him until he fell asleep, then she dozed off.

When she awoke, she left the baby sleeping in the tent and stepped outside. Nidhad and Fitela sat in front, talking. The other women weren't in sight.

"Where are the others?" Annoure asked, sitting down beside Fitela.

"They were taken to a slave auction," Nidhad said. "Ingeld thinks he can get a better price for you two since you're the best looking of the thralls."

"I didn't even get a chance to say goodbye to them," Annoure said, missing them even though they hadn't been friendly after she cursed Ingeld.

Fitela clasped Annoure's hand. "Perhaps we'll be sold together."

Annoure nodded. Everything was happening so fast now that they were in Bulgar.

Before long, Ingeld appeared with two swarthy-complexioned men in tan robes and scarf-like coverings on their heads. Both were shorter than Ingeld and carried long, curved swords. One man had dark eyes, black hair, a beard and a hooked nose. The other had a weather-wrinkled face and a white beard.

"Get up so the Arabs can see you," Ingeld said. Both women stood and Ingeld sneered at Annoure. "It's lucky they can only see your unearthly beauty and don't know you're a witch."

Annoure didn't respond, not wanting to give him the satisfaction of getting a rise out of her. Ingeld turned to the Arabs and said a few faltering words in an unfamiliar tongue.

Fitela smiled invitingly at the Arabs.

The younger Arab slid his fingers along Annoure's cheek. She tensed as he continued to examine her as if she were no more than an animal for purchase. The Arab pulled open her kaftan and pushed it off her shoulders. It slid to the ground.

She didn't resist or show any emotion, refusing to be humiliated. As the Arab began to bargain with Ingeld, Annoure picked up her kaftan and pulled it back on. Her fingers shook as she fastened it closed.

The Arabs offered a pile of silk, small bags of spices, and gold coins. Finally Ingeld reached an agreement with them. "I'm glad I didn't kill you; you've brought me a good price."

Annoure looked him directly in the eye, feeling power flow through her. "The shadow of death hangs over you."

The color drained from his face and he quickly turned away.

The black-haired Arab signaled Annoure and Fitela to follow him. Annoure turned to get Ban from the tent and the younger Arab grasped her arm, stopping her.

"I have to get my baby!" she exclaimed. The Arab pulled her away from the tent. "Let me get Ban! Ingeld, tell him I have a baby. Please, I beg of you!" The Arab stopped dragging her away and looked expectantly at Ingeld.

Ingeld smiled cruelly at Annoure. "Your baby can be tossed into the sea for all I care."

"Either you get these men to let me keep my son or I will curse you and your men so none of you ever return home. The sea will break apart your ship and you'll all drown!"

"You don't have the power to sink my ship."

The Arab tightened his hold on Annoure's arm. She kept her eyes on Ingeld, terrified of not being able to take Ban with her. "I'll draw on the power of the Celtic Goddess Brigit. Her power of fire will burn your ship at sea."

"I'm not afraid of your curses, witch."

A surge of panic sliced through Annoure, she didn't know how to save her baby.

Ingeld sneered. "Still the sooner we get rid of you and your evil offspring the better." He looked at Nidhad. "Get the baby."

Nidhad reappeared a moment later with the child and handed him to

Annoure. The white bearded Arab shook his head.

Annoure clutched Ban to her chest. "Ingeld, tell the Arabs I'll be an obedient slave and do whatever they ask if only they show mercy and let me keep my baby."

Her eyes met Ingeld's, her heart in her throat. Finally he nodded and spoke again gesturing with his hands and speaking the strange language slowly.

The older Arab stepped forward and unwrapped the baby. Annoure drew in her breath, not wanting him to touch Ban. The infant stared at the man with interest, then his little hand clutched the man's finger. The man laughed and nodded his head. He started off again and Annoure quickly followed, pressing the baby to her heart.

Fitela walked alongside her. "Bless the gods. Ban softened the old Arab's heart and now you can keep him." She smiled broadly. "And we, too, are still together."

"It will be good to have a friend to talk to among all these strange men."

"Já, it will."

They left the city gates and Annoure paused in amazement at the sight of hundreds of people erecting brightly colored tents, spread as far as she could see in both directions. "Look at their horses," she said, pointing at a prancing white stallion an Arab was trying to keep away from a mare. "They are the most beautiful horses I've ever seen. My brothers would love to have horses like these. Look how high that stallion holds his tail." She paused. "But what is that odd brown animal?"

A robed Arab walked past leading tall, strange-looking creatures with long legs and two humps on their backs. The animals were weighed down with supplies.

"I don't know," Fitela said, staring at them.

The black-haired Arab leading them turned back and gestured for them to keep walking. Before long the men stopped in front of a cloth tent that looked like it was made to keep out sand rather than cold. One of the men lifted the tent flap and pointed inside.

Annoure entered after Fitela. The tent was empty except for large pillows and brightly patterned rugs that covered the ground. Annoure sat on one of the pillows, wondering how Thorstein would ever find her among a thousand Arabs.

Chapter 28

Searching Bulgar

SO THIS CROWDED, NOISY CITY was Bulgar. Thorstein wrinkled his nose at all the strong smells made more intense by the summer heat. He preferred the spaciousness and quiet of the farm. His small party had joined a much larger group of Rus traders traveling east on the Volga River to Bulgar. The trip had gone without incident. Even though they made good time, Thorstein was worried that Ingeld had already sold Annoure.

He paused to look over a group of female thralls chained together in front of a shop. They were dressed in dirty rags and their eyes had a hollow, defeated expression. Not spotting Annoure among them, he walked on. His stomach churned as if he'd eaten something rancid. He wondered if Annoure would look like these women when he found her.

"How will we ever find Annoure in this huge city?" Ketil asked, his eyes widening with dismay. "I haven't heard a single person speak Norse."

"Many Rus traders come here," Erik replied. "They've probably set up camp near one another. It shouldn't be hard to find them."

"If we don't get lost in this maze of streets." Ketil scanned the brick buildings surrounding them.

"Don't worry. I'm used to finding my way in new places," Erik said.

"I never imagined a city could be so large." Ketil loosened his pants and urinated on a wall. A woman in a kaftan hurried by, not slowing her stride as she stepped around the yellow puddle seeping into the street.

"It's so much bigger than Hedeby," Erik said.

"There's an open market ahead," Thorstein said, quickening his pace. Soon they were among familiar-looking Norsemen dressed in tunics and pants similar to theirs. The sound of their own language filled the air as merchants hawked their wares.

Thorstein asked a Rus merchant if he knew Ingeld the Much Traveled. The man shook his head, so they continued on.

Farther down the street, he saw a group of thralls on a slave block; some were just children. Thorstein realized his son would someday be one of them if he couldn't find Annoure. He crossed over to a heavy-set man who said, "This one is young and strong. What will you give me for her?"

"I'm not interested in buying a thrall," Thorstein said. "I'm searching for Ingeld the Much Traveled. Do you know him?" Thorstein asked.

The man's eyes lit with recognition. "Já, I know him. He brought some of his thralls here to auction off."

Thorstein's heart speeded up. "Did one of them have a baby with them?" Erik drew closer and Ketil's hand tightened on the handle of his battle-axe.

"Nei." The slave dealer shook his head.

Realizing the baby might not have survived the journey, Thorstein said, "Were any of the thralls an especially beautiful Northumbrian woman?"

The man scratched his round belly, thoughtfully. "None stuck out. They all looked rather scrawny. It's a hard voyage for women. Of course, Ingeld doesn't auction his best thralls. He finds a buyer willing to pay a high price for finer merchandise."

"Is Ingeld still in town?" Thorstein asked.

"I don't know."

Thorstein continued to ask Rus traders if they knew Ingeld's whereabouts. Finally one said, "I saw him go into that tavern." He pointed to a nearby wooden building.

Thorstein strode toward the tavern. *Ingeld was here—the man he'd hunted for all these weeks.*

"We should have a plan," Erik said. "I don't care to be beaten a second time."

Thorstein heard the tension in Erik's voice, but didn't bother to answer. If he found Ingeld, he wasn't going to take time to formulate some plan while Ingeld slipped away. He and his companions were armed and that was enough.

"Erik, how many men does Ingeld have?" Ketil asked.

"I'm not sure. But a trade ship would need a crew of at least ten men."

"Maybe we'll find Ingeld alone in the tavern," Ketil said.

"Nei." Erik shook his head. "He's a coward and is sure to have some guards with him."

They walked into the tavern and Thorstein paused near the door, waiting for his eyes to adjust to the dim light. The place was loud and crowded with Rus, Fins, Arabs and Slavs.

"Which one is he?" Thorstein asked Erik.

Erik scanned the room. "I don't see him. Let's walk around. It would be easy to miss him in this crowd."

"What are you going to do when you find him?" Ketil asked.

"Ask him where Annoure is."

Ketil and Erik exchanged uneasy looks.

When they moved deeper into the tavern, Erik pointed to a bearded man, sitting at a table. His large nose and unsmiling face gave him a hard, uncompromising look. A thick gold chain hung around his neck. "That's him."

"Are you sure?" Thorstein asked.

"Já. Move with care. The heavy-set man to his left is the one who broke my lyre. More of his men may be here as well."

Thorstein pulled *Grimmr* from its sheath, crossed to the table and put the blade to Ingeld's chest.

"Ingeld! I'm Thorstein Garthson. I'm told Annoure was sold to you. Where is she?" Thorstein heard swords being drawn, but kept his eyes on Ingeld. Erik and Ketil would guard his back. "Tell your men to lower their swords or I'll run you through."

Ingeld flushed angrily, then said to his men, "Do as he orders." His hand twitched at the jeweled hilt of his sword, but he didn't draw it. His eyes narrowed. "She told me you'd come for her, but I didn't think any man would journey so far for a thrall. You're well rid of her. She's a witch."

"She's not a witch," Thorstein growled, pressing the sword against Ingeld's chest. "Where is she?"

"You'll never see her again. I sold her to a caravan of a thousand Arabs. She'll spend her life as a slave."

"Where is this caravan now?"

"How would I know?"

"I'll lop off one of your ears to help you remember."

Ingeld flinched. "They left here four days ago, traveling south along the Volga River with armed guards. You better forget her. Look around. My men far outnumber yours and we can easily kill all of you in a fight."

Ingeld pointed to Ketil. "He is the one to blame for your misfortune. He sold her into slavery. I merely resold her at a higher price. Lower your sword and have a drink to cool your temper." His steel-blue eyes met Thorstein's.

Thorstein suppressed the urge to kill him. He had the information he needed and it wouldn't help Annoure if he and his companions died in a fight. He lowered his sword and started to turn away when Ingeld shouted, "Kill them!"

Ingeld sprang to his feet with a drawn sword and attacked. Thorstein blocked the blow with his shield, then thrust *Grimmr* at Ingeld.

Behind him, the sound of clashing weapons echoed repeatedly as Ketil and Erik fought Ingeld's men.

Ingeld swung his sword toward Thorstein. "I should have cast Annoure and her offspring into the sea."

Rage poured through Thorstein at Ingeld's words and he fought like a berserker. He backed Ingeld against the bar and was about to deliver the deathblow when he saw movement in his peripheral vision. Thorstein turned and sliced his sword into the gut of a warrior who had attempted to assault him from the side. Pulling his blade free, his sword met Ingeld's as it slashed toward him. Thorstein leapt back, preparing for Ingeld's next move.

Ingeld swung again and Thorstein jumped aside as the sword whistled past his ear. An image of Ingeld throwing Annoure into the sea flashed into his mind and in frenzy Thorstein hammered his sword into Ingeld's, knocking it from his hand. "This is for Annoure," he cried. He swung *Grimmr* through the air and separated Ingeld's head from his shoulders, spraying himself with blood.

Thorstein raised his shield to his shoulder, grabbed Ingeld's sword and spun around with a sword in each hand just as two men attacked. He fought them both at once, his fury unquenched. He killed one man and Erik wounded the other while Ketil drove several warriors back with his battle-axe. Together the three companions fought their way to the door, thrusting, cutting and slashing, not knowing how many they killed or maimed. They burst out of the tavern and raced through the marketplace with Ingeld's men chasing after them. Other Rus joined in.

"This way!" Erik shouted, heading down a narrow lane, leading Thorstein and Ketil back through the maze of streets. He pushed his way through crowds of people and ran past shops and houses.

Thorstein lost sight of Erik for a moment as a horse crossed his path, then he caught a glimpse of his blue tunic rounding a corner.

"This way!" he yelled to Ketil who was right on his heels. They ran down a narrow alleyway and Thorstein glanced over his shoulder. Ingeld's men and the Rus still gave pursuit.

At last the guarded main gate came into view. Erik paused, panting for breath. "How will we get by the guards?"

"We can't stop. Ingeld's men are right behind us!" Thorstein headed straight toward the two guards, a sword still clutched in each hand. The guards drew their swords, yelling for him to halt.

"Let us pass!" Thorstein yelled.

The guards swung their swords up in answer. Thorstein fought them both at once. Ketil caught up with him and slammed his axe into one guard's head. The sound of the man's skull being crushed barely registered in Thorstein's consciousness as he buried his sword in the other man's side.

Thorstein dashed down to the wharf with Erik and Ketil right behind him. He ran to their boat and scrambled into the first seat, Ketil took the second and Erik the rear. They rowed in unison, moving swiftly away from the pier and entered the current of the wide river.

"Duck!" Erik yelled as a series of arrows flew toward them. Erik raised his shield and several sliced into it. Another hit the side of the boat and one pierced the oar while the rest disappeared into the water. A second batch of arrows fell harmlessly into the river behind their boat.

"Do they give chase?" Thorstein shouted, glancing back at Erik.

"Not yet. Raise the sail. The wind's strong." Together they hoisted the sail and it caught the wind, billowing out. The boat skimmed across the river.

Thorstein looked toward shore and saw that now two small boats were headed after them, probably Ingeld's men. He wasn't worried; they should have enough of a lead to make their escape. Erik was overseeing the sailing of the boat and there was nothing Thorstein needed to do at the moment so he tended to the swords. He used his pant leg to wipe the blood off *Grimmr* then examined it for nicks. Satisfied it wasn't damaged, he slid the blade back into its sheath. Next he cleaned Ingeld's blade in the same manner. It was an expensive weapon, worth a fortune with its jeweled handle and fine steel blade. He wrapped the blade in a cloth and placed it on the bottom of the boat, keeping an eye on the other boats that pursued them. Ingeld's men had rowed their boats into the middle of the river.

Erik steered with the steeringoar, making best use of the wind and waves. Water sprayed Thorstein's face as their vessel flew over the water.

"They've put up their sails!" Ketil yelled.

"We still have a good lead," Erik said. "Thor's thunder, I can't believe we're still alive after taking on Ingeld and his men. Thorstein, I've never seen such fighting!"

"If Thorstein had fought *me* like that, I'd be in Valhalla," Ketil said.

"We all fought well," Thorstein said.

"We fought well," Erik said. "But *you* fought like a Norse hero."

"Battle fever consumed me." Thorstein gazed at the boats following them. "We need to lose them and rescue Annoure."

"You still plan to go after her!" Ketil exclaimed. "You heard what Ingeld said. She's in a caravan of over a thousand Arabs. Even you can't kill that many men."

"What would you have me do? Should I turn back now when we're so close?"

Ketil shook his head. "In the name of Odin, I don't know, Thorstein."

"Annoure and my son will not be thralls!"

"How will we steal them back from the Arabs?" Erik asked.

Thorstein had no idea but he said, "I'll come up with something."

Erick raised an eyebrow. "I saw your last plan in action. I hope this one is better thought-out."

"I agree," Ketil said. His brow wrinkled. "Thorstein, your arm is bleeding. I'd better take a look at it."

Thorstein pulled up his bloody left tunic sleeve and studied the slice across his forearm. He wasn't sure exactly when he'd received it during the fight. "It's not serious," he said.

"Maybe not, but it should still be taken care of. It's bleeding a lot." Ketil bound the wound with a cloth he'd taken from one of the hudfats.

They sailed for several hours, always keeping ahead of the other boats. It was past time for their evening meal so Thorstein pulled out a flask of water, took a drink and passed it to Ketil, then he dug some dried fish out of his hudfat and shared it as well.

The long summer day kept the sun up until late into the evening. When it finally set, the wind died down and the men lowered the sail and started rowing. As Thorstein pulled his two oars through the water the wound in his left arm began to complain. He ignored the pain. They couldn't let Ingeld's men catch up to them.

After awhile Erik said, in a panting breath, "We can't keep up this pace forever."

Thorstein glanced over his shoulder. "They're gaining on us."

Erik started chanting "row" with each stroke so they were all rowing in unison and the boat cut through the water with greater speed. Soon Thorstein's arms burned and his breath became labored. He wasn't accustomed to the stifling heat. He shifted his attention to rescuing Annoure—he had to survive for her.

The setting sun cast pink and purple light across the water, then lowered over the forest. The boats following them disappeared into the darkness of night. Erik stopped chanting and the only sounds were the oars rippling through water and the waves lapping against the boat.

"When we reach the bend in the river," Thorstein whispered. "Let's land and hide the boat in the woods. If the gods favor us, the Rus will go right by without seeing us."

The men increased the force of their strokes and soon rounded the bend. They quickly rowed to shore and Thorstein stepped into the water and pulled the front of the boat into the weeds. Erik and Ketil climbed out and together the men carried the boat into the woods, then crouched down to wait.

After a short time they heard the sound of men talking as the Rus rowed their boats down the river and passed by only a few feet from where they lay on their stomachs.

Thorstein waited for Ingeld's men to get further downstream, then stood, gesturing to Ketil and Erik. They picked up their boat and brought it further onto land, then covered it with branches. Thorstein crept back to the shore and waited to see what Ingeld's men would do. The moon had risen by then. In its pale light he saw the boats coming back slowly.

"We've lost them," one man said in Norse.

"They're probably hiding on land."

"Let's find and kill them."

Thorstein clenched his teeth, worried that they'd pull to shore right where he lay.

"Nei," a gruff voice said. "We need to head back to bury our dead and take care of the wounded."

The voices faded away as the Rus boats disappeared from view into the dark night. Thorstein took a drink from the river, then crawled back to the others.

"They're headed back to Bulgar," Thorstein said. "Get some sleep. We'll leave at sunrise and try to catch up to the caravan. The Arabs can't travel as fast by land as we can by water." He stretched out on the ground, for the night was too warm to sleep in his hudfat. His arms shook with fatigue from the strenuous rowing, his calloused hands hurt from new blisters and the cut on his arm throbbed. He needed sleep, but was too agitated. Since finding his kin dead, his father wounded and Annoure stolen, he carried around a bitter rage that clawed at his soul. Now he felt hollow and unsure he'd be able to save Annoure and his sonr. He closed his eyes and saw the faces of the men he'd killed in battle, wondering what had given him such strength.

At first light, Erik woke Thorstein and Ketil. Thorstein stood, feeling restored and casting aside his fears from the night before. With luck, he'd find Annoure and their sonr today. He knelt in the sand and prayed to Thor for help in finding them, and then set out a piece of dried fish as an offering.

They ate a quick meal before setting off down the river, just as the world began to take on color. As Thorstein rowed, the muscles in his back, arms and shoulders protested. "By Odin's Raven, it hurts to move!"

"Já, we fought and rowed hard yesterday," Ketil said.

The discomfort gradually eased as Thorstein continued rowing.

Later that morning, the wind began to blow in the right direction and they raised the sail. Ketil and Erik played a game of backgammon while Thorstein steered the boat with the steeringoar. His desire to find Annoure was too great to relax and play a game. He wondered if she was all right after giving birth in the wilderness and being abused by Ingeld.

"Have you figured out how to rescue Annoure and the baby?" Erik asked.

Thorstein frowned, realizing the other two men looked to him for leadership.

"We'd have to be crazy to go in swinging swords against a thousand men," Erik added.

Ketil chuckled. "I agree. We could offer to buy her. I have the thick coin purse I stole off Ingeld after Thorstein separated his head from his body. And Thorstein has Ingeld's jeweled sword."

"How can we trade with them when we can't speak their tongue?" Thorstein asked. "And if we could, why would they sell such a beautiful woman when they came all this way to buy thralls? More likely they'll kill us as soon as we approach their camp. I think we're safer to steal Annoure in the middle of the night."

"How will we find their camp?" Ketil asked.

"They'll need water and so they'll camp near the river," Thorstein said. "With such a large caravan we can't miss them."

Although they traveled late into the evening, they didn't catch up with the caravan, so they decided to set up camp while it was still light. Thorstein wearily fell asleep almost as soon as he lay down.

The next day they rose at dawn and spent the day on the river. Thorstein was discouraged when the sun began to set and they still hadn't come upon the caravan. Erik and Ketil urged him to stop for the night, but he was too desperate to find Annoure. A short time later, Thorstein paused in the middle of a stroke. The sound of voices and a horse's whiny drifted across the water. "Did you hear that?" he exclaimed.

"Já, we must be near the camp," Erik said.

They rowed to shore and tied their boat to a tree where it was hidden by bushes.

"Let's spread out and try to locate Annoure," Thorstein said. "Stay out of sight. We'll meet back here, then go after her together."

They disbanded and Thorstein moved silently through the dark woods. At the edge of the caravan, Thorstein crawled on his belly through thick bushes until he had a good view. Guards walked around the edge of the encampment, which was lit by campfires.

The size of the caravan astonished Thorstein. Men, animals and tents were in every open area between the trees. His quest seemed hopeless. How would he ever figure out which tent held Annoure?

He studied the robed Arabs; they were short in stature with black hair and olive or brown skin, and armed with knives and curved swords. The guards talked among themselves, looking relaxed, as if they didn't expect trouble.

Thorstein crept back into the woods and circled to the left side of camp. The fires were starting to die down and Arabs were retiring for the night. He started back to meet Erik and Ketil when he heard voices. He ducked behind a large pine tree as group of people with water jugs walked by him on their way to the river. He moved closer to them, drawn by the sound of women's voices.

Three armed Arabs guarded a group of five women. A delicately framed woman placed a bundle on the ground and waded into the river up to her knees. She lowered her jug into the water. It was too dark to make out her face, but her movements reminded him of Annoure.

Thorstein squatted lower as one of the Arab guards looked his way. The loud wail of a baby's cry pierced the air. The woman headed back to the bundle she'd left on shore. Thorstein's pulse quickened when he caught a glimpse of her face. *Annoure!* His beloved! He fought the impulse to tear out of the bushes and strike down all the guards, knowing he'd be throwing away any chance of rescuing her. Clutching the hilt of his sword, he watched her lift the baby into her arms and sway gently back and forth.

Annoure started back to camp with the others. As she drew closer, he saw deep sorrow etched in her face. Her long hair was bedraggled, her kaftan dirty, and her walk weary. It pierced his heart to think about all she must have gone through.

Annoure paused and looked straight at where he was hidden. He knew he was well-concealed by the thick foliage, yet it seemed as if she saw him. She continued walking and he followed at a distance, keeping to the gloomy shelter of the trees. Once he saw which tent she went in, he raced back to the boat where Erik and Ketil waited.

"I found her!" he exclaimed as soon as he reached them. "She and the baby are here and alive."

"You saw her!" Erik said, his face lit with excitement.

"She went down to the river with a group of women to fill water jugs. They were guarded by three men."

"How will we rescue her?" Ketil asked.

"I saw which tent she went in. We'll go there after it gets dark."

"What about the guards?" Erik added.

They spent the rest of the evening discussing possible ways to rescue Annoure and by nightfall they had worked out a plan.

When the moon rose, the three men used its light to creep toward the Arab camp. Thorstein and Erik each carried a bow, quiver of arrows, and a sword and Ketil had his battle-axe. When Thorstein spotted a guard, he notched an arrow into his bow and let it fly. The arrow soared through the air, sailing past the man's head and struck a tree behind him. The guard turned toward the arrow right as Erik let another loose. It pierced the man's throat and he fell silently to the ground.

Thorstein and Erik dragged the body into the woods. Thorstein pulled the Arab's robe on over his clothes and put on the man's turban. They killed two more guards on the perimeter of the camp to gain robes for Erik and Ketil. Once they were disguised, Thorstein led the way through the enormous camp, moving past guards, goats, horses and camels. A few Arabs still sat around campfires, but most had retired to their tents.

Thorstein thought he could remember which tent Annoure was in, but now he was uncertain. The tents all looked alike under the cover of night and at least a hundred of them were spread out among the tall pines and alders.

Chapter 29

Arab Camp

BAN CRIED LUSTILY AS ANNOURE put fresh moss, she'd found in the woods, under his bottom. She wrapped him in a blanket to keep the moss in place, then held him to her breast.

He refused to nurse and continued howling. She felt the Arab's annoyance in the crowded tent—seven of them shared it with her and Fitela—and no one could sleep with the noise Ban was making. She worried the men might decide to leave Ban in the woods if he continued to disturb their sleep.

Not knowing what else to do, she stepped over the men trying to rest beside her and carried Ban outside. At the campfire, she rocked Ban in her arms and sang a Celtic lullaby. A guard followed her out of the tent and walked over to the horses.

Annoure and Fitela had been with the caravan for nearly two weeks. The first week they stayed in Bulgar while the Arabs traded. Many slaves, mainly women, were purchased and brought back to camp where they were kept in chains. Annoure and Fitela were closely watched, but not chained up with the others, nor had any of the men molested them.

One morning they were awakened early and given dates and a piece of mutton. While they ate, the large camp was broken down and packed onto the horses and humpback creatures she learned were camels. Their efficiency impressed Annoure.

Before the sun was fully overhead, they started the journey south. Some of the men rode on horses or camels, but most walked. Annoure strapped Ban to her chest with her shawl then she and Fitela walked alongside the other women. They trekked through a wooded, hilly land, keeping close to the river. After several hours, Annoure grew tired and her legs began to ache. She wondered if they'd walk all day without rest.

One of the women tripped, fell and began weeping, saying she was too tired to keep walking. The nearest guard brought his whip down on her back several times, yelling at her in Arabic. The woman rose with another woman's help and kept walking with her friend's assistance.

Soon Ban started fussing and Annoure knew he must be hungry. She didn't dare stop so she adjusted the baby in the shawl and nursed him as she walked. Once the baby was feed, Fitela carried him to give Annoure a break.

In the early afternoon, they were finally allowed to rest and given some bread and cheese. Then they walked until evening and the camp was quickly reassembled. The next three days went by much like the first. Annoure began to lose hope that Thorstein would ever find her.

Now as Annoure sang Ban lullabies, Fitela emerged from the tent and joined her at the fire. The two women had grown even closer in this strange new life.

"I'm sorry to keep you awake," Annoure said. "I don't know why Ban's so fussy."

"Maybe I can calm him. The poor baby's feeling your distress." She took Ban from Annoure and rubbed his back. His cries softened. "What's wrong, Annoure? You've been distracted ever since we set up camp."

"I sense something's about to happen."

"Perhaps a storm's brewing and you feel it in the air."

"Nei, look, the sky is clear, yet I'm tingling with expectation."

Fitela looked up. "It's a full moon. Perhaps it's magic."

"It's not magic. At the river, I felt Thorstein's presence." Annoure lifted a branch from the pile of firewood and placed it on the campfire.

A twig snapped and she looked up. A robed Arab approached their camp. The way he walked reminded her of Thorstein and her heart began to race. As he came closer, the firelight lit up his blond hair.

"Thorstein!" she gasped. Her hands went to her mouth and tears sprang to her eyes. She jumped up and raced toward him.

The guard yelled something in Arabic. When Thorstein didn't reply, he drew his sword and charged forward. Thorstein swung up his shield and the Arab's sword clashed into it.

Terrified for Thorstein, Annoure grabbed a thick branch and slammed it into the back of the guard's head. It hit with a thud and he collapsed.

Thorstein and Annoure flew into each other's arms. "Annoure!" he exclaimed as their mouths met in a passionate kiss.

She clung to him, joy filling her.

"Watch out!" Erik yelled as he and Ketil raced toward them. Annoure tried to make sense of Ketil being there as Thorstein spun around. The guard had regained his feet and his sword flashed in the firelight as it came toward Thorstein. *Grimmr* met it and sparks flew. Thorstein lunged, parried and thrust again. The Arab shouted for help.

A man emerged from the tent and Erik cut him down. Ketil swung his battle-axe into the next man's chest. Three more men appeared with swords drawn. Erik attacked one and Ketil another, but the third slipped by and grabbed Fitela, who still held Ban.

Annoure snatched a sword off the ground and advanced on the man holding Fitela. He released Fitela and slammed his sword into Annoure's. The impact on the blade vibrated through her arms and she lost hold of the weapon. As it fell to the ground, she took a panicked step backward. The Arab smiled cruelly and stepped toward her, his sword raised.

Thorstein sliced his blade across his opponent's chest, then sprang in front of Annoure. He twisted his blade, turning the Arab's sword away.

Annoure glanced frantically around as Thorstein and the man continued fighting. More men ran toward them from nearby campsites.

A few feet away, Erik dodged a blade slashing toward him and then sliced his sword across his adversary's leg. The man screamed in pain and fell to the ground, clutching his wound while Erik turned to face a new enemy.

Thorstein stabbed his sword into his opponent's gut, then grabbed up the sword Annoure had dropped. With a sword in each hand, he fought two more Arabs who had joined the fight.

Ketil crashed his battle-axe into his opponent and the man fell moaning to the ground. Ketil spotted Annoure and yelled, "Come with me. We have a boat."

"Nei, you son of a serpent! I won't go anywhere with you."

"Go with him," Thorstein yelled as he fought the two men. "Erik and I will follow."

"I want to stay with you," Annoure said.

"Nei! Get our baby out of here!" Thorstein blocked one opponent's sword with his own weapon, then swept his second sword toward another Arab. "Go now! We'll hold them off so you can escape."

Annoure looked at Fitela and Ban, feeling torn. "Hurry, Annoure!" Fitela cried, running over to Ketil. Annoure started to follow when a tingling sensation shot up her spine. She looked back right as Erik's opponent knocked the sword from his hand and thrust his blade toward Erik. He dodged away. Annoure ran back, grabbed Erik's sword and tossed it to him, hilt first. He caught it in midair right as the Arab slashed his sword into Erik's belly.

"Nei!" she exclaimed as Erik dropped to one knee clutching his stomach. She moved in front of him to shield him from further injury. The Arab shoved her aside and sliced his sword toward Erik. Erik grabbed his knife from its sheath and threw it. The knife lodged in the man's eye and he fell backward onto the ground, screaming in pain.

Annoure put her arm around Erik and helped his rise. "Can you make it to the horses, Erik?"

"Save yourself. It is too late for me."

"I won't leave you. Come on." Annoure struggled under his weight as they staggered to the horses. After she helped him onto the nearest one, she untied the reins and tossed them up to him, then slapped the horse on its rump. An Arab grabbed her as she started to mount another horse.

"Let her go!" Ketil yelled, running up to them. The Arab released her as he turned to defend himself. Ketil slammed his axe into his head; then he hoisted Annoure over his shoulder and ran into the woods.

"Put me down! We can't leave Thorstein!" Annoure raged, beating her fists against his back. He carried her over to where Fitela waited with the baby and set her down. "We need to go back and help Thorstein!" Annoure cried.

"He can better defend himself if he doesn't have you and Ban to worry about," Ketil said.

"Come, we must escape!" Fitela exclaimed, shoving Ban into Annoure's arms. Ketil and Fitela each grabbed one of Annoure's upper arms and started forward.

Annoure struggled to free herself, terrified of losing Thorstein. "I can't leave him."

"Don't worry," Ketil said. "The gods favor Thorstein in battle."

"Think of Ban," Fitela added.

Annoure clutched the infant to her chest and began to run alongside Fitela and Ketil. Under the cover of night, they wove their way through the trees and scattered tents.

When the river came into view, they left the shelter of the woods and sprinted toward the boat.

Annoure heard the pounding of hooves behind her and glanced back. A black-haired man on horseback bore down upon them. Fitela kept running, but Ketil raised his battle-axe and waited for his approach.

Thorstein galloped out of the woods on a chestnut horse, chasing after the horseman, but the Arab rider had nearly reached Annoure and Ketil.

Ketil glanced at Annoure. "Get to the boat." His eyes shone with emotion.

Annoure fled with Ban. The thunder of hooves drew closer; she looked back and gasped. The horse and rider were nearly on top of Ketil! It looked like he'd be trampled.

At the last possible moment, Ketil leapt into the air and smashed his battle-axe into the man's side, knocking him from the saddle. Ketil mounted the frightened horse as Thorstein came galloping up to him.

"Get Annoure!" Ketil shouted. When Thorstein reached Annoure, he swept both her and the baby into the saddle in front of him and kept riding. Ketil raced over to Fitela and lifted her onto his horse.

At the river, Thorstein sprang from the horse, then lifted Annoure and the baby down. Erik was already there, but was too weak to dismount. Thorstein helped him off the horse and into the boat. Fitela, Ketil, and Annoure, who held the baby, scrambled in after him.

Thorstein splashed into the water as he shoved the boat further into the river. An Arab warrior galloped toward him swinging his sword. Annoure screamed, "Behind you!" Thorstein twisted around, reaching for his sheathed sword.

An arrow zinged past Annoure's head and pierced the Arab's chest. He tumbled from his stead. Annoure looked back at Ketil, whose bow was still extended.

As they rowed away, a group of Arabs stood on the bank with raised fists and shouted at them. The men on shore gradually faded from sight as they rowed steadily across the wide river.

Upon reaching the opposite shore, Ketil and Thorstein carried Erik to land. When they carefully set him down on a hudfat, he groaned in pain. "I'm sorry, we tried to be gentle," Thorstein said, placing his hand on Erik's shoulder.

"My wound is not important," he said weakly. "Today I was part of an amazing saga. I fought beside Thorstein the Fearless as he stole his beloved from a thousand Arabs!"

"I am worried about you, not some saga."

"And Ketil the Bloody-Axe will be in the saga as well," Erik continued. "The courageous warrior, who knocked an Arab from his galloping stallion, to save the woman he loved though her heart belongs to another man."

He groaned, grasping his stomach, then said, "Let there be peace between us, Ketil. You are a brave man and a furious warrior. Whatever wrong you did, you've done your best to right it."

"It lightens my spirit to have your goodwill again." Ketil's eyes met Annoure's. In the moonlight shining off the river's surface, she saw concern for Erik etched in his face. She held the baby close to her chest, drawing comfort from him.

Ketil lit an iron lamp. By its light, Thorstein removed Erik's robe and body armor, then lifted up his tunic. Erik's stomach was sliced open, exposing his inner organs.

Vomit rose in Annoure's throat and she looked away, trying not to retch. She doubted Erik would survive the night.

Thorstein pushed the two sides of the wound together and bound it with a cloth. Erik reached out and clasped his hand. "Don't look so distressed, Thorstein. I thought I would die a straw death; instead I'll die as a warrior and go to Valhalla."

"A straw death?" Annoure asked, not understanding.

"Dying in bed," Erik said. "It's more honorable to die in battle." He looked at Thorstein. "Tell my faðir of my deeds so he'll be proud of me."

"I'll tell him you're a great warrior," Thorstein's voice broke. "And a true friend." Thorstein helped Erik into the hudfat, then gave him some water from a flask. "Are you in a lot of pain?"

"Já, it is a bad place to be wounded." Erik closed his eyes and

Annoure wiped the sweat off his forehead with a cloth. The baby started fussing so she reluctantly moved a few feet away from Erik to nurse him.

Thorstein moved beside her and touched the baby's cheek. "He's a beautiful baby. I feared he'd die on such a hard journey."

"Nei, he's strong and a true seaman like his father." When in her mind she'd imagined presenting Ban to his father, it was always a happy occasion—not like this, with Erik dying.

Thorstein examined the baby. "He's so small and perfect. What did you name him?"

"Ban after my grandfather."

"That's not a good Norse name."

"He is Ban Thorsteinson."

Pride shone in Thorstein's eyes. "It sounds good when said like that."

Thorstein returned to Erik's side. "Is there anything I can do for you, my friend?"

"Share the saga of our adventures with our people back home."

"I'll tell our story to a skald and he will create a saga that will be remembered by our Norse children's children."

"And make your peace with Ketil and his kin."

Thorstein's throat thickened and he nodded. "I swear on my honor to try to end this feud."

With shaky hands, Erik pulled off the silver chain hanging around his neck. A hammer amulet hung from it. "Thor's hammer has brought me good luck for many a year. I want you to have it."

Thorstein held the amulet, looking grief-stricken. "You still need it," he said, his voice filled with anguish.

"It's yours now. Put it on."

"Don't give up, Erik. We've been through too much together for you to die."

Erik smiled sadly. "I'm not afraid."

"I know, but the world will be a lesser place without you."

"Wear my gift, please. You are like a bróðir to me."

Thorstein slid the chain over his head. "And you are like a bróðir to me."

Annoure's heart ached as she watched the exchange between the two men. Then Thorstein placed a dried fish on the ground and begged Odin to let Erik live. The baby fell asleep and Annoure moved back to the skald and said, "Thank you, Erik, for telling Thorstein of my fate and joining him in my rescue. You've suffered so much for me and I can do nothing for you."

"I did what I felt was right. A man can do no less. You should be proud of Thorstein. He's a great warrior of rare courage."

"Don't try to talk; you must save your strength."

"I'm dying, Annoure. If I don't speak now, I won't have another chance."

"Don't die. I can't bear it." Tears dampened her cheeks. "We need you. *I* need you. I need your wisdom, guidance and friendship."

"You've grown strong and no longer need my guidance."

"I still do. And who will journey from farm to farm, to brighten the cold winter days with music and stories of the Norse people?"

"There will be a new skald. The songs and sagas will live on."

"None can replace you." Annoure began weeping. Thorstein came over and drew her into his arms. She clung to him, grateful for his comfort.

Nearby Fitela and Ketil unloaded the boat and put up the tent. Then Ketil squatted beside Erik and asked, "Do you want us to move you into the tent?"

Erik shook his head. "Nei, it would hurt too much, but I *am* getting cold."

"We'll build you a fire."

The men gathered sticks and branches and soon a fire blazed.

"I'll take the first shift guarding camp," Thorstein said.

"Wake me when you need a break." Ketil went into the tent where Fitela had already retired.

"You need to rest too, my love." Thorstein said to Annoure.

"Nei, I'll sit up with Erik. You go to sleep. I can rest tomorrow on the boat."

"There's nothing you can do for him."

"I can keep him company. He's dying because of me."

"It's not your fault." He placed a cape over her shoulders.

"Thank you," she said, glad for its warmth. She took Erik's clammy hand in hers and he clasped it tightly.

"Sing to me, Annoure, to distract me from the pain."

She sang a Celtic folk song, thinking of home and happier times. Sitting beside her, Thorstein kept nodding off and jerking back awake. She finished her song and said, "Get some rest, Thorstein. I'll keep watch."

"You must be just as tired."

"Nei, I'm too distraught to sleep."

"Wake me if you need me." He built the fire back up, then kissed her tenderly and stretched out on the ground. She gazed at Erik. His eyes were closed, but he still squeezed her hand.

"Water," he moaned.

She held a flask so he could take a sip. "I wish I could ease your pain."

"Your presence is enough, Annoure. I sense you've moved more fully into your power and embraced your gifts. You're becoming the woman you're meant to be."

"I had to embraced them to survive."

As the hours dragged by, his breathing became increasingly labored and ragged. Annoure hated seeing him suffer so much.

Ban awoke and she nursed him, then wrapped him in a fur and placed him on the ground beside his sleeping father. Her head spun and back ached, but she didn't give in to the need to sleep. She didn't want to leave Erik alone with his pain. She wiped Erik's sweaty forehead and took a hold of his hand again. He squeezed it tightly and rasped, "By the gods, it hurts. Let it be done with."

His hand went limp in hers. A shudder went through Annoure as she realized he was gone. She closed her eyes and focused inwardly, then shifted her awareness to a spot above her physical body and soared into the sky. She found Erik's spirit hovering above his dying body.

"Let's move on, Erik." Annoure clasped his hand and they rose into the air together. Below them the woods and river became smaller. Erik's face was transformed with amazement. In that moment, she recognized him as someone she knew from another life.

A being of light appeared and Erik started forward. At the last moment, he paused and turned back to Annoure, smiling. "We'll meet again someday, Annoure. You can't come any further."

"Erik!" she cried out, her heart breaking.

"You'll be all right. You're stronger than you realize." He and the being of light flew away.

Opening her eyes, Annoure looked at Erik's lifeless body. Terrible anguish arose within her and she clutched his head to her heart, weeping softly, rocking back and forth. She hadn't realized how much she'd come to love Erik. Theirs was a deep friendship.

She wept until she felt empty, then gently set Erik's head down on the hudfat and lay beside Thorstein, who still slept soundly. She put her arm around him, taking comfort in the sound of his steady breathing and the warmth of his body.

In the predawn light, she studied her beloved's face. Dark circles shadowed his eyes and his face had a gaunt, haggard look, as if he'd been ill. He had a beard and his tangled blond hair had grown to his shoulders. Gratitude and love for him filled her as she thought of all he must have endured to find and rescue her.

Unable to relax, she rose; a wave of dizziness washed over her. Once it passed, she walked to the river to watch the sunrise. Pink, orange and red hues lit up the sky and reflected in the rippling river. Its beauty contrasted with her deep sorrow.

Chapter 30

Funeral Pyre

AWAKENED BY LOUD, ANGRY VOICES, Thorstein started to reach for his sword when he realized it was just Ketil and Annoure arguing by the shoreline. Annoure's hands punctuated her words as she yelled, "Erik's dead because of you!"

Erik's dead! Thorstein thought, his gut twisting. He turned toward Erik's lifeless body. Grief clutched him like a band drawn tight around his heart. He wished he'd stayed awake and been with Erik until the end. His hand shook as he touched Erik's cold face. "Goodbye, my friend. Thank you for helping me rescue Annoure and Ban." His voice broke as he continued. "Without you, I wouldn't have known where Ingeld was taking them."

"I hate you, Ketil!" Annoure cried. Her anguished voice penetrated Thorstein's sorrow and he turned toward her. She flew at Ketil, who made no attempt to defend himself, and beat her fists against his chest.

"If you hadn't sold me, none of this would have happen!" She burst into tears and Thorstein started to go to her. But then Ketil put his arms around her and surprisingly she stopped hitting him and clutched his jerkin.

"You said you loved me! How could you sell me?" she sobbed.

Thorstein stood frozen in place, distressed by the intense feelings between Annoure and Ketil and by the intimate way Ketil held her.

"I'm sorry," Ketil said. "I regretted it as soon as I did it." His voice sounded hoarse. "I couldn't live with myself afterwards."

Annoure shoved him away. "Regrets are useless!"

Ketil reached for her. "Forgive me."

"I can *never* forgive you."

Thorstein charged over to them. "Stay away from her!" He clenched his hands into fists, restraining the urge to hit Ketil.

"I was only trying to comfort her. She's upset that Erik died."

"She's upset because you stole her from her home and sold her into slavery." Suddenly all of Ketil's crimes seemed to overshadow the good he'd done since then. "I should have let Erik kill you in the tavern."

"Nei, I should have left *you* to die from your well-deserved wounds. You killed my bróðir and my cousin!"

Thorstein moved angrily toward Ketil and Annoure grabbed his arm. "Stop! Please! You promised Erik you'd end this feud."

"Did Ketil rape you?"

She shook her head, looking stricken. "Nei. He never touched me."

"Do you swear it on your Christian Bible?"

"I swear it! Please, Thorstein, you must believe me."

"Did Edgtho?"

"Nei. Ketil protected me from Edgtho and saved our baby from drowning after Edgtho cast him into the sea. We owe him a blood debt. I'm sorry I started this quarrel. It's not Ketil's fault that Erik is dead."

"We should mourn Erik, not dishonor him with a quarrel," Ketil said. "Let's build a funeral pyre." Without waiting for their agreement, he walked away and began picking up driftwood.

Shaking with emotion, Thorstein drew Annoure into his arms. He gripped her tightly, needing her close to him. Gradually his turbulent emotions lessened. Erik was in Valhalla and, beyond all odds, Annoure and his child were with him.

The baby began crying. Fitela picked him up, but his wails continued to pierce the air, jarring Thorstein's already frayed nerves.

"I better feed Ban," Annoure said. When she moved away from Thorstein, he immediately missed the feel of her body pressed to his. She sat on the ground and put the baby to her breast. Blessed silence followed as he began to suckle.

Thorstein joined Ketil in collecting driftwood and branches that were scattered along the shoreline. Once the pyre was constructed, he and Ketil reverently placed Erik's body on top of it.

Ketil lifted two burning sticks from the campfire and handed one to Thorstein. Together they placed them on the funeral pyre. Thorstein watched transfixed as the wood began to burn. Annoure came over carrying Ban and she placed a blazing stick beside his.

Before long, the smell of burning flesh filled the air, making Thorstein want to gag. He covered his nose to block the odor as he watched Erik's body burn.

Ketil raised his hands in the air and said in a solemn voice, "Lo, Erik the Skald is in Valhalla with Odin. He died the death of a brave warrior and we honor him."

As Thorstein stood gazing at the fire with Ketil and Annoure, he felt a strong bond between the three of them, despite everything they'd been through.

When the fire died down, Ketil and Fitela started packing their provisions. Thorstein stayed with Annoure, mesmerized by the burning embers.

After a while Annoure said, "When Erik died, I saw an angel take him to heaven."

He looked at her, puzzled. "Surely she was a Valkyrie, not an angel. His brave deeds earned him a place in Valhalla."

"Perhaps she was a Valkyrie since Erik was a Norseman. Though I doubt he'll want to go to a world where there's always fighting. He was more of a priest than a warrior. He told me to embrace my gifts. I was uneasy at using them because the Christian priests warn against unnatural powers. But now I've embraced them."

"I'm glad you've come to see your powers as gifts for they bring you closer to the mysteries of life." Thorstein glanced toward the boat where Ketil and Fitela were loading supplies. They had to leave, but he wanted to eat first. "Are you hungry?"

She nodded. He took out a bag of dried fruit and nuts he'd bought for her in a village along the Volga. Her face lit up when she saw the food. "It's good to have something to eat besides dried fish," she said.

After they ate, he remembered the things he'd brought for her and removed them from his hudfat. There were two hangerocks and under-dresses, baby blankets and baby gowns. "These are for you and Ban."

She hugged him. "Thank you. You don't know how much this means to me."

"Kalsetini's the one who thought to pack clothes for you."

"But you were the one who carried them all this distance." She eagerly began looking through the clothes and baby blankets.

It pleased him that she was so grateful and excited. He'd carried the clothes across several difficult portages and, until this moment, hadn't been sure they were worth the trouble. As he rolled up his hudfat, Annoure changed Ban into a gown and swaddled him in a blanket.

"Is there time for me to bathe?" she asked.

He shook his head. "I'm sorry, but we need to leave as soon as possible. We have a long trip ahead of us and have lost enough of the day. You can bathe when we camp for the night."

Annoure washed her face and hands at the riverbank, then lifted Ban into her arms and walked toward the woods.

"Where are you going?" Thorstein called after her, his voice sharp with concern.

She jumped nervously and turned to look at him with frightened eyes. "I . . . I was just going to change. Is that all right?"

"Stay close. It's dangerous to wander off." He hadn't meant to scare her, but he didn't want to lose her now. She disappeared behind some bushes and he busied himself by making a comfortable place for her and Ban to sleep in the boat. Annoure would be tired as she'd been up all night with Erik. Once he finished, he looked toward the woods, trying not to worry.

Shortly Annoure reappeared with the baby, wearing a new hangerock and under-dress. Her radiant beauty stunned him. She'd brushed her hair, which flowed down her back to her hips in dark waves and shimmered in the light. Ketil smiled at her from the front of the boat and she smiled back, causing Thorstein a stab of jealousy.

Thorstein waded into the water with Annoure and the baby in his arms and placed them in the boat. He didn't mind getting his pant legs wet for the sun was out and the day was already warm. After pushing the boat into the river, he climbed in.

Fitela already sat on the middle thwart, clasping an oar in each hand. Working together the three of them began to row. Thorstein was disheartened as he thought about the return voyage on the Volga. They had to travel seven hundred miles against the current of the river.

Annoure curled up on the hudfat to nurse Ban, then they both fell asleep. Thorstein was glad she had a chance to rest, though he craved a chance to talk with her after their long separation. His heart filled with pride as he looked at Ban. Up until he'd found Annoure he hadn't dared hope that the baby would still be alive. He smiled, someday he'd teach Ban to fish, hunt and sail a boat.

They rowed until the wind turned favorable, then put up the sail and sailed against the current. After a few hours the baby started crying and woke his mother. Annoure looked wildly around, disoriented worry in her eyes, as if she didn't know where she was. When she saw Thorstein, her alarm dissolved. "How much further to Bulgar?" She sat up and put the fussy baby to her breast.

"A few days since we're sailing against the current, but we won't stop there."

"Why not?"

"We had some trouble in Bulgar. At a tavern we battled Ingeld and some of his men. And then when escaping from Bulgar, we killed two guards at the gate."

"Thorstein sliced off Ingeld's head," Ketil said.

"You killed Ingeld!" Annoure exclaimed.

"Já, the gods favored me."

The color drained from Annoure's face.

"What's wrong?" Thorstein exclaimed in dismay.

She shook her head. "I . . . he . . ." she stammered, looking close to tears. "I can't speak of it."

Thorstein stared at her, not knowing what to say.

"You should be glad," Fitela said. "Ingeld can never hurt you again."

"I *am* glad he's dead. That's not what distresses me." Annoure leaned forward and clasped Thorstein's thigh, her eyes filled with agony. "Ingeld was marked for death. I saw its shadow over his shoulder. But his death does not change what happened. I should have drowned myself rather than come to you defiled."

"You're not to blame," he said, hating to see her pain. He felt fiercely protective of her and wished he could hold her in his arms, but it was impossible in the boat.

They traveled late into the evening before setting up camp. After eating, Thorstein and Annoure crawled into his hudfat and she placed the baby between them. Thorstein leaned over Ban and kissed her, then lay back with his arm around her, cherishing being with her again. He wanted to make love to her and his body began to ache with desire, but he held back, sensing she wasn't ready.

The next morning, they rose early and were soon on the water. Thorstein was tried and rowed with less vigor than the day before. Annoure and Ketil also rowed while Fitela tended the baby. The day was still new when Annoure tilted her oars out of the water and turned to look at him. Her pretty face was flushed. "Rowing against the current is hard work."

"Rest when you need to. Ketil and I will keep rowing. When the wind changes we can use the sails. We need to reach the farm before winter."

"Do you know what month it is?" she asked.

"Nei, but it must be late summer."

"What if we don't make home by winter?"

"Then we'll stay in Hedeby."

Annoure frowned, looking worried. "What will we live off of?"

"Ketil and I can work. I can also sell Ingeld's sword. It'll bring a lot in trade."

"And I have Ingeld's purse and gold necklace," Ketil said.

"And the blood money you made from selling Annoure," Thorstein snapped. His remark ended the conversation and he realized belatedly that the voyage would be long and unpleasant if he kept up his antagonism toward Ketil.

Chapter 31

River Volga

EARLY IN THE MORNING A few days later, Annoure waded into the Volga. Cool water lapped around her legs as she scrubbed her hair with a bar of soap, then rinsed out the suds. On shore, she combed her snarled, wet hair, thinking of Thorstein. She wanted the closeness they shared before, but they hardly had a chance to talk.

Thorstein walked over from the nearby campsite where Ketil and Fitela sat by the cooking fire. "You look melancholy," he said.

"I miss Erik."

"I miss him, too. I've known him most of my life and he was my constant companion all summer." Thorstein pulled off his shirt and tunic, squatted by the river and splashed water on his face. A large purple scar marred his side.

"You have a new wicked-looking scar. What happened?"

"Ketil and I had a sword fight after I killed Edgtho. Ketil nearly killed me." He ran a hand through his blond hair, looking troubled. "Most likely I'll be fined at the *ting* again."

"Why should you pay a fine after all Edgtho did?"

"Dylan will want to end this blood feud. Ketil will probably be outlawed."

"Why are you traveling with Ketil after he nearly killed you?"

The muscles tightened across Thorstein's muscular shoulders. "I had little choice. I was gravely wounded and Ketil used my boat as a funeral pyre for Edgtho."

"He burned your boat!"

Thorstein nodded, grimly.

She slapped a mosquito on her arm, then another on her leg. She longed to get back on the water, away from these bloodthirsty pests. “Why would Ketil offer to help you?”

“He claims to regret selling you into slavery.”

“He told me that, too.” She remembered the tortured look in Ketil’s eyes when he said it. “He feared you wouldn’t know I’d been kidnapped until you returned home at the end of the summer.”

“When Ketil and Edgtho didn’t show up at camp to go a-viking, I knew something was wrong. I’m sorry I didn’t listen to your pleas and stay home to protect you last spring.”

She looked down, a lump forming in her throat. “I understand if you no longer want me for a vif.”

“Not want you? Thor’s thunder, Annoure, why would you say such a thing? I left my home and family to come after you, even though my faðir was fatally wounded, my bróðir dead and the farm my responsibility.”

“You seem . . . distant.” *And I’ve been Ingeld’s pleasure thrall*, she thought but she didn’t have the courage to voice it aloud. Shame filled her.

“I’m just worried. It’s dangerous to travel the Volga.”

“Maybe we can find another party to travel with.”

“We would have if we’d stopped in Bulgar.” He stood. “We’d better get going.”

* * *

In the afternoon, the wind whistled through the leaves of the trees on the shoreline and kicked up waves on the river. The men and Fitela made little headway as they rowed against it.

Finally Ketil said, “Let’s go to shore. We can rest a while and set off again when the wind dies down.”

Thorstein agreed and they headed for land. Once there, Thorstein pulled out his bow and arrows. “I’m going hunting. We’re short of food. Will you guard the women, Ketil?”

“Do you think they need guarding? We’re more apt to get something if we both hunt.”

Thorstein’s eyes met Annoure’s and she saw his uneasiness. ”I don't want to take any chances. The Slav and Finnish tribes are always warring and I've seen signs of bears and heard howling wolf packs."

"True enough." Ketil sat on a log near Annoure. "I can use the rest."

Thorstein disappeared into the woods.

"I'm going to see if I can find some berries or roots to eat," Fitela said, going into the woods.

Ketil smiled, looking at the baby. "Can I hold Ban?"

A stab of resentment shot through Annoure. *How dare Ketil ask to hold Ban after selling him into slavery?* She shook her head.

Ketil's smile faded. "I'm sorry. I shouldn't have asked."

Ashamed, Annoure held out the baby. "You've risked a lot to save me and Ban from a life of slavery. You've earned the right to hold him."

Ketil took Ban and smiled at him tenderly. The baby studied his face. "He's grown a lot. He makes me miss my dóttirs."

"How old are they?"

"Three and four. My vif's been dead for over two years. I still feel her loss keenly. Hanna and I knew each other since childhood and I loved her deeply. The best part of me died when she died and I haven't been myself since. I've been angry with the gods, life, even at her for leaving me. I dared the gods to kill me and would have welcomed death. When Thorstein killed Rethel, it gave me somewhere else to direct my rage. I'm sorry I stole you from your home. The mischievous god Loki must have twisted my thinking."

"You can't blame Loki."

"Loki causes trouble for humans." When she didn't object a second time, he continued. "On the journey to Hedeby, I was drawn to you. You were large with child and it reminded me of my sweet, gentle Hanna. I wanted to protect you.

"On the night Ban was born, I was reborn as well. I cared about something and wanted to live again. I thought you were the way out of the pain I'd been in. I wanted you to love me and make me happy again. When you refused to marry me, I went berserk."

He gazed at her sorrowfully. "I feel terrible for selling you to Ingeld. It is the worst thing I've ever done." He continued after a long pause. "On the night Thorstein killed Edgtho and I seriously wounded Thorstein, I thought about all that happened. When the anger left me, guilt filled me because I knew Thorstein acted honorably in avenging his family and searching for you. I decided if the gods let him live, I would help him find you. I know you can't forgive me, but I want you to know I am truly sorry for selling you and Ban into slavery."

Annoure sighed. "You've done dreadful things, but you've also done good things. I don't want you banished at the *ting*. It would be hard for your daughters to lose their father when they've already lost their mother. I wish none of this happened."

She looked to the woods where Thorstein disappeared. "I'm worried about Thorstein. He's pushing himself and us too hard."

Ketil handed the baby back to Annoure. "He has to. It's getting colder and soon the trees will change color."

Annoure stood with Ban in her arms. "I'm going to gather some moss for Ban."

"Leave Ban with me. I'm going to fish."

She set the baby down on a hudfat and went into the lush forest. Moss grew in abundance and she quickly filled her leather bag. When she returned, she saw Ban was asleep and Ketil had caught a large fish. They'd have a good dinner even if Thorstein didn't have any luck hunting. She curled up beside Ban and fell asleep.

Ban's crying awakened her sometime later and she began nursing him. Her stomach growled as she breathed in the aroma of roasting meat. A skinned rabbit cooked over the fire, hanging from a structure made of sticks.

"You're finally awake," Thorstein said, smiling at her from where he and the others sat by the fire, eating fish.

"I didn't realize how tired I was."

"Ketil thinks it will rain tonight," Fitela said, looking up at the dark clouds.

Thorstein removed the rabbit from the stick structure, cut off some meat and brought it to Annoure in a wooden bowl. "You must be hungry."

"I am. That smells delicious." She sat up and switched Ban to the other breast.

Thorstein cut off a piece and held it close to her mouth. She saw the love in his eyes as she chewed the warm, rich-tasting meat. Thorstein gave her another slice.

"I can feed myself." She grinned. "Just cut up the meat, so I can eat with one hand."

"I like feeding you." He put another piece in her mouth. She licked the grease off her lips. Thorstein's eyes dropped to Ban and he watched the baby nurse. "Your breasts have grown larger," he whispered huskily.

Annoure felt her face flush. Desire darkened Thorstein's eyes as he looked back up at her. Ban fell asleep in her arms. She covered her breast, then took the baby to the tent and wrapped him in a fur. Fitela and Ketil entered the tent. She bid them good night and went to sit by the fire with Thorstein.

Flames lit up his handsome face in golden-red tones. "I thought you would go to sleep as well," he said. He reached out and tucked a lock of hair behind her ear.

"Nei, I'm not tired. I had a long nap."

"Do you want to take a walk?"

She nodded and they ambled along the river. "What are you thinking about?" she asked.

"I'm wondering if we can get home in time for harvest. With Njal and Faðir dead, it's my responsibility to be sure there's enough food for winter."

"Walfgar and Herjulf will be home by harvest and I'm sure Thyri's family will help."

"I doubt Volsung, Olaf and Sturlee will want to help after I broke off with Dahlia. And what about us? How are we going to make it safely home?"

"Your neighbors are the kind of people who will help in times of need, and together you and I can survive anything."

He frowned, still looking troubled. "You and Ban are so vulnerable." He put his arms around Annoure and drew her close. "I shouldn't be burdening you with my worries. It's so good to be with you again."

"It is good; despite the difficulties of the journey, I'm happy. I used to lay in my hudfat at night and think of how much I loved you. I couldn't bear the thought of never seeing you again."

Thorstein leaned down, his lips so close to hers she could feel his breath. "I love you, Annoure." He kissed her and she melted into his arms.

The kiss deepened and turned passionate. Annoure responded willingly, but when his hand slid to her breast she panicked and pushed him away. "Don't!"

"What's wrong?"

"When you touch me like that, it makes me of think of Ingeld. Please don't be angry."

"I'm not angry." He cleared his throat. "Maybe it would help to talk about what happened."

"Maybe." She shuddered, thinking of how she almost drowned herself after the first time with Ingeld. "Once I'd recovered from childbirth, Ingeld forced himself on me almost every night and was violent when I resisted." She bit her lip, trying to hold back tears.

He drew her to him again. "He'll never touch you again."

"I'm no longer pure—I've been soiled."

"You're not soiled. I love you deeply."

Annoure began to cry. He lifted her into his arms and sat down on a log. She wept against his shoulder, letting all the pain she'd been holding inside pour out. When at last her tears were spent, her head felt thick and stuffy. She lay limply in his arms, relishing the fact that she wasn't alone anymore. Thorstein had found her and still loved and wanted her. Deep inside she'd been afraid he'd reject her since she'd been Ingeld's bed thrall.

She blew her nose on some leaves, embarrassed by her tears. "Ingeld was the only one who touched me—I swear it—and even he left me alone toward the end of the journey. As for the Arabs, they didn't even talk to us."

"Why did Ingeld start leaving you alone?"

"One night I drew on the power of the Goddess for strength and told Ingeld his manhood would shrivel up and he'd never be with a woman again if he touched me. He tried to force himself on me and couldn't. He didn't touch me after that and spread word among his men that I was a witch."

Thorstein's eyes widened and he swallowed, looking uncomfortable. "I wondered why he called you a witch."

She put her arms around his neck, aware of his strong thighs beneath her. "I didn't really have the power to unman him. He was just superstitious."

"Nei, I've felt the magic that surrounds you when you contact the Goddess. You have powers I don't understand."

She kissed his forehead and said in a teasing voice, "Are you afraid of me?"

"I haven't the sense to be afraid of you." Thorstein kissed her tear-streaked cheeks, then found her lips again. She tasted the salt from her tears on his lips. As the strength of his arms and his need for her brought an answering need from within her, the horror of Ingeld's rough use began to fade.

Thorstein finally raised his mouth from hers, his breathing ragged. "If you aren't ready to make love, we'd better stop. It's been far too long since we've been together and I want you so much I ache with need."

She scrambled off his lap, uneasy with his desire for her. "It's starting to drizzle. We'd better get back to the tent."

He clasped her hand and they dashed through the darkening woods to their tent. When they entered, she heard the sound of rhythmic movement and realized Fitela and Ketil were coupling.

She flushed, wishing she and Thorstein hadn't returned so soon. She removed her rain-dampened hangerock and crawled into the hudfat in her under-dress. Thorstein slid in next to her. He drew her close and she felt his arousal against her thigh. Ketil's heavy breathing and Fitela's moans filled the small tent. Embarrassed, Annoure rolled on her side, facing the side of the tent. Thorstein curled his body around hers.

Annoure was surprised that Fitela and Ketil were sharing pleasure. She hadn't noticed them being affectionate to one another, but from the sound of things Fitela was a willing partner. She could understand Ketil wanting Fitela. It had probably been a long time since he had a woman and Fitela was quite pretty. But she couldn't understand Fitela submitting to Ketil now that she was a free woman.

The rain grew stronger and beat against the tent. Rainwater began leaking under the sides and dripping down the walls. Thorstein rose. "I'm going to make a trench around the tent."

He left and she followed him outside. "Nei, stay inside," he said.

"I'd rather help."

He found two stout sticks and handed her one. The rain ran down Annoure's face and into her eyes as she used the stick to help Thorstein dig a trench in the hard ground, diverting the rainwater away from the tent. Her hair and under-dress quickly became soaked and plastered against her body.

Lightening flashed and a few moments later thunder boomed. Frightened, Annoure wanted to hide from the storm in the tent; instead she kept working.

Finally the trench was complete and Annoure dashed inside the tent. She couldn't find any dry clothes in the dark, so slid off her wet under-dress and crawled into the hudfat. After stripping off his clothes, Thorstein climbed in beside her and drew her against his cold, naked body. She tensed, wondering if he'd make love to her. When he didn't, she gradually relaxed.

In the morning, it still rained heavily. Thorstein wanted to leave, but everyone else protested so he and Ketil went back to sleep. Annoure drew on her kaftan, then she and Fitela played backgammon while the baby contentedly played with a scrap of leather.

Annoure shook the dice and moved a playing piece. "Fitela, you don't have to submit to Ketil. You're a free woman now."

"I'm still a thrall. I've only changed masters."

"Nei, you're free."

"I'd rather have a master. I need someone to provide me with food and shelter. I don't own anything."

"Thorstein will provide for you until you marry. Free women are expected to be virtuous. Next time Ketil wants you, you must refuse him."

Fitela smiled slyly. "You never understood what a woman must do to survive. Sex is a tool you can use to get things. From Nidhad, I got extra food and information. You should've used Ingeld's infatuation with you to your advantage. It would have made things a lot easier for you."

"I hated Ingeld."

"Well, I like Ketil and we share a hudfat. We might as well share pleasure."

"Your future husband will want a chaste woman."

"No Norseman will marry me. They're too proud to marry another man's cast-off pleasure thrall." Fitela moved her playing piece.

Annoure's stomach turned acid—*she was Ingeld's cast-off pleasure thrall*. She glanced at Thorstein who was an oldest son now and could marry any woman he wanted—one with a large family and rich dowry or Dahlia perhaps. She pushed her fears aside. Thorstein loved her. "I'm sure a landless second or third son will want you."

"Since Thorstein killed Rethel, Ketil is no longer a landless son." Fitela tossed the dice.

"I hadn't thought of that. Though it's likely he'll be banished for his crimes. Do you want to marry him?"

Fitela frowned. "A thrall doesn't think of such things."

"But you're free now and have a choice of whom you marry."

"Nei, women are not free. Even girls with wealthy families have to marry the man their faðirs pick for them. You're not free. Thorstein stole you from your home and will decide if he wants to marry you, keep you as a pleasure thrall or sell you. You must please him if you want his protection."

"Thorstein loves me and I love him. We're going to marry."

"Thorstein needs a woman, not a girl reluctant to share pleasure."

"I don't need your advice."

"I'm just trying to help. If you want, I can satisfy his lust and spare you, like I spared you from Ingeld's men."

"I don't want you to spare me from Thorstein," she snapped. "He's my betrothed." Annoure looked at Thorstein. In the peacefulness of sleep, he looked young and unthreatening. She clenched her hands into fists, determined to get over her misgivings.

When the rain died down to a light drizzle, they continued their journey. In the afternoon, the sun came out and they spread out the supplies in the boat to dry. They journeyed until dark to make up for lost time.

That night, Thorstein laid their hudfat on the other side of a group of trees away from where Ketil and Fitela slept. Annoure wrapped the sleeping baby in a fur. She was nervous about sleeping with Thorstein and she delayed getting into the hudfat. The moon gave off enough light for her to watch Thorstein undress. She always liked his tattoos, his broad shoulders, muscular torso and arms, and his flat stomach. She liked watching him move with smooth masculine grace.

He sat on the hudfat and said, "I heard you and Fitela talking. Is it true that you're reluctant to make love to me."

"I'm just nervous after being ill treated by Ingeld."

"Our lovemaking was always good."

"I know, but the thought of coupling brings up bad memories. You wouldn't satisfy your lust with Fitela, would you?"

"The use of a thrall wouldn't satisfy my desire for you."

"You don't want her, do you?"

"I don't want anyone but you. I'll wait as long as needed." He started planting kisses on her cheeks, throat and ears. She wrapped her arms around him and kissed him back, expressing her love for him. She knew he'd been through so much for her, sacrificed so much. She was sure of his love on a much deeper level than before.

He lay on his back and lifted her on top of him, running his hands over her back as they kissed. She felt less threatened in this position and an ache for him began to grow inside her. She sat up straddling his hips and smiled down at him.

He smiled back, his hands running lightly up from her waist, over her breasts to her shoulders and back down. "You are so beautiful, Annoure. I wanted you from the first time I saw you and my desire has only grown with the passing of time. I love you more than I've ever loved anyone, even my own kin. Let me see you without your kaftan."

In her mind sprang up the memory of Ingeld demanding she undress or he'd bash Ban's head against a tree. She moved off Thorstein and drew her knees up against her body, trembling.

Thorstein sat up. "What's wrong?" He reached for her and she flung her arms up over her head, as if to fend off a blow.

"Annoure, don't be frightened," he said gently. "You're safe now."

She hugged herself, rocking back and forth. He drew her between his thighs and held her. She broke into a sweat, still shaking. He whispered words of love until she calmed down.

Chapter 32

Sea Voyage Home

THE NEXT DAY AS THEY rowed near a Slav village, Fitela pointed toward shore and exclaimed, "Look! Those houses are on fire."

Thorstein paused his rowing to look back over his shoulder. Smoke rose from several wooden houses.

"What's going on?" Annoure asked.

"It looks like a raid on the village," Ketil said.

As they drew closer, they saw Slavic men fighting. Thorstein, Ketil and Annoure began to row to the opposite side of the river. The cries of battle, clash of weapons and smell of smoke followed them.

Thorstein dug his oars deeply into the water with each stroke, wanting to get as much distance as possible between them and the village. They might be attacked if they were spotted. The water was rough in the middle of the expansive river and the force of the current pushed them backwards. Sweat ran down Thorstein's forehead and back as he rowed.

Annoure, seated in front of him, was also tiring and her breathing became labored. They finally neared the opposite shore where the current wasn't as strong. Annoure pulled in her oars and turned to face him. "I need to rest," she gasped.

He was breathing heavy as well. "Fitela, help Annoure row."

Fitela set the baby on a fur, made her way over to Annoure. The two women sat side by side and each took an oar, then they began rowing in unison.

The baby cooed contentedly and waved his arms in the air. Thorstein smiled at his son. Ban was usually happy at sea and enjoyed the swaying of the boat. He'd make a good Norseman—though as a first son he'd inherit the farm and never have to make his living by going a-viking.

Ban reminded Thorstein of Brandi as a baby with his vivid blue eyes and fine blond hair. Now that he was a father, Thorstein understood better how Njal must have felt when Edgtho struck down Brandi.

They didn't see any more signs of fighting that day, but Thorstein wanted to travel through this land as quickly as possible. He took advantage of the long sunlit hours and didn't stop until late that night. The group decided to leave most of their supplies in the boat and didn't put up the tent, so they could leave quickly if needed. Thorstein took first watch guarding the camp as the others slept.

After a while Annoure rose from her hudfat and walked over to him. She looked like a child with her long hair worn loose and dressed only in her light-colored under-dress that glowed in the moonlight.

"What are you doing up?" he asked, wondering if she'd had another nightmare.

"I can't sleep. Why don't I keep guard so you can rest?"

Thorstein drew her close and rested his chin on her head.

"You don't know how to use a sword. Try to go back to sleep. I'm not expecting trouble; just keeping guard as a precaution."

Just then they heard a distant shout. "Get down!" Thorstein exclaimed, lowering her to the ground. "Your dress stands out. Stay here."

He drew the fur off his shoulders and placed it over her to make her less visible before heading in the direction the shout came from. As he went deeper into the forest, tall trees blocked most of the moonlight, until he was forced to hold his hands in front of him to keep from running into anything.

Soon he heard voices and crept forward, moving as silently as possible. He came upon a large camp of heavily armed Slavic men. Tents were set up and some of the men sat around campfires. Thorstein faded back into the cover of the forest and hurried back to Annoure. She'd stayed on the ground where he'd left her.

"We're leaving," he said. "Get Ban and go to the boat."

He awoke Ketil and Fitela, then grabbed his hudfat. They all quickly boarded and were soon were back on the river.

Thorstein and Ketil rowed through the night while Annoure and the baby slept in the front section of the boat and Fitela slept in the stern. The muscles in Thorstein's arms and back knotted up from many hours of rowing and his buttocks hurt from sitting on the hard thwart. At dawn, they took a short break to eat dried meat and drink some water. Then they put up the sail and tacked upriver.

The wind turned against them in the afternoon, so they were forced to go ashore and wait it out. Thorstein and Ketil collapsed on their hudfats and slept while Annoure and Fitela kept watch.

When the wind finally shifted, they continued the journey. Before long, they heard voices on the river. They quickly lowered the sail, rowed to shore, pulled the boat on an embankment and hid in the bushes.

Several boats full of Slav men rowed past where they were hidden. The baby started to cry and Thorstein's heart leapt to his throat. Annoure bared her breast and held the infant to her nipple. Ban continued to fuss for a frightening moment, then finally began sucking. Thorstein watched for signs the men on the boats heard the baby. Several men looked their way, but kept rowing.

Thorstein drew in a deep breath, realizing he was overly jumpy. Even if the men heard Ban cry, there was no reason for them to stop. A mother and child were no threat to fighting men.

* * *

After many weeks of hard travel, they finally reached the portage that led to the Volkhov River. Annoure set Ban on the riverbank, then waded into the water and grabbed the gunwale. With all four of them pulling together, they managed to drag the boat out of the water onto a row of horizontal logs placed at the bank for portaging boats. Although their boat wasn't large, its thick oak planks made it too heavy to carry.

After Annoure tied Ban to her chest with a shawl, she helped the others push the boat over the logs until they reached the last log in the row. Then they walked back to the last log. She and Thorstein lifted one end of the log and Ketil and Fitela lifted the other. Together they carried it to the front of the vessel and set it down. They put several more logs in front of this one, then pushed the boat again, rolling it over the newly placed logs. It was slow, tedious work.

The portage was easier with Ingeld and his crew, for there were enough men to carry the dugout boats. The remembrance of that portage made Annoure's chest constricted; Bergthora had died along the way.

The day wore on miserably. Annoure's tattered leather shoes gave her feet little protection from the rocky ground, insects swarmed around them and Ban was fussy. She began singing Celtic lullabies to entertain him. His cries turned into wails and she sat down on a log to feed him, glad for the break. While Ban nursed, she ate a piece of dried fish she'd stored in her pocket. The men usually ate two meals a day in Norse fashion, but she was always hungry. There never seemed to be enough food.

After several days of hard portaging, they finally reached the Volkhov River. The river flowed toward Lake Neva and they were finally able to travel with the current. They shot through some rapids unharmed and finally reached the Norse settlement of Aldeigjuborg. There they bought more provisions, including food and new shoes for Annoure.

When dusk arrived, Annoure was pleased to discover there were fewer mosquitoes than last time she was in Aldeigjuborg.

The following day they set off again and soon reached Lake Neva. They sailed across the south side of the lake and camped one night on shore. The next day, they reached the Neva River. Again they were able to sail with the current and make good time.

As the days got shorter, the weather became cooler and the trees turned golden with spots of red.

One evening it began to drizzle and they stopped early because Ban and Annoure had colds and Annoure didn't want the baby exposed to wind or rain. The men grumbled about not being home for the harvest as they put their hudfats in the tent.

Annoure crawled inside, glad to be out of the rain. She removed her wet clothes and slid into the hudfat. Her throat hurt and she'd been coughing and sneezing all day.

Thorstein joined her in the hudfat, his body cold alongside hers. The baby cried off and on all night. By morning his cries turned shrill and he was hot with fever.

Annoure felt miserable as well. Her head ached and she couldn't breathe through her nose. Neither Thorstein nor Ketil suggested moving on. As Annoure lay feverish and sweating in the hudfat, she was grateful she didn't have to endure another day of travel.

She awoke in the afternoon to discover it had stopped raining. She and Ban were the only ones in the tent, but before long Ketil entered and lay down for a nap.

The baby became fussy again. Close to tears, Annoure said, "What if he dies, Ketil?"

Ketil sat up, yawning and rubbed a hand over his thick beard. "He'll be fine. He just has a cold." He took the baby from her. "My little girls get them every fall."

"Babies often die in their first year."

"He's a healthy boy. See, he's already quieted." Before long the baby fell asleep. Ketil placed him on his hudfat and slept beside him the rest of the afternoon.

They didn't push to travel long hours over the next few days. The baby and Annoure gradually recovered. As they sailed through the Gulf of Finland, they stayed close to shore and spent nights on land.

One evening Annoure nursed Ban in the tent, then left him sleeping there. She felt restless and more energetic than she had felt in days. It was an unusually warm night and a full moon shone down on Ketil as he fed sticks to the cooking fire.

"Have you seen Thorstein and Fitela?" she asked.

"Thorstein's swimming. I'm not sure where Fitela went."

Annoure strolled down to the sea, stopping abruptly when she saw Fitela standing on the beach. Thorstein emerged from the water; his tattoos looked alive, like dragons crawling up his muscular arms.

Annoure stepped behind some bushes so he wouldn't see her. He walked over to where he'd left his clothes and his face registered surprise when he saw Fitela. He picked up a cloth and dried his back.

Fitela stepped forward and put her hand on his muscular chest. "I thought you might need a woman tonight."

"I have a woman."

"She's not much more than a child. A virile man like you must want more."

"Annoure is all I want."

"She hates coupling. I enjoy it." She slid her hand down lower and he grabbed her wrist. "I know how to satisfy a man's lust."

"What game are you playing? We've hardly spoken this whole trip."

She laughed low and sensuously. "That doesn't mean I haven't noticed you. You're a handsome man, strong and courageous."

"Why come to me when you have Ketil?"

"I wasn't thinking of me, but of you. A man like you needs a woman. I'm concerned that you'll force Annoure and hurt her as Ingeld did. She always returned from his tent with bruises. He wanted to break and control her, but she wouldn't give in."

"I'd never hurt her."

"She'll never be a good vif. She'll submit to you eventually, but she'll never enjoy lovemaking. I can make it easier for you. Annoure will appreciate it as she did when I spared her from Nidhad on our journey to Bulgar."

"Annoure won't appreciate it." He pulled on his pants.

Bunching her hands into fists, Annoure stalked back to the fire.

"Did you find him?" Ketil asked.

"Nei, I went for a walk instead," she lied, impatiently swatting away a swarm of insects that buzzed around her head as she sat on a log.

Ketil put another branch on the fire and watched it blaze. The flames played across his face, revealing a pensive expression. "I heard you wake up crying last night from a nightmare."

"Sometimes I dream of Ingeld."

"Was he a cruel master?"

"Sometimes," she replied, her stomach tightening. A crack sounded from the bushes and soon Fitela appeared.

Annoure contemptuously narrowed her eyes at Fitela. Oblivious, Fitela sat beside Ketil and put her hand on his thigh.

Annoure abruptly rose and went into the tent. She yanked off her hangerock and lay on top of the hudfat, too hot to get inside. Before long Thorstein entered the tent. She heard him undressing although she couldn't see him in the dark. He joined her on the hudfat and pulled her close so her back was against his chest. She stiffened uneasily.

"Are you awake?" he asked, his breath against her ear.

"Já."

"Will you ever want to make love with me again?"

She let out a shaky breath. "I don't know." She turned in his arms and faced him.

His ran his hand down her back. "Frey, the god of love, has lit a fire in me tonight."

"More likely Fitela put it there. I saw you with her after your swim."

"Then you know I rejected her." Thorstein nuzzled her throat.

"You didn't bother to cover yourself when you saw her."

"I don't care if she sees me naked."

"Well, I do!"

"Why are you annoyed with me? I've been patient." He rolled onto his back. "Thor's hammer, I'll not be able to sleep tonight."

"I don't mean to make it hard for you." She rolled over to face him.

"I know. I'm sorry for being grumpy. It's just been a long time and I want you so much."

She lightly ran her fingers through the fine hairs on his chest and kissed his temple. "I love you."

"Don't!" he said in a strained voice.

She snuggled closer to him. "I only feel safe when I'm with you."

He lifted her so she lay on top of him. "Don't you know how hard it is for me to hold you and sleep with you without making love to you?"

"It's hard for me, too. I want the closeness we had before. I'm just nervous."

"There's no reason to be nervous. Making love only brings pleasure." He started kissing her and she returned his kiss, getting to know the feel and taste of him again. His beard and mustache rubbed against her face.

In her mind's eye, she visualized how he looked naked in the moonlight and the way his muscles flexed when he rowed the boat. She remembered how exciting it was when they made love. She liked the way his body felt under hers, solid and hard. She liked the way he kissed, sometimes gentle with just his lips, at other times, sensual with his tongue playing with hers.

Their kisses grew heated, then his mouth moved to her ear and his hand to her breast. "Can I take off your gown?" he whispered.

"What if Ketil and Fitela come in?"

"They went for a walk."

She sat up and he slid her under-dress over her head and drew her close. She liked the feel of his bare chest against her breasts. His hands moved to her waist and he lifted her so one of her bared breasts was over his mouth. He sucked as little Ban did, only in a way that made her feel much different.

"You are so perfect," he said reverently. He lay back and adjusted her so she was straddling his hips. As he caressed her breasts, she closed her eyes and leaned back, giving in to the sensations he built within her. He sat up with her still on his lap, facing him. "Stop me if you don't want to go further."

"I like it," she said trembling. His mouth covered hers in a heated kiss and she wrapped her arms and legs around him. "Help me heal. Make it beautiful for me again," she whispered when their lips separated.

He groaned and lay back down, taking her with him. His hands continued to arouse her until finally she found the courage to explore his body as well. She liked the feel of his muscular chest and taut stomach, the way he responded when she touched him.

Breathing hard, he rolled over, sliding her under him. She felt a moment of panic, but the fear passed with the feeling of goodness that came when his familiar male body settled over hers. It felt right to be with him—this loving man who was the father of her child.

They joined as one and moved in perfect rhythm with one another, giving and receiving pleasure, loving and being loved.

The exquisiteness of the sublime feelings within her came as a surprise. She'd forgotten how good making love with Thorstein was and her uneasiness faded. She immersed herself in sensation, going beyond thought. Her breath quickened, blending with his. Urgency drove both of them to the moment of exquisite release. Waves of pleasure rolled through her and she grasped Thorstein's shoulders, crying out his name.

Afterward a feeling of peace and fulfillment settled over her. She no longer felt tension between them. It had been replaced with a new level of closeness. A satisfied smile touched her lips as she realized her body was no longer dirty and defiled, but purified by Thorstein's loving touch.

This is how it's supposed to be, she thought, relaxing beneath him. His weight felt good and welcome. Finally he rolled off and held her in his arms.

"I love you, Thorstein."

"I love you, too. I felt guilty for leaving my family to come after you, yet now I realize you and Ban are my family. I never really had any choice. You are where my heart lies." Annoure beamed at his declarations of love. He continued, "When I'm with you and Ban, my life has greater purpose and meaning. Life is more precious. We'll marry as soon as we get home."

In the morning, Annoure awakened feeling happy and full of life. Ban was fussing and she took him from Thorstein and began to nurse him, pleased to be alone with her small family. She smiled and slid her leg between his. “I enjoyed last night.”

He grinned. “Good. I’m hoping for many more like it.”

Chapter 33

Dangers at Sea

OVER THE NEXT FEW DAYS a strong wind blew as they sailed the Baltic Sea. They stayed within view of shore and Annoure enjoyed the magical looking trees at the height of fall color. One evening the men kept sailing even though it was growing dark. Tired of being confined to the boat, Annoure said, "I want to stretch my legs and my arms ache from holding Ban for so many hours. Can we please stop for the night?"

"We're almost to Kolobrzeg," Thorstein said. He was steering while Ketil and Fitela talked in the front of the boat. "If we sail all night by moonlight, we can reach it tomorrow and get supplies."

Disappointed, Annoure set the sleeping baby on her lap and watched the sunset. Gold and pink rays danced across the rolling waves that spread out endlessly. "Don't you find it hard to stay awake at night?" she asked Thorstein.

"Sometimes, but usually I enjoy it. It's peaceful and I feel a part of something bigger than myself, almost as if I'm part of the world of the gods. I look up and wonder what it would be like to see Thor riding across the heaven in his chariot drawn by two sacred goats."

She smiled, visualizing the red-haired god in his chariot. She'd come to accept Thorstein's beliefs. On her journey, she'd discovered nearly every village they stopped at believed in their own gods. Perhaps it didn't matter what god or goddess a person worshipped as long as it helped them make sense of the world. She curled up beside Ban, reflecting on the mysteries of life.

Annoure awoke to howling wind and rough waves that tossed the small boat up and plunged it into deep troughs. In the predawn light, everything appeared to be gray images. She sat up and the wind tore through her long hair. She shoved the thick tresses away from her eyes.

A huge wave with a foaming white cap curled toward the ship and slammed into it, spraying her and Ban with cold water. The baby began to cry and she lifted him into her arms and dried him off. Another raging wave followed the first. She grabbed the gunwale with one hand and tightened her grip on the baby with the other, bracing herself as it sprayed over them.

"Thorstein, what's happening?" she asked, shouting to be heard above the roar of the wind.

He turned toward her, eyes wide with concern, his hair standing on end from the wind. "A storm came up quickly. We're headed to shore."

"What if we capsize?"

"We won't, the boat's seaworthy." Then he added, "But if we do, hold onto the boat. It'll float."

"But what about Ban?"

His brow furrowed, then he dumped the contents of a leather food bag into the boat. "Put him in here and tie the bag to you." He gave her the bag and a length of rope.

She slid Ban inside so only his head was exposed and tied him to her chest, all the while wondering how she could keep herself and the baby alive in the churning sea if the boat *did* turn over. Ban didn't like being in the bag and his whimpers turned into angry wails.

A wave crashed over the side of the boat on the portside, filling it with cold water. "Bail!" Thorstein yelled.

Wet and shivering, Annoure seized a wooden bowl and began bailing. Mixed in with the water were the dried fish, nuts and cloudberries that Thorstein had emptied out of the food bag. Her sleeves were immediately soaked. She rolled them up and kept working. Ketil and Fitela also bailed, but seawater splashed in faster than they could dump it out.

The boat bucked and Annoure struggled to keep her balance, afraid she and Ban would be swept overboard. Water swirled over the gunwale and sloshed back and forth in the bottom of the boat as it rocked with the waves. Annoure knelt in the water that now completely covered her lower legs.

"Ketil, can you tell which way is land?" Thorstein shouted.

"Nei, I lost track in the dark."

Annoure searched for sight of land as the boat rose to the top of an enormous wave. In the distance, the waves looked like the mountains that surrounded the fiord where Thorstein lived. No land was visible. The boat plunged into a deep trough and she could see only walls of water.

With the dawn of a new day, the tumultuous waves turned bluish-green, but there was still no sign of land.

Annoure heard a rumbling overhead and looked up. Cool drops of rain splashed on her face. Soon the rain fell heavier and the waves grew more violent.

"We're going to drown!" Fitela cried. "We're going to drown!"

"No, we won't!" Annoure shouted. Shaking with cold, she pulled up her cape hood and dumped another bowl of water over the side. Then she kissed the top of Ban's head, glad he was tucked in the leather bag with only his head exposed to the storm. His crying had died down to a soft whimper.

"We need to lower the sail!" Thorstein yelled to Ketil. "The sea's gotten too rough."

The fierce wind pounded Thorstein as he untied the sail rigging, then he stood to lower the sail. The wind fought him, threatening to rip the rope out of his hand. His wet hair was plastered against his forehead and cheeks and his clothes billowed out from his body. A flash of lightning lit up the dark, turbulent sky. The boat rocked and Annoure was thrown against the starboard side.

Another shard of lightning struck the mast of the boat. It burst into flames and snapped in two.

"Thorstein, look out!" Annoure screamed as the mast crashed down. The yardarm hit Thorstein in the shoulder and knocked him from the boat. He disappeared into the rolling waves.

The woolen sail fell down around those in the boat. Ketil stripped off his tunic and jumped into the water after Thorstein.

"We're all going to die!" Fitela moaned again.

The rain continued to pour down, putting out the flames that engulfed the bottom half of the mast.

Annoure searched the churning water for signs of the men. Heavy rain obscured her vision. “Find him, Ketil! You have to find him!”

Finally Ketil broke the surface. He drew in a breath of air before diving under again. The boat bobbed away from where he’d gone down.

“Fitela, row!” Annoure cried. Fitela didn’t move; her eyes were frozen on the water.

Ketil resurfaced with his arm across Thorstein’s chest and swam toward the boat, pulling his unconscious friend through the waves. Annoure crawled to the thwart and sat on it backwards, then picked up the oars and dipped them into the water. She started rowing, struggling to maneuver the boat through the roiling sea. A wave doused her with cold, salty water. Ketil drew close and she held out the oar. He clasped it and she hauled the two men to the side of the boat.

Annoure grabbed Thorstein’s upper arm, her movements awkward with the baby bound to her chest. As she fought to pull Thorstein into the boat, Ketil tried to push him up from below.

She managed to haul Thorstein to the gunwale, but couldn’t pull him any higher. Her strength gave out and he fell back into the sea with a splash. Ketil kept him from going under. She leaned further over the side, clasping Thorstein once more and the boat tilted dangerously, nearly dumping her and Ban overboard.

“Fitela, move to the opposite side!” Annoure shouted, leaning backwards. Fitela slid to the other side of her seat and the boat leveled out.

“Can you hold him?” Ketil asked. “I think I can drag him into the boat once I’m on board.”

“I’ll try,” Annoure tightened her grasp on Thorstein’s sleeve, beseeching the Mother Goddess to help her. In her mind’s eye, she blocked out the waves, the sea and her fear. Gradually a surge of renewed strength flowed though her.

Ketil grabbed onto the gunwale and worked his way down to the stern, then heaved himself onto the boat and crawled to Annoure. He clasped Thorstein’s belt and shouted, “Heave!” Together they succeeded in rolling Thorstein into the boat. Then Ketil dragged him to the stern and rolled him onto his side.

Thorstein moaned and spat up water, but didn’t awaken. Ketil shoved a bag under Thorstein’s head to keep it out of the water, which had collected at the bottom of the boat. Then he moved back to the middle thwart.

Ketil's teeth chattered and he shook with cold. "By Odin's Ravens, I can't feel my feet." He pulled off his tunic, got a dry one out of his hudfat and drew it on. "It's up to the gods if Thorstein will live. I did what I could." He removed his shoes and changed into dry pants.

"Thank you. You easily could have drowned."

"I couldn't let him die."

Annoure made her way back to where Thorstein lay, careful not to rock the boat, and put her hand on his cold, pale cheek. She kissed his bluish lips. "Dear God, let him live! Let him live!" She knew he could freeze to death if she left him in wet clothes, but there was no way she could remove them in the small confines of the boat. She cut them away with a cooking knife. Once she removed them all, she covered him with a hudfat.

"Bail water!" Ketil shouted as he rowed.

Annoure found the bowl she'd been using before and began bailing. The storm was starting to let up and little additional water was accumulating in the boat. She and Fitela bailed most of what was left, while Ketil tied down the torn sail and yardarm.

Ban began crying and Annoure took him out of the bag to nurse him. She worried all the while that Thorstein might never awaken and that they might be lost at sea and never reach land.

Gradually the rain stopped and Annoure pushed off her hood, grateful the boat now rode gently up and down on waves that no longer threatened to toss them into the sea.

The hours dragged as Ketil rowed. At last Thorstein moaned and opened his eyes.

"What happened?" he asked. He started to sit up, then grasped his shoulder groaning, "By Thor's hammer, I feel like I was kicked in the shoulder by a horse."

"You were hit by the yardarm and knocked overboard," Annoure said, relief and joy surging through her. He'd awakened! "I was afraid you'd drown."

"Is that Thorstein I hear awake and already complaining?" Ketil asked. Good humor and cheer radiated in his voice.

Annoure smiled. "Já, he lives."

"How is it I didn't drown?" Thorstein asked.

"Ketil dove in after you."

"I owe you my life, Ketil." Thorstein sat up, pulling the hudfat around his bare shoulders. He looked at Annoure. "Is Ban all right?"

"He's fine." She lifted the edge of her cape so he could see the baby underneath it.

Tension eased from his face. "The gods are merciful. What happened to my clothes?"

"I cut them off. You were frozen from being in the sea."

He rummaged in his hudfat until he found his other set of clothes and awkwardly pulled them on in the rocking the boat. Once dressed, he studied the sea and sky with a trained eye. "Ketil, do you know how far off course we are? We need to get to shore and repair the boat."

"Nei. But I've seen birds and seaweed, so I don't think we're far from land."

"Perhaps I can spot it." Thorstein rose, bracing his feet wide to keep his balance. Annoure felt as if a huge weight lifted from her shoulders, not just because Thorstein awakened, but because he was already taking charge.

Thorstein looked in all directions, before pointing across the sea. "I see a dark landmass that way."

"Thank the gods," Fitela said, "I've had enough of the sea."

Thorstein traded places with Annoure and joined Ketil in rowing the boat.

Annoure changed the baby into dry clothes, packed fresh moss around his bottom, then wrapped him in a wool blanket. She smiled as she remembered weaving the blanket for him while she was pregnant. A yearning for the farm rose within her.

The land mass gradually began to take shape and the men determined they'd passed Kolobrzeg and were approaching the island of Rügen where Arkona was located.

After several hours of hard rowing, they reached the Slavic port. Annoure remembered coming here previously with Ingeld. It was their first port after leaving Hedeby. Here was where he'd taken her to the temple with the many-headed gods. She touched her neck, remembering how awful it felt to wear an iron band.

The men docked the boat between two rowboats at the wharf. Fitela hopped out and ran to land. She knelt down and grabbed a fistful of grass. "Land! We made it! I didn't think we would."

Ketil grinned. "By the gods, land *is* a welcome sight." He lifted his hudfat and swung it over his shoulder, ignoring the water dripping from it. Once they'd gathered up most of their supplies, they walked to the earth rampart and tower marking the entrance to Arkona.

Annoure shuddered as she walked down the town's wooden platform that was still wet from the recent rain. When she'd been here last, Ban was but a few days old and she was still weak from childbirth, nearly three months ago. She moved closer to Thorstein, wishing her arms weren't full so she could clasp his hand.

They walked through the marketplace and stopped to buy a warm loaf of bread and fresh fruit. She put her hudfat down, tore off a chunk of bread and stuffed it in her mouth, breathing in the flavorful aroma as she chewed. Thorstein broke off a piece for himself and handed the rest of the loaf to Ketil and Fitela. Once the bread and fruit were devoured, they walked on until they came to an area filled with tents. They found an open site near other Norsemen and spread their supplies on the ground to dry.

"The women can repair the sail while we make a new mast," Ketil said. He dug wool fabric, scissors, needles and thread out of the seal bag and gave them to Annoure.

Annoure set the baby on a blanket and examined the sail. It was made of squares of wool fabric trimmed with leather. The leather held up well, but the wool was burned and ripped in places and needed mending.

Ketil rose. "Let's go to an inn, Thorstein, then see about the mast." The men left together.

"They'll come back drunk," Fitela said as she started repairing the sail. "Did you mean it when you said I was free?"

"Já, you're no longer a thrall."

"Then I've decided I want to stay in Arkona."

Annoure drew in a sharp breath and paused in her mending. "Why would you stay here?"

"I never want to get back into a boat again. I was sure we would all drown."

"You don't know anyone here. How will you live?"

"I'll get work at an inn. I know how to cook and I don't mind cleaning or drunken men. I'll do well enough. I'd rather be in a busy town than isolated on a farmstead. I'll have a chance to find a verr here."

"We're friends. You must come."

"I've no wish to die. Thorstein and Ketil are both determined to be home before winter. They don't mind the long days at sea or stormy weather."

"They're good sailors. They wouldn't risk our lives merely to reach home before winter."

"They did yesterday. They're both the eldest sons now. They feel honor-bound to provide for their families and run their farms."

"They didn't expect a storm to come up."

While they worked it grew cold. Finally Annoure said, "I'd better gather some wood for a fire. Will you watch Ban for me?"

"Já, he'll be fine with me."

Annoure left the city and went into the forest where she gathered sticks and small branches. On the way back to the city gates, she saw Thorstein hurrying toward her.

"What are you doing here?" he demanded, glancing around, his hand grasping his sword hilt.

"We needed firewood."

"You shouldn't be out here alone. It's too dangerous."

"I didn't think it would be dangerous during the day." Annoure maneuvered the conversation to another topic. "Fitela's upset about the storm and doesn't want to continue the journey with us."

"It's her choice."

"We can't just leave her. She plans to get work at an inn, but she doesn't know the language or anyone here."

Once they crossed through the city gates, Thorstein took the heavy wood from her. "I doubt you'll get her back in the boat. Even an experienced sailor can become unnerved after being in such a violent storm."

"You must convince her it's safe."

"Then I'd be lying. There's always danger at sea. We'll leave her some coins. It's better if she doesn't come to the farm with us. I don't want to share our home with her."

Annoure frowned, realizing she didn't want Fitela to share their home either. She no longer trusted Fitela around Thorstein. "Maybe Ketil wants to marry her."

"I don't think so."

"Why not? He obviously likes her."

"He still misses his vif."

"I'll talk to him about it."

"If Ketil wants to marry her, he'll talk to her. It's not our place to interfere."

When they had reached the campsite, Annoure approach Fitela. "Thank you for watching Ban." Annoure started a fire and the men set to work on a pine tree they'd cut down in the forest. They sawed off the branches and began stripping the bark to make a mast.

Fitela watched the men work. "Do you really think Thorstein will marry you? He's a man with land and he can marry a woman with a large dowry."

"He loves me. A dowry isn't important to him!" A knot formed in her stomach and she wished they were *already* married.

That night in the hudfat, Annoure snuggled closer to Thorstein. "Why don't we get married while we're here?"

"We'll marry once we reach the farm so my family and friends can celebrate with us. Besides I doubt there's a Norse priest here."

"I don't like not being married when we already have a baby."

"We'll be home in a little over a week if the weather favors us. It's not so long to wait."

She slid her arm around his chest and put one leg between his. "So I'll be a bride soon."

He kissed her. "You'll be my *vif* soon." He sounded pleased and she returned his kiss with amorous intent.

The next morning Annoure and Fitela went to market. Annoure bought vegetables, fruit and bread, then they stopped at a tavern. It was a dark, dreary place reeking of smoke and stale mead. Fitela asked about work, communicating with gestures and the few Slavic words she knew. The owner agreed to take her on as a serving girl. Fitela seemed content as they walked back to the campsite.

The men put the new pine mast on the boat and attached the repaired sail with a walrus hide rope. Annoure and Fitela broke down camp and carried the hudfats and other supplies down to the sea where the men packed them on the boat.

"How will we get home from here?" Annoure asked.

"We'll go straight north to Kaupang," Thorstein said. "From there we'll sail around the peninsula to the Hordaland fjord where our farmsteads are located."

Ketil gave Fitela a pouch of silver coins, then he pulled her close and kissed her.

Fitela and Annoure hugged. "Are you sure you want to stay here?" Annoure asked.

"I'm sure." Fitela stared at the waves rolling in and crashing against the rocky shoreline.

"God be with you and keep you safe," Annoure said. "I'll miss you. I never would have survived without you."

"Já, you would have. You're a strong woman."

Annoure held Ban close as Thorstein helped her into the stern seat of the boat, then waved to Fitela. The men rowed out to sea, fighting the incoming waves. The boat rose and fell with the sea and she uneasily clasped the gunwale.

Once the men raised the sail, they glided over the water and Annoure's mood lifted. Soon she'd see Herjulf, Asa, Kalsetini and the others. Her happiness was tainted by the knowledge that Njal, Brandi and Garth were dead.

She had to be strong for Thorstein. He'd need her in the quiet of winter when there was time to grieve for his lost kin. When spring came he'd plant the crops, but unlike other years he'd stay on the farm instead of going a-viking. She breathed the salty sea air and watched the sail billow out as it filled with the wind. The cloudless sky was deep blue and the day was warm.

Thorstein faced her and she grinned at him. His fine-looking mouth curled into an answering smile. "You look especially lovely with the sun shining on you," he said.

"I'm excited to be so near the end of our journey. The farm will be a good place to raise Ban."

"Já, it's a great place to grow up. I'm looking forward to seeing my family again."

Chapter 34

The Wedding

A BROAD SMILE SPREAD ACROSS THORSTEIN'S face as his family farmstead came into view across the water. He'd done it—found Annoure and the baby and brought them safely home! Thorstein and Ketil lowered the sail and began rowing. The setting sun glowed on the houses and outbuildings, gilding the harvested fields. Everything was as he pictured it in his mind so often on his journey. Soon he'd see his loved ones again.

His smile faded as he wondered how the women and children fared without his father and brother to run the farm over the summer. He'd hated leaving them in search of Annoure.

Once he, Annoure and the baby were on the dock with their supplies, he said to Ketil, "Have a safe journey home." He wanted to thank Ketil for saving his life and helping rescue Annoure, but it didn't seem right when Ketil was the one who had kidnapped her and caused so many deaths. So he merely said, "It's been quite an adventure." The words belied all the deep emotions churning inside him.

"It's a relief to have made it home before winter," Ketil replied.

"Goodbye, Ketil." Annoure's eyes filled with sorrow.

Thorstein put his arm around her, wondering if she was distressed about parting from Ketil or perhaps she was saddened by the memory of what happened here. In the distance, he caught sight of Herjulf approaching the shore. "Ketil, you'd better leave, Herjulf's coming." Thorstein pushed the boat away from the dock and Ketil rowed into the fjord.

Herjulf let out a joyful whoop and broke into a run. Upon reaching

Thorstein, he gave him a hearty hug. "I can't believe you all made it home safely. The gods are merciful." He embraced Annoure and the baby, staring over her shoulder as the boat rowed swiftly away. "Is that Ketil?" he asked, all the former warmth in his voice gone.

"Já."

Herjulf stared hard at Thorstein. "Why would *he* bring you home?"

"It's a tale that will take some explaining."

The baby started fussing and Herjulf said, "So this must be your little one."

"He's my son Ban," Thorstein said proudly.

"He looks healthy."

"He thrived at sea and is a true Norseman."

Herjulf took one of the hudfats from Thorstein and swung it over his shoulder. "Come to the house. Your móðir will be overjoyed to see you. It's been difficult around here—too much sorrow."

"Is Faðir . . ."

Herjulf grimly shook his head saying, "Nei, he didn't make it. He died soon after you left."

"I didn't think he'd live long. I didn't dwell on it while I was gone, but now that I'm back home it doesn't seem possible he and Njal are dead. They were so central to my life and running the farm. I miss them both."

"As we all do."

"Were the crops harvested before the weather turned cold?"

"Já. Walfgar and I were home by harvest and the neighbors helped. There will be plenty to eat over the winter."

Freydis gasped when Thorstein and Annoure stepped through the door. Thorstein swiftly crossed the room and embraced his mother, noticing new, deep lines around her eyes and mouth and the grey strands in her hair. Her hands shook as she held him close. Kalsetini hurried over, her eyes filling with tears. Thorstein caught her in one arm while the other still encircled his mother. He was relieved to see that they were both all right.

Thyri rose from where she sat in a dark corner of the room.

"Did you kill Edgtho and Ketil to avenge our family?" she demanded with a wild look in her eyes. Her hair was messy and her hangerock dirty. Sandey clung to her mother's shirt and sucked her thumb.

"Já, are they dead?" Walfgar asked sharply as he and Asa entered with their two children, Astrid and Rothgar.

"Edgtho's dead. Ketil's still alive," Thorstein replied.

"Ketil brought them home," Herjulf said. Everyone stared at Thorstein in disbelief, waiting for some explanation.

Thyri's eyes narrowed and she hissed, "How can that be?"

Thorstein stared at his brother's widow, not knowing what to say.

"Have all of you forgotten your manners?" Asa said. "Annoure and Thorstein must be hungry and tired. Let them rest before demanding answers to all your questions." She embraced Annoure, who still stood near the door. "I didn't think I'd ever see you again. And your baby is a bonny child. Is it a boy?"

"Já."

"May I hold him?"

Annoure handed her the child. "He looks like Brandi at this age," Asa said. "Doesn't he, Walfgar?"

Walfgar drew closer and looked at the baby, a smile touching his lips. "Já, he does."

Thyri glared at Thorstein. "So your thrall has a healthy son while my boy is dead and one of his murderers yet lives."

Thorstein looked compassionately at his sister-in-law. "Edgtho did the killing and died for his crimes. As for Annoure, she is not a thrall, but my betrothed. We will be married as soon as I can make arrangements."

His mother let out a wail. "We're in mourning! There can't be a wedding for a year."

"Annoure and I already have a son. We don't intend to wait any longer to marry."

"Have you no respect for the dead?" Thyri demanded.

"Waiting to marry won't bring them back." Disappointment welled within Thorstein. He didn't want the joy of his homecoming dampened by a quarrel.

"We can't possibly prepare for a wedding." Freydis wrung her hands, her eyes anxiously sweeping the house. "There are so many preparations to be made."

"It will be a small wedding," Thorstein said. "Annoure doesn't have any family here so there won't be negotiations with her faðir concerning a bride's gift."

"Or a dowry," Freydis added sullenly.

"I'm head of the family now and plan to marry before winter!" Thorstein exclaimed, losing his patience. "I'm not waiting a year for Annoure to be acknowledged as my vif and for my sonr to be recognized as my legal heir."

A tense silence filled the room.

Finally Freydis said, "The gods and goddesses brought my sonr home. It's a happy occasion. Let us celebrate. Kalsetini, bring out some food." She crossed to Annoure and kissed her on both cheeks. "Welcome home, dóttir. Let me see my grandson." Freydis took the baby from Asa. "What healthy plump baby and such rosy cheeks! The sea must agree with him." She smiled at Ban who reached up and touched her face, cooing. "I'm your *amma*, little one. I'll see that you are well cared for. I'll bet you'd like a nice warm bath and some clean clothes. Then I'll wrap you in the soft wool blanket I made for you." She looked up from the baby. "Asa, go haul some water and warm it for the baby's bath. Kalsetini, bring out the best cheese. Thorstein, sit. We have a new crop of apples and I just made bread and churned the butter."

She held her hand out to Sandey. "Come and meet your new cousin." The little girl released her mother's shirt and walked over to see the baby. Rothgar and Astrid also came over to gaze at the newest member of the clan. Rothgar made funny faces at the baby until Ban started to laugh.

Thorstein sat down and took a bite of his mother's delicious bread topped with a thick slice of goat cheese. The tension melted from his shoulders. Tonight he'd sleep in a warm house in his own sleeping bench with Annoure by his side.

* * *

Two-and-a-half weeks later on her wedding day, Annoure sat in the sauna, attended by Freydis and Kalsetini. It was Friday, the day the Norse called Freyja's day. Freydis told her proper weddings were always held on this day of the week because Freyja was the goddess of love. Kalsetini poured more water on the rocks and steam rose up. Sweat ran down between Annoure's breasts. The heat felt good on such a cool day.

The wedding would be held outside in front of the stone altar where the family worshipped. Annoure had met the priest Jamsgar at breakfast; he'd arrived the night before. He was a friendly man with a take-charge attitude. He explained the ceremony and her part in it. She'd always thought she'd have a Christian wedding in a church with her father walking her down the aisle and her brothers there to share her joy. A wave of homesickness washed over her.

"Annoure," Freydis said, interrupting her thoughts. "The sauna is symbolic of washing away your maiden status and purifying you for the next stage in your life. Thorstein will use the sauna once you're done to wash away his bachelor status. He is now considered the head of the family as the eldest son. You'll become the mistress of the farm and be given the keys to the house."

"I don't want to take the position from you."

"It is tradition. Your duties are to keep track of finances, see that the farm animals are cared for, be sure the food lasts the winter, and run the farm when the men are off hunting or trading."

Annoure swallowed. "That's a lot of responsibility and I don't have much knowledge of your ways."

"I'll help you learn your duties."

"Móðir, don't scare her with so many responsibilities," Kalsetini said. "She'll decide not to marry Thorstein."

"I'll never change my mind about marrying Thorstein," Annoure said.

Kalsetini laughed. "Já, you're in love with him. I hope I love the verr Thorstein picks for me."

"Let's return to the house," Freydis said, "and get ready for the wedding."

They wrapped themselves in blankets, then hurried to Asa and Walfgar's house. Asa was inside preparing a tub of hot water. Annoure stepped into the tub and sank into the fragrant, rose-scented water, enchanted by the rose petals floating on the surface. After her bath, she dried off with a clean drying cloth, then put on a pleated white underdress. Then Asa combed her long hair by the fire, while Kalsetini and Freydis bathed and dressed in their best clothes.

Once they were dressed, Freydis and Kalsetini helped Annoure put on an exquisite scarlet hangerock. "Let me put on the crown!" Kalsetini exclaimed. Her eyes shone with excitement as she carefully set a well-crafted straw crown on Annoure's head.

"You're beautiful," Asa said and the other two women agreed.

Annoure felt her face flush. "It's such a pretty hangerock. Thank you for making it, Freydis."

Freydis smiled. "My sonr's bride must be well dressed."

A knock sounded at the door and Kalsetini exclaimed, "Oh, is it already time? Thorstein must not have spent long in the sauna." She opened the door and let Walfgar inside.

Freydis hugged Annoure. "Thorstein is lucky to have you for a vif."

Asa lifted the sleeping baby off a sleeping bench and all the women, except Annoure, left the house.

"We go last," Walfgar said. His beard was freshly braided and he wore a crisp navy cape. It was flipped up over one shoulder so he could easily reach the sheathed sword on his back. "I'll walk you through the crowd to Thorstein. He and the priest are in the front by the horgr."

"Horgr? I don't remember what that word means."

"It refers to the stone altar. I'm carrying Thorstein's sword *Grimmr*. I'll give it to you when the priest asks you for it."

"What if I do something wrong? Your weddings are so different from ours."

"You'll do fine. I'll be close by if you have any questions about the ceremony."

She nodded, feeling reassured. She trusted Walfgar who'd been the one to patiently teach her the Norse tongue.

He placed a cape over her shoulders and held out his bent arm. She put her hand on his forearm and he led her outside. As they walked to where the wedding was to take place, Annoure noticed more tents were set up in the barren fields.

A crowd of people surrounded the altar and she couldn't see Thorstein or the priest. People started murmuring as she and Walfgar approached and soon everyone turned to look at them. The guests moved to either side to make way and Annoure got her first glimpse of Thorstein. He wore a fine fur cape and looked tall and handsome. She smiled at the friendly faces surrounding them as she and Walfgar walked down the aisle, but her main attention remained on Thorstein. Soon they would be married and she would finally be a proper wife and a free woman.

Thorstein clasped her hand when she reached him and said, "You're a lovely vision."

She tightened her grip on his hand, too emotional to speak.

They turned to face the priest who smiled serenely at them. "We will begin the ceremony." He held his arms out to the statues of the gods on the altar. "We ask the gods and goddesses Odin, Frigga, Thor, Frey and Freyja to bless this wedding."

Herjulf walked down the aisle with Thorstein's stallion Gunner and the priest said, "This horse is given as a gift to the gods and goddesses."

Annoure's eyes flashed to Thorstein's, worried they'd sacrifice the horse.

"A living gift," he whispered.

The priest Jamsgar made the sign of Thor's hammer, a short downward motion followed by a movement from left to right, then blessed the water contained in a bowl that rested on top of the stone horgr. Next he dipped fir branches into the water and sprinkled it over Thorstein and Annoure. He dipped the fir branches in several more times and sprinkled it on Thorstein's family and the friends who stood closest to them.

Jamsgar gazed into Thorstein's eyes. "Thorstein Garthson, give Annoure Garth's sword. The giving of the sword signifies the continuation of your bloodline."

Thorstein handed Annoure his father's sheathed sword. It was heavier than she expected and she held it with both hands.

"Annoure, dóttir of Earnwald, give Thorstein *Grimmr*. The giving of the sword symbolizes the transferring of your faðir's guidance and protection to Thorstein." She and Walfgar traded swords and she handed *Grimmr* to Thorstein.

"You may now exchange the rings."

The priest lifted two rings off the stone horgr. Thorstein held out the hilt of his sword and the priest put the rings on top of it. The priest said, "The circle of the ring represents the unbreakable nature of your vows."

Thorstein picked up the smaller of the two rings and Annoure took the larger one. He sheathed his sword, then gazed lovingly into Annoure's eyes. "With this ring, I promise to love, honor and protect you." She held out her hand and he slid the gold band onto her ring finger; the tiny hammer dangling from it sparkled in the sunlight.

Annoure slid the matching man's ring onto his finger, her heart overflowing with love. She could only get it as far as his knuckle and he pushed it on the rest of the way.

"With this ring I promise to love and honor you, and hold my vows sacred all of my life," she said. Then she lowered her voice so only he could hear, "And beyond this life as I have in other lives, my dream friend."

"You may kiss your new vif," the priest said.

Thorstein gathered her close. Trembling with excitement, she put her arms around him and they kissed. They joined hands and turned to face his family and friends.

Closest to her were Walfgar and Asa, who held Ban in her arms. Annoure's heart expanded with love as she realized that she, Thorstein and the baby made a complete family circle.

Freydis seemed to glow, looking happier than Annoure had seen her since arriving back on the farm. Thyri looked less disheveled; her hair was neatly combed and her cape well made.

"Time for the Bride's Run," Thorstein said.

Annoure squeezed his hand and together they dashed down the aisle toward the main house. Everyone raced after them. When they reached the front door, Thorstein drew *Grimmr* and faced the crowd, speaking the ritualistic lines. "No one can enter until Annoure and I are inside."

He turned to Annoure. "Crossing the threshold symbolizes your new life as my vif. Be careful not to trip over the raised threshold. My people consider it a bad omen if you fall." He didn't release her arm until she was safely inside.

Annoure looked around, pleased to see that the house was decorated with brightly embroidered tapestries hung on the walls and long tables heaped with food for the feast.

People packed into the house and watched as Thorstein thrust *Grimmr* into the ceiling as far as he could to demonstrate his virility. Walfgar slapped him on the back. "You drove *Grimmr* far into the ceiling. You'll have many sonrs."

The house was warm from a blazing fire in the hearth. Thorstein lifted Annoure's cape from her shoulders and removed his own, handing them to Walfgar. "You're a beautiful bride," Thorstein said, his eyes drifting over her scarlet hangerock.

"And you're a fine-looking groom." He wore a new patterned tunic cut to show off his muscular torso.

"Come with me, Annoure," Freydis said. She led Annoure to a bowl with birds carved on either side, filled with mead smelling of fermented honey.

"When everyone has their mug filled for the toasts, serve this bowl to Thorstein." Her eyes twinkled. "The people who were last in the Bride's Run must serve everyone."

Annoure noticed all the guests had their own mugs hanging from their belts. They held their mugs out to be filled with the mead as the servers cheerfully moved through the room.

"Everyone's been served," Kalsetini said, smiling widely as she came over to them.

"Give Thorstein the bowl, Annoure," Freydis said, "Do you remember your verse?"

"Já." Annoure lifted the bowl and carefully made her way through the crowd to Thorstein, who sat at the head of the table. She handed him the bowl and said,

"I bring you mead my warrior verr
You are strong, honorable and courageous
It's mixed with magic and great songs.
May you have the blessing of the gods and goddesses.
And may your adventures be written on rune stones."

"I dedicate this drink to the god Thor," he answered. He made the sacred hammer-sign.

"I make a toast to the Odin." He lifted his bowl and everyone in the room lifted theirs and cried, "Odin!" He took a drink and handed it to Annoure. She drank from the bowl and the sweet-tasting alcoholic liquid slid down her throat.

She raised the bowl. "I make a toast to Freyja, the Goddess of Love."

"To Freyja!" Everyone cheered.

Annoure took another swallow and handed Thorstein the bowl, grinning mischievously. "Drink my pagan lover," she whispered. "It's fortunate my father is not here to see this heathen ceremony."

He took a drink and she sank onto the bench beside him, relieved that the ceremonies were nearly over.

"May you have many children," Herjulf called out and they had a third toast. Thorstein placed a small, sacred hammer on her lap and recited the traditional verse.

"Bring the sword to the bride to bless
On the maiden's lap lays Mjölnir, Thor's hammer
In Freyja's name, our wedlock is hallow."

Freydis supervised serving the food. Mutton, beef, fish, cheese, eggs, bread, onions, apples and dried berries were set out on the table. Annoure and Thorstein filled their plates, then the guests began filling theirs. The room was crowded with only enough room for the elderly to sit; most guests stood or went outside.

"The food looks delicious," Thorstein said, starting to eat.

"The women have been cooking for days and the guests brought food," Annoure replied.

"Usually wedding celebrations last a week. I hope you don't mind that most of the guests will leave tomorrow. I didn't want to make it too big of an event with my family still in mourning."

"This is perfect. One day of celebrating is enough."

The room quieted as the skald Gylfi recited a saga about a god who fell in love with a goddess.

When he finished, Olaf stood and told a wild "lying story" made up for the occasion to amuse the guests. The mead and wine flowed freely and Annoure could tell Walfgar and Herjulf had enjoyed their share of it when they began an amusing "insulting contest." The other men soon joined in, each trying to outdo each other with the most outrageous affront.

After the feast and merriment, the newlyweds went outside. Some of the men participated in wrestling and fencing matches while the children played ball games.

Thorstein and Annoure walked over to where people gathered around a large bonfire. Nearby musicians assembled: Olaf with his horn, Kalsetini her pan flute, Danr his fiddle and the skald Gylfi his harp. They began to play as Thorstein and Annoure drew near.

"They are waiting for us to dance," Thorstein said.

She smiled. "Then let's not keep them waiting." Thorstein drew her close and they started dancing as the crowd cheered. Soon Walfgar and Asa and other couples joined in.

Later in the evening, Asa sought out Annoure to tell her Ban wanted to nurse. When Annoure entered the main house, Freydis was walking the crying baby. No one else was in the room.

Annoure's milk immediately let down in response to the baby's wails. She took Ban from Freydis, sat on a bench and put the hungry baby to her breast. After nursing on both sides, he fell asleep in her arms and she placed him in the cradle. She drew a cover over the baby, remembering when Thorstein built the cradle and carved a dragon on the headboard.

"It's time for you to get ready for bed," Asa said. She and Freydis helped Annoure change out of her wedding clothes and into a deep-blue sleeping gown.

"You'll sleep in the main sleeping bench now," Freydis said.

Annoure climbed into the sleeping bench that used to be Freydis and Garth's. She sat up with the covers drawn up to her waist. Then Freydis set the straw crown back on her head while Asa left to get Thorstein.

Before long, Thorstein entered the house, followed by a crowd of well-wishers. He walked over to her and grinned as he quickly stripped down to the linen breeches he wore under his wool trousers, ignoring the kidding and suggestive comments from the onlookers. Annoure felt her cheeks heat in embarrassment and wished they'd leave.

Thorstein climbed into the bed and lovingly removed the crown from her head. The crowd hooted as he leaned down and kissed her. Freydis, Herjulf and Walfgar began ushering everyone out, saying the fun was over and to leave the newlyweds in peace.

The door closed, leaving Annoure and Thorstein alone. Outside the sound of music and laughter floated into the house. "That was embarrassing," Annoure said.

"They didn't mean any harm. They came to see the removing of the crown, which symbolizes consummating our marriage."

"Oh!"

"Your first duty as my vif is to make love to your new verr."

She arched an eyebrow. "Your móðir never mentioned making love to you as one of my duties."

"She's the only one who didn't; everyone else has made lewd suggestions all day and all evening long. Our duty is to produce a hoard of children."

She grinned merrily. "Well then, we'd better get started."

Chapter 35

Hard Choices

ONCE THE LONG WINTER PASSED and spring finally returned, Annoure attended the *ting* with Thorstein and his family. It was held on a high cliff overlooking a fjord, where she could hear waves crashing on the rocks and the cry of seagulls.

Thorstein took his father's place as a landowner and could now vote on complaints brought before the court. Her heart swelled with love and pride. He took his new responsibilities seriously and looked handsome in the new tunic and pants she made for him.

She and Thorstein had grown closer in the six months they'd been married, but their happiness was overshadowed by not knowing what would happen at the *ting*. She felt uneasy every time she thought of it, although Walfgar had assured her that Thorstein's only punishment would be a fine for killing Edgtho in a duel.

The elderly konungr, Dylan, presided over the legal assembly. As usual, he wore a thick gold necklace to signify his wealth and importance and a finely-made fur cloak. The equally well-dressed priests, jarls and chieftains stood near him. The only familiar face among the men was the priest Jamsgar who'd performed her and Thorstein's wedding.

Annoure couldn't keep her attention on the proceedings, feeling as agitated as the churning sea. She wondered when Walfgar would bring charges against Ketil before the council.

Ban pulled on her amber necklace and she pried his small hand open before he broke the strand. She shifted his weight onto her right hip. At almost a year old, he was getting heavy. She had held him all morning as one case after another was heard before Dylan. Asa and Kalsetini stood beside her, listening intently to the proceedings.

A tall, proud woman stepped forward. She'd recently divorced her husband in front of witnesses and now demanded to keep her business raising sheep and selling their wool. Much discussion ensued among the council after several neighbors and her brothers testified that her husband was a drunkard and hadn't taken care of his family.

"I've never heard of a woman getting a divorce in Northumbria," Annoure whispered to Asa. "Women have no legal rights in my country. Did she get to keep her children?"

"She kept the baby and toddler."

"Her sonr stayed with his faðir," Kalsetini interjected.

The konungr put the case to a vote and the majority of landowners voted in the woman's favor.

After Dylan made his ruling, Thorstein and Walfgar stepped forward and Walfgar made a formal complaint against Ketil. The konungr ordered Ketil to come before him to hear the charges.

Ketil stood across the clearing with his kin and two little girls who had wispy blond curls and pink cheeks. He spoke briefly to his daughters, then walked over to stand near the konungr opposite Walfgar and Thorstein. Unlike most people who attended the *ting*, Ketil wore old clothes and his hair was messy as if he didn't care how he looked.

Annoure wondered if he'd fallen into despair over the winter. It was hard for her to see him again after all he put her through and all the harm he'd done to Thorstein's family. Helping rescue her hadn't made up for all the pain he'd caused.

In a deep voice that carried across the crowd, Walfgar told about the attack on the farmstead. His voice rose as he told of the deaths of Njal, Brandi and Garth, and of Annoure's abduction.

The elderly konungr listened without interruption, letting Walfgar tell his entire story. Walfgar ended by demanding Ketil's death. Annoure looked anxiously at Ketil to see his reaction, but he kept his head bowed.

The konungr called Nesbjörn forward as head of Ketil's clan to speak for him.

"The *ting* was wrong in their ruling last year!" Nesbjörn said angrily. "Thorstein should have been made an outlaw for killing Rethel. Edgtho and Ketil had the *right* to seek retribution. Now Thorstein has killed my nephew Edgtho as well, yet Walfgar dares asks for Ketil's life? With two kinsmen dead, we need Ketil's help on the farm more than ever."

Ketil lifted his head for the first time and looked directly at Thorstein. "I challenge you, Thorstein Garthson, to a *holmgang*. We will settle this with a duel."

Annoure gasped. She felt as if she'd been hit in the stomach. Could Ketil legally challenge Thorstein at the *ting?* she wondered.

Color drained from Thorstein's face. "How can you suggest that after all we've been through together, Ketil?" he asked so low that only those closest to him could hear.

"A holmgang is the honorable way to end this feud," Ketil replied. "Our families will have to abide by the outcome and not seek further retaliation."

The konungr looked at Thorstein. "Do you accept this challenge?"

"Ketil saved my life when I was knocked overboard at sea. I can't honorably fight a man I'm so deeply indebted to."

Ketil exclaimed, "You're *nithigar* if you don't accept!"

"I'm not a coward."

"Thorstein Garthson, you'll be an outlaw if you refuse," Dylan said. "No one can give shelter or aid without endangering their own lives."

Thorstein stared at Ketil, feeling trapped. "I accept your challenge."

"The challenge's been made and accepted according to the laws of our people," Dylan said. "You will each have a sword and three shields. The *holmgang* will be held tomorrow when the sun is directly overhead on sacred Norns Island. Only one of you will leave the island alive."

"Nei!" Ketil exclaimed. "We're to fight only until first blood is drawn." A deafening roar drowned out his voice as the men banged on their shields and rattled their spears in agreement.

When it quieted, Dylan said, "It is decided. Go make a sacrifice to the gods."

The blood drained from Annoure's head and she swayed unsteadily. Asa grabbed her as she started to fall and Kalsetini lifted Ban out of her arms.

"Annoure, are you all right?" Asa's voice seemed far away. Annoure's head started to clear as Thorstein hurried over to her, his mouth drawn in a straight line. He drew her into his arms and held her tightly. She felt the pounding of his heart. Finally he released her and they walked a short distance away from the assembly.

"Why would Ketil challenge you?" Annoure asked, not able to make sense of things. Ketil was their friend.

"He said he challenged me to end this feud and only wanted to fight until first blood was drawn. I believe him, but if he wins, he can claim everything I own, including the farm, now that I am the eldest sonr. Without a holmgang, he'd probably be declared an outlaw and never see his family again."

"It's too terrible to contemplate either of you dying. But if he did win and took the farm, where would your family go?"

"Thyri and her dóttir would return to her parents. I don't know where the rest of the family would go. But rest assured that Walfgar and Herjulf will see to it that you and Ban are taken care of no matter what happens."

"Surely Ketil wouldn't be so cruel as to kill you and take the farm."

"I don't know what to think. He abducted you and in the process my bróðir and nephew were killed and my faðir fatally wounded. What is challenging me to a duel compared to that?"

"Edgtho did the killing and Ketil regretted his part in it. Regardless, this is not justice! You didn't do anything wrong!"

"I killed Edgtho."

"In a fair fight."

"True, but Nesbjörn still lost a sonr and nephew. My people believe when a man kills another man, he must either pay the family for their loss or settle the matter with holmgang."

"Won't the loser's family want revenge?"

"Families usually accept the outcome, but not always."

Herjulf and Walfgar joined them. "Let's leave the *ting*, Thorstein," Herjulf said. "You need to prepare yourself for the fight."

"Nei, I'm a landowner now. It's my responsibility to vote on the rest of the cases."

"You haven't sparred all winter and Ketil is a good swordsmen," Herjulf said.

Thorstein frowned. "Well, I know. I have a wicked scar to prove it."

Walfgar grasped Thorstein's shoulder. "You are a man of unusual courage and can easily defeat Ketil."

"But what if he doesn't?" Annoure said.

Walfgar shot her a piercing glance. "Thorstein is a hero. Sagas are sung at market about his skills, though I agree he should prepare himself for battle. Go and make a sacrifice to the gods and goddesses, Thorstein. I'll stay and vote for our farmstead."

Thorstein and Annoure left the assembly with Herjulf. "Let's spar," Herjulf said.

"I need to be alone," Thorstein said. "I never thought it would come to this." Thorstein pressed the heels of his hands against his forehead. "By Thor's hammer, I don't know what is right anymore. Ketil fought beside me and Erik against Ingeld and his men, and later, against the Arabs and he saved my life at sea. How can I fight a man I owe my life to? Yet if I don't fight him, my people will consider me a man without honor and make me an outlaw."

"He killed Njal and —"

Thorstein interrupted. "I know what he did! I blame myself for killing Rethel and starting this feud." He strode away, without giving anyone a chance to reply.

Annoure stared after him, her heart sinking.

At last Herjulf said, "This is bad. A duel is won in the head before the fight even begins. If Thorstein hesitates when fighting Ketil, he'll lose. Maybe Walfgar can talk some sense into him. He's good with words."

"Thorstein needs to work it out for himself," Annoure said. "He'll just argue if Walfgar tries to reason with him right now."

"He should welcome the chance to fight Ketil after his betrayal," Herjulf said, sounding puzzled.

"There must be a way to settle this without Thorstein or Ketil dying."

"There's no way to change the decision. It was voted on."

"There's always a way," Annoure said. She headed into the woods, away from the booths and contests, away from the sounds of laughter, merchants hawking their wares, children playing, and the aromas of meat, bread, clams and fish cooking. She walked deeper into the woods, needing to move. If she stood still, feelings of helplessness would catch up to her. Eventually she found herself in a grove of ancient oaks. She paused, attuned to the energy of the forest, wondering how to stop the duel.

Annoure raised her hands in the air and gazed upward, letting the power of the sky and earth fill her. Then she called out to the creator of all life to give her the wisdom to end this feud, the courage to face whatever happened and the strength to fight for a new type of law. She knew the Norse people valued justice. There must be a means to make them see a better way is needed to deal with feuds than a fight to the death, she thought.

She felt loving energy flow through her and knew she was not alone in this trial she must face. She saw Thorstein in her mind's eye. He turned into her dream friend, wearing the clothes of a Druid. His clothing and appearance changed as lifetime after lifetime revealed itself to her and she knew he would be a part of her life again. Everything that happened was for a reason. She had to trust the force that guided her life to continue to show her the way.

Light streamed down through the leaves and branches of the tall oaks. As Annoure gazed at the light, a woman manifested, shimmering with a bright glow. Trembling in awe, Annoure recognized her as the celestial maiden who'd come for Erik.

"Are you an angel?" she asked.

The being smiled benevolently and sweetness radiated from her angelic face. "I appear in whatever way a person feels most comfortable seeing me."

"Are you the Virgin Mother?"

"No, I'm not a Valkyrie either, although to Thorstein I appear as one. I bring comfort where needed."

"Can you help me?"

"I don't interfere with mortal lives."

"You have power. I can feel it."

"You have power, too. That's why you can see me. Use your power tempered by love."

"How can I use my power to stop this fight?'

"Wait for an opening."

"I don't understand."

"Surrender to the higher powers and you'll be guided." The maiden faded away. Annoure stared into the sunlight caressing the ground and pondered her words.

At last she headed back to find Thorstein. Her heightened state of awareness stayed with her. She felt removed from all the people buying and selling wares as she entered the marketplace. She passed Ketil who stood with his two daughters, looking at wooden toys in a carver's booth. Ketil noticed her and called out, "Annoure, stay a moment."

She froze, torn with uncertainty. His eyes had a sunken, haunted look with dark shadows beneath them. He was leaner than when she'd last seen him. She felt her chest tighten as they stared at one another in strained silence. She almost moved away when at last he spoke. "It was a hard winter."

She waited for him to go on.

"I missed Edgtho and Rethel. The only way I got through the dreary winter was by thinking of you."

"I'm sorry the winter was so hard for you."

He looked at her earnestly. "I didn't challenge Thorstein so I could take the farm from him and his family. I don't want any of Thorstein's possessions; I have a farm now that Rethel is dead. I only want my own freedom so I can raise my dóttirs." He looked down at the two little girls who each held one of his hands.

"So you would kill Thorstein rather than be an outlaw."

His face became clouded. "Annoure, can't you see that you and Thorstein's family weren't the only ones hurt in this feud? My family and I grieve for our lost kin, too, especially Rethel's vif and four bairns. You started this by pushing him overboard, causing him to lose his sword. Do you know how valuable that sword was?"

Not waiting for her answer, he continued, "It was in my family for generations, handed from faðir to sonr. It was proven to be a good sword by numerous battles and had the skills of our ancestors in it. It was Rethel's most valuable possession and he didn't have the money to replace it. A sword is worth a half-mark of gold. That's enough to buy sixteen cows or even a small farm. But *you* were too proud to lie with him when he sought retribution."

"He threw Brother Tondbent, a holy man, overboard and laughed when he sank beneath the waves. What is a sword compared to a man's life?"

"Tondbent was a Christian monk and bad luck. Our ship could have sunk if he hadn't been thrown overboard."

"He wasn't bad luck! His only crime was worshipping a different god than yours. I'm sorry Rethel died, but I can't be sorry Thorstein stopped him from killing me."

"He wouldn't have killed you."

She lifted her chin and touched the scar on her neck. "This is where his knife cut me."

Ketil frowned and shifted his weight from one foot to the other. "You were booty from a raid. He would only have paid a fine if he killed you."

"Would you rather I died?"

"Of course not, dearest." He gazed at her affectionately. "Annoure, I didn't stop you to quarrel. I wanted to see you one last time while there might still be a scrap of warmth for me in your eyes. After the holmgang, I'll be dead, or Thorstein will be and you'll hate me. I only wanted to fight until first blood was drawn the way holmgangs are usually fought. But Dylan is old and used to feuds being settled with an *einvagi*—a duel fought outside the law to settle arguments. Those battles often end in death. Please believe me when I say I don't want Thorstein's death."

She sighed. "I believe you. I was there when you saved Thorstein's life. I wish you hadn't challenged him to a holmgang, but I don't hate you for it." As she gazed into his gray-blue eyes, the world faded. She saw a vision of Ketil with his wife Hanna, surrounded by light. He looked happy and the dark shadows were gone from his face. The vision lasted only an instant. She wondered if it foretold the future. Her heart felt heavy. "I don't wish for your death, Ketil, but I don't want to lose Thorstein." Heavy-hearted, she said, "I can't speak to you any longer. It's too painful. I *do* care about you and your young daughters." Tears sprang unexpectedly to her eyes. "I don't want you or Thorstein to die, but I don't know how to stop the battle."

He released one of his daughter's hands and clasped hers. She felt a jolt of warmth go through her. Their eyes held for a moment, then she gently pulled her hand free and hurried through the crowd of people shopping at booths.

She heard a skald singing and paused to listen, recognizing his voice. It was Gylfi who'd traveled to their farm for the wedding. His voice was tenor like Erik's, but not nearly as rich in tone. A small crowd gathered around him. He ended his song and smiled at Annoure as he began another.

Thorstein the Fearless rescued his beloved Annoure from a thousand Arabs.
He became one of Odin's berserks, savage in battle.

He fought with his sword Grimmr in his hand and his two companions at his side.
Erik the skald, his trusted friend, traded his lyre for a sword.
He fought like a strong bear until a sword pierced his armor.
Light appeared and a Valkyrie carried him to Valhalla.
Ketil Bloody-Axe, his warrior companion, swung his battle axe
He fought like a snarling wolf to rescue Annoure
The woman he loved more than his own life.

Annoure trembled as she listened to the words of the saga. They cut into her heart. It was as Erik predicted: the tale had caught the imagination of the Norse people. Erik should be the one singing it, she thought. He should not have died. It struck her that Thorstein must have honored his vow to Erik and told Gylfi the story.

The song continued:

Tomorrow when the sun reaches its zenith.
A holmgang will take place on Norns Island.
Between Thorstein the Fearless and Ketil Bloody-Axe.
Two warriors once friends.
Once sworn enemies
Now friends again
A friendship forged by trials,
Both caught in a deadly feud.
tNorns Island is named after the Norns,
Three sisters whose names together mean fate.
They spin a thread upon which the life of every person and god hangs.
Even the destiny of the universe hangs from their strong thread.
They measure time and control the past, present, and future.
The Norns will decide the fate of Thorstein the Fearless and Ketil Bloody-Axe.

Annoure moved away, grimly realizing that the *holmgang* was an event looked forward to with anticipation. A dark sort of entertainment, heightened because it would end in death. Those were the highest stakes a man could fight for.

She pushed her way through the crowded, noisy marketplace, feeling as if she couldn't bear it another moment.

Once free of the press of bodies and profusion of sounds and smells, she ran to their campsite, hoping Thorstein had returned by now. As she drew closer, she saw Thorstein and Walfgar sparring while others watched. She stayed out of view so as to not distract Thorstein. He fought with skill and agility, yet as a mortal who could die.

Walfgar yelled a stream of running orders, still playing the role of an older cousin. "Don't leave yourself open. Keep your guard up. Watch your footwork."

Thorstein lowered his sword and leaned over with his hands resting on his thighs, breathing hard. He wasn't wearing a shirt and his chest shone with sweat. "I'm tired. Let's break for a moment."

"You've got no stamina!" Walfgar exclaimed.

"You're fresh while I just sparred with Herjulf."

Herjulf handed Thorstein a flask of water and he took a long drink, then poured the rest over his head before handing it back. His eyes swept over the people gathered and he spotted Annoure. He held her gaze and she felt his strength of character. His expression remained bleak as he turned back to Walfgar and raised his sword. "Let's continue." He swung Grimmr and his cousin blocked it with his shield. Thorstein slammed his sword into the shield a second time before Walfgar had fully recovered. The fight was more aggressive than before and Annoure knew it was because Thorstein fought for her.

She heard a baby crying and hurried over to Kalsetini who was trying to satisfy Ban with a bone to suck on. Annoure sat on the bearskin beside Kalsetini, took Ban from her and began to nurse the baby. "I saw Ketil and his little girls at the marketplace," Annoure said, wondering if Kalsetini still loved him.

Kalsetini stiffened. "Did you speak to him?"

"Briefly. He said if he wins, he won't take the farm. He just wants his freedom."

"His word can't be trusted. Whatever good was in Ketil died when his vif died. I hate him."

"Hate is a heavy burden to carry."

"You should hate him, too!" Kalsetini jumped to her feet and disappeared into the crowd.

Thorstein finished the match and came over to sit beside Annoure. He smelled of sweat and fresh air as he leaned over and kissed her. He smiled at the contently nursing baby, then took out a sharpening stone and carefully whetted the edge of his sword blade, to take out the nicks.

She remembered the first time she'd seen him sharpening his sword and asked what the runes etched on the blade meant. He said Grimmr, meaning fierce, a name that gave the sword power. Now he would need its power at the holmgang.

"You were gone a long time," he said.

"I found a sacred oak grove."

"That explains why I sensed your presence as soon as you returned."

"What do you mean?"

"Whenever you tune into your god or goddess—whoever it is that speaks to you—you come back vibrating with light and magic."

"You sensed my presence because you love me. Thorstein, let's take Ban and leave. We can start a new life somewhere else."

"I'm not a coward." He finished sharpening his blade and slid it into its scabbard. "Besides if I leave, Herjulf or Walfgar will have to fight in my place. I fight my own battles. Moreover, the farm is my responsibility now; I can't leave."

She told him of her conversation with Ketil, that he didn't want to fight to the death.

Thorstein nodded. "I know. I heard him say that to the konungr. He didn't expect Dylan to cling to the old ways."

"Ketil saved your life, but he also did you grave injury."

"Do you want me to kill him?"

Her throat constricted. "You haven't any choice."

"What about my mistakes?"

"You fought both Rethel and Edgtho in a fair fight. Thorstein, I loved you even before we met in this world and I will love you beyond this life. What we have is rare. We found each other against all odds. It seems like my god or yours wants us to be together. Fight for me and Ban and our future together. Fight because you love me, not because you hate Ketil. Fight because you have no choice. If you can't fight him with the determination to win, then let Walfgar. He is an able swordsmen and will not hold back for friendship or honor."

"It's my fight."

"Nei, all your family suffered from what happened, not just you!"

"I owe Ketil a blood debt for saving my life. If I kill him, I won't be the same man you love."

"I'll still love you. The agony you suffer over fighting Ketil makes you who you are. But don't die for some misplaced sense of honor." She lifted Ban to her shoulder to burp him.

Thorstein's expression softened as he looked at his son. "He's a fine boy, Annoure. Thank you for my sonr." He gave her a kiss, his lips soft and sensual on hers.

"He's growing quickly."

"Let's retire to the tent," he suggested.

"It's still early."

His eyes darkened with desire, which set her heart racing. "I know."

Thorstein helped her up and they entered the tent. She sat cross-legged on the hudfat and let Ban nurse on her other side. Thorstein sat across from her, watching the baby tug at her nipple. Heat radiated from him as he flexed the muscles of his bare chest.

"I'm stiff and sore," he complained. "And out of shape from not fencing all winter."

She stretched out her leg and slid her foot up his inner thigh. "Já, you're stiff."

"Feeling bold, are you?" He untied the straps of her leather shoe, slid it off and kissed the tender skin on the sole of her foot. He worked his way up her calf, each kiss sending a chill up her spine. He removed the other shoe and kissed that foot as well.

As soon as Ban fell asleep in her arms, she placed him on the hudfat and leaned toward Thorstein. "Let me rub your sore back."

"My sword needs rubbing more," he said suggestively.

"In due time. Turn around." She began to massage his thick shoulders, wondering how not fencing for so many months would impair his skills. He was tense; she felt hard knots in his neck and shoulders. She pushed her thumbs into a muscle. He groaned in ecstasy. "You've got a magic touch."

She pressed her breasts against his bare back and kissed the back of his neck. Her hands slid around his chest, feeling his blond hair soft and silky against her cheek.

He shuddered as she untied his pants, slipped her hand beneath the waistline and breathed into his ear, "You're still stiff."

He turned his head and their mouths met in a heated kiss. He moved so they faced each other and he slipped off her hangerock and underdress. "You smell of spring flowers and woods," he said, "and the taste of you is making me intoxicated, as if I drank mead."

"Has my barbarian become a poet?" She wrapped her legs around his waist and rocked against him "I heard a saga about you at the marketplace. I think I shall enjoy making love to a great hero." Her words were light, but her stomach was tied in knots. There was a real chance he would be killed the next day. This could be their last time together.

"Is that why you came to find me?" He lightly nipped her lower lip between his teeth.

"Já, I've seen how you thrust your sword to your advantage."

"Shall I slide it into your sweet sheath?" Thorstein set her on a fur and slid off his pants. Then he moved so his body was over hers, poised to put his words into action, but delaying as she throbbed beneath him. "By Thor's hammer, you are most beautiful when your face softens with desire."

"Lust, not desire. Don't tease me any longer. I want you." He held her with his eyes as he slid into her; she gasped and started to move her hips. She dug her fingers into his back, making love to him with her whole being. She wanted to strengthen their bond so if he died, they'd find each other again in another life. Tears began to slide down her face.

Her exquisite release caused him to crest with her. She couldn't distinguish herself from Thorstein for they were spiritually, mentally, emotionally and physically attuned. Thorstein rolled off her and held her as she continued to weep. "Hush, my love, it's going to be all right."

"I'm so scared. I can't bear it if you die."

"I'm scared, too. Not of death, but of leaving you."

She sniffed back her tears. "The gods brought us together. Surely we won't be torn apart so soon."

He didn't reply as he continued to hold her. After a while his arm became heavy as he drifted off to sleep. Annoure lay awake; they had so little time left before the duel. She had to figure out a way to keep Thorstein and Ketil from fighting to the death. What did the woman of light mean by "wait for an opening?"

Chapter 36
Holmgang Saga

IN THE MORNING ANNOURE AWOKE to find Thorstein gone. She dressed quickly and scooped up the still sleeping baby. Thorstein and his family gathered a short distance away around statues of the Norse gods. She winced as Walfgar sliced open a lamb's throat. Asa held a bowl beneath to catch the blood. Thorstein noticed Annoure and he moved over and put his arm around her. Freydis said a prayer, her face pale and strained.

"Why didn't you wake me?" Annoure whispered to Thorstein.

"I know you don't like sacrifice."

"Today it seems like the right thing to do."

When the sun was nearly straight overhead, Annoure walked down to the ocean with Thorstein and his kin. They filled two boats and rowed over to Norns Island, a small rocky island where Ketil's family, the konungr, priests and Jarls had already gathered.

Annoure watched the proceedings with a feeling of unreality. This can't be happening, she thought. How can people gather to watch two friends fight to the death?

The konungr called Thorstein and Ketil before him. Thorstein kissed Ban's cheek, then kissed Annoure. "I love you, Annoure."

She clutched him around the waist. "I love you. Please live."

"Avenge me!" Thyri said, her eyes narrowed.

Freydis clasped his forearm. "And your faðir."

"Remember to guard your left side," Walfgar said.

Thorstein and Herjulf walked over to where an ox hide was staked out on the ground. Thorstein carried a sword and shield. Herjulf carried the other two shields Thorstein was allotted. Ketil was already there with his sword and shield. His cousin Ljot stood beside him with his two extra shields.

Dylan poured a cup of mead on the ground with a shaky, brown-spotted hand. "I give this mead to honor Odin, the chief of the gods. All have agreed this battle will end the feud and restore peace among our people. Thorstein will have the first blow since Ketil is the challenger. You each have three shields. When one is broken, you are to allow your opponent to get a new one until all three have been used. You must stay on the hide. If you step off, you'll be considered nithigar."

Thorstein and Ketil both stepped onto the ox hide. Thorstein swung Grimmr and Ketil met it with his shield. Ketil was allowed the next blow. He fiercely thrust his sword at Thorstein, who blocked it and slashed his own sword toward Ketil. Ketil parried the blow, then slammed his weapon against Thorstein's shield.

Each lunge made Annoure cringe until she felt like a lyre string wound too tight. Sweat poured down Thorstein's brow; he lacked the aggressiveness that marked his usual style of fighting. He fought defensively: rarely attacking, deflecting blows, yet holding back as if it was a sparring match—not a fight to the death.

Ketil pounded his sword against Thorstein's shield until it broke in two. Thorstein threw it aside and took a new one from Herjulf.

"You fight with no heart!" Ketil said. "I've seen you fight like a god. Did you go soft over the winter?"

He drove Thorstein back to the edge of the hide where Thorstein was forced to hold his ground. "I do what I must.

"Have you forgotten I sold Annoure into slavery?

Thorstein said through gritted teeth. "Nei, I haven't forgotten."

"Then in Odin's name, fight me!" Ketil closed in and delivered another blow. Thorstein parried and their blades flashed in the sunlight. Thorstein forced Ketil back and broke away, moving so he was back in the center of the hide

"I am fighting you," Thorstein said, his breathing heavy. "Do you wish to already lie on the ground bleeding to death?"

"Do you wish to give me Annoure?"

"Why do you seek to goad me?"

"I want to rouse your fighting spirit. I have as much responsibility for Njal's death as Edgtho. We fought him two to one. It could have easily been me who slid my sword into his belly and carved out his guts."

"You go too far," Thorstein said, his voice low and threatening.

"Too far! Thorstein, we're fighting to the death. I want to win, but not against a man who isn't even trying."

Thorstein rushed forward and sliced Grimmr with a forceful arc. He hit the flat side of Grimmr against Ketil's sword with deadly force and the weapon flew out of Ketil's hand and spun across the ground.

"Kill him!" Thyri yelled.

Thorstein stepped back as Ketil dove for his weapon and sprang back into fighting stance with his sword and shield held ready. The fight continued with renewed fury, the swords swinging repeatedly against the shields until both men were down to their last shield.

The tip of Ketil's blade sliced across Thorstein's shoulder, drawing first blood. The wound brought Thorstein to life and he fought with renewed energy.

Annoure knew if she was going to find a way to intervene, it had to be soon. She handed the baby to Kalsetini, listening inwardly for guidance from the lady of light. Thorstein's blade ripped across Ketil's forearm, and his sleeve turned red.

A silence descended over the onlookers, in anticipation of death. Annoure heard Thorstein and Ketil's heavy breathing, the sound of their feet moving on the ox hide and the repeated pounding of swords against shields. More wounds bloodied both men as the fight continued with violent intensity.

Blood sprayed in the air as Ketil lunged at Thorstein. Annoure was so close she breathed in the metallic smell mixed with sweat and dirt. Though both men were tired, they embraced the fight and fought on grimly, reluctant to kill and not yet ready to die.

Thorstein leapt forward, slicing his sword through the air. Ketil held his shield in front of his chest, but Thorstein swung low and the blade sliced deeply into Ketil's upper thigh.

Ketil stepped back, raised his sword, then lowered it. He staggered back a few feet and collapsed on the hide. Thorstein stepped forward and put Grimmr to Ketil's throat. Annoure drew in a sharp breath, watching in fascinated horror, wondering what Thorstein would do.

The konungr yelled, "End this! Kill him!"

Thorstein raised his eyes to Annoure before stepping away from Ketil. "I can't kill him. I owe him my life. Let him live."

"Nei, he must die," Dylan said. "If your honor won't let you deliver the death blow, then let one of your kinsmen do it."

Walfgar stepped forward and drew his sword. Annoure rushed forward, grabbed Ketil's fallen sword and stood between Walfgar and Ketil. "Stay back!" She felt the power of the Druids flowing through her, giving her strength. "There will be no more killing!" Her voice was pitched so all present could hear. The very air around her throbbed with expectation. "It ends here!" She paused to let the weight of her words descend like a blanket. "Blood has been spilled, balance restored and honor won."

She sensed the presence of the celestial maiden who appeared at the oak grove. "The blood of your kinsmen is on this sword. Isn't that enough? Do you want more? How many more women must be widowed, how many children orphaned before you are satisfied?" She turned in a circle as she spoke, the sword held out as if to strike. "Where will it end? When all in both families are dead? If Ketil dies or Thorstein, it will not change the thirst for revenge. It will only increase the sorrow and rage. What will it take to satisfy you? Isn't the life of a courageous warrior valued here? The gods will be angry if you force Thorstein to kill Ketil. You all lose from Ketil's death. All of you.

"You are a just people. Your laws are fair. The way you reach decisions by bringing up disputes, discussing them, and then voting on a discussion is good. A holmgang should be fought until first blood is drawn. Fighting until one man dies just causes more antagonism. It doesn't end a feud."

She faced the konungr. "You are a wise man. I've watched and listened to your decisions over these past few days. End this fight. Thorstein won. Slaying Ketil won't make it a clearer victory."

Everyone looked expectantly at Dylan, waiting for him to speak. Ketil lay on the ground, his face white, blood flowing from his wounds. The leg wound needed tending soon or he would die. Thorstein didn't look much better. He was unsteady on his feet and it was hard to know how much of the blood that covered him was Ketil's and how much was his own. He looked beyond weary. His eyes sought out hers. He looked as determined as she was to protect Ketil.

The konungr rose and turned powerful eyes upon Annoure. "This man wronged you and your family. Why do you want him to live?"

"In his terrible grief, Ketil made some bad decisions," Annoure said, her arms shaking from holding the heavy blade upright. "He tried to rectify them. His death serves no purpose. Spare him."

Dylan looked at Thorstein's clan. "Is there anyone here who objects to Ketil being spared?"

Walfgar advanced toward Annoure, his sword drawn. "My uncle, cousin and nephew are dead. Ketil's life is forfeit." Walfgar swung his blade toward Annoure and she met it with hers. The force of his strike vibrated through her arms.

Thorstein was instantly beside her, parrying Walfgar's next blow. "Cousin, revenge doesn't end the pain. Show mercy."

"I can easily kill you. You are battle-weary."

"Try it."

Walfgar's face darkened and Annoure trembled, terrified he would slay Thorstein in his rage.

Thyri rushed forward, wild-eyed. "I demand justice! Ketil killed my verr and bairn. Njal was gutted and Brandi's head split open. Ketil must die."

"Ketil didn't kill them; Edgtho did and he died for his crimes," Annoure said.

"Ketil and Edgtho fought Njal two to one!" Thyri shouted. "He's equally responsible for Njal's death."

Annoure looked at her with compassion. "I was there, too, Thyri. I know how terrible it was, but Ketil did not come with the intent to kill anyone. I don't think he would've killed Njal. And Ketil's death will not bring Njal back."

Thyri began to shake and tears rolled down her cheeks. "My life was destroyed that day."

Walfgar put his arm around Thyri. "Perhaps Annoure is right. This feud has to end someplace." He looked at Dylan. "Let the gods decide if Ketil lives or dies."

Dylan looked over the spectators. "Annoure has wisdom beyond her years. There's no justice in two men fighting a holmgang to the death. We made laws so men of wisdom make fair decisions instead of letting fate decide. Thorstein Garthson and Ketil Nesbjörnson, you are both pardoned."

Annoure knelt down beside Ketil and pressed her hand against the gaping wound in his thigh, trying to stop the bleeding. His face was deathly pale from the pool of blood that had formed around his leg. “Give me something to tie off the leg and stop the bleeding,” she cried. She felt faint and bit her lip to stay focused. Thorstein took off his belt and tightened it around Ketil’s thigh above the wound. The bleeding slowed.

“Thank you, Annoure,” Ketil gasped. He looked upward as if seeing someone and a faint smile touched his mouth. He reached out his hand. “Hanna.” His eyes became vacant and his hand dropped to the ground. Annoure shuddered, knowing he was gone.

His little girls ran over to him and began crying on his chest. The sunlight cruelly reflected off their blond heads like halos. Tears streamed down Annoure’s cheeks as she rose and stumbled into Thorstein’s arms. “I couldn’t save him,” she cried.

“Not him, but you made the konungr and my people see that death isn’t a good way to settle a feud. Perhaps next time a man won’t have to die needlessly.”

“Let me tend your wounds.”

“Not here. A hero whom sagas are written about doesn’t collapse on the field of battle. Let me have a little pride.” He put his arm around her shoulder and leaned heavily against her as they walked to their boat. Once there, Thorstein sank down on a boulder to rest.

“How bad are your wounds?”

“I’ll heal. Thank you for intervening so I didn’t have to kill Ketil when he lay gravely wounded.” He smiled sadly. “I was proud of you. You looked like a goddess, standing regally before the konungr with power surrounding you like a cape. You have grown into a woman of strength and wisdom, instead of being defeated by all you have suffered.”

“If I were wise, Ketil would be alive and you wouldn’t be wounded. Remove your shirt so I can tend to your wounds.” After he’d removed his tunic and shirt, she poured water from a flask on a piece of cloth and began to wipe the blood off his shoulder. She was relieved to discover the cut wasn’t deep.

He cupped her cheek in his hand. “We can’t control everything that happens to us and those around us. We can only meet each challenge with courage and do our best to act with honor and integrity. You haven't turned bitter, angry or vengeful and you have taught my people something."

"They are my people now. I'm glad to be one of them." She cleaned a wound on his forearm. "Thank you for fighting Ketil despite your misgivings." She impulsively embraced him. "I'm so glad you're alive."

"I won because I had more to live for than Ketil. He will go to Valhalla and feast with Odin. I stayed to be with you. Perhaps my fate is to die a straw death instead of one with Grimmr in my hand."

"More likely Ketil will go to join Hanna. I saw her waiting for him."

"Then perhaps he can find happiness again."

"I hope so." Overwhelmed Annoure said, "I was scared you would die and leave me."

"I'll never leave you."

"Good because I think we started another baby last night and I want him to know his faðir."

Thorstein smiled and his blue eyes sparkled. "I'll be there when this little one is born. A new baby will bring joy and healing to my family."

Author Notes

I'm excited to finally see *Annoure and the Dragon Ships* make its entrance into the world of literature. Annoure and Thorstein are finally getting a chance to share their story.

I carefully researched this period of history and did my best to make it accurate. Although the Norsemen had runes for writing on stone and labeling things, they didn't have books that would have left a more detailed picture of their lives.

Much of what we know about them has comes from archeologists and the people who they invaded who didn't portray them in a favorable light.

We do know the Norsemen's longships were an important part of their culture. They were fast, sleek and shallow-drafted, which allowed them to travel up rivers and come into shallow water.

In writing the book I used some Norse words to make the story more authentic. Since the Norse language was before the time of dictionaries, the names given to words varies, as does the spelling of those words. I chose to take the most commonly used words and their spellings of the words such as "sonr" for son.

Even the word "Viking" is a more modern term to refer to the Norsemen. They didn't call themselves Vikings. They would say they were going "a-viking" when they planned a trading expedition or went on a raid.

The Viking Age began with an attack on the monastic settlement of Lindisfarne, an island off the northeast coast on England in Northumbria.

My story starts a year later when five dragon ships sailed the River Thyne and attacked St. Paul's Church at Jarrow. They burned the two monasteries, killed or kidnapped the priests and monks, and fought the soldiers and villagers who tried to stop them. Their war leader was killed during the attack.

As the Norsemen left, a terrible storm arose and two of the dragon ships sank. The Norse warriors who survived the shipwrecks swam to shore and were killed by the villagers and soldiers.

Historians disagree as to where the Norsemen who attacked Jarrow came from. For the purpose of my book I chose to have them come from what is now known as Norway.

While researching the book, I traveled to England and visited St. Paul's Church. The church is still in use after over a thousand years. Beside it are the remains of the two monasteries that were destroyed in the Viking raid.

Nearby was an exhibit of a reconstructed medieval village complete with live animals. I was delighted to see what a village would have looked like back then with its thatched-roofed houses and twisted-branched fences.

Later I made a trip to Norway with my husband who is a one-hundred-percent Norwegian. I wanted to visit Rosendal where Thorstein's family homestead was located on the west coast of Norway, an area famous for its fjords.

We flew into Stavanger where we rented a car and started our journey. We drove through a tunnel cut out of bedrock under a bay, traveled by car ferry, and drove on narrow mountain roads though some of the most beautiful country in the world. The area has changed in over a thousand years yet the mountains, ocean, the nearby island (where Thorstein's neighbors lived) and fjord are the same. Being there helped me write more realistically about the area.

I hope the story depicts the Norsemen in a way that shows their strengths and weaknesses and gives you a glimpse into their lives.

If you enjoyed the novel please leave an online review so others can discover it as well.

In 2016 I plan to publish the next book in my Star Rider Series, an exciting series that takes places in a different galaxy in a time of interplanetary war. Please follow these books too, if you enjoy reading action, adventure and romance books that feature strong, spiritually inquisitive heroines!

Acknowledgements

My sincerest gratitude to the readers of my drafts of *Annoure and the Dragon Ships* who encouraged and believed in me.A special thanks to my critique group who gave me feedback and helped ensure that the historical facts were accurate. All of their input has helped make this a better novel.

Thank you to Coleen Rehm for her careful editing and friendship. Thank you also to Deranged Doctor Design for the cover treatment.

And as always, every day, thank you, Jim, for everything.

About the Author

Heidi Skarie lives with her husband Jim and cat Lucky in Minnetonka, a suburb of Minneapolis. She has three grown children and two grandsons. *Announre and the Dragon Ships* is her second historical fction novel. She previously published *Red Willow's Quest,* about a Native American girl training to become a medicine woman. She has also published *Star Rider on the Razor's Edge, the frs*t book in a science fiction series that came to her in a dream. Her novels are an exciting blend of action, adventure and romance that feature strong, spiritually inquisitive heroines. When Heidi is not inventing characters and putting them in dangerous situations, she enjoys other creative outlets such as blogging, gardening, knitting, oil painting and teaching writing classes.

In 2016 Heidi plans to publish the second book in her Star Rider series.

Readers can contact her by email at heidi.skarie@gmail.com, visit her website at www.heidiskarieauthor.com, or friend her at Facebook, Twitter or Google Plus.

Thank you for reading *Annoure and the Dragon Ships.* If you enjoyed it, please leave an online review to help me get the word out to other readers.

Readers Group Guide

Discussion Questions

1. Do you think Annoure caused the feud by pushing Rethel overboard?

Do you think there is anything Thorstein could have done differently to prevent the feud?

2. The Norsemen convened at a ting, a leadership assembly that all land-owning men participated in. Women also had rights, such as being able to own land and a business and being able to get a divorce. Do you see the rudiments of modern-day democracy in their system? What do you think led the Norse people to adopt this form of governance when other areas in Europe at that time had aristocracies and feudalism?

3. Why do you think farmsteads were always left to the eldest son, leaving younger sons to turn to earning a living by going on trading expeditions or raids? Do you think this was a fair system? Why or why not?

4. Annoure's life was shaped by being kidnapped (first from her home and later from Garth's homestead). How effectively do you think she dealt with these ordeals? Do you see her as a strong character or a victim? How does Annoure's Druid background help her? What did you think of her Grandmother and Erik's roles as guides in her life?

5. Thorstein kidnapped Annoure from her home, but later saves her from a life of slavery by rescuing her from Arabs. Did you find him a flawed character or a noble character and why?

6. Ketil participates in abducting Annoure from Garth's homestead and sells her into slavery. Do you feel he is still a sympathetic character?

Why do you think he helped Thorstein save Annoure? Do you think someone can love another person and still do something terrible, such as selling them into slavery?

7. If you were put in Annoure's position, would you have married Ketil to avoid being sold into slavery with your baby?

8. Why do you think Annoure was still unsure about Thorstein wanting her after he traveled so far and risked so much to rescue her from the Arabs? Is her uncertainty understandable? Why or why not?

9. Why do you think it was so hard for Thorstein to kill Ketil in a duel after Ketil participated in the attack on his family homestead and sold his wife and child into slavery?

10. Some historians feel that the Norsemen attacked Christian churches because Christians were growing too powerful and threatened their way of life. Do you think the attacks were part a clash in religious ideology?

11. The Vikings are often portrayed as savage pirates who plundered other countries. After reading *Annoure and the Dragon Ships* and learning about the Viking culture, do you see them in a new light? Why or why not?

Praise for Red Willow's Quest

"A powerful spiritually invocative story about a woman taking her power."

~Lynn V Andrews, best-selling author, Love and Power and Medicine Woman

"*Red Willow's Quest* not only is a good story but a primer in learning to follow your dreams and listen to your heart."

~June Rouse, The Monthly Aspectarian

"In *Red Willow's Quest* Heidi Skarie displays a talent for mystical and spiritual writing. She explains the meaning and symbolism for each tradition mentioned, then adds action, adventure and romance, bringing them all together into one powerful epic. . . I enjoyed *Red Willow's Quest* from beginning to end."

~Kristen Woodruff, Bloomsbury Review of Books

"Ms. Skarie has a wonderful voice for the character and obviously has extensive knowledge about the life and customs of the Shoshoni tribe."

~Sandra Avery, reference librarian, Jefferson County Public Library

Praise for Star Rider on the Razor's Edge

"The author does a great job of immersing the reader into the story from the very first page. From then on it is a fast, entertaining story with plenty of excellent characters and well-crafted plotline—with a healthy dose of romance!

~Michael Diack, author of Shadow in the Sand

"Without a doubt, *Star Rider on the Razor's Edge,* by the author Heidi Skarie, instills creative imagination. It takes you to realms where illusions of power for the enslavement of the many are soon uncovered. I felt visibly transported; actively participating, holding a child's Obi-wan Kenobi lit sword in the Star War battle dramas, which ensued so the light of truth could emerge! It was exciting, spell-binding, artfully choreographed, and provocative!"

~Jean Weber, author of Pets Are Soul Too

"Heidi Skarie is definitely a talented writer, and it shows in Star Rider. This was indeed a fun, interesting novel. I found myself especially intrigued by the characters. There was a lot to like about each one. Their different personalities shined, and it was easy to become emotionally invested them. Passion, pain, sorrow, and action-packed fights are good ingredients for any novel, and this one has them all."

~Michael Brooks, author of Exodus Conflict

"Science Fiction at its best. . .With a rugged setting and intimate character detail, *Star Rider on the Razor's Edge is c*ompelling and creates a lasting impression. Overall, a playfully entertaining read that connects a sense of realism while she (Toemeka) takes on the ultimate quest for restoring peace to the people of Jaipar."

~Catherine Kimball, Top 500 Reviewer on Amazon

Made in the USA
Columbia, SC
26 September 2019